Untamed Bachelors

ANNE OLIVER
KATHRYN ROSS
SUSAN STEPHENS

D1099386

 MILLS

Published in Great Britain 2015
by Mills & Boon, an imprint of Harlequin (UK) Limited,
Eton House, 18-24 Paradise Road, Richmond, Surrey, TW9 1SR

UNTAMED BACHELORS © 2015 Harlequin Books S.A.

When He Was Bad..., Interview with a Playboy and *The Shameless Life of Ruiz Acosta* were first published in Great Britain by Harlequin (UK) Limited.

When He Was Bad... © 2010 Anne Oliver
Interview with a Playboy © 2011 Kathryn Ross
The Shameless Life of Ruiz Acosta © 2012 Susan Stephens

ISBN: 978-0-263-25214-9
eBook ISBN: 978-1-474-00393-3

05-0515

Harlequin (UK) Limited's policy is to use papers that are natural, renewable and recyclable products and made from wood grown in sustainable forests. The logging and manufacturing processes conform to the legal environmental regulations of the country of origin.

Printed and bound in Spain
by CPI, Barcelona

WHEN HE WAS BAD...

BY
ANNE OLIVER

Anne Oliver was born in Adelaide, South Australia, and with its beautiful hills, beaches and easy lifestyle, she's never left.

An avid reader of romance, Anne began creating her own paranormal and time travel adventures in 1998 before turning to contemporary romance. Then it happened—she was accepted by Mills & Boon in December 2005. Almost as exciting: her first two published novels won the Romance Writers of Australia's Romantic Book of the Year for 2007 and 2008. So after nearly thirty years of yard duties and staff meetings, she gave up teaching to do what she loves most—writing full time.

Other interests include animal welfare and conservation, quilting, astronomy, all things Scottish, and eating anything she doesn't have to cook. She's traveled to Papua/New Guinea, the west coast of America, Hong Kong, Malaysia, the UK and Holland.

Sharing her characters' journeys with readers all over the world is a privilege and a dream come true.

You can visit her website at www.anne-oliver.com.

With many thanks to my fabulous critique group—
for good ideas, good food, good company.

And a special thank you to Piers for your inspired idea
of a golden horned unicorn for Belle's garden!

CHAPTER ONE

'IMAGINE him naked.'

Ellie Rose barely heard her friend's voice above the night-club's musical din, but she recognised the lusty tone. She knew why. And she knew to whom she was referring. The six-foot-something male-model type standing not more than fifteen feet away. As the gyrating crowd parted briefly beneath the swirl of dimly coloured neon lights and bone-jarring bass, she was treated to her first full-length glimpse of him.

He was turned away from her, but she could see that he was tall and dark and... She had a thing for cute rear ends. One butt cheek tightened and... Nice, she thought with a little sigh that tickled like a guilty pleasure down to her toes. Very nice.

Then the crowd closed around him and she cursed her height-challenged five foot two. But no way was she admitting to ogling him with the same lustful thoughts her friend had voiced. She hadn't known Sasha long, but she did know that she was more than likely to up and invite him over. From what Ellie had observed, Sasha didn't wait for men to find her; she found them.

Ellie feigned ignorance. 'Who?'

Sasha lifted her bottle of wine cooler in salute and raised her voice over the noise. 'You know perfectly well who—the guy up close with that tall chick in leather pants. Better still, imagine yourself naked *with* him.'

Ellie could. Very well. Too well. On indigo satin sheets... Except that the stunning brunette leaning in for a kiss insisted on sabotaging the image. Ellie swallowed and said in a ridiculously tight voice, 'We're not here to pick up guys. We're here to enjoy the music.'

'Speak for yourself.' Sasha tipped her bottle to her lips. 'If you want to enjoy music, go see a musical. Uh-oh, I think he's looking at us,' she said. 'At you,' she amended as the crowd between them thinned. She pressed her knuckles into Ellie's spine, prodded her forward. 'He's coming this way. Go on. You could get lucky tonight.' Sasha leaned closer, spoke into Ellie's ear. 'Ask him if he's got any friends.'

Ellie's legs began to tremble. She didn't want to get lucky. Did she? No. Not with a guy who had the potential to make her want things she knew she couldn't have with a guy like him. He had *permanent playboy* written all over that cocky smile and confident stride.

He wore black trousers and a white open-necked shirt that reflected the ceiling's changing light show. His hair was dark, short and spiked with a touch of gel in such a way that it looked as if he'd just rolled out of his lover's bed. The designer platinum watch adorning his wrist screamed money, money, money.

The lighting changed to an intermittent strobe—it seemed to flash in time to her pulse—as he drew near. And then he was so close that a quick yank of her arm would bring him within lip-smacking distance, and it was like watching one of those flickering black-and-white movies.

His eyes were dark bottomless pools. Mesmerising, magnetic, reeling her in. 'Hi, there. Can I buy you a drink?'

His voice, liqueur over dark chocolate, slid down deep, coating her insides with its lusciousness. She raised her all-but-empty bottle of cola. 'I already have one, thanks, and I'm with a friend...' She trailed off as she saw Sasha making off into the knot of dancers, hips swaying. The rat. This little dinghy was doomed.

'Looks like your friend knows how to have a good time,' he said, his gaze following Ellie's briefly before turning back to her. 'I haven't seen you here before.'

'Because I haven't been here before. I'm not a regular club-ber.' Sasha had dragged her along despite her protests, insisting Ellie needed more fun in her life.

'Let's make you one.' He reached for her hand. 'Dance with me.' A tingling sensation zipped all the way up her arm and settled low in her abdomen. His hand was warm, hard, firm. The way she imagined the rest of his body would feel. She recalled her sheet fantasy—and the brunette. Tension gripped tight in her lower belly.

'What about your friend?' She slipped her hand from his. Smoothed the tingly palm over her little black dress. Hitched her miniscule embroidered bag higher on her shoulder.

Uh-oh. Big mistake, voicing that observation, because now he knew she'd been checking him out. But he couldn't know what she'd been thinking...

Or perhaps he did, because he grinned—the way a man like him *would* grin if he knew—and Ellie wished she'd never given him the satisfaction.

'Yasmine's a colleague,' he said, that sexy confident grin still in place. 'I haven't seen her for a while. I've been working in Sydney.'

Hence, the up close and personal, Ellie supposed. She darted a quick glance behind him. She saw a well-endowed blonde in a white halter neck watching him with avaricious intent, but she could no longer see Yasmine. Or maybe her name wasn't Yasmine at all; maybe she'd just given this guy the flick and he'd moved on to his next target—Ellie. She didn't know him; he could be lying, looking for an easy lay.

And when it came right down to it, who here wasn't?

She wasn't.

Her body wanted, desperately, to refute that claim—*with him*—but she injected the zap of excess hormonal energy into her spine instead, straightened and stuck to something inanely neutral. 'You're from Melbourne originally?'

He nodded. 'I work on multiple projects, so I commute between the two cities on occasion.'

And he obviously took the high road to town, whereas she lived on the low road.

'The name's Matt, by the way.'

No surname, Ellie noted. Obviously not interested in more than a passing flirtation. Fine. Long-term relationships and becoming attached to people always ended in disaster. At least, it did for her. She lifted the bottle to her lips and drained the contents to soothe her throat which felt as if it were coated in sand. 'I'm Ellie.'

'How about that dance, then, Ellie?'

A ribbon of heat shimmied through her as the music changed to a slow, thrumming love song.

Body contact.

Perspiration broke out between her breasts, on her upper lip. She tugged at the neckline of her dress a couple of times to create a draught. It didn't help. 'I'd rather not at the moment, if you don't mind...' Except that the bosomy blonde was sure to pounce...and Ellie found herself smiling up at him. 'It's so airless and loud in here, I—'

'Outside, then?' he suggested. 'I could do with some fresh air myself.'

Even better, Matt thought as, with a light hand at her back, he guided her around the sway of dancers toward the club's secured outdoor area. The sensation of skin-warmed fabric was a tantalising heat against his palm. Anticipation—a different kind of heat—nipped at his skin.

But she stopped midstride and swivelled to face him, looking for all the world like a bunny frozen in headlights, and for a moment there he thought she'd changed her mind. He was prepared to do whatever it took to change it back again, but she gestured to the cloakroom.

'I…I'll want my jacket. It might be hot in here, but it's bitterly cold outside.'

He watched her walk towards the cloak check. He hadn't intended picking up a woman tonight. He'd come to get away from the pressures of work for an hour or two, but the petite woman with the short flyaway bob had captivated him. Perhaps it was because she was nothing like the women he usually dated.

He liked his women the way he designed his million-dollar constructions—tall, clean-cut lines, elegant sophistication and a sense of style. This girl was tiny, delicately boned but curvaceous. Moreover, every curve looked real. She reminded him of fairy floss—pretty and sweet and fragile.

That warm nip of anticipation struck anew. Harder, hotter. He ran a finger around the collar of his shirt. His suggestion to step outside had been inspired because suddenly he couldn't wait to find out if she tasted as sweet as she looked. And then…then he wanted to take his time to enjoy, something not easily achieved on a crowded dance floor.

He watched her hand over her ticket to the attendant, her spiky stilettos drawing attention to the smooth, well-turned ankles, her short hem riding up her thighs as she reached over the countertop to collect her coat.

'Hi,' a sultry feminine voice said beside him. 'I couldn't help noticing your friend leaving.'

He barely glanced at the woman who'd materialised beside

him. Blonde. Big...teeth. 'She's not leaving,' he said, his gaze finding Ellie again.

Ellie turned and wide wary eyes met his. She looked away, then looked back, nibbling on her lower lip, and for the second time in as many moments he thought she might bolt to the exit.

To forestall that possibility, he stepped forward quickly to meet her, cupping her elbow as he drew her towards the outdoor area. 'Everything okay?'

'Why wouldn't it be?'

'You looked a little edgy for a moment there.'

'Did I?' A tentative sound between a laugh and a cough escaped her as she accompanied him outside.

An almost solid wall of cold air laden with cigarette smoke met them. Bright lanterns swung overhead, reflecting pools of colour on aluminium tables and overflowing ashtrays. Clubbers huddled in groups around tall gas heaters, smoking, drinking and laughing while couples smooched in shadowy spots around the high-fenced perimeter. And by an amazing stroke of luck one of those spots appeared to be reserved for them.

'This is better.' He took her jacket from her hands—a little black number with embroidery on the pockets—and settled it around her shoulders. Her bobbed hair, cut just below chin length, brushed silkily against his fingers.

Her fragrance teased his nostrils. Not perfume, but something that smelled like spiced raspberries. 'Now we can talk without risk to our vocal chords.' Her eyes intrigued him. Beneath their placid reserve he glimpsed the promise of passion. 'So, Ellie, if you're not into the club scene, what do you do for fun on a regular Saturday night?'

'I read. Science fiction and fantasy mostly.' Shrugging deeper beneath her jacket, she said, 'I know...that probably sounds pathetically solitary and boring to someone like yourself.' She rolled her eyes to the star-studded sky. 'But haven't you ever wondered what's out there?'

'Sure.' He shifted his gaze—not skyward but to the tempting column of her throat. 'For now, though, I'm perfectly satisfied with what's right here in front of me.'

'Oh...'

He blinked. *Oh? That was it?* Most women would respond with a smile or a giggle or a flutter of lashes—some hint that this game was definitely going somewhere.

Not Ellie. And yet there was no mistaking the latent heat behind her gaze. She tugged the edges of her jacket together with tightly curled fingers and switched topics. 'What's been happening in Sydney?'

He rocked back on his heels. 'To tell you the truth, I've been too busy to notice.'

'Doing what?'

'I'm working on a harbour-side housing project at the moment. How about you? What line of work are you in?'

She moved her shoulders. 'A bit of this, a bit of that. I like to move around, so I pick up work wherever.'

'Travel. So I'm guessing you've been overseas?'

She coughed out a laugh. 'I'm afraid nothing near as exciting as that. Name a town between Sydney and Adelaide and I've probably been there at some stage in the past few years. I don't like to be tied down.' She laughed again but the humour didn't seem to reach her eyes. 'Call me irresponsible.'

'Okay, but at some point, you'd probably like to settle in one place, build a career and take on the responsibility of raising a family?'

She shook her head once. 'Not me. I'm a free spirit. I go where I please, when I please. And I like it that way.'

Do you? he wondered, watching the play of mixed emotions flicker across her gaze.

'And I can eat the whole darn cheesecake in one sitting

if I want. Now that's what I call freedom.' Her smile broadened. This time her eyes danced with devilment and he found himself totally entranced by the way her lips curved, making apples of her cheeks.

'I guess it is,' he agreed, smiling back. 'Free spirit, huh.' His lips tingled in anticipation of his first taste of her luscious-looking lips. He could almost feel their sweet heat, the warmth of her breath against his cheek.… 'Ellie, I want to kiss you,' he murmured. 'I've been wanting to kiss you since the moment I laid eyes on you.' And a lot more besides, but he didn't voice that yet.

Her head snapped back, her eyes locked on his and the slow-burning sexual tension which had been simmering along nicely evaporated in a puff of frosty air. Her tongue darted out to lick her lips, then they disappeared altogether as she pressed them into a tight flat line.

His body howled a protest. *That's what you get for being a gentleman, McGregor.* He'd not had much experience with women knocking him back. Or he was right and she wasn't as *free* spirited as she was making out. 'Is there someone else?'

'No.' Her face reflected the light from the pink lantern hanging nearby as she shook her head.

'So…?'

Nearby, someone's glass shattered on the concrete but her eyes remained locked with his. They seemed to say yes, but her behaviour indicated otherwise. The wind scuttled along the high brick fence, scattering dried leaves at their feet and riffling through her bright hair, gleaming like moonlight.

Then her shoulders tightened as she drew in air. 'So…do it, then.'

Her surprisingly breathy demand had his libido leaping to attention. He leaned closer, watching her chest rise sharply as she drew another swift breath, watching her eyes flare with a mix of vulnerability, hesitance and anticipation.

He barely laid his lips on hers, just enough to feel the warmth there, the texture. It was like tasting summer's first ripe peach. Sweet, soft. Sensuous. Eliciting a low throaty murmur from her that sang like honey through his bloodstream.

More. It was more than he'd anticipated and it threw him for a loop. He lifted his head to gaze down at her, saw that she was as surprised as he. He hadn't expected to feel his heart beating oddly out of time, as if he stood on the top of the Sydney Harbour Bridge in the middle of a storm without a safety harness.

Willing to believe it had been a fluke, again he lowered his lips, felt her hesitance dissipate like autumn mist in sunshine as she shifted nearer. Her mouth, tentative and unsure, softened and opened beneath his. He took swift advantage, lifting his hands to cradle her jaw for more intimate access and angling his body so that they aligned in the all right places.

He felt her tiny frame quiver against him as he swept his tongue inside her mouth to tangle with hers where the flavours were richer, darker, hotter.

Ah, *now* she didn't resist. In any way. She was right there with him—he knew by the way her tongue curled with his, the way her body turned fluid and malleable against him. He stepped closer, her legs tangling against his.

Either she didn't notice or she didn't care. Her hands slid up the front of his shirt. He could feel his heart pounding into her flattened palms. Then she slid them down again and wrapped them around his waist, and leaned in so her breasts pushed against his chest.

He let his hands wander too, over the smooth creamy column of her neck, the delicate heart pendant she wore, inside her jacket until they found the neckline of her dress. Down, palms skimming the outside of her breasts, the womanly shape where her waistline dipped, then flared again as he traced her hips. She was perfection. He wanted more. And with the way she was melting against him, it would appear he was in luck.

Ellie's knees were so loose it was a minor miracle she didn't collapse right there on the pavers. Her pulse thundered, her blood sizzled. Her only thought was she couldn't believe that she was letting this man—this *god*like man who smelled sinfully good and probably did this every night of the week with a different woman—kiss her to kingdom come.

Then her eyes closed, her mind shut down and all she felt was sensation. His hands warm and firm on her body, his unfamiliar hot, potent flavour, the sound of fabric shifting against fabric as he drew her closer.

And she was clutching his shirt without even realising she'd reached for him. Her body was burning without any recollection of who'd lit the fire.

His hands began a more intimate journey, seeking out her hardening nipples, drawing them into stiff peaks against the bodice of her dress. Rolling them between finger and thumb. She gasped as wetness accumulated between her thighs and, like a wanton, thrust her breasts forward, willing, *willing* him to keep doing what he was doing.

He did. Oh, yes, he did. But the ache only intensified, his clever hands sending ripples of desire straight to all her secret places. Her belly rubbed against a powerful ridge of masculinity. A moan rose up her throat at the sensation of the contrasting hardness against her softness.

A ragged answering groan seemed to come from the depths of his being. 'How far to your place?' he murmured thickly against her neck.

His voice and the message conveyed broke the lust trance she'd been momentarily lost in and her eyes snapped open. The harsh streetlight over the wall haloed his head, leaving his features obscured. All she was aware of was a dark silhouette looming over her and the unfamiliar scent of a man she really didn't know at all.

Oh. My. God. Panic clawed up her throat and she pulled free. 'I...I need to go to the ladies'.' Clutching her jacket about her shoulders, she took a couple of steps away, and from the safety of distance she pulled her thrumming lips into some semblance of a smile and said, 'I'll be back in a moment.'

She plunged back into the overheated room, saw Sasha amongst the dancers and caught her eye. Sasha winked over some guy's shoulder and twirled her index finger in the air— their prearranged 'goodnight' signal should they decide to leave separately.

Ellie nodded, manoeuvred her way through the dancers, past security at the entrance and out onto the street, still busy with traffic despite the late hour.

A car filled with loudmouthed teenagers cruised past, their car stereo's bass competing in an out-of-sync rhythm with the club's. Cold air stung her face and bare arms as she clung to her jacket, desperately willing a taxi to appear.

'Wait, Ellie.' She jumped at the sound of his voice behind her, but she didn't turn around.

No, no, no. If she looked, she might reconsider and she couldn't risk that. A fleeting kiss was fine, a little flirting... probably. But a kiss like *that*, with a man like *him*... A man who could sweep away her common sense without raising a sweat...

A frantic wave brought a taxi screeching to a halt in front of her. She dived inside, slammed the door and ordered the cabbie to *drive*.

But before he could pull into the stream of traffic, the door swung open again. Her breath caught and her fingers tightened on top of her bag. Matt whoever-he-was filled the space with his unique brand of woodsy midnight cologne, his smile, his charisma. 'You dropped your jacket,' he said, and laid it on the seat beside her. He didn't attempt to climb in.

'Ah... Thank you.' She hadn't even realised it had slipped off her shoulders and felt like a fool. He hadn't done anything she hadn't wanted him to and she'd taken the coward's way out and ditched him without one word of explanation. Worse, she could see the blonde who'd eyed him up earlier watching the proceedings from the club's entrance.

'You sure you don't want to change your mind?'

No. She dragged her eyes back to his. 'Yes.'

'"Yes," you're sure, or "yes," you want to change your mind?'

She shook her head. 'You know what I mean.'

His smile faded. 'Maybe, but I'm not sure you do.' He withdrew a wallet from his hip pocket, flipped it open and pulled out a black-and-gold business card. 'When you do... change your mind...'

When I do? That's why she stayed away from men like him. They messed with your head; they were dangerous... and addictive. And when they were finished with you, what did you have? Emptiness, pain and regrets.

When she didn't take the card, he reached inside and grasped her hand with his large warm fingers, turned it palm up. He pressed a kiss to the centre, then replaced his lips with the card, folded her fingers over the top. 'Until I see you again.' Spoken with all the arrogance and confidence in the whole damn universe.

Her palm burned and she curled her fingers into a fist. *Protecting the imprint of his mouth or screwing up his card?* 'I don't think so.'

But he just grinned, as cocky as ever. He peeled off a one-hundred-dollar note from his wad. 'Cab fare home. Pleasant dreams, Ellie.'

* * *

Ellie unlocked the door to her one-room studio apartment, stepped into calming darkness and solitude, grateful none of the other tenants she shared the building with were around to witness her dishevelled state.

Leaning back against the door, she let out a sigh. She could hear her own breathing, still ragged, her pulse, still rapid. What had she been thinking? Letting him kiss her and then… *oh*…and then letting him come on to her that way? And what was she supposed to do with all that change from the cab fare?

Closing her eyes didn't help. It didn't block the images or shut out the memory of how she'd responded to him. 'Idiot!' she snarled. 'I am an idiot.' She recited the words slowly through clenched teeth. Her fingers closed tightly over the business card she still held. She hadn't been able to make herself drop it in the gutter like she should have.

Crossing the room, she tossed the crumpled cardboard on her night stand *without* looking at it, flicked on her bedside lamp and flung herself onto her narrow bed, pulling her comforting pink rug over her body. Then, just to be sure, she sent Sasha a text telling her she'd gone home. Alone—in case Sasha got smart and sent her a fun text about 'getting lucky'. *Lucky?* She stared at the ceiling as if she could read answers in the ancient water stains.

She didn't want to get lucky. She didn't want to get involved. With anyone. Not that Matt had come even close to suggesting any such thing. It had been obvious where his intentions had been focused. But a late supper, maybe a few dates and who knew where that would have led? On her part, at least. *You know exactly where,* the little voice in her head whispered.

She didn't know how, but Matt was unlike any man she'd ever met, and that made him dangerous. Didn't mean she didn't know his type. He'd probably already forgotten her.

She'd always been one to get easily attached to people. And

when they left, for whatever reason, they took another piece of her with them.

Like when her part-time father walked out on her and Mum for the final time. She'd been three. Then three years later there'd been the car accident which had taken her mum and both grandparents. Her father had come back into her life to take care of her, but he was and always had been a wanderer. It had been a glorious adventure, travelling with him around the country chasing work, but she'd been a hindrance, and at the age of nine he'd left again, tearing out her young heart, and she'd found herself in foster care.

As she'd grown up she'd had boyfriends, and two and a half years ago her first and only serious relationship.... She shook her head against the pillow. No, she wasn't going to think about Heath. But the memories slinked back anyway, like wolves waiting to pounce.

They'd been inseparable for six months. Ellie had thought Heath was serious, but no... Instead, it seemed the gorgeous Brit she'd fallen for had an expiring work visa and the not-so-little complication of a fiancée waiting for him back in London. He'd told her it had been great while it lasted but she'd been a fling, didn't she understand that?

Her hands clenched around the sheets. Matt whoever-he-was hadn't only ignited a fire in her belly; one look into his eyes, one brush of his lips over hers and she'd forgotten everything she'd taught herself about self-preservation.

No. Those days were *over.* She'd never allow herself to get close to a man again. To fall in love. And most definitely, absolutely, she'd never risk marriage and kids. Matt was wrong about that. So wrong. 'No, Matt whoever-the-hell-you-are,' she said to the ceiling. 'I will not change my mind.'

CHAPTER TWO

On Tuesday morning, after he'd seen Belle safely off at the airport, Matt headed upstairs. Belle's century-old six-bedroom Melbournian mansion was maintained in spotless condition, but she'd left his old bedroom alone and a good clean-out was well overdue. He planned to slot it in between appointments he'd arranged at the city office over the next few days.

He'd get started while waiting for this mysterious employee—Eloise someone—to put in an appearance tomorrow.

Eloise. The name reminded him of Ellie, which brought back memories of Saturday night. He'd thought he had it made. Until she'd pulled her disappearing act. He'd spent the rest of the night in acute discomfort and his body still hadn't quite recovered. A week or so of mutual enjoyment would have filled the evenings here very nicely. He dismissed the fact that he could have enjoyed a few hours with Belinda the busty blonde and frowned as he reached the top of the stairs. It had been Ellie he'd wanted.

He knew the interest had been reciprocated. The eternal question would always be why she'd changed her mind. Obviously she had some hang-up that she hadn't deemed fit to enlighten him about.

Still, for a few moments there in the shadows, gazing

into those captivating amethyst eyes, he'd been completely charmed.

He shook the memory away. Right now he had a more immediate concern. Until Belle had phoned last week, he'd never heard her mention anyone by the name of Eloise. And seeing that look in Belle's eyes today when he'd waved her off on this impulsive trip—visiting Miriam, some woman she'd not seen in fifty-odd years in North Queensland—was a real concern.

'Miriam's the sister of a man I once knew,' she'd told him when she'd rung to see if he could house-sit while she was away—something else she'd never done.

'After all these years, why now, Belle?' he'd asked.

'Because something's happened and I need to make a decision and she's the only one who can help me make it. I'm sorry, Matthew, I can't tell you more. Not yet.

'There's something else,' she'd continued. 'A new employee you haven't met will be working there while I'm away. Her name's Eloise and I want you to look out for her.'

He'd agreed. Of course he'd agreed.

Then this morning… 'Don't forget, I need you to be nice to Eloise,' she'd reminded him as he'd escorted her to the departure gate.

'I'm always nice.'

For once, Belle didn't smile. 'Matthew, this is not a frivolous matter.'

Belle was the closest person to a mother that he had, and he'd known her for more than twenty-five years, but he'd never seen this particular expression in her eyes before. Fear? Desperation? Hope?

He frowned. 'If you're worried about leaving her unsupervised, why can't you just tell her to come back when you return?'

'She needs the work. Moreover, I'm afraid she might leave.'

'If she needs the work, she won't leave.'

'I don't want to take that chance. She—' Biting off her words, she smoothed a finger over his furrowed brow. 'And don't scare her off with that stern all-business facade.'

'I am in business, remember?' Which always made him wary of others' motivations. 'What's so special about this particular employee?'

Her short caramel-coloured hair was permanently tamed to within an inch of its life but Belle ran a restless hand through it. 'It's complicated. That's why I need to take this trip. To talk to Miriam, to consider and then to make a decision. And I need you here to keep an eye on…everything.' She wrapped her fingers around his forearm. 'Promise me, Matthew.'

'Of course, Belle, you know I will.'

She presented her boarding pass to the attendant. 'I know you have questions and I appreciate you not pushing me for answers.' She reached up, kissed his cheek. 'Thank you for coming. I think you'll like Eloise—you might even become friends. She'll be there tomorrow. You might take her out,' she suggested. 'Get to know her better…'

He felt his eyebrows lift. *Friends? Take her out and get to know her better?* Was that *hope* in Belle's voice? She'd never been a matchmaker, so there was something else she wasn't telling him. He returned the kiss absently. 'Why the urgency, Belle? Come back with me, let's meet this Eloise person together and we can discuss whatever it is that's worrying you.'

But she shook her head again and moved into the stream of passengers heading for the air bridge. 'A few days, Matthew. I'll explain everything when I come back….'

She'd told him that *she'd* phone *him* when she was ready. At least he'd made her promise to text him that she'd arrived safely. Still pondering his concerns and whether he should intervene in some way, he pushed open the door to the familiar bedroom.

Cartons he'd never got around to sorting were crammed against one wall. Age had faded the once-bright carpet square. Grime from storms past dulled the mullioned windows.

But nothing could dull the memories of waking up in this room to sunlight streaming through the glass and spilling rainbows across his *Star Wars* quilt. To the aroma of hot toast and bacon. Belle had always insisted on a good breakfast.

Unlike his biological mother, who'd not even bothered to stick around, nicking off in the middle of the night and leaving no more than a note saying she was sorry. *Sorry?*

Zena Johnson, single mum—and pole-dancer on her evenings off, it had turned out—had been Belle's housekeeper until she'd skipped town, leaving her only son with her employer. The best decision Zena had ever made, for all concerned, Matt reminded himself, without a lick of regret for the woman who'd given him life.

Belle had taken that scared, lonely, introverted kid, who'd never formed attachments since they'd never been in one place long enough, and treated him as her own. Loved him as her own. To Matt, Belle was family, and fourteen years ago at the age of eighteen he'd taken her surname to prove it.

He hefted the first carton, overloaded with his old school books. Time for the recycling bin. But the box was flimsy and slid out of his grip, spilling the contents over his feet. Dust billowed over his sneakers and jeans, then rose to clog his nostrils. He swiped a dust-coated forearm over his brow. Okay, the job might take longer than he'd anticipated—

A flash of movement somewhere beyond the window caught his eye. He saw a female figure walking up the leaf-littered path. Frowning, he moved nearer, rubbing a circle on the glass with the hem of his T-shirt for a better look. Not walking, he noted now—more like bouncing, as if she had springs attached to the soles of her worn sneakers. Or a song running through her head.

Young—late teens, early twenties? Hard to tell. He couldn't see her face, shadowed by a battered black baseball cap, nor her hair, which she'd tucked out of sight. She wore a baby-pink T-shirt under baggy khaki overalls with stains at the knees. What looked like an old army surplus backpack covered with multicoloured daisy graffiti swung from one slender shoulder.

She slowed and, with her face in shadow, uncapped the bottled water in her free hand and stood a moment, staring at the old unicorn statue in the middle of the lawn. Something about her tugged at the edges of his mind.

He tracked her progress along the carefully tended topiary and gnome garden statues. How had she slipped past the gate's security code? She wasn't the first trespasser on Belle's property—the reason he'd had the damn thing installed for her in the first place.

Only one way... She'd climbed the fence.

Every hair on his body bristled. Young, agile, probably doe-eyed and short on cash—she was just the sort to take advantage of a trusting woman living alone.

Not this time, honey.

He crossed the room, descended the stairs, half expecting the front doorbell to ring. He yanked open the door but saw no sign of her.

Where the hell had she gone?

He hotfooted it through the kitchen, his sneakers squeaking over the tiles, and shoved through the back door. Scouring the grounds, he spotted her slipping inside the old garden shed, partially obscured by ivy at the far end of the estate.

Heading grimly across lawn damp from last night's rain, he barely noticed the stiff autumn breeze whistle through his threadbare T-shirt. But he noticed the scent she'd left on the air. Subtle and clean and...somehow familiar...

Barely visible in the shed's gloom and with her back to him, she was inspecting gardening tools, discarding some, dumping others in the wheelbarrow beside her, all the while humming some unfamiliar tune slightly off-key.

He stopped at the open doorway, leaned an arm on the doorjamb. What was her game plan? he wondered, watching her add a pair of gardening gloves to her stash.

She couldn't be more than five foot two and what he could see of her was finely boned. She didn't look dangerous or devious, but he knew all too well that looks were deceiving. A gold-digger in overalls? Something niggled at him and he waited impatiently for her to turn around....

Ellie knew she wasn't alone when the light spilling through the doorway dulled. A tingle swept across the back of her neck, cementing her to the spot. The tune she'd been humming stuck in her throat. The fact that whoever it was hadn't spoken told her it wasn't Belle.

And he was blocking her only escape route. Her mouth dried, her heart rate doubled. Trebled. The stranger was male. She could feel the power and authority radiating off him in waves. And something else. Disapproval. Red-hot disapproval, if the heat it generated down her spine was any indication. Was he a cop? She tried to recall if she'd jaywalked on her way here but her brain wasn't computing anything as simple as short-term memory.

A cop wouldn't sneak up on her.

She could smell sweat and dust.... Barely moving, she closed the fingers of her right hand around the handle of the gardening fork which, by a stroke of luck, already lay in the wheelbarrow beside her hip.

Heart jumping, she grabbed the fork with both hands and

swivelled to face him at the same time. 'That's close enough.'
Her voice grazed the roof of her mouth like the dry leaves at
her feet. To compensate, she jutted her chin, aimed the fork
in the direction of his belly and hoped he hadn't noticed the
tremor in her hands.

In the windowless shed all she could see was his silhouette.
Tall, dark. Broad-shouldered. One bulging arm holding up the
doorframe. Why hadn't she flicked on the light as she came
in? She aimed the fork lower, straight at his crotch. 'I'm not
afraid to use this.'

'I don't imagine you are.'

There was something familiar about that deep, dark voice
which made her stupid heart jump some more, but in an
entirely different way. More of a skip.

She jabbed the fork in his direction. 'You're trespassing.
Miss McGregor'll be coming out at any moment.' At least,
Ellie hoped she would…or maybe not, since Ellie would be
forced to defend the woman as well as herself. 'She's probably
already ringing the police.'

'I don't think so.' His voice, frost-coated steel, sent a chill
down Ellie's spine.

'Back off. Now.' Heart thumping hard again, she lunged
forward, rotating the fork's tines to a vertical position so that
they lay a dangerous whisker away from his jeans. From this
position he towered over her and it belatedly occurred to Ellie
that all he had to do was open his hand and her weapon would
be his.

But he didn't attempt to confiscate it, nor did he step back.
As if he knew she couldn't carry through with her threat,
and there was nothing overtly menacing or desperate in his
demeanour when he said, 'How did you get in and what are
you doing here?'

'I used the code Miss McGregor gave me. Did you think I
scaled that seven-foot fence?' She shook her head, realising

that was probably what he thought. 'I'm the gardener—who are you?'

'You're Belle's gardener?'

She drew herself up at the barely veiled sarcasm. 'That's what I said.'

'What happened to Bob Sheldon?'

'He still comes in to do the heavy stuff.'

This man knew Belle's name and was obviously familiar with her staff. Still... Ellie's fingers relaxed some on the fork. Her arms ached with holding the thing but she didn't lower it. Not yet. 'You haven't told me who *you* are.'

Then he stepped back, into the sunlight, and said, 'Matt McGregor.'

Brown eyes met hers. *Familiar* brown eyes. Eyes she'd dreamed about for the past couple of nights.

Her entire body went into lockdown. *Oh, no. Not him. Please, please, please. Her Saturday night almost-lover couldn't be Belle's nephew. Couldn't be.*

'What are *you* doing here?' Her words came out on a wheeze.

A tiny twitch in his right cheek was the only sign that he recognised her. Her fingers slid off the fork as he took it from her boneless grasp and let it drop to the ground beside him. 'I might ask you the same question, *Ellie*. Or should I call you Eloise?'

'I already told you, I work here. And only Belle calls me Eloise and gets away with it.' Forcing herself to meet his gaze, she squinted up at him from beneath the bill of her cap. Same eyes—without the heat. Same beautiful mouth. The same mouth that had kissed her crazy. A tremor rippled down her body, her nipples puckered in loving memory.

That mouth wasn't smiling now.

'I'm here to keep an eye on things in Belle's absence.'

By sheer force of will, she drew herself up and attempted

casual. 'Belle's gone already? I thought she was leaving tomorrow.'

'She left at six this morning. As you'd have discovered if you'd knocked at the house first.'

She glared up at him. So *this* was Belle's hot-shot architect nephew with the million-dollar business—which she'd have known if she'd only looked at his card. What were the odds? She should buy a lottery ticket.

'Belle sometimes sleeps late,' she informed him coolly. 'I like to start early. I usually greet her when she comes outside with her morning coffee. I'm running late today because—'

'You had to wash your hair?'

How did he know? Her hand rose automatically to her cap and she sighed. 'Several times, actually.' But it hadn't made much of a difference. It was still pink.

'Ellie.' The sound of her name rolled out like a boulder over a grassy knoll. 'Ellie...what?'

She straightened her spine. 'Ellie Rose.'

'As in hyphenated?'

'As in Rose is my surname. My mum's surname, actually,' she explained. 'My father didn't want a kid so Mum...' She trailed off. *Too much information, Ellie.*

'Well, Ellie Rose,' he said, still eyeing her as if she might pick up the fork the moment he turned his back. And, by crikey, she was tempted. 'If you'd come up to the house...'

A sense of foreboding slid through her. 'Pardon? Belle doesn't—'

'Belle's not here. *I'm* asking you.' He inclined his head. 'Please.'

'Is this because I didn't come to work last Friday? I went on a field trip to the botanic gardens and I thought I'd make it up today, so that's why I'm a day earlier.'

'Just come with me,' he said, gesturing towards the house, and she realised her tongue had run away from her. Again.

Stress, that's what it was, but trying to explain would only make it worse. Was it because she'd left him on Saturday night without any explanation?

He was already walking away, his lanky stride putting more distance between them every second. Ellie couldn't help it; she couldn't drag her eyes away from those tight jeans clenched around that familiar butt. Temptation on legs.

No, she told herself and darted back into the shed to grab her backpack. Never again. Gorgeous overbearing men were *not* her type.

Lose the attitude, Ellie. You need the work. Focus on the *work.* Swinging her pack over her shoulder, she hurried to catch up, the nervous fingers of her left hand twirling around the button on her overalls strap. And wouldn't you know it—the pesky thing came away in her hand. The bill of her cap bumped into him, knocking it off and sending the brass disc spinning over the grass in front of him. 'Oops,' she mumbled to his back. His very broad, very hard back.

He spun around, firm hands closing around her upper arms. She barely had time to absorb their heat and the long lean feel of them before he let her go.

'My button... Sorry,' she muttered again, and while she was rubbing away the tingles his touch had wrought, he was bending over and searching for her button in the grass. She watched the muscles flex and roll on either side of that long curve of spine, the enticing sliver of bronze flesh below his T-shirt. She wondered what he'd do if she just reached out now and ran her fingernail across—

He straightened abruptly as if he knew exactly what she'd been thinking. She cleared her throat, attempted a smile and held out her hand. 'Thanks.'

He didn't smile back or answer. He was too busy staring at her hair.

And she'd been too busy checking out his butt—his

back—to pick up her cap. She swiped it up, aware that her cheeks probably matched her hair by now. 'Supermarket brands... Never mind.' She jammed her cap back on. She was never, *ever* going to put a colour through her hair again.

'Fairy floss,' he murmured to himself, still eyeing her cap as if he could see through it.

He dropped the button into her outstretched palm before turning and continuing to the back door, leaving her to struggle with the strap as she followed. She slipped its end through the bib's buttonhole and tied it into a temporary knot and prayed it held.

The kitchen smelled of lemons, cinnamon and rosemary. A homey room with sparkling red and white china and a friendly collection of ceramic cows on the pine dresser. The fragrant miniature potted herbs on the windowsill had been a gift to Belle from Ellie.

'Have a seat.' He pulled out a chair at the table for her.

Their knees bumped as he sat and his eyes flicked to hers, as if he, too, had felt that zing of sensation. She shifted her legs out of harm's way. Wringing her hands beneath the tabletop, she chewed on her lip to stop herself speaking before he got started on whatever he had in mind.

He set his hands, palms down, in front of him on the table and considered them carefully before he looked at her. 'I have some questions.'

About Saturday night? Why she'd changed her mind? Rushed off? Not called him?

No. His eyes weren't asking those questions. This was more like a job interview. It didn't seem to matter to him that Belle had already hired her. 'I thought Belle would've told you about me.'

While she spoke he pulled out a fancy-looking black and silver electronic organiser and began tapping. 'Not enough,

I'm afraid.' His finger paused over the buttons. 'First up, how did you come by this job?'

'Belle contacted me through an ad I posted in the local paper. And she hired me on the spot because I'm a damn good gardener,' she finished, leaning back and crossing her arms. 'That was a month ago, and it must be true because I'm still here.'

He didn't reply, just continued to study her with a steady, impenetrable gaze. Not a hint of Saturday night's heat there. Ellie refused to be disappointed. Refused.

Maybe if she explained why he could trust her to do a good job... Leaning forward again, she said, 'This house holds a special significance for me. When I was a kid my mum and I used to walk past here on the way to the tram. She told me the property had been in my grandfather's family at one time. The house was a little girl's fantasy and I loved it—especially the unicorn statue in the front garden. Its horn used to be gold, you know.'

His gaze turned considering. 'I know.' He studied her in silence a moment longer, then tapped his fingers on the table. 'References?'

'I've moved around a lot.' *Call me irresponsible*. Her words spoken in part jest, part bravado last Saturday night spun back to haunt her. Racking her brain, she tried to recall what else she'd said, but unfortunately could think of nothing that would instil confidence.

'Ah, of course, the free spirit.'

She watched those long fingers punch more buttons while heat bled up her neck and her nipples tingled. Those fingers had—

'No references. Your address and phone number?'

Her gaze whipped up to his face. That tiny muscle twitched in his jaw again but his eyes betrayed nothing. Not a thing. The heat continued to rise, suffusing her cheeks. She twisted restless fingers around the locket at her neck. 'Look, I really don't see that this is any of your concern. I'm Belle's employee, not yours.'

'Belle can be a little too naive sometimes. I'm making sure she's taken care of. Address? Phone number?'

'Belle has them.'

'She's incommunicado. What if something comes up? I need to be able to contact you.'

Holding his gaze defiantly, she snapped out the information.

'What days do you work?'

'Wednesdays and Fridays and I alternate Mondays and Tuesdays, but—'

'I value responsibility. Belle values responsibility. You call yourself irresponsible. So I'm wondering where that leaves us. Or more to the point, where it leaves you. I'd like you to think about that while you're working here.' He leaned back in his chair and placed his hands on the table. *Interview over.*

Thank goodness his unfathomable dark eyes didn't drop below her face. Thank goodness her chest was hidden beneath her overalls, because no way her skinny T-shirt would have been enough to hide the sudden way her nipples begged for more of that attention he'd given so generously Saturday night.

But then the cool business facade disappeared. His eyes thawed to a warm chocolate, lips curving into that lazy smile she'd seen across a crowded nightclub. 'Now we've got that out of the way,' he said in that deep sexy tone she'd been fantasising about in her daydreams. 'Have dinner with me tonight.'

CHAPTER THREE

DINNER? She stared at him, incredulous. He looked genuinely serious. 'Excuse me? You expect me to go to dinner with you?'

'Why not?'

'After that…that *inquisition*?'

'You need to understand my first concern is for Belle. But we've discussed the terms of your work here. I'm satisfied—' plucking a violet from the little vase in the centre of the table, he twirled it between his fingers '—with the business aspect of our relationship.' He flashed her a look that had her heart rate picking up again.

'But we haven't talked about the personal. We need to. If we don't, it's going to get in the way.' He leaned towards her, tucked the violet behind her ear, just beneath the edge of her cap. 'Never mix business with pleasure, Ellie.'

Her insides rearranged themselves at the intimate tone of voice. She didn't want business *or* pleasure with this man.

Liar. Okay, it wasn't wise or sensible to have anything more to do with him—certainly not pleasure. Already *un*-sensible thoughts were racing through her head.

Which reminded her of Belle's comment over a coffee break one day. *Matthew's always been a bit of a playboy when it comes to the ladies*, or some such. Ellie hadn't taken much notice—until now. Well, she did not intend to play second fiddle to anyone, ever again.

'I'm thinking I'll give this job a miss until Belle returns,' she said slowly. She placed her hands flat on the table and forced herself to meet his eyes. 'It's probably best for everyone concerned.' Particularly Ellie. 'I don't think the employee-employer relationship bit's going to work for us.'

His jaw firmed; his gaze turned thoughtful, then speculative. 'In which case, there'd be no reason not to have dinner with me, would there?'

She shook her head. 'I still can't have dinner with you.'

'If you're worried about your hair...mishap, we can dine in.'

Oh, way to charm the girls, Mr Ladies' Man.

She tugged the bill of her cap lower, tossed him a narrow-eyed glare and didn't deign to reply.

Or maybe it was just her. She bet he wouldn't say *that* to the type of high-maintenance, *high-class* Yasmine look-alikes he probably dated. He'd told her he was in Melbourne for a couple of weeks. Saturday night proved he was simply out for a good time, and if she hadn't left when she did they'd have ended up in bed. And that would have been a monumental mistake.

Pleasure had definitely been on Matt's agenda, but if that wasn't going to happen, so be it; he intended keeping his promise to Belle. Somehow he needed to keep Ellie happy in her job and ensure she stayed on. And what better way than to keep her close, keep an eye on her? Smiling at her, he switched to his most persuasive tone. 'Ellie, it's just dinner. I'd like your company this evening.'

Unmoved, she met his gaze squarely. Her eyes were the most amazing colour—amethyst with a sprinkle of gold dust... Bewitching...

Focus, McGregor. 'Okay, you may as well know up front. Belle asked me to look out for her employee while she's away. I'd like to be able to tell her I've done so.'

A tiny frown furrowed between her brows. 'I don't need looking after. Why would she ask that of you?'

Wouldn't we both like to know? 'Seems she's grown very fond of you and was concerned about you working at the house alone. Since I was going to be around, it seemed like a good solution.'

She waved a dismissive hand. 'It's all irrelevant because I have to work tonight. At least Red's Bar doesn't give their employees the third degree. I was hired on the spot, no questions asked.'

'Red's Bar.' Surely they'd eat a girl like her alive? 'That's not a reputable bar and it's not in a safe part of town.'

'*Some* of us can't be choosy. *Some* of us need cold hard cash to pursue our dreams.'

He didn't bother telling her he'd been there, done that and had the scars and papers to prove it. 'And what's your dream, Ellie?'

'To build my own landscaping business. Oh, and did I tell you I'm studying landscape and garden design? In modules. When I can afford it. At the rate I'm going I should be qualified in the next fifty years or so. Which is why I need Red's pay packet at the end of the evening.'

Landscaping business. He nodded to himself. Good, honest work. But what job did she hold at Red's? he wondered, eyeing the defiant lift to her chin. Kitchen hand, bartender, waitress? Or pole-dancer, like his long-lost mother? The thought made him feel physically ill, with a whole bunch of complicated emotions he didn't want to think about whenever his mother came to mind.

But the stubborn image that gyrated before his eyes had

his blood plummeting below his belt. If Ellie chose to pole-dance, he wanted it to be for him. In private.

Back on track. He cleared his throat and chose the safest option. 'Waiting tables?'

'Yes, *waiting tables*, what else would it be? Oh…' A rosy pink bloomed on her cheeks—those apple cheeks that had blown him away the first time he'd met her. When he'd just had to kiss her…

Ignoring his body's response, he focused on the valid reason he was still pursuing this line of questioning. She was playing in an adult playground—did she know the rules and, more importantly, the dangers? But perhaps she was already an experienced player. After all, he hardly knew her.

He knew he wanted her.

Her heightened colour intensified. 'What?'

'How long have you worked there?'

She lifted her shoulders, avoided his eyes.

'How long?' he demanded.

'It's a trial shift.' She pushed up. For once she had the height advantage and her eyes met his, bright with defiance. 'And your *babysitting* duties do not extend to telling me where I should or should not engage in paid employment. Now, if you'll excuse me, I have a kitchen garden to be getting on with. Since I'm already here, I'll work out today's shift.'

She pushed the chair beneath the table with a sharp scrape. 'And in case you're wondering, I use the outside loo, I brought my own packed lunch and can let myself out the gate when I'm through for the day. I'm sure you have work too. Lots of work. So if you want to go to the office and catch up with Yasmine…or whatever, don't let me spoil your day.'

Sparks, he noted. Promising. Where there were sparks there was emotion. Passion. Possibilities. He felt a smile kick up at the corners of his mouth. 'My day's going just fine, thank you.' Even better when he saw her fingers tighten around the back of the chair as she glared at him.

'Before I leave, there's still the matter of what went on between us Saturday night,' he said, unable to resist looking at her lips one more time. 'As I said, ignoring it won't change things.'

She sucked in a breath, studied her hands. 'It was just a kiss....'

A snort escaped him. 'Hey, I was there, remember?'

'Okay, it was more than a kiss.' Cheeks blazing, she lifted her gaze. 'It was a *mistake*. You're Belle's nephew, Belle's my employer and—'

'So you *are* going to reconsider working here.'

She shook her head and continued. 'I don't want, nor do I have time for, anything complicated.'

'It doesn't have to be complicated. You and me and a mutual attraction. It doesn't come much simpler than that.'

'Good times—is that all you're about?' She shook her head again. 'Of course you are. Men like you always are.'

'Men like me?'

'Attractive, arrogant, ego as wide as the blue Aussie sky.'

He studied her. The *you-don't-fool-me-for-a-moment-McGregor* stance, the nervous way her fingers played over the back of the chair. 'You're a contradiction, do you realise that? You say you don't want complicated, yet you're rejecting simple. What *do* you want, Ellie?'

Her mouth flattened and she swept to the door, yanked it open. Then she turned and glared back at him from the safety of distance. 'With you, Matt McGregor? Nothing. Not a thing.'

Uptight young lady, he mused. Damned if he wasn't going to enjoy finding out why. 'You know, Ellie Rose, I'm going to prove you wrong about that, and believe me, it's going to be a pleasure.'

He grinned as the door shut firmly behind her. 'Yes, a real pleasure,' he murmured. 'For both of us.' He was in for an interesting week.

Matt rode the glass elevator to the Melbourne offices of McGregor Architectural Designs, watching a rain shower draw a grey curtain across the cityscape. He never failed to feel the thrill of the ride up to his office on the forty-second floor. The award-winning precinct of glass and brass and green, with its unique interior-walled gardens cascading over half a dozen floors down towards a pool in the main lobby, was his first major achievement. Proof that one could turn possibilities into something real.

And his rapidly expanding Sydney branch was proof that success bred success. He'd worked bloody hard for it. In a roundabout way he had Angela to thank. His ex-lover was the reason his was one of the top architectural firms in Australia. After she'd given up trying to make something of their relationship and eventually walked out on him, he'd put his heart and soul into building his dreams.

Not that he blamed her for leaving. She deserved better than a guy who was incapable of the everlasting love and long-term commitment she'd obviously been looking for. And no-one could tell him he wasn't pleased to know she'd found it with an accountant in rural Victoria.

The current Sydney project was nearing completion. He trusted his hand-picked team of specialist engineers to handle it for a couple of weeks, enabling Matt to think about relocating back to Melbourne in the near future. The city he'd been raised in. Home.

The elevator slid to a soundless stop and he stepped out. Light spilled through the floor-to-ceiling windows and over miles of pearl-grey carpeting and polished wood.

Joanie Markham, the first face the public saw, glanced up

from the sleek polished reception desk as he approached, her middle-aged smile sparkling at him over her slim reading glasses.

'Good morning, Joanie.'

'Mr McGregor, good morning. We weren't expecting to see you today. Didn't Miss McGregor have something she wanted you to take care of?'

An image of Ellie shot into his mind with the force of a blowtorch. And not the image he *should* be focusing on—Ellie in cap and sexless khaki overalls wielding a gardening fork. Instead, he saw Ellie *not* in her little black dress and toothpick heels. He could almost taste that soft skin just below her jaw, her spiced berry scent.…

She was something to be 'taking care of', all right. He pinched the bridge of his nose, concentrated on bringing his wayward libido under control.

'Mr McGregor…are you okay?'

'Fine. Fine.' Amazed that his eyes had closed—not surprising with the lack of sleep he'd had over the past few nights— he blinked them open and pasted a reassuring smile on his lips. 'All under control, Joanie.'

Moving past reception, he skirted desks, design boards, pot plants, greeting staff along the way.

'Matt.'

He turned at the familiar sound of Yasmine's voice. As usual, she looked stunning in a slim grey suit with a modest scrap of white lace at her cleavage, her raven-black hair tied back in a tidy knot. He admired her clean-cut lines from an architectural viewpoint.

As a friend, he valued her inner qualities. 'Hi, Yasmine.'

The love of Yasmine's life worked as a geologist at the Mount Isa mines in Queensland and was sometimes away from home for weeks at a time. She and Matt often found themselves unattached at work functions and had forged a friendship. If either had a problem, they used each other as a sounding board.

Didn't mean he wanted to discuss his current problem, but he had a gut feeling he was about to be interrogated as she rounded her desk and accompanied him towards his corner office with its spectacular one-hundred-and-eighty-degree city views.

'Well, aren't you the man?' she said with a smirk, the moment they entered.

He closed his door. Firmly. 'Last time I looked, yes. You have something you want to say, Yaz?'

'You and that little slip of a girl against the wall on Saturday night,' she said cheerfully. 'Then dashing after her that way. Hmm.'

'I wasn't *dashing*.' He felt a prickle between his shoulder-blades and rolled his shoulder. He didn't pursue women. Didn't have to. 'I was making sure she got away safely.' *Hell*. He set his laptop on his desk with a *thunk*, discarded his jacket and laid it carefully across the back of his leather chair. Was it him or was the thermostat set too high in here? 'No law against that, is there?'

She slid her elegant backside onto the corner of his desk. 'No. But…you? You're usually so—' she waved an airy hand '—totally cool and sophisticated and together with women.'

When he didn't reply—because right now he really couldn't think of a comeback—she cocked her head. 'So, what's her name?'

'Ellie.' He switched on his laptop, drumming his fingers on the desk while it booted up. 'Fancy a coffee? It must be break time.'

'Just had one, thanks. Are you seeing her again?'

He shot her a dark look. 'As fate would have it, turns out she works for Belle, so the answer's yes, I'm going to be seeing her again.'

'Fate.' She arched a smooth dark brow at his choice of words, eyes twinkling. 'Serious stuff.'

He shrugged it off. 'Not at all. Just one of life's quirky coincidences.'

'Of all the nightclubs in all of Melbourne...' she purred, leaning closer. 'Yep. Has to be fate.'

'For heaven's sakes, Yaz, give it a rest.'

As always, undeterred by his scowl, Yasmine swung one long leg while she twirled her fingers through a container of paperclips. 'Are you bringing her to the staff do?'

'Staff do?'

'Have you forgotten? You approved the idea. Twenty-first of June—next Monday night for those who forget to look at the calendar. Formal or fancy dress or Celtic, yet to be decided. A money raiser. Charity to be determined by the boss.' She tapped his chest. 'That would be you.'

He grunted. Someone had come up with the idea in February for a winter solstice celebration as a morale booster, he remembered, but he'd been working in Sydney for most of this year and it had slipped his mind.

'So are you going to bring her?' she asked again.

'No.'

'Why not?'

Because...? He preferred the idea of something more intimate for their first date, not a roomful of colleagues garnering Ellie's attention. When he and Ellie got together—and they would—he didn't want an audience. 'We're not involved.'

'Yeah, I noticed,' Yasmine said dryly. 'Bring her anyway. Make Belle happy.'

It *would* be a way to keep his word to Belle that he was looking out for Ellie. 'We'll see,' he muttered, more to shut Yasmine up than any promise on his part. But for now... He clicked open a folder on his computer. 'Moving on to more important matters,' he said, ignoring Yasmine's grin. 'Bring me up to speed on the Dalton project.'

'Six beers, two tequilas, one rum and Coke,' Ellie recited to herself, sliding the requested drinks order onto her tray. She started towards the table of rowdy guys, wishing her black skirt was a few centimetres longer.

The atmosphere inside the club oozed sweat, cheap aftershave and testosterone. A lone pole-dancer was doing her thing to bad music over a poor sound system. According to Ellie's fellow waitress, Tuesday night wasn't usually busy, but an entire football team had turned up after training and were jostling for viewing space.

Her throat felt scratchy with the constant strain of having to raise her voice over the noise. They were one staff member short. Sasha, who'd arranged the shift for Ellie and was supposed to be here to help her through the first night, hadn't turned up. Ellie suppressed her annoyance. Perhaps Sasha was sick, but she should have phoned.

Well, she was doing just fine tonight without her help, thank you very much. Only a few more hours with Sleazy in the cheap business suit mentally undressing her from his corner table and she was out of here.

She offloaded the beers, carried the rum and Coke to Sleazy's table.

'How about a nightcap when you finish up here?' he asked her breasts as she set the glass down.

'No, thanks.' Booze had made him more obnoxious than he'd been an hour earlier.

'Come on, babe. We'd make a good team, you and me.'

'I don't think so.' She turned to leave but he grasped her wrist. She wrenched her arm away, toppling his drink. Liquid splashed the table, sloshing over the edge and onto his shiny polyester trousers.

'Everything okay, here, Ellie?' A familiar deep voice behind her.

She darted a look over her shoulder, glimpsed Matt and groaned inwardly. With relief, with embarrassment. 'How long have you been here?' And how come she hadn't seen him arrive?

'Long enough.' Then to Sleazy, he leaned low and murmured, 'I suggest you leave while you still can.'

Sleazy glared at Ellie a moment as if deciding to make something of it, then rose. 'You'll pay for this,' he muttered, swiping at the damp patch on his leg. He didn't give eye contact to Matt, she noted, but he sent Ellie a final glare, then pushed his way towards the bar.

'You okay?' She felt Matt's hand at her back but shrugged it off before she did something stupid—like arch against it and purr. 'I'm fine. Please let me get on with my job.'

He stepped back. 'Fine. Get on with it.'

His clipped reply reminded her that she'd been prickly and ungrateful—a survival mechanism, but rude nonetheless—so she followed up with, 'Would you like a drink? On the house.'

He nodded. 'Mineral water. Thanks.'

She watched him return to an empty table on the far side of the room, away from the tables she was serving, and flick open a folder he'd left there. His dark eyes met hers again, sending ripples of awareness down her spine.

Smoothing her skirt, she headed to the bar to place his order and paid for it herself. She couldn't remember the last time someone had bothered to come to her rescue. Even if she hadn't needed it. She reminded herself she didn't need anyone, particularly Matt McGregor, stamping all over her independence.

So when she came by with his drink a few moments later,

she couldn't help herself. 'There are much better strip clubs in town, as I'm sure you—'

'Yes. I know.' He studied her a moment, an almost-grin lurking around his mouth. Then picked up his glass, raised it to her, took a long slow swallow. 'But the evening's young yet.'

Something hot quivered low in her belly, prompting her to say, 'Unless the stripper's a personal friend of yours?' She saw his eyes narrow and leaned towards him a fraction. 'You're checking up on me,' she accused. 'Did you think I was lying to you this morning?'

'Would you lie to me, Ellie?' His gaze slid to her lips. 'About how you feel, for instance?'

Her pulse jumped up a notch and she took a swift step back. Away from the incredible aura he seemed to exude. 'Why would I?'

'Only you can answer that.' Still watching her, he took another swallow from his glass.

'Listen, I don't need a minder—'

'Belle's idea.'

She huffed an impatient breath. 'I'm sure she didn't mean for you to intrude on my private life.'

'I have a moral obligation since I don't consider this a safe working environment. And hasn't that been proven justified?'

She looked away, only to catch the disapproving eye of the bar manager. So it seemed it was okay to be sexually harassed and threatened but chatting with the customers was frowned upon. 'I need to get back to work.'

He set his glass down, flicked an eye over his folder, then drew out his phone. 'And I need to make a call.'

She knew Matt was there, was conscious of his eyes following her for the next couple of hours, even though whenever she glanced his way he had his nose buried in his folder or was speaking into his mobile phone. At one point he was smiling while he talked and she just knew he wasn't talking business—unless it was funny business. And that, she told herself, was none of *her* business.

It was sometime after midnight when the manager paid her at the end of her shift and told her that her services were not required. He told her there'd been a complaint, that she'd come on to a customer, then deliberately spilled his drink when he'd knocked her invitation back. So the manager had docked her the cost of the drink for the damage that the *customer* had caused.

Resentment spiked through her bloodstream. 'That's not how it was and you know it.' Giving him the best evil eye she could manage, she stuffed what was left of her night's pay into her bag, buttoned her coat with quick jerky movements. 'You can take your lousy job and stick it in a very dark place,' she snapped out on her way to the nearest exit.

Ellie was accustomed to people expecting her to be an easy walkover. Usually she fought back. She could have argued her case; she was the injured party here. Tonight, as she manoeuvred her way through testosterone city, all she wanted to do was get out of this pit and lay her throbbing head on a pillow and sleep for a week. Was she coming down with a bug?

She shook it away. Not going to happen. She had to rise and shine early tomorrow. At this point she really, really needed Belle's part-time job. And *now* it came with an additional problem... Speaking of which, did she say goodbye to Matt or what? Would he think she was angling for a lift home? Or more? She glanced to where he'd been sitting moments earlier but he'd left. Without a word.

Good, she told herself as she veered back towards the exit. One less problem. Tomorrow morning was way soon enough to be interacting with him. She wasn't in the mood to deal with complications. And despite his views about their *non-*

relationship, Matt McGregor was *complication* in flashing lights. Big red warning ones.

Doing his gentlemanly duty as he saw Ellie preparing to leave, he exited the bar and waited for her outside.

She'd told him she wanted to be left alone, but safety concerns aside, knowing where she'd be this evening had been too much of a temptation for Matt to ignore. He'd wanted to see her again, simple as that. He stepped towards her the moment she appeared. 'I'll walk you to your car.'

Her head swivelled towards him and her eyes widened. 'Why are you still here?'

The damp air teased her hair so that it curled in wisps around her face. She must have washed it again because it was lighter—honey blonde with only a streak or two of pink—but the austere light from the street lamp turned it silver-white, making her appear smaller, more fragile.

'You think I'd leave you here at this time of night without ensuring your safe journey home?' Wherever that might be.

She pulled her coat tighter, straightened her spine, hitched her bag higher. 'I can take care of myself.'

'Yeah, right. Alone, past midnight, in this seedy area. Where's your car?'

'I don't own a car. And I happen to live in this seedy area.' He didn't miss the light of contempt in her eyes.

Along with her list of criticisms, did she think him prejudiced? He couldn't decide whether it amused or annoyed him. 'How are you getting home?'

'Public transport.'

'My car's across the road. I'll drop you off.'

'It's—'

'Non-negotiable.' He placed a silencing finger against her lips.

Heat, as her sharp exhalation of breath streamed over his

fingertip. Friction, as his finger drifted lightly over her lips. Desire, sharp and swift, as her lips parted the tiniest bit. In surprise? Or something else? He couldn't be sure, and for a pulse beat or two he thought she might yield and open further. But she remained completely still.

'Non-negotiable, Ellie.' He pressed his thumb to her lower lip, watching her eyes darken to an intense charcoal in the dimness. 'So get used to the idea quickly.'

CHAPTER FOUR

ELLIE didn't move, didn't pull away, even as a throng of raucous patrons spilled from the bar and ambled past, their voices raised in some tuneless song. The night breeze, pungent with the sting of exhaust fumes, wrapped around them. In the distance an alarm wailed. He wanted to press his momentary advantage, replace his thumb with his mouth and relive that first kiss.

He could almost smell the desire on her skin, but he didn't push it. She stepped back, eyes flicking away, as if giving him eye contact might betray her. She scanned the row of parked cars. 'Let me guess—yours is the champagne-tinted convertible.'

'Sorry to disappoint—it's the little bent and black ninety-six Ford.' He couldn't resist adding, 'My Ferrari's in Sydney.'

Her laugh was spontaneous and unexpected and she seemed as surprised as he. 'I *knew* it,' she said with a half-smile. 'Red?'

'Is there any other colour?' With a light hand at her back, he steered her across the road.

Ellie practically fell onto the seat, willing her pulse to settle down while Matt rounded the car. Good Lord, just that single thumb print on her lower lip had turned her inside out. If he hadn't stopped—oh, she did not want to think about it. He made her weak. Made her want…what she couldn't have.

By the time he'd climbed into his seat she'd managed to halfway calm herself. She directed him to a street about a kilometre away. She spent a moment studying the car's interior rather than the width of Matt's more than capable hands on the steering wheel, focusing on the engine's rough-throated purr rather than the scent of clean masculine skin.

But as they neared her apartment her breathing changed for very different reasons. And with every passing moment the band beneath her breastbone tightened.

She'd always sensed Heath's low opinion of her previous apartment even though he'd never voiced it. As if her living conditions reflected her worth as a human being. She might have been in love with him but her self-confidence and sense of self-worth had taken a battering and never fully recovered. Compared to this dump it had been a palace.

Would Matt the squillionaire businessman judge her the same way? And why did it suddenly seem to matter if he did? 'You can drop me off here,' she said, ready to jump out and flee the moment they stopped.

The building she lived in was crammed between the abandoned car park of a graffiti-covered warehouse and a row of currently untenanted shops.

Matt slowed to a stop. 'This your place?'

His tone didn't change but her stomach clenched tighter. 'Yes.' She knew what he was thinking. She just knew it. She would *not* let it bring her down.

She reached for the doorhandle. Before she could thank him and escape, he was out of the car and rounding the bonnet.

'No need to see me inside—I live upstairs,' she said, climbing out. Somewhere nearby a cat yowled and the din of metal rolling down the street broke the night's stillness.

'How long have you lived here?'

'A couple of months.' She remembered him quipping about his Ferrari. 'Would it help if I said I used to live in Toorak?'

she said, forcing humour into her voice as she mentioned one of Melbourne's most affluent suburbs.

He didn't return her smile. 'Only if it helps *you*.'

It didn't and her smile faded. Those days were gone. Once upon a time, before the people she loved had been erased from her life for ever, her world had been very different.

But his voice helped. Smooth and steady and even, like a still lake, soothing the rough edges around her heart. Until she looked up into his eyes and saw the storm, all dark and brooding and beautiful. Reminding her that she didn't want to get involved. With anyone, ever again.

'Thanks for the lift.' She paused before adding, 'And thanks for your assistance at the bar tonight.'

'No worries.' He didn't seem in a hurry to leave.

She hesitated. 'I'll see you tomorrow, then.'

He nodded. 'You're coming. Good.'

'I didn't get the bar job, so yes.' She shrugged, trying for philosophical, failing miserably.

'Because it wasn't the right job for you.' There was something in his eyes. Not sympathy—she didn't want sympathy, nor did she need it. Understanding?

She stood, rooted to the spot, watching him while he jingled his car keys. What the hell would he understand about the tough non-corporate world of low finance?

'Goodnight, Ellie.' He touched his lips to hers. A token kiss, almost impersonal. No sexual undertones. Nothing she could call him on.

And nothing to get herself in a lather about.

Because now he'd watched her lose a job on the first night and seen where she lived, what other kind of kiss could it be?

She stepped away before she kissed him back and made it into something it wasn't. 'Goodnight.'

She turned abruptly and made it through the entry door and

halfway along the common hallway before the door behind her opened again. She looked over her shoulder. Matt's silhouette filled the space and a thrill of excitement shivered down her spine before she could stop it. 'Is something wrong?'

'Damn right something's wrong.' He stepped inside and walked towards her, his shoes echoing on the worn concrete floor, his features growing clearer as he neared. 'I should be ashamed of myself. Kissing you that way.'

Huh? Her mouth fell open in astonishment and she remained where she was, sure her heartbeat would wake the entire building. 'It's okay.' The words trembled out. 'I didn't—'

'Since when do you let a guy kiss you like that and get away with it?' He gripped her shoulders. Walked her back until her shoulders touched the wall, eyes glittering in the dim stairwell's light. His face was close, his hands possessive, stroking down her upper arms.

With what little strength she had left, she hugged her handbag in front of her like a shield. 'Depends... On who's doing the kissing.' Oh, good Lord, had she said that aloud, and in that thin reedy voice that seemed to be coming from someone else?

His sensuous lips curved and he moved nearer. His jeans brushed against her bare legs. Hard thighs rubbed hers...and heat speared into her lower belly. Her arms slid uselessly to her sides, leaving her bag dangling from one shoulder.

'I am,' he murmured before his mouth descended on hers.

She could no more hold back her response than stop the sun from rising. Her lips fell open beneath his and her whole body shuddered against him. Without any idea of how they got there, her hands slid to his waist and grasped fistfuls of his shirt beneath his jacket.

His taste was as she remembered, only more. Richer, fuller, more intoxicating—

'Excuse me, Ellie... Perhaps you could take your displays of...affection upstairs?'

Ellie jerked back, her head bouncing off the wall. 'Um, hi. Mrs Green.' From apartment two. And looking less than impressed that they were all but standing in front of her door. Ducking under Matt's arm, Ellie spun away into the passage, fumbling with her slippery hold on her bag at the same time. 'Um. Sorry.'

Matt and Ellie regarded each other without speaking until her downstairs neighbour's door closed and they were alone again.

It gave Ellie time to gather her jumbled thoughts. She considered it a minor miracle that she was able to say, 'It's late and I'm tired,' in a reasonably steady no-nonsense voice. And she meant it. Every muscle felt sapped of energy and she had no idea whether it was Matt's fault or the bug she seemed to be coming down with.

Matt, who'd propped himself against the wall, watched her with a hint of the devil in his eyes. 'Mrs Green's suggestion sounds good to me.'

'Not to me.' Straightening, she pulled out her keys. 'I've worked two jobs today. Goodnight, Matt.' She caught a glimpse of that sexy grin before she forced herself to turn away and head for the stairs.

It was way, way harder than she wanted it to be.

Ellie was woken by a dull throbbing headache when her alarm trilled at 7:00 a.m. And when she swallowed, it was like forcing a razor blade down her throat. To her surprise, she realised she'd slept the entire night, probably because she'd been so exhausted.

So how come she felt as if she hadn't slept a wink?

With a groan, she dragged herself out of bed and peered through her dust-spattered window at the heavy-bellied clouds just visible in the dawn sky. A dark rain shower swept across the distant suburbs, wind whistled with malice around the ill-fitting pane.

A perfect day to burrow back under her quilt and nurse her sore throat. But she didn't have that luxury, so she grabbed a couple of painkillers at the kitchen sink before stumbling to the bathroom.

She stepped beneath the ancient showerhead, shivering as she soaped up quickly under the meagre lukewarm stream. She'd just bet Matt McGregor was still tucked up nice and warm in *his* bed.

And after that kiss last night...well, she might have been sharing it with him. His hot, hard body pressing her into the mattress, springy masculine hair rasping against her nipples. That deep voice, gravelly with sleep and sinful suggestions while his fingers played out those sinful suggestions over her—

'Get those X-rated thoughts of your *employer's nephew* right out of your head,' she ordered herself, whipping the shower curtain aside, creating a shivery draught. Grabbing her towel, she rubbed briskly to get the blood flowing beneath her skin. 'Concentrate on important matters. Like an income.'

Belle paid her generously, but she needed to supplement it with another part-time job and somehow fit both jobs in around the volunteer after-school shifts she worked at the children's centre around the corner.

She loved kids but she'd never fall in love again, could never risk a failed marriage. Which meant no children, ever. But her maternal instincts were very much alive, and working with underprivileged children was her way of satisfying that natural urge.

Grabbing a muesli bar, she swung her gear onto her shoulder and headed out into the wintry day. The tram was crowded and stuffy with early-morning commuters, and Ellie was glad of the fresh air when she disembarked just after eight and walked the last few minutes to Belle's place.

Remembering yesterday, she knocked on the back door to let Matt know she'd arrived. She could always hope he'd already gone to work. On the other hand she could hope she'd gotten him out of bed. To see him dishevelled and disgruntled at her early arrival. Bleary-eyed, unshaven…

'Good morning, Ellie.'

She turned at his voice. He was none of those things.

Fully dressed in dark jeans and a soft-looking cream jumper that probably cost more than her entire wardrobe, he ambled from the garage, morning newspaper and a carton of milk in hand. He'd obviously showered and shaved already; the fresh smell of sandalwood soap carried on the breeze. And his eyes were bright, alert and focused. On her.

Memories of last night's kiss hung in the air between them. But this was a working day, a working environment, and she intended keeping it that way.

'Good morning.' She cleared her throat, wincing at the raw pain as she did so and trotted down the back steps with an officious, 'I'll be getting on with it, then.'

'Want a coffee before you start?'

'No, thanks. I want to make some headway before it starts to rain.'

'What are your plans today?'

'I have to finish digging over the plot.' Which she should have finished yesterday, but with Matt calling the meeting and all, it had put her behind. She kept moving, walking backwards as she spoke. 'Then it's the fertiliser and seedlings— Belle left everything in the greenhouse. Are you going to the office?'

'I don't plan on it,' he said, dashing her hopes for a day

without the prospect of further interruptions. 'I've a costing to finish and a computer link-up with the Sydney crew.'

She nodded. 'I'll come by the door when I'm done.'

When she stopped for lunch, she ate her sandwich and drank her thermos of coffee alone. Despite what she'd told Matt about being self-sufficient, Belle always invited Ellie inside to share her break.

On the last day Ellie had seen her, Belle had offered her a key to the main house, allowing her access to the bathroom and hot water. But she'd felt awkward about the whole idea and refused it. If anything happened in Belle's absence Ellie didn't want to be held responsible; it was bad enough that she'd given her the code to the gate.

She'd not glimpsed Matt since she'd started work this morning. Seemed he was in accord with her—business hours were just that. She didn't know whether she was relieved or disappointed.

Her mobile rang as she was packing away her lunch box. She glanced at caller ID and answered straightaway. 'Sasha. I tried calling you last night. Where did you get to?'

'I called in sick. I just opened your message.'

Her friend sounded distant and Ellie felt that all-too-familiar clutch in her belly. 'Are you okay now?'

'Never better.'

'So are you up to checking out that Healesville job with me sometime soon? We need to let them know—'

'Ah, about that…' A pause, then Sasha went into excitement mode with, 'I met this great guy at a club last night. Anyway…' she went on when Ellie didn't reply, 'I've got the chance to work onboard a cruise ship leaving Sydney in a week's time.'

Disappointment ripped through Ellie. 'I thought you said you were sick last night?'

'Everyone chucks a sickie now and then, right?'

No. Not when it mattered they didn't. 'I was counting on you to show me the ropes at the bar last night.'

'Oh. Sorry. Did you get the job, by the way?'

'Let's just say I'm not cut out for that sort of waitressing. Which is why this Healesville job is important to me.' She closed her eyes, surrendered to the inevitable. 'Sasha, obviously your heart's not in this, so take the cruise job and forget Healesville.' *Forget everything.*

The bed-and-breakfast place out of Melbourne was offering a four-week stint to landscape their garden, and Ellie had persuaded Sasha to come along. Ellie had explained that she didn't want to let Belle down while she was away and had promised to get back to them by the end of next week. She intended winning the job, with or without Sasha.

'Hey, you there, Ellie?'

'I'm here.'

'So…I'll call you when I get back and maybe we can—'

'There's no point, Sasha, it's just not practical. Good luck with everything. Goodbye.' *And have a nice life.* She stabbed the disconnect button.

She'd thought they were friends. But true friends didn't let each other down. When was she going to learn? Ellie had some kind of in-built radar that sent people running in the opposite direction.

Remember that when you think about Matt McGregor.

As befitting her mood, ten minutes later it started to spit—a cold, ugly, misty spit. Ellie pulled on her thin plastic poncho and continued digging. She would *not* quit on account of rain. Unlike Sasha, she'd prove herself reliable and responsible and accountable if it killed her.

Matt pulled himself mentally and physically out of his work. He glanced at his watch, surprised to find he'd worked through the lunch break he'd set himself. He'd intended talking Ellie into sharing a coffee. Stretching fingers cramped from working the keyboard, he wrapped them around his neck and glanced at the window. Rain spattered the glass.

He walked to the kitchen window and saw her. Mud splattered her overalls up to her knees. She was measuring and pouring pellets into her hand, sprinkling them over the earth, then moving on to repeat the procedure. The misty rain speckled the flimsy plastic she'd pulled on but the cap had blown off, leaving dark honey locks damp and curling over her head.

His gaze narrowed. Yesterday he'd raised the question of her responsibility. After all, it was she who'd labelled herself irresponsible. Was she now trying to prove a point? Responsible was all well and good, but there wasn't much point to it if the woman came down with pneumonia.

He stalked to the back door, grabbing an umbrella from the coat stand on the way. Rain spattered his soft leather shoes. It wasn't heavy but constant, and obviously had been for some time. But the wind was fierce—it snuck under the umbrella, threatening to turn it inside out.

She was facing away from him and didn't hear his approach. Or was she choosing not to?

'Why the hell are you still out here in this weather?' He reached for her shoulder to swing her around but she squealed and jerked and he lost his footing in the slimy mud her digging had created. The umbrella was forgotten as he fought the inevitable and ignominious slide to the ground, taking her with him.

At the last second he managed to twist them both so that she landed on top of him in a blur of limbs and bad language. While he was still trying to catch his breath, he stared up at the rain-spattered sky, contemplating this example of life's little jokes. Cold muddy moisture seeped through the back of his jumper, a striking contrast to the warm wet body plastered against his chest.

When she didn't move, he raised his head and wheezed, 'You all right?'

'Oh, yeah, never better,' she snapped. Apparently unconcerned that he might be on his last breath, her only movement was to disentangle her legs from his and tug on the strap of her overalls.

He would have laughed at the situation but what air was left in his lungs exploded out of him as her elbow jabbed him in the solar plexus.

'Sorry.' She twisted some more, the sound of plastic crinkling as she continued struggling to free herself. He didn't try to help. Giving up the attempt for the moment, she glared down at him. '*What* were you thinking?'

Rain-spiked lashes blinked at him over those gorgeous lilac-coloured eyes. When he could breathe again, he smelled summer raspberries and her own brand of hot feminine scent. The scent a woman exudes after a healthy bout of exercise. Or sex. He took this unique opportunity to draw it in slowly.

What had she said? Something about thinking... 'I wasn't.' If he'd been *thinking* he'd have engineered this scenario somewhere dry—on Belle's Persian rug in front of a roaring fire, for instance. Minus the wet clothing.

'I was reacting,' he continued, 'to your hare-brained idea of working outdoors in these conditions.'

'It's where most gardening's done.' She rolled a shoulder, the movement shifting her breasts against his stomach. He wasn't sure, but he imagined he could feel two stiff nipples jutting just above his navel.

A spear of heat shot through his body, angling straight to his groin. Doing his damnedest to ignore it, he stared up at the sky again and continued with, 'So is this your attempt to prove you're responsible or stubborn or both?'

Her hips chafed against his as she dragged a trapped hand from between their bodies to push at her crinkled hair. 'What's a little rain, for heaven's sakes?'

His gaze shifted to her face. To her eyes, irises dark with some unnamed emotion she refused to admit to. Her mouth, damp with rain and a tempting whisper from his own. He could kiss her now, drink in the freshness of raindrops and Ellie. 'For one thing, it's wet. And damn cold.'

She stared back at him, shook her head. 'You indoor career types are too soft.'

He didn't feel soft. And if she didn't quit squirming against him like that she was going to find that out for herself.

And bingo: She went completely still, and when he looked, her eyes had widened. He watched the colour intensify, her cheeks turn a shade pinker before she scrambled up on her knees and pushed away. Up. Pieces of her now-shredded plastic poncho flapped like flags in the wind.

'Stubborn, then,' he muttered. He pushed up too, his jumper peeling away from the mud with a slimy sound. An instant chill cloaked his body. 'We'd better get out of these wet clothes.'

Without looking at him she picked up her trowel. 'You go ahead, I need to clean up here first.'

'Leave it, I'll come out later and tidy up.'

'My job, I'll do it.'

'Fine. Catch pneumonia.'

Without looking at him, she stacked everything in the barrow, including the mangled umbrella, with infuriating slowness, then wheeled it to the garden shed. So be it. He could be as ridiculously stubborn about this as she.

He waited until she locked up, put the key in its hidey-hole, then took her sweet time walking back with her pack on her shoulder. Even from metres away he could see she was shivering, that now the blush had faded, her cheeks were pale and there were dark circles beneath her eyes.

He met her halfway across the lawn. He didn't think about whether she'd object, just took her chilled wet hand in his. 'Come on.' He hustled her up the path to the verandah, pulling away the plastic remains of her poncho as they shuffled under shelter and into the laundry. 'A hot shower will warm you up. Or a bath. Whichever you prefer.'

'No. I'll be all right.'

'Ellie.' Concerned now, he shot her a stern look. 'You're wet through. You're going to take that shower if I have to put you under it myself.' He peeled off his sodden jumper, tossed it on the floor.

Her gaze slid like a hot silk glove down his chest. He was about to make a joke of it all, but something warned him she wouldn't see the humour right now. She gulped, then lifted panicked eyes to his. 'I'm all muddy.'

'That you are. I'll find you some of Belle's clothes.'

She shook her head. 'I'm not trailing mud and water all through the house.'

'Take off your shoes.' He stepped out of his, removed his socks.

Ellie did the same, then looked up at him. *Not* looking at that gloriously exposed chest. Oh, why had she thought working in the rain was a good idea? At the time she hadn't given any thought to the mud factor. Nor had she counted on them wallowing in it. Together. 'My shoes aren't the only things covered in mud.'

She regretted those words instantly. She felt the heat in his gaze as it travelled over the rest of her and wondered why her clothes weren't steaming.

'Same here.' If anything, he was in a worse state than her. The entire length of him was iced in shiny brown mud. He unsnapped his sodden jeans.

Ah... 'What are you doing?'

'Someone has to do *something* if we're going to find clean dry clothes,' he said, being entirely too practical.

It took a moment for him to ease his jeans over his hips and step out of them. Involuntarily—that's what she told herself—her eyes followed his fingers down the length of his strongly muscled thighs and over his knees to the hairy calves and long knobbly toes as he shucked the denim off.

And, oh... My goodness. Except for a pair of navy boxers which rode low on his lean hips, he was stark-staring naked. She sucked in a breath.

Imagine him naked.

But the perfection of his golden-toned body was even better than her imagination had been able to conjure up. She could smell his skin. Two steps closer and she'd be able to reach out and touch. Another step and she'd be able to taste.

No. If she let him close again, she was going to fall for him; she just knew it. And it would be a much harder landing than that soft mudslide a few moments ago. Safer to keep her distance. And the only way to keep that distance was to *not* give him any encouragement.

If he'd noticed her indulging in her little fantasy, he didn't show it. He was all matter of fact and purpose, rescuing his clothes from the floor and dumping them in the laundry trough.

Ellie remained where she was. Did he expect her to follow his lead? She could take off her overalls and still be no more exposed than she would in her bikini...but that wasn't going to happen. Not with Matt McGregor watching on.

'Use this,' he said, handing her a sheet which he pulled from a nearby cupboard. 'You can slip out of your things and wrap it around you. When you're ready, meet me in the kitchen.'

Moments later, down to her underwear, and clutching the

sheet around her, Ellie followed Matt through a formal lounge and dining room. If she could just keep her sex-starved eyes off his broad-shouldered, near-naked body along the way... She bit back a sigh at the way the light played over the muscles beneath that healthy olive-toned skin and his hairy masculine thighs before making a conscious effort to avert her gaze.

She'd never been upstairs, but as she followed Matt, it was clear Belle paid the same loving attention to detail throughout the grand old house. She passed a pretty feminine bedroom, then a bedroom with a huge four-poster bed and a mountain of maroon quilt. A pair of shiny black men's shoes were placed neatly on the floor at the foot of the bed. A perfectly pressed snowy shirt hung on a hanger on the wardrobe door.

Matt slept in this room.

Her blood thickened and, without realising, she slowed, hoping for a glimpse of something that told her more about the man beyond the obvious fact that he was tidy. She shook it away, reminding herself she knew all she needed to know. She wasn't here for a tour. She was here to get clean.

'This is the guest room,' Matt said, opening a door further down. 'The en suite's through there.' He gestured to another door on the far side of the room. 'You should find everything you need. Meanwhile I'll rustle up some clothes and leave them on the bed for you. When you're done, can you find your way back to the kitchen?'

'Yes. Thank you.'

'Take your time.'

She didn't reply, just waited until he left before relaxing enough to take it all in. Beautiful in shades of green and white and gold. Big double bed, snow-white quilt. Elegant pictures of a bygone era on the walls. A view over the rose garden, dark spikes now, in the dead of winter.

In the bathroom, light spilled through a skylight, bathing a froth of fernery in one corner. She flicked a switch and an instant flood of heat rolled over her shoulders. Absolute decadence.

There was a double-headed shower and a bath big enough for three. The bath won. When it was full she sank in and let frangipani-scented bubbles soak away the grime.

Not so easy to soak away thoughts of Matt and the way their bodies had clashed out there in the muddy garden plot. It put another spin on getting down and dirty.

He'd been turned on.

At the memory of that hard, hot masculine wedge beneath her a bolt of heat shot to her core. Had he been turned on before or after she'd wiggled? And she'd reacted to that subtle prod like a frightened virgin.

Which was best all-round, she decided, diverting her concentration to scrubbing her skin until it tingled. It would give him yet another reason to think she wasn't interested in him and leave her alone.

Admit it, Ellie. You want him. You want him bad.

As her sex slave, she told herself. That was all. That was *all*?

Yes, she decided, swirling the bubbles through her fingers, *turn the social tables on him.* So...if he was in here with her... She flopped back against the bath's edge. She'd command him to start with her back. Keeping the best bits for last. Keeping the delicious anticipation to the max.

She have him kneel behind her, so close that she'd hear his heart beating, feel his breath against her hair. He'd lave beneath her ear, move on to her neck, her collarbone. Then he'd soap up those long, tanned fingers and drag them over her shoulders, down her breasts, stopping to massage her nipples, draw them out. Slowly...

She sneezed, an unwelcome explosion, dragging her out of the moment and back to reality.

And that reality appeared to be that she was, indeed,

coming down with a bug. She could not afford to get sick. She needed as much work as she could get. Which reminded her she was in her employer's bathroom, using Belle's lotions and potions and fantasising about her nephew. For goodness' sake.

She yanked out the plug and snatched one of the thick jade towels off the rack. Damn Matt. For making her want things she had no business wanting. Her employer's nephew. A man way out of her league.

Impossible.

CHAPTER FIVE

MATT knocked at the partially open bedroom door. When there was no answer, he entered carefully. He'd found one of Belle's jumpers, a pair of soft jersey sweatpants and thick socks. As for underwear... She'd have to go commando for now.

And wouldn't that be something to think about over steak and salad? He should have put the items on the bed and left, but the sweet floral scent seeping from beneath the door was too tempting to resist.

It had been a long time since his own bathroom had smelled like this. Feminine. Alluring. Inviting...

When he and Angela had shared an apartment. His jaw clenched. Those times were over. These days when he took a lover, it was his way or the highway. They used her place. He rarely slept the night. Sleeping implied a degree of intimacy he simply didn't have. Didn't want. Didn't need.

He breathed the scent in again, deeply. What did he know of the girl on the other side of that door? By her own admission, she was a drifter. How long before she up and left? Where did she go and what did she do, and who did she do it with while she was there?

Still... Until then, he didn't see a problem with them sharing something a little more personal when the gardening tools were packed away for the evening. And he could keep his word to Belle at the same time.

Unfortunately it couldn't be tonight. He'd organised a meeting with the construction manager on one of his latest Melbournian projects but Cole had been tied up elsewhere until this evening. They'd arranged to meet over a beer later.

He didn't intend to start something with Ellie tonight and not be able to finish it. When he got her naked, he wanted everything right. He wanted to take it slow, enjoy—

The sound of the bathroom door opening warned him to leave but it was already too late. Ellie wafted out on a cloud of scented steam and he waged a quick tug of war within himself. Her stifled yelp and the way she stood clutching her towel and damp underwear almost had a grin tugging at his mouth.

Until he got a better look at what she held in her hand. Fire-engine-red G-string, matching satin and lace bra. Surprise. Who'd have thought that beneath those ugly overalls…?

Remember Saturday night?

This was that same woman, and his pulse quickened, his mood sobering to something darker as the primitive side of him stirred to life. Her skin glowed a delicate peach. He imagined it was as soft and luscious as it looked. It took all his will not to stride right over there and sample it. Her legs, bared to her upper thigh, were perfection and she reminded him of a long-stemmed rose on a foggy day.

He couldn't seem to look away. Couldn't move. Felt as if his body had turned to stone. Inside his skin was another matter. His mouth was dry and his blood was surging south. Somehow he remembered why he was there, cleared his throat and lifted the bundle of clothes in his hands. 'I'll just put these on the bed.… I've put the rest of your clothes in the washing machine. Would you like me to add those?' He gestured to her bundle.

'No.'

Her fingers tightened into a fist around it and he got that she was thinking of his hands on her G-string.

He almost groaned aloud. *Way* bad timing. A fleeting thought that he could ring Cole and postpone darted through his mind, but their meeting was important and he was a professional first and foremost. Business took priority.

'Okay.' He swallowed, then continued with, 'If the trousers are too long you can roll the legs up or whatever....' He thought it wiser not to mention underwear again.

'Thanks.' She didn't move. 'Was there something else?'

'I'm fixing us a bite to eat when you're ready. How do you like your steak?'

'Steak?'

'You're not vegetarian, are you?'

'No, rare, and why are we having this conversation right here, *right now*?'

'Rare. Okay.' He made himself step back. 'I'll leave you to it, then.'

The instant he'd gone, Ellie rushed to the door and locked it before the man decided to come back to ask her wine preferences. He was fixing steak? For her? For *them*?

Dropping the towel, she hauled on the clothes he'd provided her with. In front of the mirror, she ran a comb through her unruly hair, then, with no hair straighteners in sight, gave it up as a lost cause. And what did it matter? She didn't care what Matt McGregor thought. Nor was she going to be impressed—or swayed—by his cooking prowess. She stuffed her damp undies in her backpack and started down the hallway, following the aroma of frying onions.

When she entered the kitchen Matt already had the steaks on the grill and was chopping tomatoes into a salad bowl. His freshly shampooed hair gleamed under the light and he wore another of those soft-looking jumpers.

She looked around for something to do. 'You want me to finish that?'

'All under control.' He inclined his head towards a jug of juice topped with mint leaves and ice. 'Help yourself.'

'Thank you.' She noted he already had one at his elbow and poured herself a glass. She felt dumb standing around without a task so she hefted herself onto a breakfast stool. 'Do you cook often?'

'Not as often as I like. Too busy. This week's going to give me a good opportunity. You?'

'Hate it.' She sipped the juice. Freshly juiced orange, pineapple and passionfruit. 'This is nice.'

'Juicing it at home's a vast improvement over supermarket brands. So...Ellie.' Multi-tasking Matt gave the onions a stir, flipped the steaks, reached for the cucumber. 'You mentioned you lived around here as a child. Do your parents still live in Melbourne?'

'No.' She didn't want to talk about her parents. It reminded her of how alone she was. But in the ensuing silence she knew courtesy demanded an elaboration of sorts. 'Mum and my grandparents died in a car accident more than eighteen years ago.'

His knife paused midslice, a measured compassion in his dark eyes. 'I'm sorry, Ellie. That must've been tough. How old were you?'

'Six.' A misty image of her mother singing a lullaby stole through her mind and her heart twisted. Even after all this time, the pain would shoot back at the most unexpected times.

'After, it was just my father and me for a couple of years travelling country Victoria and South Australia while he took the odd job....' *Then played the odd game of chance and lost what he'd earned.* She didn't tell him her father had only come back into her life when Mum had died.

Before Matt could ask, she said, 'In the end I held him back.'

He looked up sharply. 'What do you mean, you "held him back"? He was your father.'

'He couldn't look for work and care for me.' But deep down that nine-year-old inside her still cried. *He could have if he'd wanted to.*

Matt turned to slide the steaks onto two plates, muttering something she was probably better off not hearing. Because then she'd want to defend her father and tell Matt she'd forgive him in a moment if he ever came back. *She was that weak.*

She often wondered if that's why she felt compelled to move around the country. Was she hoping to find him? Or was she running from him? Running from any involvement that might tear open those childhood wounds that had never quite healed.

She turned the focus to him, or rather, away from her. 'What about your parents?'

His lips tightened as he set the sizzling plates on the breakfast bar. 'It's just me and Belle.'

Old pain. She heard it in his voice. Tight and angry. Saw it in his avoidance of eye contact. Recognised it because she lived with it herself, every day.

He pushed the salad bowl her way. 'Help yourself.'

'Thanks. Avocadoes too—my favourite,' she said to lighten the atmosphere as she spooned salad onto her plate.

So he didn't want to talk about it. She understood that. Men didn't delve into personal and emotional issues. Matt's mother's absence in his life—for whatever reason that he wasn't inclined to share with her—had left scars. As it would, of course. But she had a feeling it went much deeper than grief. There was a bitterness and anger there too.

They ate in silence for a few moments, listening to the

sound of the rain lashing the window. The stormy weather had intensified over the past hour.

'Do you ever—' The jingle of Matt's mobile phone in the adjoining room cut Ellie off.

'Excuse me.'

Matt rose, leaving her alone in the kitchen with a jumble of thoughts running through her head. The family he didn't want to discuss and the walls he'd erected.

He'd made no attempt to disguise his attraction to her, but obviously that was as far as it went. His interest was purely physical. Unfortunately it was becoming more and more obvious that, for her, it went beyond that. His sheer magnetism drew her, sparking an undercurrent of excitement which flowed constantly just beneath the surface of her skin, so strong she wondered that she didn't glow in the dark, and leaving her in a perpetual state of anticipation. She'd never known anything this intense.

But despite his unwillingness to open up, he also had a nurturing, caring side no other male had ever shown her. In fact, he could be downright chivalrous, and that was so... attractive. Seductive. Alluring as it was alarming.

Which meant she needed to be on her guard at all times.

His voice carried through the open doorway. She heard the name of a five-star hotel mentioned. And then the lobby at 8:00 p.m. He'd be a little later than they'd arranged. Unavoidably detained... Looking forward to catching up...

Was his tone an indication that he was talking to a woman or did he speak to everyone in that deep velvet voice? She didn't know him well enough to tell...was this just Ellie being slightly paranoid Ellie?

'Matthew's always been a bit of a playboy....'

Something hard and heavy lobbed dead centre in her chest. She jabbed the point of her knife into her half-eaten steak, hacked off a piece, jammed it in her mouth. Why the hell did it matter who he met? She chewed vigorously. Or what he did with whomever it was tonight? At 8:00 p.m. In one of the best hotels in the city.

She tried to swallow but the food lodged behind the knot which had formed in her throat over the past couple of minutes.

'Meat not to your liking?' Matt took his seat once more and resumed eating.

'It's…very nice,' she managed and swallowed carefully. 'Just a bit of a sore throat.' She reached for her juice to wash it down. 'I need an early night. In fact…' She made a show of glancing at her watch, didn't note the time. 'I'll get going. There's a tram due in ten minutes. I'll collect my other clothes later.'

'I'll drop you home.'

'Not necessary, I've an umbrella in my bag.' *And you have a date.*

'I insist. I have to go out in any case—I'll drop you off on the way. Just give me a moment.'

She accepted because she really didn't feel one hundred percent and it was easier than arguing. But she almost changed her mind when he reappeared in dark trousers and a smart charcoal jacket that looked as if it had been tailored exclusively for him. A few wisps of masculine hair were visible at the open neck of his shirt.

He'd splashed on that cologne she'd smelled the other night. Something free and fresh and foresty that reminded her of secret midnight trysts.

She thought about that—and him—when she climbed into her narrow bed after he'd dropped her outside her apartment building a short time later. And reminded herself that permanent playboys were not for her.

* * *

Matt rolled over, peered at the digital readout on his clock and swore. Seven-thirty.

He dragged a hand over his face. He felt as if he hadn't caught more than ten minutes' shut-eye at any one time. Erotic dreams had plagued him from the moment his head had hit the pillow. The kind of dreams he'd not experienced since puberty.

Ellie was entirely to blame.

Pushing the quilt down to cool his overheated body, he stared at the ceiling's blank canvas, hoping to rid himself of the images still dancing behind his eyes.

No such luck. It didn't make a scrap of difference that he'd chatted up a tall well-constructed New York advertising executive after his meeting with Cole. Lysandra. Lissendra? He'd bought her a cocktail and they'd discussed… Global warming. A couple of cocktails on, she'd had a few interesting suggestions to help cure his insomnia. And he'd come close to letting her try.

Until a vision of Ellie Rose wearing nothing but that towel had sauntered into his mind like a siren from days gone by… He sat up in bed, scratched his morning stubble. Damn it.

Since when had he turned down a woman like Lissandra whose requirements ticked all the right boxes? Why would he pass up an opportunity like that for a girl who didn't want to get involved, despite her eyes and the way she kissed telling him otherwise? A girl nothing like the women he dated.

And that girl would be turning up at any moment, if she wasn't here already. Easing off the bed, he padded down the passage and into a spare bedroom for a view of the backyard. Low on the horizon, the early morning's thin lemon sunlight was sliding obliquely between the clouds, glistening wetly on the lawn. He scanned the boggy patch where Ellie had been working yesterday. The garden shed. The back porch.

No sign of her.

She'd be here, he told himself; she wanted the job. Still, he felt oddly disappointed she hadn't arrived yet. He wanted to see that glimpse of sunshine turn her hair to old gold and watch the jaunty, carefree way she had of moving.

He folded his arms across his chest as chilly air prickled his skin. Yeah, right. Watching her while he stood here naked. Scowling, he scrubbed a hand over his jaw. *Lucky for you, you're not here yet, Ellie Rose.*

Meanwhile he needed a cold shower and he needed it fast.

While he shivered and soaped up under the spray, he made a decision. This thing between them needed serious attention. Tonight. Get it out of their systems—two rational, consenting adults—then they could move on.

He turned off the taps, reached for his towel. Satisfied with his plan, he lathered on shaving cream and reached for his razor.

He checked his emails over fruit and toast. Coffee in hand, he made a follow-up call to last night's meeting with Cole. Then he phoned the office to inform Joanie he'd be in before ten and took the next little while to look over a new project.

When Ellie still hadn't turned up by nine o'clock he grew annoyed. He paced to the window. The devil of it was, he had no good reason to be so ticked off. Ellie kept her own timetable and Belle hadn't expected him to wait around. But he was here now, and in Belle's absence he felt he was entitled to know Ellie's plans for today. Keep an eye on things. Keep his finger on the pulse.

He swung away. *No, not Ellie's pulse.* Although if she didn't get here soon he might have to throttle her.

He was a busy man. He didn't have time to... He checked his watch. Nearly nine-fifteen. ...Didn't have time to *waste*.

At ten o'clock he rang Joanie to tell her he'd been detained, that he'd phone again when he was on his way.

Responsibility. They'd talked about it. Ellie had worked two days and been on time. Perhaps that was her limit. He tapped in her phone number. Swore when her phone was switched off. She had no answering service so he couldn't leave a voice message.

He paced to the window, glared at the front gate. When she arrived he'd tell her his expectations: While he was here, he preferred—wanted—her to keep regular hours... Damn, why wait until she'd arrived? He'd go inform her himself. That way he could drive her here if she was running late.

A short time later he parked and stared up at her sorry-looking apartment building. Daylight showed the dull facade in all its unspectacular glory. Grey peeling paintwork. Dusty windows.

He climbed out of his car and walked to the door. In this instance he was relieved it wasn't a coded entry—except that anyone could walk in off the street. He took the stairs two at a time and followed a dingy passage until he found apartment number four, then knocked on the door.

No answer. Impatience snapped at him; he barely waited before knocking again, louder, longer. 'Ellie, are you in there?'

A scruffy-looking sort in a grey hooded jacket with straggly blond hair and teenage fuzz above his upper lip exited an apartment down the hall. Mid- to late teens, Matt figured. The odour of sweat and dirty sneakers preceded the guy as he approached.

Matt's nostrils flared in distaste. But Ellie had no choice; she couldn't afford anything better. Matt understood that all too well.

'She ain't left yet,' Scruffy said as he passed Matt.

He studied the youth through narrowed eyes. 'And you'd know this how?'

Scruffy popped a wad of chewing gum in his mouth. 'See everyone from my living room window. You dropped her off last night. Night before too. Black Ford, right?'

A twinge of concern jolted through Matt. 'Do you watch everyone's comings and goings?'

'Pretty much,' he said cheerfully. 'Ain't safe round here. It's just me and Mum, and she's in a wheelchair, so I keep an eye out.'

'And you are?'

'Toby.' He stuck his hands in the pockets of his hoodie. 'You Ellie's new boyfriend?'

'I'm... Yes,' Matt decided. One could never be too careful and any woman living alone was always a potential target, even if Toby seemed harmless enough. 'My name's Matt. I'll see you around.'

'Okay. See ya.' Toby hunched into his hoodie and headed to the stairwell.

Matt resumed knocking. 'Ellie, I know you're in there. Answer the door.' Finally he heard a muffled sound and the door cracked open. Her face was only partially visible and what he could see didn't look good.

'What are you doing here?' She sniffed, dug a tissue from the pocket of her dressing gown, held it to her nose.

No wonder she hadn't turned up. 'You're ill,' he said unnecessarily. 'You should have phoned me.' He pushed the door wider, took in the dark circles beneath her glassy eyes before closing the door behind him.

'Why?' She turned away and headed over the worn lino-leum floor towards her bed. She wore flannelette pyjamas under her robe, he noticed, and fluffy pink slippers.

'To let me know you weren't coming in...' His voice was tight and clipped to his own ears. He saw the way her shoulders drooped and softened it with, 'To let me know if you need anything.' He glanced about him at the tiny studio apartment. The place was basic at best. And colder than an antarctic winter.

'On my day off?'

'Your day off?'

'I don't work Thursdays. I told you that at our *interview*.' Stepping out of her slippers, she crawled onto the bed, dragging the covers over her. 'So, if there's nothing else... Pull the door shut behind you on your way out.'

Even with his jacket on, his skin goose-bumped beneath his cashmere jumper. 'Don't you have heating?'

'It's broken down,' she mumbled.

'I can't leave you here like this.'

'Sure you can. Don't you have appointments to keep? Five-star hotels to frequent?' A hand appeared from beneath the quilt to grab another tissue.

Five-star hotels? 'What are you talking about?' He crossed the room, stared down at her, shook his questions away. 'Forget appointments, forget work. You shouldn't be on your own and this place is an icebox. You're coming home with me.'

CHAPTER SIX

'No.' Her reply was razor sharp.

'I don't want to argue with you, Ellie.'

'Good.' A beat of silence. 'I'm better off here. If I can sleep it off today, I'll be right for work tomorrow.'

He lowered himself to the edge of the bed, his shoe skittering against something as he sat. He looked down...

His business card. Crumpled. By one very tight, very deliberate fist, if he guessed correctly. He picked it up, lowered the quilt so he could see her face and waved it in front of her. 'I must've made a good impression Saturday night.'

Her eyes flicked open, then widened as she realised. 'Oh.' She blinked up at him. 'How did that get there?'

He felt a corner of his mouth tip up. 'You didn't throw it out.' He smoothed it out, tapped it against his chin. 'This tells me something, Ellie.'

Her eyes slid shut again. 'It tells you I'm environmentally aware, that I was waiting for the paper recycling day to come round.'

'Yeah. Right.' He slipped it beneath her pillow with a smile she didn't see.

He glanced about the apartment. Her fridge was covered in kids' paintings held in place by frog magnets. 'Whose artwork?'

'I volunteer at a homework centre for disadvantaged kids,' she mumbled into her pillow.

A volunteer? She was more than he'd given her credit for and something deeper stirred inside him. Willing the somewhat disturbing feeling away, his gaze landed on a small but familiar figurine on the scarred night stand.

He looked back at Ellie, her eyelashes resting on pale cheeks, then picked it up, rolled it between his palms. 'Where did you get this?'

Her eyes opened halfway. 'Belle gave it to me. She said everyone needs a guardian angel.'

Matt knew it wasn't a simple trinket. It was one of a kind, according to Belle. She'd bought it in Venice a few years back and paid a fortune in tourist dollars for it. Did Ellie know its true value?

He folded the quilt back and tucked the edge beneath her chin. 'Guardian angels won't cut it today. You can sleep in Belle's guest room.'

'No.'

He tightened his jaw. 'I can carry you downstairs in your pyjamas and put you in the car myself or you can get dressed first—your choice. But you're coming with me in five minutes.'

'I'm staying here. I'm going to try to sleep. *Here*. Thanks for your offer, now go away.'

He pushed up. So be it. He found an empty supermarket bag, then scouted the room for something she could wear later—a black tracksuit sprawled over a chair and a pair of sneakers with socks spilling out nearby. 'Four minutes.' He opened drawers till he found underwear.

Behind him, he heard her gasp. 'You are *so not* touching my—'

'Think again, honey.' He pulled out a filmy white bra and panties, tossed them in the bag. Added a pair of socks.

Ellie's eyes narrowed to slits as she watched Matt's broad-shouldered shape disappear into her tiny bathroom. Her heart thudded erratically against the mattress. She pushed the tissue against her lips to prevent a whimper when she heard the clatter of bottles being scooped up. Squeezing her eyes shut, she willed him to leave. She was an independent woman. Had to be. If she refused to move, made it obvious she didn't want his assistance, didn't *need* it, he'd respect that. He'd—

Her eyes snapped open again when the quilt's warmth vanished. A tide of cold air and defeat washed over her as she gazed up at one determined man. Mouth resolute. Jaw squared, brow furrowed. Her bag of stuff on his arm.

A man accustomed to having his demands met.

Well, she had news for him. 'Listen, I...' His dark eyes challenged hers and she felt her words drain away with her resolve.

'Since you're obviously not going to cooperate—' he continued, sliding his hands beneath her armpits '—why wait the extra two minutes?'

As he dragged her upright, she saw the glint in his eyes and her heart leapt with a contrary thrill in her chest. 'You wouldn't...'

The glint remained as he slid her slippers onto her feet. He tightened the sash on her dressing gown, fastened the top button of her pyjamas. 'Yes, Ellie, I would.' Then scooping her up, he swung her into his arms.

His jumper tickled her nose, his hold was so tight the only air she could breathe was full of his scent. She kicked—uselessly—since her legs hit nothing but air. 'Put. Me. Down.' Her futile demand was muffled against his chest.

'Not until we reach the car.' His voice rumbled against her ear. She felt herself being carried across the room. He passed the kitchen table, dumped her handbag on her lap.

'This is crazy. I'm not ill. I have a cold, that's all.'

He gave her a disbelieving look. 'Keys?'

She thought about refusing to tell him, but she doubted it would make any difference, and being locked out wasn't a sensible idea either because she was *coming back tonight* if she had to walk it. 'On the hook by the door.'

Grabbing them on the way, he stepped into the hallway and pulled the door shut behind him. The click echoed in the dimness. He started down the stairs and she had no choice but to hang on and let him do his macho-hero thing.

His car was parked right out front. She flopped down in the seat with a scowl, but couldn't help sighing at the sun's warmth through the windscreen.

Sniffing, she turned her head away so she wouldn't have to look at him when he climbed in and set the car in motion. Lucky for her, she wasn't looking for a man in her life. And even if she was, it was lucky Matt McGregor was far too domineering.

Because it meant she could relegate him to the back of her mind and only deal with him when it was absolutely necessary. Like now, unfortunately.

She watched the streetscape change from concrete and retail to the upscale mansions behind hedges and greenery as they neared Belle's place.

She frowned. So why did her insides still insist on turning themselves about when she thought of him? And how could she help thinking about him when she couldn't seem to avoid him? Like this morning. How many darn times had he felt that manly need to come to her assistance?

She didn't need him or his help.

Her inconvenient sneeze prompted a tissue to appear in front of her face. She took it with a scowl and a muttered, 'Thanks.' She was *not* going to be that weak, needy, ditzy woman he seemed to think she was.

'Asking for help isn't a sign of weakness, Ellie.'

She swiped her nose, then stared at him. Did the man read her thoughts now? 'I *didn't* ask.'

His face was in profile; his eyes were hidden behind his sunglasses. 'Because you *misplaced* my business card and didn't know how to contact me?'

'Because I...' She let her head fall back and rolled her eyes up to the car's interior light. 'I have Belle's home number. If I'd needed to, I could've contacted you.'

'And if I'd left earlier for the office, as I'd intended?'

'Why *didn't* you leave earlier—and why are we having this conversation?'

The moment the car came to a halt near the front porch, she swung the door open. Her dressing gown flapped around her ankles in the wind as she walked up the path. How she must look—bed hair and flannel pyjamas and handbag. Yesterday's make-up. Rudolph's red nose and it wasn't even Christmas. She pressed her lips together. She hadn't even cleaned her teeth this morning.

He unlocked the door and ushered her inside. 'Go on up. Belle always leaves the bed made in case of unexpected visitors,' he told her, handing her the supermarket bag. 'I'll bring you a cup of lemon tea before I leave.'

She stared at him. Did he not know when to stop? And yet...someone doing something nice for her, looking after her, warmed her insides like Gran's bread-and-butter pudding.

His brow rose. 'Unless you want me to carry you again?'

She shook her head and walked towards the staircase.

Ten minutes later Matt appeared with the promised tray of lemon tea, one of Belle's delicate dishes arranged with sticks of carrot, cheese, olives and celery and an unopened packet of her favourite chocolate biscuits. He set it on the little doily-covered table beside the bed. 'Help yourself to anything in the fridge. Get some sleep. I'll be back by teatime.'

'Thanks. I...appreciate it.'

He reached for her hand and for a furious pulse-beat she thought he was going to bring it to his lips, but he pulled out a pen and wrote a string of numbers on the inside of her wrist.

'If you need me,' he told her.

And just like that her whole body melted at the subconscious message those words conveyed. She closed her eyes. 'I'll be all right.'

When Ellie woke, her stuffy head had cleared somewhat and her throat was a little better, courtesy of the cold-and-flu medication Matt had included on the tray.

Early-winter gloom had plunged the room into semidarkness, but rather than the dank chill of her apartment, the afternoon sunshine's warmth still lingered in the room, the fragrance of fresh linen filled the air.

And for a moment she was a little girl again, in her own bedroom with the fairyland wallpaper and chintz curtains. A time when she'd been too young to understand the meaning of loss, or to appreciate the value of family.

Snuggling deeper into the lavender-scented sheets, she indulged in those long-forgotten memories of safety and warmth, love. All the more precious because once upon a time this home had belonged to her grandfather's family.

As she shifted position, she caught sight of Matt's mobile number on her wrist. Heat flooded through her when she remembered the feel of his hand brushing her arm as he'd penned the numbers.

And another thought occurred to her. Was it only the history of the house or was Matt also partially responsible for bringing all these feelings to the surface?

She'd seen a different side to him over the past couple of days. He might be hot, but whether she wanted to admit it or not, there was a comfortable warmth there too. A warmth had nothing to do with sexuality and everything to do with the kind of man he was. The kind that made you want to cuddle right up and share…what? Your deepest secrets? Hopes and fears?

How could she reconcile that with the sexy Matt who made her want to cuddle up and share a whole lot more than confidences?

Matt was also a take-charge kind of guy. How would that translate in the bedroom? she wondered, her mind straying into forbidden territory. Would he expect to make all the moves? Or did he like to lie back sometimes and let a woman do the work? Her body tingled, grew languid at the new and dangerous direction her thoughts had taken.

Until she remembered that he'd had a date last night. The feeling seeped out of her, leaving a cold empty space in the pit of her stomach. Probably someone like Yasmine from the office. Tall, career-oriented, killer body, long smooth *straight* hair. Unlike her own flyaway frizz that hadn't seen a pair of straighteners in the past forty-eight hours.

She needed to ignore that warm cosy feeling that kept creeping up on her whenever she thought of Matt's caring side. She needed to ignore those hot forbidden fantasies that sprang to life whenever he looked at her.

He wasn't in Melbourne for long, she reminded herself. She only had to survive a few more days, and in the meantime she'd give him no reason to think she was interested in pursuing what they'd started any further.

So it wouldn't be a problem when he left.

And she'd go back to her life the way she preferred it. with promises they didn't keep, no unrealistic expecta-ken heart.

* * *

The house was in darkness when Matt let himself in around 6:00 p.m. He headed straight for the guest room, a strange anticipation twirling through him like streamers at Sydney's Mardi Gras parade.

A glimmer of light slanted across the hallway. Her door remained partially open as he'd left it. The lamp on the night stand, dimmed to its lowest setting, cast subtle shadows over Ellie. He'd intended asking her what she fancied eating but quickly decided she needed sleep more than sustenance.

Her hair formed a curly halo around her face; long lashes rested on porcelain cheeks. The top button of her pyjamas had slipped undone, revealing the gold locket she always wore nestled in her dusky cleavage. Beautiful.

And vulnerable.

He should step back, give her privacy, but his eyes refused to look away. His feet held fast and his hand tightened around the edge of the door.

He wanted to cross the room, brush his hand over her hair and enjoy its texture. To skim her cheek, lay his lips on hers and reacquaint himself with her taste.

He imagined her waking to his touch. Amethyst eyes blinking up at him, turning dark as he slid his palms between flannel and warm skin. Then he'd soothe that innate caution she seemed to have with soft words, softer kisses. His fingers itched and his mouth watered.

He dragged his gaze away from the bed to the darkened window while his thoughts drifted back to yesterday. She wasn't as carefree and irresponsible as she'd initially have had him believe. And perhaps she wasn't the type of woman he could easily walk away from without it playing on his conscience.

He'd need to make it clear that there was no chance of anything serious developing between them. He didn't do long-term. He'd been unable to give Angela the happy-ever-after marriage and children because long-term commitment didn't work—he'd been witness to that too many times to count. He knew Belle's heart had been broken when the man she'd loved had walked away, even though she'd never discussed the details.

And the innocent kids when two people decided they'd had enough—where the hell did that leave them? Ellie's father. His own mother. He didn't want to hurt Ellie the same way.

Didn't mean he wanted her in his bed any less. As soon as she'd recovered, he told himself.

The following morning Matt stood at the kitchen window watching the rain while he scooped up cereal, racking his brains for a reason other than gardening to keep Ellie here for the day. Assuming she was well enough. Hoping she was recovered because having her sleep so near that he could practically hear her breathing was playing havoc with his libido.

Ellie appeared in the doorway, already showered and dressed in her tracksuit. Her complexion was pale, her nose still red, but other than that, she looked...like Ellie.

He couldn't believe the way her presence lifted the kitchen's ambience. And his mood. 'Good morning.' He hefted the coffeepot. 'You'd be feeling like a coffee, I imagine?'

'Hi. Yes. Please.' She walked a few steps, hesitated. 'I didn't mean to sleep all night. Sorry if I inconvenienced you in any way. I intended going home.'

'I hardly knew you were here.' Yeah, right. He'd not been able to think of anything else. For most of the night he'd been uncomfortably awake and aware that she'd been a few quick steps down the hall. He set a mug of coffee on the kitchen table. 'How are you feeling this morning?'

'Much better, thanks.'

'I'll let you know now, I don't expect you to work in the rain.'

'Oh. Good.' She picked up the mug but remained standing.
'So, I…'

'So, I…'

Both spoke at the same time. She raised her mug at him.
'Yes?'

'I was going to say if you'd like to work today and you're
feeling up to it, I've got an indoor job for you.'

'Oh?' Relief crossed her expression. 'Great. I could do with
the extra money.'

'The downstairs windows could do with a wash. I'm sure
Belle would appreciate it.'

She smiled. 'Just show me where the gear is, point me in
the right direction and I'll get started.'

'No rush. Finish your coffee while I make you some
breakfast.'

'You don't have to go to all that trouble, the caffeine hit's
fine.'

'Belle would skin me alive if I forced you to work on an
empty stomach. How does scrambled egg sound?'

'Wonderful, but I can do it if you need to be somewhere.…'

'I've got a luncheon appointment but that's hours away.
Why don't you find what you need in the laundry and set up
while I cook?'

Ellie set to work as soon as she'd eaten the meal Matt had
prepared for her, which had been every bit as tasty as she'd
expected. To her relief, he didn't sit with her while she ate because a business call came through requiring his attention.

She started in the dining and living rooms, admiring the
exquisite cream, rose and jade furnishings against the dark antique furniture as she set up the stepladder and got to work.

Next she chose a cosy little room down the hall which
would catch the afternoon sun and give hours of pleasure on

a cold winter's day. Bookcases overloaded with classics lined one wall.

Another shelf was crammed with fifties memorabilia. A selection of old vinyl 45s sat atop a small record player. Bill Haley's 'Rock around the Clock,' Pat Boone's 'Love Letters in the Sand.' The Platters, Elvis.

A photo album caught Ellie's eye. On the front was a black-and-white image of a teenage Belle. Ellie recognised the shape of her face, the wide eyes and broad cheekbones. But the hair was a surprise—pulled back in a curly ponytail, not unlike her own unruly locks. She was dressed in a full-skirted gingham-checked dress cinched at the waist with a wide belt and wore a heart-shaped locket around her neck.

Ellie's fingers tangled in the slim chain of her own locket which had belonged to her mother. A tingle danced over her nape, as if someone had stroked a finger down her spine.

Shaking the sensation away, she set the album back in place. But for just a heartbeat or two she'd been mesmerised by the image and a strange feeling that she was missing a piece of a puzzle.

CHAPTER SEVEN

A SHORT time later she was halfway up the stepladder when Matt appeared to inform her he was leaving. He wore a white shirt, silver-grey silk tie, dark trousers and a chocolate-brown suede jacket. Smelling fresh and masculine and entirely too sexy to be heading out to anything remotely concerned with business.

But then…he hadn't mentioned *business*, had he? Only that he had a luncheon appointment. Which was open to all manner of interpretation.

Something slithered through Ellie's belly and coiled tight around the top of her already stuffy chest, making it hard to breathe. Something that felt horribly, unimaginably like… possessiveness. Her fingers tightened on her little bucket of water, her other hand clutched the top rung of the ladder. *No*. It was *not* that. No way.

She saw his brows pull down. 'Are you okay?'

And before she could blink he'd crossed the room and was beside her, his face too close, his hands reaching for her shoulders. With Ellie on the ladder, they were the same height. His eyes almost lined up with hers. His mouth was… too close.

'You startled me, damn you.' *Damn his luncheon date. And damn her dumb reaction*. She jerked away from his touch.

A few drops of water splashed out of the bucket and onto his shirt.

'Ah…'

'Yes, *ah*.' He took the bucket from her nerveless fingers, set it down out of harm's way, then straightened to face her.

Biting her lip, she stared at the damp splotch, but then her traitorous gaze shifted to the dark hairs barely visible beneath the fine textured fabric. To his neck, and the pinpricks of newly shaved stubble. His Adam's apple.

She sucked in a breath, bringing the scent of his aftershave with it, and she forgot all about luncheon dates and being snippy.

She was too busy being turned on.

An image of her loosening his tie, slipping his buttons undone and spreading his shirt open, sliding her hands between fabric and olive skin danced behind her eyes. Setting her mouth to that masculine throat…

Swallowing hard, she dragged her eyes away…and up…to meet a pair of dark assessing eyes. 'Sorry—' she lifted one finger of her free hand '—about the shirt.'

He leaned nearer. She could see flecks of hazel in his dark irises. A tiny bald patch in his left eyebrow.

'What are you going to do about it?' His breath whispered against her mouth, a current of energy arcing between them.

'Um, I have a dry cloth somewhere.…' She didn't try to find it. Sparks. She was sure there must be sparks.

'Won't help.' He slid his free hand over her shoulder, traced a line over her shoulderblade. Used the move to draw her closer. She could feel his masculine heat and strength radiating off him. 'Ellie?'

Her legs threatened to give way. They weren't even touching but his lips were heating hers, making the blood rush to

her cheeks, sending those sparks sizzling through her blood.
'Yes?'

'Kiss me.'

Her breath stalled in her throat. 'What?'

His deep chuckle vibrated along her bones. 'You know how
it goes. You put your lips on mine and I...reciprocate.'

'I'm working. And it's business hours.' But, oh, the temptation. It tingled on her lips, her tongue. Tap-danced over her
skin and twisted through her limbs.

'I won't tell the boss.' He leaned in, lips puckered. 'Your
call, Ellie. You're in the driver's seat with this one.'

She huffed, 'Fine, then, if it'll get you to leave quicker,'
and leaned in to meet him.

Hah. From the instant their lips touched, any notion that she
held the upper hand was whipped away by a blast of astonish-
ing masculine know-how. She should have known better with
a man like Matt McGregor. In a response that screamed need,
Ellie relinquished that control. She wanted more—craved it
as his hands cruised up and down her spine, as he tilted his
head for better access.

Her mouth fell open beneath his. She tasted temptation and
desire—his and hers. Heard both in the soft throaty sounds
scrambling up her throat. Felt it in the heavy hardness that
rocked against her belly as his hand slid over the curve of her
buttocks and tilted her toward him.

It should have been enough, this fleeting sensory indulgence; temporary was all she knew he was looking for. It
should have been enough for her too.

But he lifted a hand to cup her jaw as if he held antique
china, and the determination behind her resolve melted like
frost on grass on a bright winter morning. This man was...
more. Dangerously more.

Because he drew emotions from her that she'd learned
to keep buried down deep, that she no longer wanted to

acknowledge. The warm feeling of being wanted, valued as a person. Cherished, even, for who she was. She'd become an expert at holding that part of herself back until Matt McGregor had strolled into her life. And it came at a price. Vulnerability.

She yanked herself out of his hold. Gripped the ladder with both hands. Her arms felt leaden, her muscles had turned to water. And it was only marginally comforting to see that he was as breathless as she. That his eyes blazed with the same heat she was sure hers signalled.

But his interest was skin deep. And that heat would cool soon enough, she knew. It always did. Turning away, she reached for the cloth she'd left on top of the ladder. 'You'll be late for your luncheon appointment.'

Who he was meeting was none of her concern. They'd kissed. So what? It didn't make them an item. Permanent playboy and gardener did not a couple make.

'Have dinner with me tonight.'

His deeper-than-midnight voice had her turning back to look at him. 'Dinner?'

He shrugged. 'Why not? It's after-hours. There's a new Moroccan restaurant not far away I've been wanting to try. Or we can do something else, if you'd prefer....'

'Dinner's good,' she said quickly. Dinner was probably the lesser of two evils. The way he'd said 'something else' sounded decidedly risky if the way her pulse had tripped was any indication.

'I'll make a booking.' He passed her the bucket of water. 'I'm calling by the office after lunch so I'll pick you up from your place around 6:00 p.m.'

'Umm,' she murmured, her mind all over the place. 'Oh— It's Friday.'

'Is that a problem?'

'I'm at the homework centre Friday afternoons. I'm there till six. Never mind about dinner, another—'

'We'll make it seven. Where's the centre?'

'In that old church building with the peppercorn tree out front a couple of blocks from my place, but—'

'Okay. I'll see you later.'

Ellie worked furiously for the next few hours, stopping only to put together a sandwich while she stressed about the upcoming evening. It felt strange helping herself to the contents of Belle's fridge, but what choice did she have? She'd been practically kidnapped here.

Matt was weakening her resolve not to get involved, that's what he was doing. Breaking down her defences with serious acts of gallantry, seducing her with searing hot looks and that deep velvet voice.

She plunked her backside on the bottom rung of the ladder. No fancy wine—she'd stick to mineral water. Just because she didn't intend getting involved—with anyone—didn't mean she couldn't enjoy some company, and he was going to turn up at seven o'clock in any case.

Next problem—what to wear? Her one and only black dress? She frowned. It might give him the impression she'd dressed up especially for him. So jeans and T-shirt with her black jacket for warmth.

Decision made, she packed the belongings she'd brought with her to Belle's and headed off for the kid's centre.

'Okay, crew, who wants to help plant the pansies?'

A chorus of 'Me, me, me' chimed around Ellie as the kids clustered eagerly about her.

'Okay, here we go.' She handed out the punnets she'd paid for herself. 'Careful, there's plenty for everyone.'

Ellie had established a garden plot at the back of the

building with the help of half a dozen interested kids. They'd planned what they wanted as a team, designed the plot and purchased the plants, giving them pride and ownership. An older girl, Jenny, was helping Wayne to separate parsley seedlings and plant them into prepared holes.

But Brandon was having none of it. He lounged on the sideline, all skinny limbs and attitude, but Ellie knew he wanted to join in, and her heart went out to him. She knew he lived with a father who didn't give two hoots. If she only knew how to involve him.

'How about hunting for wildlife, then?'

Ellie's head swivelled at the sound of Matt's voice behind her. He gave her a quick look and a murmured, 'I've cleared it with the boss inside,' then approached Brandon and squatted beside him, holding a box. He was still wearing the suit jacket he'd left home in earlier.

'There's no wildlife here,' Brandon scoffed, rolling his eyes. The corner of his mouth curled...as if a grown man could be so dumb.

'Sure there is. Slimy snails and creepy crawlies. Huge fat spiders with hairy legs, if you know where to look. Want to help me find them?'

'Nope.'

'Okay... By the way, my name's Matt and I'm a friend of Ellie's.' He produced a couple of magnifying glasses from the box. 'Ever watched the forensic scientists on those crime scene investigation programs on TV?'

Brandon gave him a cursory glance. 'We don't have a TV.' He scuffed a worn sneaker along the ground. 'But I've seen it on Nan's.'

'Well, you'll know that sometimes they look for insects and stuff to help solve a crime scene. I'm going to have a look round here and see what I can find. I need an assistant with good investigative skills to help me. How about it?'

And just like that, Matt had Brandon eating out of his hand.

Ellie watched them scour the seemingly lifeless asphalted area a few moments later. Watched their heads bent close together as they studied something in the weeds along the perimeter. Who'd have thought the man would have a way with kids? Yet she knew nothing of his past or how he'd come to live with Belle, except that the memories still haunted him.

A short time later she saw the pair of them sitting on a log seat away from the rest of the kids. This time Brandon was doing the talking, Matt was listening. Nodding. Sharing. And Ellie's heart rolled over like a giant tumbleweed in her chest.

'…And we want to extend the rear of the building into a music-cum-dance-cum-drama room,' Ellie said as they exited the centre and walked towards Matt's car. She'd given him a tour of the place and told him all about the grand albeit pie-in-the-sky plans they had. 'And if we had the finances we'd employ artists and musicians and offer a breakfast program. These kids need all that and more.'

'You're really passionate about it, aren't you?'

A warm feeling that he understood burrowed through her. 'You'd better believe it. Thanks for your help with Brandon. He's a tough little nut to crack.'

Matt pulled out his car key, pressed the remote. 'Next time I come, I'll bring my microscope.'

She stared at him over the top of the car. 'You'd come again?'

'Sure.' He grinned at her. 'Why should you get to have all the fun?'

Ellie nearly melted right there. He liked kids. Oh, dear. She was a goner.

CHAPTER EIGHT

DARKNESS was already swallowing what little day was left when Matt dropped her outside her apartment building to change for dinner. The rain clouds had blown away, leaving a hard indigo sky. The aroma of damp bitumen and a charcoal grill somewhere hung on the still air.

A car cruised the street, slowing as it neared. Ellie tugged her tracksuit jacket a little higher. She never let thoughts of murder and mayhem bother her. If she did, she'd never go anywhere. But she breathed a little easier when it passed by.

Climbing the stairs in the dimness—the darn stairwell light hadn't been replaced for three weeks—she dug in her pocket for her keys. Her thoughts were focused on a quick shower in her draughty bathroom, a little make-up…

But rational thought evaporated when she lifted her hand to put her key to the lock. *Splintered wood.* Her whole body tightened and her blood drained into her legs.

While she'd been overnighting at Belle's place someone had intruded on her sanctuary. The one place she should be able to feel safe. How long she stood there she didn't know—listening for noises from within, hearing only her heartbeat pounding in her ears.

Gradually she became aware of other sounds. Down the hall the reassuring sound of Mrs Larson's TV and, intermittently, Toby's voice. Outside, city sounds. Inside…silence.

Scarcely aware that she was holding her breath, she reached out, fingers touching the scarred wood. The door opened with a light push. Keeping her gaze dead ahead, she felt for the switch to her left. Light flooded the room and spilled into the bathroom beyond. Empty. The one advantage to having a studio apartment was the ability to see everything in a single glance, she thought grimly, stepping inside and pushing the door closed behind her.

The inspection didn't take long. Then she sat on her bed and started to laugh, a touch hysterically. The laugh was on them—financially challenged Ellie Rose had nothing of value to steal. But they'd obviously taken exception to the time and effort they'd wasted and left the contents of her fridge strewn over the floor.

She realised her hands were shaking and her throat was dry. Someone had touched her things, breathed the same air, invaded her space. Chills crawled over her flesh and down her spine. Grabbing her quilt, she tugged it around her, then almost as quickly pushed it away—irrational, but it felt dirty somehow and a chill shuddered down her spine. What if whoever-it-was had touched it? She felt violated and alone.

Jerking up, she paced to the kitchen sink, adrenaline and anger pumping through her body.

Matt found her crouched by the refrigerator, mopping up the mess with a kitchen sponge. The fact that her door was open and damaged and that she hadn't answered his knock had struck him with fear like he'd never experienced. A primitive instinct to protect what was his drummed through his body. 'Ellie.'

She jolted at the sound of his voice, then froze for a second like a trapped animal. 'I'm… Okay.' She resumed her task with a choked attempt at a laugh. 'The scumbag hung around here long enough to drink my last can of Coke.'

Crouching down beside her, he took the sponge from her fingers. 'Leave it, Ellie.'

'I have to clean this mess.'

'No. You don't. I'll have a cleaning service come in tomorrow.'

'I need to keep busy.' She waved a hand. 'Nervous energy and all that.'

He tipped her chin up, hating the naked distress he saw written all over her face. 'Busy, hmm?' He smiled into her eyes, taking his time about it. 'I can help you with that.' He kept his voice light, teasing even, but inside...inside he wanted to punch the living daylights out of the low-life who'd done this to her.

He rose, pulling her up with him, his hands beneath her elbows to steady her. 'Did they take anything?'

'I don't think so.'

'Have you rung the cops?'

'No.'

'I'll do it now, then.' He smoothed his hands down her back, drawing her closer. 'It's going to be all right, Ellie. I'm here.'

The last words didn't surprise him, but the emotions they invoked did. Feeling the fragility of her bones beneath his hands and that tiny slender frame against his...it drew up a well of tenderness he'd not known existed. He wanted to go on holding her and— *Protect what was his?*

His whole body tightened. Where the hell had that come from? He'd seen the broken lock and Ellie on the floor and had simply reacted. He was no knight in shining armour.

Loosening his hold, he stepped back, uneasy with the emotions she'd conjured in him. Assured himself it was a momentary thing. She'd proclaimed herself an independent woman; she had no need for such masculine displays of chivalry.

'I can manage,' she said, backing up at the same time.

As if she'd read his thoughts. But beneath that *I-don't-need-you-to-take-care-of-me* facade he could see the little-girl-lost lurking in her eyes and he had to clench his fists at his sides so as not to reach for her again. If he touched her, he might give her more than she was willing to accept. More than he was willing to give.

Swinging away, he paced to the other side of the room. 'I'll double-check everything's okay—you might have missed something. I'll look into finding you alternative accommodation tomorrow.'

'But I don't have the finances to—'

'Don't worry about that now.' He waved a hand. 'I'll arrange something. I know people. There are studio apartments near the university. Safe and clean. It'll be fine, trust me. I'll make those calls, then we'll get something to eat. Takeaway's probably best under the circumstances.'

'Something hot with a bite to it,' she said, swiping at her damp-kneed sweatpants with a muttered curse. 'Beef vindaloo with teeth.'

Over the next twenty minutes he rang the police, organised a cleaning service and someone to fix the door and add extra security—no way was he waiting around for some absent landlord—while Ellie showered and changed.

A couple of hours and a police report later, they were in the car on the way back to Belle's place with Ellie's requested Indian takeaway.

How had she gone from living in relative comfort as a child to…this? 'You don't have to answer this, Ellie,' he said as the car idled at an intersection. 'But wasn't there some sort of inheritance when your mum passed away?'

She was silent a moment and he thought she wasn't going to answer. Finally she said, 'My family invested in a company that went bust. They lost a substantial amount of their wealth only months before the accident.'

'That's tough.' Damn, he should have kept his mouth shut. As the lights changed, he set the car in motion again. 'Forget I asked.'

'I don't mind.' From the corner of his eye he saw her chin lift. 'I'm not ashamed.'

'Nor should you be.'

'Mum left what she had to my father. When Dad walked out on us, she obviously gave no thought to changing her will, which she'd made before I was even born. I only learned about it when I was old enough to understand.'

So that's why Ellie's father had turned up after her mother's death—not out of any sense of parental duty but because he thought he'd come into wealth. Matt's lip curled in disgust. 'What about his family?' he asked. 'Your paternal grandparents? Couldn't they help?'

'Both dead, back in England. He emigrated here on his own. Of course he used what money there was to keep us together,' Ellie hurried on. Seemed she was determined to defend him. 'Even though we moved around a lot, we lived in nice places, ate at the best restaurants. But he was a gambler,' she finished quietly.

Ah. It didn't take a PhD to figure the man had left his daughter again when the money had run out. 'Didn't the courts make provisions for you as her daughter?'

'They did. It was kept in trust for me until I turned eighteen....'

Something in her voice alerted him, pushed him to say, 'Let me guess, your father turned up.'

She didn't reply.

He shook his head. 'Ellie, Ellie. Don't you know feeding a gambling problem only makes it worse?'

'He said he'd changed. He's my father. The only family I have left.'

Her tone tugged at something deep down inside him. 'He used that against you—you know that, don't you?'

He could feel the pain his words caused across the space between them and felt like a jerk, but she said, 'I insisted he use it to get help. And at least I used some of it to finance most of my horticultural course.'

'I didn't mean to insult you.'

'I know. It's just that people like you don't have a clue about people like me.'

He let it pass. *You don't want to talk about yourself, Matt— don't bring it up.*

They turned into the driveway; the gates swung open, revealing the magnificent home in all its eccentric splendour. Proclaiming wealth from the tip of its spired turret to the landscaped front garden with its statues, ponds and carefully tended topiary.

He knew how it must look, but Ellie had no idea how much they had in common.

Matt switched on the TV and left Ellie in the lounge room while he found plates and set their meal out on the table.

Then since they weren't eating out, he headed upstairs to change into something casual. A shadow of movement alerted him as he passed Belle's room. He saw Ellie place Belle's angel on the night stand.

'Ellie?'

She jerked at his voice and spun to face him. 'Don't sneak up on me like that. I'm jittery enough as it is.'

He stepped into the room, intrigued. 'Why would you return a gift?'

She turned her attention back to the angel, caressed it. 'It's safer here. Thank you. For helping me out. And for this afternoon with the kids.'

She looked over then, and smiled at him—just a hint but,

ah, God, it was as if the sun came out. He wanted to pull her close, kiss away the demons he saw in her eyes, but that special kind of intimacy was more than he had in him to give. He didn't want to get emotionally involved. For her sake as well as his own. He turned away. 'Anyone would do the same. Let's go put a dent in that curry.'

They sat down to tandoori chicken and beef vindaloo with rice, servings of crisp pappadums, cool cucumber raita and tangy mango chutney. Ellie attacked her meal with a vengeance which appeared to be borne of anger rather than hunger.

Finding your apartment ransacked was a rotten end to anyone's day. He picked up his glass, took a few mouthfuls of water—she'd refused his suggestion of wine so he'd opted out too—and watched her. The way her lips closed over the spoon, lightly glossed with oil. Her fingers, slender with short, unpolished nails.

He could almost feel those fingers drifting over him in pleasure, clutching at him in passion. He shifted uncomfortably on his chair. In the silence he could almost hear his own blood rushing through his veins and making his jeans two sizes too tight.

Timing again.

The best he could do was to take her mind off her troubles and his mind off his libido. 'What do you do when you're feeling down, Ellie?'

'I'm not down, just angry.' She stabbed a cube of beef, shoved it in her mouth and chewed vigorously.

'So what do you do when you're angry?'

'Run.' A small smile lifted the edges of her mouth. 'Not the running-away quitting kind of running, the simple mind-clearing act of pushing one's self to the limit. That nervous energy I mentioned? I channel it. If there was a beach nearby that's what I'd do. With the wind on my face and the sound of surf in my ears. I'd run until I couldn't run another step, then I'd stand on a cliff and watch the waves roll in. And pray for a storm.'

He set his glass down, laid his hands on the table. 'How about now?'

Ellie's brow pleated. 'It's hardly beach weather.'

'Does that stop you?'

'Well, no...'

He leaned back and watched her. 'Ever ridden a motorbike?'

'No.'

'There's nothing like it. Hitting the bitumen, outriding your problems. Ride till you come to the end of the road. Same rush, same result. I have an idea.' He rose, skirted the table and reached for her hand, tugged her up, then headed for the door.

'Wait up, where are we going?'

He turned to her and grinned. 'My place.'

'*Your* place?' Ellie stared at those beguiling brown eyes while her heart thudded loud and strong against her ribs. 'I thought you lived here when you come to Melbourne.'

'Nope. My place is down the coast a bit along the Great Ocean Road. Lorne has the best view in the world.'

'But Lorne's a couple of hours' drive away.'

'Less if the traffic's light. It's a clear night. What better way to dust off the cobwebs and get that adrenaline pumping?'

'Hang on...' A frisson of something like excitement inextricably bound with alarm zipped down her spine. 'A motorbike was mentioned. You're going to ride there?'

'No, *we're* going to ride there.' When she just stared at him while that adrenaline geysered up and churned with her dinner, he smiled. 'Don't worry, Ellie. I've got two helmets and I don't take risks.'

'But it's already nearly ten o'clock.' She did *not* add that

10:00 p.m. was her routine bedtime. Although tonight she wasn't anywhere near ready to sleep.

His eyes darkened and his voice deepened. 'Guess that means we'll be staying the night.'

CHAPTER NINE

STAYING the night. In Matt's house. Just her and him and…
Ellie's pulse leapt. *And…? And* if she wanted, she could let
herself go for once and give in to this attraction.

One night with Matt McGregor.

She steeled herself to hold his gaze and that now-familiar
current of energy arced across the space between them, sparking flashes of anticipation along every nerve ending. 'I'll need
to collect a few things on the way.'

His eyes twinkled with something like amusement. 'I have
a spare toothbrush.'

Her jaw firmed at the timely reminder. She just bet he did.
Probably a whole box for all those unexpected female guests
who slept over. She refused to let the doubt demons get to her.
Tonight Ellie was going to be that guest, and tonight was all
that mattered.

'And an efficient underfloor heating system,' he went on
smoothly. 'So you don't need a thing.'

No, she didn't imagine she did. She crossed her arms beneath her breasts. 'I hope the view's worth it.'

His gaze flicked briefly to the cleavage she'd unwittingly
created, then just as quickly back to her face. 'Oh, it will be,
I assure you.'

Her nipples tingled and tightened as heat spurted up her
neck, bled into her cheeks. Were they talking about the same

thing? She'd not participated in this kind of sexual innuendo in more than two years. Not since Heath...

'Grab your jacket and I'll meet you out front in a few minutes.'

She grabbed her backpack from the couch in the lounge room, her problems shoved to the back of her mind and a sense of anticipation rocketing through her as she slipped a cardigan over her sweater and dragged on her jacket before hurrying downstairs.

He'd changed and wore a black leather bomber jacket over his white T-shirt and jeans and was holding two helmets. The evening breeze slid through his spiked hair, giving it a reckless windswept edge. He looked more than a little bit dangerous.

Her heart skidded to a halt, then resumed at twice its speed. Beneath the canopy of inky sky with a whiff of motor oil in her nostrils and the throaty sound of the black-and-silver monster warming up beside him...well, it felt like some sort of illicit fantasy.

He must have transferred that recklessness to her. The spine-tingling prospect of freedom and being with Matt on that metallic beast as he whisked her away from reality... Just for tonight she wanted to forget everything and enjoy the ride—and it wasn't only the bike she was thinking of.

As he settled the helmet on her head, helped her adjust it, she admitted, 'I've never been game enough to ride on a motorbike.'

He climbed on, turned the key, patted the seat behind him. 'It's easy,' he said over the noise. 'Just hang on and let me do the rest.'

Still, perching herself behind him—

'Closer,' he ordered, voice muffled through the helmet as she wiggled into place. 'Don't be shy.'

Easy for you to say, your private parts aren't touching mine. She did as he requested, scooting close. His body heat warmed her inner thighs through the double layer of denim, her hands slid around his waist and over the soft leather.

At first the ride jerked and twisted as they crossed the suburbs, stopping for traffic lights and accelerating away at what felt like breathtaking speed but probably wasn't. But once they hit open road she relaxed, leaning into his sheltering body, revelling in the way the chill wind snuck under her visor and skimmed over her knees.

The cold was exhilarating, invigorating and a stunning contrast to his warmth all down the front of her body. The monotonous hum of the powerful machine vibrated through her bones, soothing her into a soporific state of well-being.

They stopped briefly near Geelong for hot coffee and cruised down Lorne's main street soon after midnight. A moment later Matt extended one arm to the view at the top of a crest in the road where she saw white foam curling and crashing over worn rocks along the shoreline.

A short distance from the township Matt turned off the main road and followed a track through tall skinny eucalypts, coming to a stop in front of a sprawling dwelling cleverly camouflaged to blend with its surroundings. He parked beneath a wide verandah, switched off the ignition.

Ellie climbed off, removed her helmet. Salty air heavy with the fragrance of eucalyptus swept through her hair and filled her nostrils. After the noisy journey the sudden silence rang with the sounds of the bush. An animal scuttled through the undergrowth, the soft clack of higher branches as the wind buffeted treetops, all against the background sound of distant surf. A gibbous moon spangled the leaves with silver.

'Here we are. Home sweet home.'

He produced a key and unlocked the front door, flipped a switch, illuminating dozens of downlights, giving the room a mellow ambience as she followed him in.

It had to be the most unique home she'd ever seen, all odd

angles and glass and slabs of colour that blended with the natural environment outside. A ceiling that soared and dipped, invoking a feeling of space and movement. 'No walls.'

'Don't need them.'

Her brows rose in surprise. 'Not even the bathroom?'

He grinned. 'The exception. Through here.'

Huge. With a spa big enough to need its own lifeguard, double shower, double vanity. It was another fantasy of glass, but private at the same time, and looked out onto a roomy columned courtyard of lush native flora accessed only through the bathroom.

'*Cyathea australis.*'

'If you say so.' Matt grinned. 'I prefer to call them tree ferns. It's easier to say.'

'You designed all this?' she said, following him to the living space.

He nodded, removing his jacket, tossing it over a wide leather couch. 'It's flexible in that I can add modules to extend living space as required. This suits me fine as it is for now.'

Ellie stared at the expensive fittings, the flow of honeyed wooden flooring. 'Not bad for a weekender.'

'Not a weekender,' he said. 'It's my home. I want you to see the view of the bay from upstairs.' He led her up a shallow flight of floating steps to the mezzanine level. Her feet made no sound as she crossed the thick carpet. The huge irregular hexagonal window framed a spectacular view of Louttit Bay filmed with moon glow. Lorne's lights twinkled through the trees. Possums partied on the roof, their bush sounds the only noise in the room's silence.

'Now isn't that a sight for inspiration?' He was standing close behind her, his voice rumbling softly at her ear.

'Oh, yeah.' His warmth spread across her back like a blanket. She placed a hand against the glass. So many contrasts. Heat and cold, the dark rise of the land against the moon-drenched water. Man-made in harmony with nature. And the man who'd built it all slid his hands loosely around her waist. Strength and tenderness. She didn't need protecting, but it was there in the way he shielded her with his body.

His hands now on her shoulders, he turned her to face him. 'Ellie.' Her name had never sounded as beautiful as it did coming from his lips. And the sight of this gorgeous man before her was more inspiring than any view behind.

And more terrifying.

She'd sworn never again to allow a man to seduce her and here she was. Yet staring up at him she sensed no intended seduction as such. Just a burning desire. One he'd carefully banked. One she shared.

She didn't need a man, yet in this moment, with the starlight reflecting in his eyes and the cool night radiating through the glass at her back, she wanted *this* man.

Neither did she need his support—unless it was the kind of support which would keep her upright on legs that were weakening with every beat of her pulse.

His hands slid over her shoulders, her arms, then inside her jacket, palms brushing the sides of her breasts, every fingertip sending sparks of excitement shooting to her feminine places.

What she needed... She *needed* his hands on more of her. On all of her. Her own hands trembled as they followed the hard contours of his chest through the soft jersey of his T-shirt. Up...until she felt his heart thud fast and heavy beneath her palm.

The fragrance of the cold night's ride clung to his clothes, his skin. Leaning up on tiptoe, she breathed him in, right in the little hollow at the base of his neck. Dizzy with his scent, his proximity, she dropped her head on his chest.

Her whole body throbbed with heavy anticipation, yet she felt as light as air, as if the slightest puff would blow her away.

Had she ever felt this way? She might have thought so once, but she couldn't have—she'd have remembered something this intense.

Cupping her face in both hands, he tilted it towards him, and what a view she was treated to. A strong jaw etched in the moon's silver glow, hair backlit with gold from the light filtering up from downstairs, lips that no artist could do justice to, eyes as dark as midnight. Eyes that could make a girl forget how to breathe, let alone her well-rehearsed lessons in self-preservation.

He whisked a thumb over her lips, just once. 'What do you want, Ellie?'

Be careful what you wish for. The little warning voice she'd learned to listen to and followed religiously dulled to a whisper, then faded completely.

One night. Her choice. Her decision.

Stepping out of his arms, she shrugged out of her jacket, let it fall to the floor. 'You. Here. Now.'

If it were possible, his eyes darkened further, but he didn't move except to let his arms drop to his sides. 'Are you sure? Because I don't know if I can stop if—'

'Yes, I'm sure,' she snapped out, unbuttoning her cardigan. She had no illusions about Matt where relationships were concerned, but now she'd made her decision she wanted to get on with it. 'One night.' She lifted her chin, every cell in her body jangling. 'That's the way you play the game, isn't it? One night at a time?'

He hesitated, the acknowledgement written on his face as he rocked back on his heels. 'But I'm not sure it's the way you do.'

No, it wasn't, but the other way hadn't worked for her in the past so perhaps it was time she tried something different. Knowing it all up-front meant no expectations, no disappointments and, most important of all, no broken heart. Without breaking eye contact she slipped off her cardigan. 'Wasn't it you who suggested the other day that we do something about this…tension between us? Get it out of the way?'

'Yes, but after what happened, you might—'

'I'm calling you on it now. I want to forget this afternoon.' Still watching him, she toed off her sneakers, peeled off her socks. Her toes curled into the warm carpet. 'I feel like I'm about to explode. I still have all this pent-up angry energy I need to get rid—'

Matt cut her off with a hard-mouthed kiss that echoed the wildness he sensed within her, barely glimpsing her surprised eyes as he dragged her against him and answered her request.

She didn't miss a beat, meeting him with the same force, the same heat, the same passion. Her hands shot upward, clutching fistfuls of his T-shirt, lush lips parting beneath his, tongues touching, tangling, thrusting in a tantalising prelude to what he wanted to do with her. To her. In her.

The hot potent flavour of her residual anger flowed over his tastebuds like dark chilli chocolate as he searched out all the hidden recesses in her mouth while his hands explored the firm flesh beneath her skinny T-shirt. Curves he'd not expected, dips he'd never seen, made all the more enticing by his long-endured anticipation—a neat little bellybutton, the indentation he discovered at the base of her spine when he slid a hand below the waistband of her jeans.

Breaking the kiss, he lifted his head, watched the same anticipation colour her eyes that deep dark amethyst he found so fascinating. Skimming his palms up her sides and taking her T-shirt along the way, he dragged it off, tossed it over his shoulder, leaving only her locket winking erotically above her cleavage.

A glimpse of white lace bra before he yanked it down to her waist so he could bury his face in the smooth fragrant valley between her luscious breasts, cupping their weight, then massaging them so that her nipples beaded tightly against the centre of his palms.

Her low keening moan triggered a thousand impatient needs, a thousand desperate desires. Dazed and driven by his own impatience to get naked right along with her, he dragged his T-shirt over his head. 'Jeans off, now.'

He watched her shimmy out of her jeans and a pair of cute white knickers with hearts on while he discarded his boots, then shoved down his own.

Like a man dying of starvation, his eyes devoured her body, shimmering in the room's soft glow. Shadows and light. Exquisite. Perfection.

Where have you been all my life?

The question hovered on the edge of his mind, unsettling him momentarily. He dragged his gaze back to her face, reminding himself she was here now, his to enjoy, his to pleasure. Reminding himself that he didn't measure his relationships by time, but by mutual satisfaction and respect.

So why did he hesitate to touch? Why did his hand shake when he reached out to trace a line down her body, from cheek to collarbone and over her left breast where he stopped to feel her heart thud in time with his?

Her eyes were taking their own erotic journey—he could almost feel the caress—a hot silk glove stroking his erection to almost unbearable hardness.

'Don't stop now,' she demanded.

He looked down at himself, choked out a half-laugh, then met her eyes once more. 'Do I look like I want to stop?'

'No...' Her eyes sparked with arousal.

His eyes remained on hers as he reached for her hands, drew her against him. And in that first glorious instant when her body melted against his, warm and willing and all woman, his toes curled off the carpet and he shuddered to the soles of his feet. When she gasped and plucked at his shoulders, he answered with a groan that seemed to come from the depths of his being.

Desire clashed with passion, impatience with hunger. His mouth fused with hers. Bodies bumping, legs tangling, he manoeuvred them both backwards and collapsed onto the bed, Ellie sprawled over him.

He twisted so that she lay beneath him, plundering her mouth while his hands raced over her. She writhed against him, her small deft fingers scraping over his neck, his shoulders, the base of his spine. Her warm fragrance teased his nostrils; her breathing was fast and shallow.

Impatience tore at him. He couldn't get enough. Enough of her scent, her moans, her taste. The room's cool air mingled with the warm scent of arousal, muted light spilled over them like gold dust and her skin glowed like fire.

The primitive race to finish what they'd begun beat like a jungle drum through his blood, vanquishing any semblance of his customary urbane finesse.

No time to linger, less to think. Pushing her legs apart with his thigh, he plunged his fingers into her wet heat…
Protection.

The world they'd created ground to a halt.

On a groan of frustration, he withdrew his hand. 'Condom,' he mumbled when she whimpered in protest. He reared up, yanking open his bedside drawer and pulling out the necessary item.

Ellie bit her lip at the unavoidable delay, momentarily appalled that she'd not given it a thought. But before she could chastise herself, his hard body was stretched over hers once more, his weight pressing her into the mattress.

He drove inside her, one long swift glide that had her bucking to meet him and gasping his name. She lifted her eyes and his all-dark, all-seeing, all-powerful gaze met hers. And in that stunning singular instant of mutual connection she surrendered freely.

He withdrew, then plunged again, deeper, harder. Closer.

Wrapping her legs around his waist, she let him set a rhythm and take her where he would. From the dark erotic realms of her most secret fantasies to the giddy heights of mindless pleasure. She'd never wanted the way she wanted Matt McGregor, never needed anything or anyone the way she needed him at this moment.

He bewildered her. He captivated her.

He lifted her on wings of wonder and sent her soaring. Muttering her name like an oath, he thrust one final time before spinning over the edge and joining her.

Ellie's body still throbbed with the aftermath of great sex. Her skin still tingled; her breathing was still shallow. In the dimness, with only the moon's glow casting an oblique path across the carpet, they lay close, but not touching. Not speaking. Her mind was overflowing with jumbled thoughts.

The space Matt had put between them was subtle, but not lost on Ellie. A reminder that what they'd shared was simple lust, nothing more. A diversion. *Ride till you come to the end of the road.*

They'd reached that point. She'd prepared for that, been ready for it. She'd even initiated it. Yet somewhere along that journey she'd lost a part of herself. To him. Had he noticed? She listened to his breathing become slow and regular as he drifted towards sleep. She hoped not. Good Lord, the last thing she needed was for him to think she expected more than what they'd shared. Sex. Good sex. *Very* good sex.

That was all.

She sighed into the silence, resisting the urge to curl up against him and reconnect in a physical if not sexual way. To her, intimacy was as important as the sex. But not for Matt.

She reminded herself again that she didn't expect more. Problem was, she'd never used sex as a diversion for her problems. She didn't know the etiquette for the morning after. Or the day after. Belle was due back Monday. Then Matt would leave and that would be it. The end. *Finito*.

And if that hurt and left her feeling empty and alone, she'd have no-one to blame but herself.

Matt stared up at the low-beamed ceiling, resisting the urge to scoop Ellie closer. Already his sex stirred to life. He wanted to tuck her bottom against him and take her from behind—slowly this time, while he— *No. Deep slow breaths*. He needed to clear the confusion of thoughts and feelings from his mind before he did.

He'd thought once he'd had her, this attraction between them would settle. He'd get on with his life, she with hers. Instead, his response had been…unnerving.

Hell, this whole impulsive idea to bring her here had been a one-off. He'd never brought a woman to his place. Not for sex, not for any reason. His bush home was his private refuge. Belle was the only woman he allowed to get close.

His thoughts shifted to Angela. She'd seemed to be everything he wanted in a woman. Sophisticated, bright and intelligent. Until she'd told him she wanted more than a no-strings relationship. She'd wanted marriage, the house in the 'burbs, the kids and the dog.

She'd wanted the promise of everlasting love.

His fists tightened against the mattress but he forced himself to remain still. He'd been unable to give it to her and he'd had to let her go when she told him she wouldn't accept less.

What did Ellie want?

She turned towards him in sleep, shifting nearer. Too near. One arm slid over his chest and a breast snuggled up against his torso. Intimacy and trust. His body tightened further. He closed his eyes, refusing to acknowledge it. Despite her assertion to the contrary, he had an edgy feeling Ellie wasn't the kind of woman who'd be satisfied with a fling either. He'd allowed himself to get too close on an emotional level. Dangerously close.

It was a long time before he slept.

CHAPTER TEN

THERE really was nothing quite like waking up next to a warm woman on a winter's morning. Particularly if that woman had hair that smelled of hyacinths and a firm smooth bottom snuggled against his hardening groin.

Unlike last night, the room glowed with a crimson dawn. Rather than the possum party, a couple of kookaburras exchanged a cheery good-morning in the gums outside the window.

But the urgency hadn't lessened. If anything, it had increased. Again Matt was hit with the same headlong, mind-blowing rush to have her. That same sweet desperation to bury himself inside her.

He fought the feeling down, throwing off the bedclothes, welcoming the cooler air over his heated flesh. He needed to get out of here, away from temptation. She did things to him he didn't want, didn't need. 'Time to rise and shine,' he said, forcing a brightness he didn't feel into his voice. 'Why don't you take the first shower. I'll make us some breakfast. I want to be on the road asap.'

'Okay.' Ellie half expected him to ask if he could join her, but no matter how attentive he'd been last night and how sensational their lovemaking, she'd sensed the barrier he'd put between them. She told herself it was a relief, *not* a disappointment. He played it casual, she would too. That's what they'd agreed to.

From beneath the covers, she watched him stroll naked to the mirrored wardrobe and pull out a thick aubergine dressing gown. That butt was magnificent, no doubt about it. Tight, taut. Tantalisingly touchable. She'd known that, but she'd only seen glimpses. Her imagination had filled in the gaps. Now, seeing him for the first time in all his glory in the full light of day... Then he turned around, and, oh, my...

He was an architectural masterpiece in himself. Hard planes over well-defined muscle, sharp angles that caught the early sunlight filtering through the window and cast navy shadows in dips and hollows. Not to mention all that...that glorious masculinity.

No, not to mention that at all. Swallowing, she struggled to pull her lust-crazed thoughts into some sort of order. Then he stepped into a pair of boxers and her lip-sucking moment was over.

She realised he'd picked up her discarded clothes while she'd been lying here like lady of the manor. He laid them at the foot of the bed with the robe. 'You'll find towels in the bathroom.'

'Thanks.' That wild fantasy of making him her love slave surfaced and she fought down a blush, but it wouldn't have mattered because he gave her no more than a glance.

She waited till he'd pulled on jeans before easing herself off the bed, clutching her clothes to her breasts and heading to the bathroom.

Ellie soaped herself up beneath the hot spray with exquisite care, every dab, every glide of her hands over her skin, a reminder of another pair of hands. Her body quite literally sang.

A tiny flash of movement caught her eye through the

fogged glass. She cleared a space and saw a black-and-yellow honeyeater flitting in and out of the courtyard's fernery.

She could get used to this, she thought. Shaking her head she switched off the taps with unnecessary force and reached for a towel. Forget it. Wasn't going to happen. Wouldn't know what to do with it if it did.

Because it would end. It always ended.

She tugged at the tangled curls, secured her hair at the back of her head with an elastic this morning and stared at her own face in the mirror. 'Repeat after me,' she told her reflection. *'Don't be fooled again, Ellie Rose. Guys like Matt aren't looking for long-term with girls like you.'*

Matt had breakfast in the oven and ready to dish up when his mobile rang. 'Hello.'

'Matthew.'

He smiled at the sound of the familiar voice. ''Lo, Belle. How's everything going?'

'Very well, dear. Or it was, but there's a bit of a problem here.'

'What's wrong?' His hand hovered over the stove, breakfast forgotten. 'Anything I can do?'

'No, no. It's just that Miriam wanted to go skydiving and she talked me into—'

'You did *what*?'

'You heard correctly,' she said with a smile in her voice. 'If ninety-year-olds can do it, why not me? When you get to my age you realise that sometimes you have to take chances before it's too late. It was a tandem dive with a fully qualified instructor. Anyway,' she hurried on before Matt could get another word in, 'Miriam landed heavily and twisted her ankle. She lives alone and I'd like to stay on a day or two to help but I don't want to put you out longer than I have to.'

'No need to hurry back. Everything's fine here.'

'That's good to hear.' She paused. 'How's Eloise?'

He smiled at her usual formality. 'Fine. The weather's been a bit wet for gardening but I kept her busy.' He was suddenly excruciatingly aware of how his response might be interpreted, so he added, 'Your windows now sparkle.'

'Oh. Thank her for me.' Pause. 'Matthew...I know when you're not saying something... Have you been seeing her?'

Seeing her— Oh, yeah, images of last night were imprinted on his eyeballs. 'She works for you, Belle, of course I have.'

'You know what I mean.'

'Don't go getting any romantic ideas, Belle.' He struggled with a feeling that he was scaling his own skyscraper with one hand tied behind his back. 'It's not...'

Then he noticed Ellie in the doorway, looking unsure, and Belle's voice faded into the background. He beckoned her in. How long had she been standing there? What had she heard? And while he tried to recall what he'd said, he watched the way her nipples poked at her T-shirt as she stretched and studied the view from the window and everything else flew out of his mind.

He turned away, rattled off, 'Have to go, Belle. We're about to have breakfast. Talk to you soon, bye.'

Ellie's arms dropped and she spun to him, the pleasure bleaching from her face. 'Oh, that's just peachy. Breakfast? You as good as told Belle, my *employer*, we're sleeping together. Slept together,' she corrected quickly, her eyes widening as if remembering that was all they'd agreed to.

'I didn't mention any names.' His voice felt tight as he dropped the phone onto the table. 'And so what if we did? We're consenting adults.' While Ellie sat down, he concentrated on sliding a plate piled with crisp bacon, eggs and buttered toast from the oven. He set it in front of her. 'Eat before it gets cold.'

She bit into a piece of toast. 'What about you?'

He moved away from her fresh scent before he said or did something unwise. 'I'm going to take a shower first.' With the safety of distance, he grinned, but it felt forced. 'Leave some bacon for me.'

They'd ridden back to Melbourne soon after breakfast, arriving at Belle's midmorning. Now Matt scowled at the garden in progress through the window while he spoke to a guy he knew about finding Ellie new accommodation.

He'd dropped Ellie back at her apartment. The cleaning crew had been; Matt had ensured her door was repaired and secure. Then he'd left. No suggestion of meeting up later. Nothing.

With arrangements to view a couple of places, he disconnected. He'd give her a call later, make sure everything was okay. Meanwhile there was a problem at one of the Sydney sites that couldn't wait. He'd already made arrangements to fly there. Business was his priority, always had been—he'd see Ellie Tuesday.

Days away. He frowned. Memories of last night played over and over in his mind. How smooth and soft her skin felt against his when she'd wrapped her legs around him. Her impatient moans of passion against his ear. Her slick hot heat as he'd plunged inside her. She'd been so responsive, so satisfying. The best sex ever. From her response she thought so too.

Why wait for Tuesday?

Swiping up his keys, he headed out into the drab winter's day.

'Matt.' Ellie pulled her door wider, staring at the man who'd left less than an hour ago. 'Did you forget something?'

'As a matter of fact...' He stepped in, closing the door

behind him and pulled her close, crushing her breasts against his chest and covering her mouth with his.

If she'd thought he'd changed his mind after last night, this hot, hard doubt-melting kiss proved her wrong. He lifted his head. 'It doesn't have to be one night, Ellie,' he murmured, cruising his hands up her back.

'What are you saying?' As if she didn't know.

As if she could think of the right response...the *sensible* response. After all, she'd heard him telling Belle not to get any romantic ideas...and despite their mutual understanding—that last night was one night and one night only—it had hurt. More than it should.

'We could spend a few more days...and nights...enjoying getting to know each other better.'

She felt the demand in his fingers and stared up into impatient dark eyes. Less than twelve hours ago she'd seen passion burning bright in those eyes. It was still there, dark and smouldering. One move, one spark, and they'd ignite.

She wanted to burn like that with him again.

But a few days, then what? He was talking about a few hours of pleasure between the sheets with maybe the odd candlelit dinner thrown in. And when put like that...was she *really* considering turning him down?

But something inside her cramped and twisted and she stepped back. Did she want to relive that familiar pain of being left behind when he moved on? To slice open those old wounds around her heart which had never completely healed?

He was suggesting a fling.

She didn't do flings. And she didn't do them for very good reasons.

She continued to back away until her backside hit the edge of the kitchen table. 'I know what you're asking.' *And you want to put a time limit on it.* 'Forget it. I enjoyed last night, and I would be lying to pretend otherwise, but—'

His mouth swooped down on hers again, cutting off her protests. His beautiful, beguiling, bewitching mouth. Tormenting her with all kinds of sweet temptation, promising all manner of dreamy delights. Delights he'd barely begun to show her last night, delights she'd barely begun to discover.

She wanted more. And he gave her more, with mouth and tongue, low-throated murmurs and clever hands. Not the blazing brush fire this time, but a hot steady burn, no less powerful in its intensity.

When he lifted his head and looked straight and clear into her eyes, she found herself clinging to his sweatshirt for support. Her head was spinning, her heart trying to catch up.

'It was good between us last night,' he murmured. 'I want to pursue it. So do you.'

She closed her eyes, denying it, denying him. Denying herself. 'No.'

'Look me dead in the eye and tell me you don't want to continue what we started.'

He cupped her jaw, thumbs whisking over her lips, and her brain shut down. 'I don't want you to—' one hand skimmed down the centre of her body from neck to navel, down '—to... stop,' she finished on a moan. She tried to move away again, but the table prevented her and it seemed her body had a will of its own. 'I can't think when you do that....'

'Then look at me, be honest and tell me you don't want me.' The trace of his lips over her chin and down the side of her neck had her arching backwards over the table, his hand warm against her lower belly. Her feminine places swelled and throbbed. One touch and she was melting....

Her eyes drifted open. 'This is crazy.'

'I agree.'

He lifted his head, watched her with a grin that promised everything she wanted if only she had the courage to take it for however long it lasted.

He wiggled his brows. 'Why don't we get crazy together?'

She felt her own lips kick up at the corners. 'You think it'd help? I mean...help with getting it out of our systems. Like you said.' Sometime. She waved a vague hand; she couldn't remember when he'd said it, only that he had. Which meant he wanted to get naked with her to scratch that pesky clichéd itch. Temporary diversion. Lust.

'We could give it another try right now...' He shifted closer, easing himself between her thighs.

'Uh-uh. Not until we make a few things clear.' Pushing him away, she straightened, her mind awhirl. Did she dare to risk setting herself up for the fall which would inevitably occur? For starters, 'If I change my mind, you respect that, no questions asked.'

He nodded. 'You got it.'

'And while we're being crazy together, you're not being crazy with anyone else.'

'Ellie, I—'

She shook her head. 'Never. *Ever.* I won't tolerate it.' She could feel herself shaking, her voice catching, remembering Heath's betrayal. While he'd made merry with her, he'd had a fiancée he'd forgotten to tell her about. 'I'll not—'

'Ellie, calm down. I'm not asking for undying love and commitment. All I'm asking is a few days of mutual enjoyment. Just you and me.'

'A few days.' She stared up at him, unable to believe he'd ask it, unable to believe she'd even consider it, let alone agree to it.

'It'll be okay, Ellie.' He searched her gaze for the longest time, then touched her cheek with a light finger. It was almost as if he knew she'd been hurt before, and his perception and understanding did strange things to her insides, quieting the shrill questions and fears, beckoning to her like a warm quilt on a cold night.

Still, she rubbed the tiny shiver from her arms that his touch invoked. 'I know it will.' She'd make sure of it.

He nodded, taking her reply as acceptance. 'I need to return to Sydney for work for a couple of days. Come with me.'

She felt her jaw drop. 'To Sydney? What about Belle?'

He smiled. 'I happen to know she'd approve.'

'I don't know that she would—what about her kitchen garden? Thanks to the weather, it's behind schedule. She's trusting me to get on with the job in her absence.'

'You're not due to work again until next week. I've organised the company jet to be ready at three-thirty and booked a table for dinner tonight at the Sydney Tower Restaurant.'

Company jet. Dinner in Sydney.

And his undivided attention.

An incredulous laugh bubbled up. She was standing here in her dim, decrepit one-room apartment, being proposi-tioned by an irresistible millionaire who'd already planned the entire thing. It was all moving so fast she felt as if she was being whisked up to the top of that tower already. 'Mr Super Confident,' she murmured.

'The only way to make things happen.'

How was she going to keep up with him? 'I don't have anything suitable to wear to such an up-market restaurant, and didn't you say you had to work?'

'Not till tomorrow. And you'll look gorgeous, whatever you wear.'

Oh, yeah? He hadn't seen her wardrobe. 'You work on a Sunday?'

'It's urgent and the only day everyone involved can fit it in. You can sightsee, shop or spend the time at the apartment, if you prefer. There's a spa with a great view over the city and plenty of bubbles.'

'Soap or champagne?'

'Both, if you so desire.'

And, oh, she did... She bit back a sigh. Her own *Pretty Woman* vision without the shopping spree.

Unlike the crowds and delays of commercial travel, they departed on time and with no fuss, leaving the dull grey Melbourne skyline behind.

Soon after take-off Matt fixed them drinks and nibbles, then excused himself to catch up on some work on his laptop, leaving Ellie to lie back on the wide leather seat and enjoy the comfort of the tiny private jet.

She watched the ice-cream clouds below them for a time, then flicked through a couple of architectural magazines. McGregor Architectural Designs featured on the cover of the previous month's issue. Matt was standing at the base of some steps, jacket slung over his shoulder, a glimmer of that sexy-as-all-get-out grin on his face. A needle-thin glass-and-steel pyramid vaulted into the sky behind him. She recognised it as one of the city's prominent buildings, but hadn't realised it was one of Matt's designs and the home of his business empire. The whole concept that she was in his jet, flying off to spend the weekend with him, blew her away.

In just over an hour they were descending over the Harbour Bridge, the water reflecting the deepening orange and indigo sky. Lights were coming on all over the city like thousands of twinkling fireflies.

A limousine picked them up and whisked them to the city centre. They stopped in front of a tall round building and stepped out onto George Street, thronged with tourists out on a Saturday night. The lobby sparkled with lights and black granite. Ellie had worked in Sydney but she'd stayed in cheap accommodation, not in...this. 'You own an apartment in this building too?' she asked as they stepped into the elevator.

'Yes.'

'How many places does one guy need?'

He grinned as they shot skyward. 'I look at them as investments and it beats impersonal and unfamiliar hotel rooms.'

The elevator doors slid open to reveal a small lobby. Matt opened a wide-panelled door and the stunning harbour view greeted them through floor-to-ceiling windows. As she followed him through the spacious apartment she noticed vibrant autumn colours of amber and taupe. A tall arrangement of black lacquered twigs in a vermilion pot stood in one corner. Comfortable couches, the latest in electronic entertainment.

He stopped at a bedroom, setting their bags just inside the door. Her pulse stepped up at the sight of the king-size bed with its dark-chocolate quilt and apricot pillows.

The reason she was here.

The air crackled with sexual awareness but he said, 'Feel free to make yourself at home. I've got some plans to go over before tomorrow morning. I'll be in my study.' *Business before pleasure.*

'Okay.' She closed her eyes briefly as he left, feeling way out of her comfort zone. *What was she doing?* She wasn't the type of girl who went with a rich man for sex.

She crossed the room to watch the changing colours of the twilight sky. Last night Matt had been just a regular guy in a leather jacket who rode bikes to relax. The guy who'd slipped over in the mud with her. The guy who'd helped her wipe the mess off her kitchen floor when she'd been burgled and looked after her when she was ill.

Here on his own turf, this Matt was someone else. The permanent playboy and businessman, wealthier than she'd ever imagined, more influential than she'd given him credit for. He managed a business empire over two cities. A man way out of her stratosphere.

He was also the man she'd had the steamiest, most sensational sex of her life with.

If she could just concentrate on that and *not* think about how he was tugging at strings she didn't want tugged. Making her feel things she didn't want to feel. Making her vulnerable.

No, no, no. Not vulnerable. In control. Swinging her case onto the bed, she unzipped it with a firm tug and pulled out her one and only black dress. She slid the mirrored wardrobe door open to search for a coat hanger...

A row of after five dresses met her eyes, neatly arranged in colour from black through to white. Her stomach clenched, her fingers went limp. But only for a moment. Had the woman left her designer underwear too? Throwing her own cheap cotton dress on the bed, she flung open cupboard doors, yanked out drawers, rifling through briefs, boxers, socks.

She found an abundant supply of condoms in the top bedside drawer. An overabundance, in her opinion. She slammed the drawer shut. At least he was responsible, but did he have to be such a boy scout about it?

'Ellie? I heard noises. What are you doing?'

She swivelled her head to see Matt the love rat at the doorway. The way he stared at her, brow furrowed, eyes questioning... Damn it, he made her feel as if she was looking for his hidden stash of cash.

She realised she was holding a pair of black briefs and dropped them back in the drawer. Lifted her hands away from his underwear.

'The condoms are in the top drawer,' he said, leaning lazily against the doorjamb. 'In case you were wondering.'

'Yes, I *know*. I was *wondering* why you've asked me here when you've clearly got plenty of female company to keep you occupied.'

His gaze followed hers to the open wardrobe and his expression cleared. 'I forgot to mention them. They're for you to choose something to wear this evening. I had the boutique from downstairs bring them up, but if the size isn't right...' He trailed off at her glare.

'So my clothes aren't good enough?' She felt like three kinds of an idiot, accusing him without cause.

He frowned. 'You were the one who said you didn't have anything suitable to wear.'

Oh. Right. 'I didn't expect... Look...I'm sorry, okay?' She waved a vague hand at the jumbled drawers. 'I don't need you to—'

'Just choose something. That purple or the turquoise.' His voice rumbled, water-smoothed stones beneath a deep-flowing river.

She could almost hear him say, *One that comes off easily at the end of the evening.* Could see it in the way his eyes seared her skin.

Or maybe he was saying, *We can be late....*

All the air left her lungs. She was tempted, so tempted, to walk on over and push his T-shirt up, kiss her way across that firm, hard abdomen and distract him from his work.... 'Okay,' she heard herself murmur as if she stood somewhere outside of herself.

He gave her a heated look, but then, just when she thought she'd been right all along, he glanced at his watch. 'We'll leave in thirty minutes.'

CHAPTER ELEVEN

POISED three hundred metres above Sydney, the scenery from the tower's restaurant was, as always, spectacular. Matt barely glanced at it, preferring to watch the city lights reflected in Ellie's eyes. To linger over the way her lips curved when she talked and admire the play of light and shadow over her cleavage in that low-cut turquoise dress.

She was different from other women he'd dated. What she lacked in sophistication she made up for in her enthusiasm. She had an appetite for the sumptuous food on offer, unlike most who picked over the salads and talked about the latest diet fad. Ellie talked about her hopes to set up a landscaping business, a financial struggle the power women in his life would never have to cope with.

She had an in-depth knowledge of environmental issues, natural and herbal remedies and sixties music. She loved her volunteer work with the kids. She loved sci-fi movies but preferred reading fantasy novels and could name every character in *Lord of the Rings* without missing a beat.

She just kept surprising him.

He let his mega-dollar-a-bottle champagne swirl over his tongue and wondered how many more surprises she had in store while he watched her break her last prawn apart with as much care as he'd seen her tend her coriander seedlings. She popped the seafood in her mouth, then dipped her fingers in the water bowl supplied, wiped each one individually on her napkin. Those small slender fingers fascinated him. He shifted on his chair, remembering the feel of them on his body last night.

And they'd barely scratched the surface, so to speak. His skin heated, his neck prickled, his groin hardened. So much to discover, so little time…

Her eyes lifted to his, warm and liquid and almost black in the light, and he knew without a shadow of doubt that their thoughts were speeding in the same direction.

She continued to watch him with those expressive eyes while she patted her mouth with her napkin. 'That was wonderful.'

'The evening's barely begun.' He dropped his own napkin on the table. 'You ready to leave?'

A spark danced across her gaze and her full lips tilted at the edges. 'I thought you'd never ask.'

'We didn't have dessert.' Ellie's voice was breathless and hot against his ear as he backed her up against the door to his apartment before the elevator doors had closed behind them.

'Dessert's overrated.' His fingers fumbled the key while he kissed his way down the exposed column of her neck. 'I have all the sweet temptation I need right in front of me.' Then the door swung open and they stumbled inside.

He kicked it shut and, grasping her wrists, rolled her with him against the wall. Right here, right now, he gave in to the firestorm which had been raging through him all evening. Beneath his skin and in his blood.

He pinned her hands above her head so he could feel all of her, from mouth to breasts to thighs and knees. Then he leaned in, grinding his erection against her softness and crushing her mouth with his until they were both delirious and dizzy and drunk on desire.

She tasted of hot wine and hotter woman and something darker, richer, more potent. One hand traced the sinuous length of an arm, from fingertip to palm, elbow to shoulder, pausing where her pulse beat a crazy tattoo at her neck, then down over one breast, to enjoy its firm fullness, loving the way she arched urgently against his palm. He tugged her closer.

All of her. He wanted all of her. Again. And in that moment of stunning contact he forgot caution, forgot that he always maintained a certain emotional distance. He wanted to give her all. Everything. Until they were both spent and neither had anything left to give. 'What you do to me,' he managed, between laboured breaths, 'should be against the law.'

'So arrest me.' Her husky voice laced with humour stirred the simmering volcano in his gut to a rolling boil.

His laugh was strained. He drew back a moment to take in the vision before him. With her arms still above her head and against the wall of their own accord, she looked like a siren calling him home. In the light slanting through the windows from the city below, he could see the sheen of desire on her face and arms. Her eyes were open and dazed and full of passion.

His fingers tensed, then twisted into the soft fabric at her waist. Curves and contours, dips and valleys—he found them all. A mess of contradictions, he wanted his hands everywhere at once, yet he wanted to savour each sensation to its fullest.

No time.

Reaching out, she grabbed a handful of his shirt. Buttons popped, he heard a rip, then her hands rushed up and over his chest.

She made a sound—part humour, part apology. 'I hope that wasn't your best shirt.'

'I have more.' Sweeping her up into his arms, he staggered

to the bedroom, his shirt hanging from his arms. Her fast shallow breaths fuelled his own. Impatience, as urgent as if it were the first time, whipped through him.

She reached around to her back, the action thrusting her breasts forward. He heard the rasp of a zipper. His hands slipped beneath the straps and her dress slid off, a whisper of silk on skin beneath his hands. A crackle of electric excitement as the rest of their clothes were stripped away and they tumbled onto the bed together.

No words. Just mindless pleasure, mutual delight. He feasted on her dewy skin, drank the honeyed pleasure at her mouth, then on a groan that seemed to come from some uncharted place inside plunged his aching erection into her warm and willing heat.

She arched to meet him as if she'd been waiting a lifetime, clutching at his shoulders, fingernails scraping down his spine. Reaching down between their joined bodies, he touched her sweet spot and watched her eyes turn indigo. 'Matt...' Her breath sobbed out. 'I can't...'

Catching her plea on his tongue, he touched her again, tracing tiny circles over her slick moisture with his thumb. 'You can. Now.' True to his promise, seconds later her body convulsed beneath him, her gasps harsh against his neck as he sent her soaring.

'Again.' He raced with her along a dark velvet road which spun up into a never-ending spiral where the air was hot and heavy, filled with the sound of their moans.

They took what they wanted, what they needed, each from the other, flesh straining against flesh, mouths fused, hearts pounding in sync. And then the hot and slippery slide to climax.

Sated and spent, they lay close, touching. Intimate. Explosions of pleasure still shuddered through Ellie's body. So Matt wasn't into pillow talk, but he'd let down some of the barriers she'd sensed last night. Like right now as he pulled her close, his hard masculine torso warming her all down her back.

She snuggled against him, not analysing, not anticipating tomorrow or the next day, but content to simply be as sleep closed in around them.

Since Matt had left for his appointments early, Ellie spent a lazy day pleasing herself and playing tourist. Darling Harbour was within easy walking distance so she crossed Pyrmont Bridge, wandered the arcades and sat in the warm winter sun and ate ice-cream. Then she returned to the apartment and spent a couple of hours catching up on sleep in the luxurious bed they'd made love in last night and into the early morning.

Late in the afternoon she couldn't resist the lure of the spa bath. White marble surrounds, a view over the sparkling aquamarine harbour and coathanger bridge, a range of bathroom products that spoke of Matt's many hours of indulgence in this room, with or without company.

'Need your back washed?'

She turned to see Matt with a bowl of strawberries in one hand, a bottle of bubbly and two glasses in the other. He set them down and started unbuttoning his shirt. He looked gloriously masculine, his jaw shadowed with the day's stubble, his chest hair gleaming darkly in the reddening glow from the sun. His eyes smouldered with intent and her pulse leapt in anticipation. 'Only my back...?'

He undid his belt, unzipped his trousers, his erection straining against navy-blue boxers, and grinned, teeth gleaming as he pulled a condom from his pocket and held it aloft. 'Whatever you want, I'm a slave to your desires.'

Her love slave. She couldn't help the smile as she sank

back against the cool side of the bath and watched him strip away the final barriers. 'In that case…'

Afterwards, she reclined against his body while he fed her strawberries. The water lapped at her breasts. 'This is true decadence.'

He dropped a handful of bubbles onto her shoulder, smoothed it all the way down her arm. 'Enjoy it—we're leaving tomorrow morning.'

She couldn't deny the stab of disappointment. 'You finished everything here, then?'

'Yes.' Water sloshed and she felt him move as he set his glass on the tiles with a *chink*. She thought he hesitated before saying, 'Ellie, I've got a function tomorrow night at the Melbourne office. A winter solstice party. Fancy dress. Come with me.'

Her pulse skipped a happy beat, but only one. A private fling with him was one thing, being seen together in the very public arena of his place of work and amongst his colleagues was something else. That he'd asked her was another surprise and one that had her heartbeat stepping up a notch. What did it mean for her? For them?

No. She couldn't even begin thinking of them as a couple; he'd made it quite clear that's not what they were. If he was asking her to accompany him, it was because they were having a fling and he needed a partner for the evening.

But her heart squeezed tight beneath her breast. Oh, how easy it would be to step into those glass slippers and play the princess, just once. But the magic wouldn't last and no prince was going to come searching for her in the cold light of morning, least of all someone like Matt. Apart from great sex the man might as well be from another planet for all they had in common.

'Ellie?' His scratchy jaw rasped against her neck; his hands slipped beneath her armpits to play with her nipples. 'You're thinking too hard. Don't analyse it, just say yes.'

'Thanks, but I don't think so.'

His fingers stilled. Obviously he wasn't accustomed to being turned down. 'It's a charity fundraiser,' he continued. 'Right up your alley. Yasmine will be there. She's loads of fun and I know you'll like her. She's organising my costume. I'll get her to organise something and contact you.'

'Thanks, but no.' Ellie the gardener didn't want to talk to the tall, stunning Yasmine with the long sleek hair and high-profile job. 'I'm not into office parties. I'd just feel out of place.'

'Out of place? Why? Other people are bringing their partners.'

'Come on, Matt, you know what I'm talking about. We're not "partners". You and me—we're just two people having sex.'

'We're—'

'*And* we both know we're on different sides of Belle's upscale wrought-iron-and-concrete fence.'

He was silent for a long time. Then he said, 'You think that makes a difference to me?' She could feel his frown at the back of her head.

'Maybe not, but it makes a difference to me.' She shrugged, not allowing herself to look at the luxury surrounding her, not letting Matt's words seep into her consciousness and—worse, much worse—into her heart.

'Only because you let it. Who skewed your thinking, Ellie?'

'A guy I knew once.' She hadn't realised she'd spoken aloud until she felt his lips touch the back of her neck. 'And he didn't skew my thinking. He opened my eyes to the hard, real world.'

'A lover?'

'Heath.' She avoided the label. 'His name was Heath.'

'Where did you meet him?'

'I was working in a nursery-cum-florist-shop in Adelaide. He was from a wealthy family, on a working holiday from the UK, and came in to place an overseas order. We got talking. Next morning the biggest bunch of roses appeared on the counter with my name on it.

'He treated me like a princess, promised me the world all wrapped up and tied with a big red bow. Weeks later he moved in with me, even though I knew he thought my apartment was the pits, but hey, I was paying the rent, so why not?'

'He was a scumbag.'

'I thought so too.' *After he'd ripped out my heart and left me behind.* 'Especially when I learned he already had a fiancée back home—they were getting married in London the following month. I should have guessed when he placed that first order but I trusted him and it was so nice having someone in my life again.' To love and be loved. 'But it turned out I was the holiday fling. I saw everything clearly after that. I am who I am, I know my place in the world and I'm comfortable with it.'

'But not with me, apparently. Ellie, look at me.' Gripping her shoulders, he turned her to face him, tucking her legs around his muscled torso. 'Do you see a guy like Heath when you look at me?'

She looked into his eyes and answered honestly, 'No.' Unlike Heath, this man had integrity. He was honest and up-front about what he wanted.

She continued watching as the last light of the day gilded his face with bronze. And, oh, that was a big mistake—huge—because suddenly her heart that she'd closed to him was thumping in a strange and different way, ribbons of warmth spiralling around it, pulling tight. Love…

No, not that four-letter word that had no place in her life.

Ever again. Deliberately she shifted closer so that his erection nudged at the apex of her spread thighs. With her fingers she smoothed the perplexed frown from his brow, determined to hold strictly to the reason she was here with him in his bath in his luxury apartment. Determined not to think about what-ifs and ever-afters. Changing the topic. 'Enjoying sex…that's what we're good at, right?' She leaned forward and watched his eyes heat, soothed her lips against his and murmured, 'Got another of those condoms handy…?'

After Matt's chauffeured vehicle dropped her home on Monday morning, Ellie decided to take the rest of her free day to inspect a couple of job prospects advertised at the local council in today's newspaper in case the Healesville one she was looking at tomorrow didn't pan out.

Sitting around her apartment feeling sorry for herself would give her too much time to think, and she didn't want to think. She didn't have anything suitable to wear to a big-deal office party, and even if she did, she didn't fit in with those high-flying career types.

She showered and dressed in black trousers and business jacket, her mind going around in circles. Matt had been pre-occupied with work during the flight. No mention of when he'd see her again. She wondered if he'd decided to call it quits since she'd refused his party invitation. Except that now she'd have to face him when she turned up at Belle's for work.

When her mobile rang, she stood a moment, chewing on her lips. If he was trying to change her mind… But when she picked it up she didn't recognise the caller ID. 'Hello?'

'Ellie? Hi, my name's Yasmine and I work with Matt at McGregor Architectural.'

Ellie gulped, sinking onto the nearest chair, her knees turning to jelly. 'Um, hi…'

'Matt's busy right now but he asked me to give you a call

and see if I couldn't change your mind about joining our festivities this evening, and before you say no, I'll tell you now that I'm afraid if I'm unsuccessful, I could be looking for a position elsewhere tomorrow morning.'

'Oh. I—'

'Are you at home now?'

'Yes, but—'

'Great, I'm right outside on the footpath. With cake.'

'Uh…' Phone in hand, Ellie yanked her door open, hurried to the window overlooking the street at the end of the building's corridor.

And directly below her stood Yasmine, her beautiful business-clad butt on the bonnet of a sexy little silver hatchback, a phone pressed against her glorious sweep of black hair.

Ellie's fingers tightened on the phone. 'Oh, crap.'

Yasmine grinned at that, then lifted her face so that the sun worshipped her stunning cheekbones and waved up at her.

This time Ellie covered the mouthpiece, swore again, then waved back. 'Come on up.' What else could she say?

Ellie rushed back inside, decided it wasn't worth trying to make the place look presentable and, breathless, met Yasmine at the door thirty seconds later. 'Hi. Come in.'

Yasmine didn't bat an eye at her lowly apartment. 'I've been looking forward to meeting you ever since I saw you two together at the club.' She set the box from a local bakery on the table, her ring finger glittering with a starburst of diamonds.

Ellie tried not to notice the sparkly jewellery and feel pleased while she busied herself clearing the clutter of mismatched dishes to one end. 'We weren't together… I mean we were just— Matt's *talked* about me?'

'*Mentioned* you. But you know men—they never *talk*, particularly about women to other women. If only they knew it's what they *don't* say that gives them away every time.' She opened the box, revealing a selection of pastries and iced cupcakes. 'How was Sydney?'

When Ellie jerked around to stare at her, Yasmine was smiling. Grinning, actually. Showing perfect white teeth. 'Um... Great.' Snapping her mouth shut, Ellie swivelled towards the sink. 'Coffee?'

'Love one.'

Yasmine pulled out a chair and made herself at home while Ellie switched on the kettle and struggled to remember where she'd put the blasted stuff. 'How did you know? About Sydney?'

'I heard him making dinner reservations for two—best table, best wine, la-di-dah-di-dah. When he asked me to contact you this morning, I realised you're the mystery woman who's had him distracted for the past week.'

Distracted? Matt? Fingers trembling slightly, Ellie splashed hot water onto the coffee grounds, carried the mugs to the table, grabbed the spare carton of milk from the cupboard and sat down gratefully. 'But we're ju—'

'So as the event organiser, I really need you to come tonight or he's going to be absolute hell to work with tomorrow.' Yasmine slid the cakes Ellie's way. 'Help yourself to a bribe. Either that or I'll be polishing up my résumé.'

Ellie shook her head. 'I don't have anything to wear.'

'Not a problem. I have a stack of costumes in the car. There's sure to be one that fits.' She sipped her coffee, eyed Ellie over the rim of her mug. 'So, I'll just shoot downstairs and grab them, shall I? Then I have to get back to work and tell the boss the good news. At least then we might be able to put in a few productive hours before this evening.'

'I—'

'Great.' Beaming, she rose, headed for the door. 'Back in a jiff.'

Ellie blew out a slow, not-so-steady breath. It seemed Cinderella was going to the ball after all.

CHAPTER TWELVE

MATT was out of the chauffeured car the moment it pulled up outside Ellie's apartment. He tugged at the sweeping emerald cloak's tie which was all but strangling him. His hands felt a little clammy, his pulse a tad faster than usual, and for a moment he felt as if he was on his first date. And, in a way, escorting Ellie to a function as his partner for the evening *was* a first date for the two of them.

Thanks to Yasmine, colleague extraordinaire and miracle worker.

He knocked on her door. Odd—his breathing was slightly elevated while he waited for her to answer. As if he was nervous. Then the door opened and his lungs all but collapsed at the sight before him.

A petite vision in a medieval long-sleeved gown of dark crimson velvet which flowed to dainty slippered feet. A matching hooded cloak lined and trimmed with snowy fur. An ivy wreath crowned her head, tiny red berries sprinkled amongst the soft blonde hair—which was sleek and straight this evening.

He took another moment to linger in the depths of those violet eyes, sparkling with nerves tonight. Her fingers gripped the strings of the velvet pouch bag she held so tightly her knuckles were white.

'Aren't you going to say something?'

'Good evening, Ellie.' He had his breath back. Barely. And her familiar spiced-berry scent washed over him like a dream. 'You look absolutely amazing.' He kissed her cheek, respectable and civilised, the way a gentleman greets his partner on a first date. But inside…inside an unfamiliar sensation stumbled around the region of his heart. Suddenly the thought that he'd be back in Sydney in a couple of days wasn't something he wanted to think about. Tonight might be the last chance they'd have to be together.

'Thank you,' she said, bringing him back to the present. 'You're looking pretty sensational yourself.'

Her gaze stroked down his cloak, lingered a moment on the black-clad torso beneath. Little darts of heat prickled his skin, fed into his bloodstream, tightened his groin. *Later,* he promised silently. Later he was going to enjoy more than just her gaze.…

'The Holly King,' she said, lifting her eyes to his. 'As befitting the boss, I guess. Yasmine told me all about it. Question, though—where's the holly wreath that's supposed to be on your head?'

Grinning, he shook his head. 'I'm not a masochist.'

'Pity.' She smiled. 'I hadn't realised there was so much tradition attached to the evening. Guess it's more a northern hemisphere event.' She closed and locked the door behind her with the new deadlock he'd had fitted.

'So you and Yaz got along well, I take it?' Matt took her elbow as they descended the shabby stairwell.

'She's a good friend to you—you're lucky to have her.' Her pensive tone reminded Matt of Ellie's wandering and no doubt lonely lifestyle.

'She can be your friend too, you know.'

'I don't think that'll happen. You're leaving soon.…'

Whether it was the chill in the air or her words, he didn't

know, but something like a shiver ran down his spine as they stepped into the cold winter street.

'In you get,' he said, making an effort to lighten up as the chauffeur opened the door.

Ellie settled the cloak about her while Matt climbed in beside her. He poured a couple of glasses of champagne, handed her one. 'To a pleasant evening.'

She clinked her glass to his. 'A pleasant evening.'

Chauffeured limos, champagne en route. She marvelled at how quickly she'd become accustomed to this kind of luxury. How easily it could be taken for granted if you'd never known anything else.

She reminded herself this was a one-off as they cruised down the street and headed towards the city centre. Their destination speared into the sky, all twinkling lights and power and wealth.

'Something to wear tonight,' Matt said, drawing a rectangular velvet box from his pocket.

'Um.' Her heart stammered at the unexpected gesture. 'It's not necessary....'

'Maybe not, but I wanted to.' Relieving her of her glass, he pressed the box into her hands. 'Open it,' he told her when she didn't make a move to do so.

Her fingers felt awkward as she lifted the lid. A delicate single strand of what could only be diamonds winked at her on their bed of black satin. A bracelet that must have cost The Earth.

Stunning. Sensational. But also shockingly, outrageously expensive. How could anyone justify spending so much on a piece of jewellery? She'd live her life worrying if someone was going to steal it. Still, her fingers drifted over the stones. 'It's beautiful,' she breathed. 'But I'd never have an occasion to wear it....'

'You have tonight.' He lifted it, draped it over her wrist and fastened the clasp.

She lifted and rotated her arm, watched it glitter in the night lights. 'I wonder how many Third World children we could feed with the money it would fetch?'

'Ellie, it's not always about the money. It's a gift because I wanted to show you how much you...'

When he trailed off, she looked up at him. His expression was unreadable. Still a thrill of illicit pleasure lanced through her.

'...how much I've enjoyed having you with me this past week,' he finished. 'Please accept it for what it is.'

If she didn't know better she'd have said his voice sounded strained. Vulnerable? Nah, not Matt McGregor. Unlike her, he probably hadn't given its value a second thought.

Rather than look at him and read into his gaze something that wasn't there, she admired the bracelet's sparkle again. Looking at him would only remind her that their time together was nearly up. 'I'm sorry, I didn't mean to sound ungrateful or mercenary.' Its beauty would always be a cherished memory of this interlude in her life.

'You didn't. Not quite.' Smiling, he leaned across the seat, tilting her face so that he could plant warm lips on hers.

Interlude. Was that really all this was? she wondered as she let herself sink into the kiss. This heart-stopping, all-enveloping, all-consuming... *Careful, Ellie*. Digging her fingernails into her palms as he drew back, she turned to watch Southbank's lights reflect on the River Yarra. Yes, interlude. She wouldn't let it be anything else.

McGregor Architectural's meeting rooms on the forty-second floor, with a one-hundred-and-eighty-degree view over the city, were decked out in abundant winter greenery—rosemary, laurel, ivy, pine boughs. The forest fragrance mingled with the scent of melting wax, beer and hot cider.

Matt felt a warm feeling of satisfaction when Ellie's first impression when they stepped out of the elevator was, 'Wow.'

He'd devoted the past fifteen years to growing the business. Day and night, often seven days a week for months at a time. 'Yasmine and the organising committee have done a terrific job.' He stood a moment, enjoying the celebrations taking place in front of them, enjoying the feel of Ellie's hand in his.

Warm colours of red and amber and gold in the tall free-standing candles, rainbow hues in the sun catchers suspended from the ceiling. Paper lanterns, medieval music, platters of cheese and nuts and winter fruits on gold cloths.

'Come and meet some of my colleagues.' He'd taken barely a step when Yasmine, in a snowy Grecian-type robe that showed off plenty of bare shoulder, pounced on them.

Her sunburst headband of gold beads swayed as she pecked his cheek. 'Hi, there, handsome.' Then she linked arms with Ellie. 'Good choice,' she said, her charcoal eyes sweeping Ellie's costume. 'Come with me, there's someone I want you to meet and then we're going to check out what exciting treasures are on offer at the silent auction tonight. You don't mind, do you, Matt? John Elliot wants to talk to you about the zoning requirements for the Dockland development anyway.' She waved a vague hand towards the knot of men in the corner and swept Ellie away before he could mutter more than, 'No worries.'

He discovered he *did* mind. For once in his life he didn't want to talk business. He glared in Ellie's direction, watching her and Yaz disappear amongst a throng of women. He *wanted* to talk to his date. To share the evening with her, not with some hardnosed guy who never knew when to quit.

A bit like an older Matt McGregor.

The realisation was a solid punch to his gut. God, did he really see himself as a future J. H. Elliot? Middle-aged bachelor on the edge of a breakdown with nothing but work to fill his later years?

And wasn't that where Matt was headed? In less than twenty years he'd be alone on the wrong side of fifty too. Not so appealing.

But it could never be anything else. He, Matt, had engineered it that way.

He needed a drink to wash away the sobering prospect. He strode to the table, helped himself to a goblet of mulled wine, then mingled with staff as he manoeuvred his way to the windows where the lights of the city centre twinkled, and further out to the inky blankness of Port Phillip Bay.

'Matt.'

Distracted, he turned to see his receptionist wearing a heavily brocaded vermilion gown. 'Joanie. You're looking lovely tonight.'

'Thank you.' She handed him a squat fat candle. 'Looks like this solstice evening idea's a success.'

He nodded. 'How's the auction going?'

'Very well. What charity did you decide on?'

He'd thought of Ellie and knew she'd be happy with the idea. He'd already considered drawing up plans. 'We're going to give a local disadvantaged kids' homework centre a generous makeover. I'll give you the details later.'

Joanie nodded. 'A worthy cause.'

He spotted Ellie amongst the crowd talking with Spencer from accounting downstairs. Must be a fascinating conversation because she was smiling up at the guy. Leaning closer to hear what he said. Enjoying herself.

Which was what he'd wanted, right? But a fist knuckled beneath his breastbone and his jaw tightened as he watched them. He'd always disliked the guy.

'...so you know the tradition?' he heard Joanie say.

His eyes remained on Ellie. 'Yaz filled me in.'

'Why don't we make a start? I think everyone has a candle now.'

A tinkle of silver on glass got everyone's attention and at Joanie's request they formed a circle. Before the ritual got under way, Matt crossed the space and clasped Ellie's hand. 'Before we get started, I'd like to introduce Ellie.' He looked into those amazing eyes, felt himself falling, heard himself saying, 'She's with me.' Something inside him rocked off-centre; he'd never heard that possessive tone in his voice before.

But then a murmur of greetings followed, Yaz requested they seat themselves on the floor and the room was plunged into darkness. Only the city lights forty storeys below lent a soft sheen to the ceiling. It cast Ellie's face into dimness, but it was enough to make out her long eyelashes and the curve of her cheekbone. The tilt of her chin.

Vaguely he heard Yaz speak about long-ago traditions around the winter solstice. The battle between light and dark. A time for releasing personal resentments and regrets. He curled Ellie's fingers into his palm and his gaze remained locked on hers in the Moment of Silence for Personal Reflection.

Who was the real Ellie behind those violet eyes? Would he ever really know before he left? He knew some of her hopes, some of her fears. What of her secrets?

Her lips—a little wistful, a lot tempting. He bent his head to touch them to his. And lost himself in the warmth, her fragrance, her whisper of breath against his cheek...

Someone shuffled, Ellie drew back and he heard Yasmine's whisper at his other ear. 'Ah, Matt, when you're ready...'

He mentally shook himself. *For God's sake.* The sooner he left Melbourne, the better off he'd be. The sooner he could refocus on his work. His reason to get up in the morning. His life's core and purpose.

Rising, he placed his candle in the bowl of water which Yasmine had set in the centre of the circle. As he lit the wick, the tiny flicker glowed yellow against his palm. In turn, each participant stepped up, lit their candle from his, then placed it around Matt's. Finally Yasmine spoke of the Sun Child and the promise of light and a glowing future.

Lights were switched on, the music cranked up and goblets filled with all manner of spiced wines, ciders, beers. Caterers began bringing out platters of skewered meats and savouries. Hot herbed bread and appetising dips. A variety of soups served in chic individual shot glasses.

As Matt took Ellie's hand to lead her to the window, he noticed her bare arm. 'Where's your bracelet?'

Ellie didn't look at her wrist. She knew she didn't have the finances to contribute, so she'd done the only thing she could; she'd donated her bracelet to the cause.

'I haven't had the chance to tell you. When I learned you were donating the proceeds to the centre, I wanted to help. It's worth a lot more there than on my arm.' Before he could answer, she jumped in with, 'I'm sorry if that offends you.'

He tilted her chin up with a finger and looked steadily into her eyes. His touch was so infinitely gentle her stomach quivered. 'It doesn't offend me, Ellie.'

'I wouldn't expect you to understand, Matt,' she said softly. 'You wouldn't know about going without.'

For an instant she thought he was going to say something but then he shot her a curious look. 'If you'll excuse me a moment, there's a matter requiring my attention.' He did an abrupt about-turn and made his way through the hanging lanterns and across the room.

Turning away, she studied the panorama below. She *had* offended him. In this particular instance she didn't care. It was just another example of how they didn't fit as a couple, another reason to ignore her heart telling her this man was different. One of a kind. Special. She pressed a knuckle beneath her nose, telling herself the misty outlook was rain, not tears.

'Ellie? What are you doing here by yourself? Has Matt deserted you?'

She didn't need to turn to know it was Yasmine standing beside her, and just as well, because she didn't want anyone to see her infuriatingly damp eyes. Self-pity was not a good look. So perhaps her voice was a little too nonchalant, even acerbic, when she said, 'I'm just admiring the view. Amazing, isn't it? Matt's literally on top of the world.'

A brief silence. 'It took Matt years of sacrifice and effort and scaling Mount Everest to get here.' Yasmine sounded defensive.

Ellie's response was cool to her own ears. 'You two have known each other a while, then, I take it.'

'Twelve years. You're wondering about our relationship,' she said. 'Friends, confidants. Never lovers. Does that help?'

Ellie nodded, blurry eyes fixed on a skyscraper in the middle distance. 'I apologise if that came across as anything other than friendly curiosity.'

'Doesn't mean I don't care about him. If he was my brother, I couldn't care more.'

Ellie's gaze flicked to Yasmine's reflection in the glass. 'He's never told me about his family.'

'It's not something he talks about, with anyone. Not even me. But I do know he's achieved all this on his own. Worked his way through university, wouldn't take a cent from Belle.'

Her stomach suddenly twisting itself into knots, Ellie turned to Yasmine. 'Thank you for telling me. I think I just said something to him that I shouldn't have.'

Yasmine's smile was genuine. 'Why don't you go find him?'

Ellie stopped at the supper table with its sumptuous aromas and filled a plate, then looked about for Matt. She saw him on the far side of the room, one hand in a trouser pocket while he talked to a couple of guys and their partners. He'd removed his cloak and was in black from head to toe. He looked divine, if one could look divine and sinful at the same time.

Matt McGregor could.

He caught her staring and the hand in his pocket fisted, a muscle twitched in his jaw. His easy-going smile dropped away and his expression turned serious. He spoke to the group, then made his way towards her while her heart tried to find its rightful place in her chest.

Time seemed to slow. Everything but Matt blurred while he increased in clarity as he drew near. A hint of dark stubble on his jaw, the creases which didn't detract but rather carved his personality into his cheeks. Midnight eyes.

'Hungry?' she murmured belatedly when he reached her. Still looking at him, she lifted the delicious-smelling plate, noticing her hands were trembling slightly.

He plucked a snack from her offering. 'Yes. But I'm not thinking food.' He took a bite, slipped the other half between her lips, letting his fingers linger when she opened her mouth for the morsel.

She swallowed, still watching him. 'I did offend you. I'm sorry.'

'On the contrary,' he murmured back, holding her gaze. 'It was more of a reality check.'

'If I don't understand you it's because you haven't told me.'

But instead of an explanation, he took the plate, laid it on a nearby table, clasped her hand and said so that only she could hear, 'What say we get out of here?'

The raw and undeniable intent in his words, in his eyes,

shot sparks through her bloodstream. She let her sudden intake of breath out slowly. 'But don't you want to mingle?'

'I can think of better ways,' he replied, and tugged her out of the room and towards the bank of elevators.

Inside her apartment, he untied her cloak, laid it across a chair and slid his hands over her shoulders, up over her scalp and into her hair. 'I've been thinking about this all night,' he said, and kissed her. Slowly, deeply, deliciously.

But the tiny room was chilly, the old linoleum creaked and crackled beneath her feet. Yesterday's stale odour of fried cabbage from along the corridor permeated the air. A couple was arguing downstairs. 'My bed's too small for the both of us,' she whispered when he finally let her come up for air.

'We can make it work,' he murmured and kissed her once more, his hands cruising down her spine, over her bottom and up again.

Was this his attempt to show her he didn't care where she lived, who she was? It warmed her deep down to the centre of her being. 'But your bed would be much more comfortable....'

Lifting his head, he grinned, pulled out his phone and called back his driver. 'We've changed our minds.'

CHAPTER THIRTEEN

IN MATT'S room upstairs in Belle's house they were a world away from thin walls and peeling paint and noisy neighbours. The air was cool but not uncomfortable and tinged with the scent of his aftershave and fresh linen. A shaft of moonbeams slanted over the quilt. An owl 'mopoked' to another in the trees outside the window.

He undressed her slowly, skilfully, without the need for words. Her beautiful gown slid to the floor, her underwear followed. When she was naked but for her locket, he reached into his pocket and pulled out the string of sparkles. 'This is yours.' He clasped the stones, warm from his body, around her wrist. 'Please wear it, no questions asked.'

'But the auction wasn't finished when we left. You didn't *take* it, did you?' she said, momentarily horrified.

He grinned, kissed the tip of her nose. 'No, I didn't take it.'

'Then how—?'

He put a finger to her lips. 'I said no questions. All you need to know is that the money's going to a good cause.'

'Oh…yes.' Its elegant beauty and those deep dark eyes of his as they searched hers caught at her chest and made her nose sting and her eyes water. The way she saw it was he'd ensured his would be the highest bid before they left, and now she knew the money was to be donated, how could she refuse his gift for a second time? 'Thank you, it's beautiful,' she whispered.

'The centre's going to have those extensions you were talking about. I'll be there next week to take measurements and have plans drawn up.'

'Thank you doubly.'

But it wasn't the time to think of tomorrow or next week. That would come later, she thought—when she'd cry and berate herself for letting things get so complicated. For now, as he divested himself of his own clothes and watched her with a reflection of her own desires, she held the moment in her heart and rejoiced.

This moment of tenderness. Quiet murmurs and sighs. Gentle hands, soothing lips and a rolling, restless anticipation tempered by a patience that stemmed from the already familiar.

Moonlight carved a silver blade across his shoulders as he lifted her to the bed, laid her on the fine linen as if she was the most treasured of treasures. He stretched out beside her, and, oh...the feel of his hands as they skimmed over her body, every fingertip a glide of pleasure over shoulders, breasts, belly, thighs.

His lips now as they soothed the places his hands had delighted, warmth leaving a trail of moisture cooling on her flesh. He lingered over her breasts, teasing each nipple with tiny nips and tugs, then moved lower to curl his tongue around her bellybutton.

Slow, languid, yet she felt her breath being snatched from her lungs. Smooth as a glide of water, yet her pulse bumped and blipped as he shifted between her thighs and she realised his intent.

Lower. Skin sliding over skin. Spreading her thighs wider, he bent his head to bring her what she was afraid to want.

What some hazy part of her mind told her she'd remember on some cold and lonely day when he was gone. A memory.

And then even that was forgotten and she was soaring, flying apart into a million pieces, an explosion that shattered her awareness of self and the world as she knew it. He brought her down gently, with skill and a perception she'd never known he possessed.

And it came to her in that brief moment of stillness and fulfilment that, whether she willed it or not, this overflowing sensation of body, mind and spirit was indeed love. Freely given and without regret. Of feeling safe, protected, desired, and yearning to give it back threefold.

And yearning, yearning, to have it returned.

With his arms on either side of her hips, Matt looked down on her. Had he ever seen a more beautiful sight than Ellie rumpled with loving on his sheets? The warmth of her gold locket around her neck, the cool silver stones at her wrist, her halo of hair washed and bleached with the mystery of moonlight.

'You're almost too beautiful to touch,' he murmured, and saw her eyes fill with a poignancy that caught at his heart. He rolled on a condom, then bent to kiss those lush lips. 'Almost…'

Sliding into her slick wet heat was like coming in out of the cold. She took him inside her with a sigh, welcomed him with mouth and hands. She warmed places inside him he'd not acknowledged in…forever.

He moved inside her, in a slow sinuous dance, and she matched his rhythm as if she'd been made expressly for him. Here was sanctuary from the day-to-day demands in the cut-throat business world that was his life. In her arms that world didn't exist.

He was wrapped around her, she around him, and he felt

himself drowning, drowning, in the deepening well of her generous and open heart.

Still inside her, but sated and satisfied and blissfully lazy, they lay together in the darkness. Even as Ellie's breathing told him she was asleep, he didn't move, couldn't bear to complete the separation. He'd never known such a connection, a sense of completeness, of oneness.

Ellie was unlike anyone he'd ever known. She was proud yet vulnerable, with a strength of will and an empathy and generosity towards others. She wasn't pretending to be anything other than who she was.

Unlike him.

The sudden sharp chill of realisation sliced to his core like an icy blade. He hadn't been up-front about his past. Perhaps he should have. But it wasn't as if they had anything permanent.

And yet... As he watched her sleep, the curve of her cheek ivory in the dimness, he could no more deny he wanted her than fly to the moon. He wanted her more than his next breath. He needed her more than his next heartbeat.

But he knew all too well that desire, needs and wants wouldn't cut it with Ellie. He wasn't being fair to her. To them. With the spectres of lost loved ones haunting her past, if anyone needed love and constancy in their life it was Ellie. She'd tried so hard to hide it but he knew that, despite her assertions to the contrary, she wanted security, a home, family.

And he couldn't give her that.

Careful not to disturb her, he eased away. Already he mourned the loss of her sleepy warmth, the feel of her satin-soft skin against his. He stared up into the darkness.

Ellie... He sighed. Fiercely independent, living-life-as-it-comes Ellie. She wasn't as single, carefree and liberated as she let on. He knew by the shadows in her eyes when she thought he wasn't looking.

But over the past couple of days he'd seen glimpses of something else.… It twisted like a fist in his gut and clamped tight around the region of his heart. He'd seen something he should never have allowed to happen.

She was falling for him. The greedy, self-indulgent bastard that he was had seen it… Seen it and continued their affair with selfish and reckless abandon.

He needed to ride.

Slipping out of bed, he dressed quietly and went downstairs, grabbing his helmet and gloves by the back door, and strode out into the cold night air. He had to let her go. Tomorrow. Yes, she knew what they had was temporary—he'd always been up-front about that—but other emotions that he hadn't anticipated had entered into the mix.

His fist rapped the side of the helmet beneath his arm as he passed the garden, glittering with dew in the predawn. Ellie's garden. *'Dammit.'* His voice cut through the silent air like the crack of a whip. Knowing Ellie as he did now—the caring, vulnerable, love-starved girl that she was—he *should* have anticipated this could only end badly.

He wheeled the bike to the gate so as not to wake her, jammed on his helmet and fired up the machine the moment he was through the gate and set off for…who the hell knew? Cared? Anywhere out of town where the road was long and straight and relatively deserted at 5:00 a.m. Somehow he had to convince Ellie that he wasn't the right man for her.

Ellie tipped out another punnet of basil. As she'd drifted off to sleep she'd decided to get an early start this morning. To lie beside Matt, to feel the warmth of his hard masculine body all down her back, his slow breathing against her ear and wonder if it might be the last time was the best and worst of tortures.

But when she'd reached for him on waking she hadn't expected to find herself alone. She'd ignored the vaguely uneasy feeling at first, telling herself he was probably making coffee. But he was nowhere to be found.

Where was he and why hadn't he let her know his plans? He'd left no note, and when she'd checked the garage she'd discovered his bike gone. Perhaps this was something he did regularly, she comforted herself, like jogging; after all, she'd known him such a short time.

Yes, such a short time, she reflected, and despite all the self-talk and warning bells, she'd fallen in love.

She'd come outside hoping that working the garden would distract her from the dark and crazy thoughts buzzing around her head. She had plans today that she couldn't change. The job in Healesville was full-time but it was more than an hour away and involved catching buses and trains if she was going to stay in Melbourne. But it sounded challenging and exciting and she wanted to see what was involved. The appointment was for this afternoon.

She hoped Matt would be back before she left so that she could tell him—calmly, clearly—that she didn't appreciate his lack of courtesy because it had made her worry. That people who cared about each other or were in a relationship—*any* kind of relationship, no matter how temporary—were naturally concerned about the other.

Or was it already too late for all that? Was their relationship already over?

The full-throated rumble on the driveway heralded his imminent return. Setting her trowel on the muddy earth beside her, she watched his bike come to an untidy halt near the garage. He pulled off his helmet and gloves, set them on the ground. His expression was grim, from the compressed mouth to the shuttered eyes.

'Hi.' She stood slowly and walked towards him, dusting the dirt off her overalls while butterflies whirled crazily in her stomach. He didn't make a move to meet her midway, just stood there like one of Belle's crazy garden statues.

She stopped in front of him, those butterflies growing to monstrous proportions. His eyes were bloodshot, probably from lack of sleep but...she couldn't read them. He'd closed himself off from her. 'What's wrong?'

No response. Nothing. A mask of stone.

Then he reached out, curled his fingers around her upper arms. He smelled of leather and man. For an instant Ellie thought she saw remorse or regret or both. Then he hauled her to him, mashed his lips with hers. Heat, passion, anger—all that and more poured from his kiss in a surging tide that crashed over her, leaving her weak and shaken. Then he lifted his head, dropped his hands to his sides, took a step away—physically and emotionally.

She felt the distance like a chill wind sweeping through her soul and stared at him, not understanding. Rather, not wanting to understand. Because it was suddenly, devastatingly clear where this was headed. She steeled herself for it. 'Why are you angry?'

'I'm not angry, Ellie,' he said. 'Frustrated, perhaps. I'm flying back to Sydney today.'

It was delivered as a cool statement of intent. With no hint of regret on his part.

The big R.

He hadn't said it but it was clear as the prize crystal vase on Belle's dining table. She'd been rejected so often, left behind so many times, she should be immune to its effects now. Surely it wasn't possible for her heart to bleed any more than it already had? But she felt its life force seeping out, drop by drop.

Why? Their relationship had never been more than temporary. She'd always known, but it didn't make it any less painful. Gut wrenching. Heartbreaking. And yet...last night she could have sworn he...cared. Really cared. 'I thought you—' *we* '—had a few more days?'

'I'm needed there asap,' he said, his voice monotone. 'It's—'

'I know—business before pleasure.' She spoke over him, deliberately schooling her tremulous voice to somewhere approaching normal. It was time to reflect on the futility of it all and take control of her own life. Time to leave. This time it would be her doing the walking, not the other way round.

Somehow she pulled her numb lips into some sort of a smile. 'I understand. I really do. I've some business to attend to myself today. It's been good, Matt, but it's time to move on, we're not—'

'There you both are.' Belle's voice from the back door had them both turning. Still in her black overcoat, she walked towards them, her fawn hair riffling in the breeze.

'Belle.' Matt did an abrupt turnabout and strode to meet her, tension visible beneath his jacket's heavy leather shoulder pads. 'You should have let me know you were coming back today. I'd have picked you up.'

'No need.' She pecked his cheek, then looked past him, smiling at Ellie while she spoke. 'I thought you might be busy. I didn't want to disturb you so I caught a cab.'

From behind him, Ellie saw his shoulders lift. 'We were just—'

'Yes.' Belle smoothed his cheek, and even from where Ellie stood she could tell by Belle's expression that she'd seen them kissing.

And the rest...had she seen the rest? *Heard* the rest?

Ellie's legs were shaking so hard she thought she might have to sit down.

'I'll just let you two finish whatever you're doing and go and put the kettle on, shall I?'

'Be there in a minute, Belle.' He returned his attention to Ellie. Once more there was nothing in his blank expression when he said, 'Let's go and have that coffee with Belle. We'll talk about us later.'

No. There was no *us.* But she nodded and they walked to the house in silence.

Somehow Ellie managed to sit at the kitchen table with Matt and Belle and make conversation over coffee and chocolate biscuits, though what she said—what anyone said—she didn't remember.

But she did remember watching Belle. Slim black trousers, a hot-pink top with black lace edging. Her skin barely touched by her seventy-odd years. Short straight hair, blond barely streaked with grey and touched with gold highlights. Eyes that vacillated between blue and indigo…and something about the shape…almost familiar somehow… She'd never noticed that before.

Then she heard Belle say that she wanted to speak to Eloise on her own, 'For a little while, if you don't mind, Matthew?'

It wasn't a question and Matt knew it, had been expecting it even, because he rose, fingers stiff on the tabletop. 'Belle…I thought we were going to talk—'

'Thank you.' She smiled at him but her tone was firm. Final.

He left without a further word or a backward glance.

'We'll go into the lounge room,' she told Ellie. 'It's more comfortable.'

Belle chose an armchair and indicated that Ellie should

take one at an angle to hers. 'Eloise, when I went to my room I noticed you returned the angel. May I ask why?'

'My apartment was broken into the other night and I thought it would be safer back here.' Ellie's discomfort made itself known in her belly and she shifted uneasily on her chair. 'I love it, Belle, really, but I think it's more appropriate that you keep it. I'm only your gardener and Matt told me it's worth a lot of money.'

Belle acknowledged this with a nod. 'It is. I should have perhaps waited till now to give it to you, but I couldn't stop myself. Guardian angels are very important.'

'I don't understand.' Her voice quavered. It was such a valuable piece, why give it to Ellie? Her blood was pumping too fast around her body and she had a sudden urge to jump up and run as far away as she could. From Matt, from Belle. Except she was sure she'd fall into a dead faint before she reached the edge of the property. Worse, she didn't entirely know why.

'Eloise.' Belle leaned forward, her eyes seeking Ellie's. 'Your locket. Remember I asked you about it? You showed me the photo of your mother as a baby inside.'

Ellie's fingers rose automatically to the gold heart suspended around her neck on its fine gold chain. 'Yes...'

Belle smiled and it was the saddest smile Ellie had ever seen. 'I put that locket on my daughter the day she was born. The same day she was taken from me.'

Ellie's fingers tightened on the metal and something inside her trembled. 'But Mum said...'

'It was 1963,' Belle continued, slower now, her eyes misting as she looked back to a time long gone. 'I was nineteen, unmarried and alone and I never saw my baby again.'

'Your baby…?' Ellie stuttered to a stop, the images colliding and coalescing like a watercolour painting in the rain.

'That baby was your mother. Eloise, I am your grandmother.'

CHAPTER FOURTEEN

'NO.' ELLIE shook her head as much in denial as to try and make sense of it. 'My grandmother—Gran—died in an accident with Grandad and Mum when I was eight.' Twisting her locket in her fingers, she looked at Belle. The eyes...now she knew why they were familiar. *Because they were her mother's eyes.* 'How is that possible?' She heard her voice as if it came from somewhere outside her.

Belle reached out, took Ellie's hand in hers. 'You also have John's surname—Rose. Your grandfather and I were lovers. He was older but I had no idea he was married. I thought he loved me. Until I got pregnant. My parents disowned me, I had no one and I was desperate.

'John's wife, Nola—your gran—couldn't conceive, so he took the child on the condition that I never made contact. That I never saw my child again. Legally the baby belonged to him and Nola. I signed an agreement to that effect.'

'Oh, Belle,' she murmured, her eyes stinging as she imagined the pain of losing a child. 'How could he make you do that?'

'In those days there were very few options and I decided Samantha would have a better life with them than I could give her. John gave me this house as a form of payment.'

'But Mum knew this house belonged in her father's family.'

Belle smiled. 'Oh, I dare say John slipped up there at some stage. Or perhaps it was his pride. He was a wealthy man and my, oh my, he loved to flaunt it.'

Using it to tempt women like the pretty young Belle, Ellie thought, and hated her grandfather with a sudden and vehement passion. He'd cheated on Gran, stolen her grandmother from her and from her mother. 'You knew all this before you went away.'

Her smile faded. 'I did. When I saw your advertisement for gardening work in the paper, the surname leapt out at me, as it always does. But, Eloise...' She paused. 'Eloise was your grandfather's mother's name.'

'I know,' Ellie said. 'And I hate it. I only put it in that ad because I thought maybe it sounded more professional and would attract more clients. I'm not sure it worked.'

Belle smiled. 'It worked for me. You'd rather I call you Ellie?'

Ellie nodded. 'Please.'

'Then Ellie it is.' Belle folded her hands on her lap. 'But the name got me thinking. I did some research into his family history and made a startling discovery. I had no idea about the accident, or the fact that I had a granddaughter. Believe me, darling, if I'd only known years ago...'

'That's why you hired me? To get to know me?'

She nodded slowly. 'But after all these years...I wanted to decide whether I had the right to turn your life upside down. I went to see your grandfather's sister, Miriam, to talk it over with her, since she was one of the few people who knew the whole story.'

'Grandad never said he had siblings.'

'That's because Miriam never spoke to him again after what he did.' She took a deep slow breath. 'So, Ellie, I need to know...did I do the right thing? Your gran was probably a very important person in your life.'

'She was, but it was so long ago.' And now...now she had Belle. A miracle. And her whole being rejoiced. 'Yes, Belle, you did exactly the right thing.' She leaned forward and took both Belle's hands in hers. 'It'll take time to get used to the idea. I've been on my own so long. Matt will—'

Matt. Ellie's heart missed a beat. 'If Matt's your nephew and I'm your granddaughter...'

'Matthew's not my biological nephew.' She turned her hands over in Ellie's. 'He didn't tell you?'

'No.' She let a relieved breath out slowly. 'Closed book on that subject.'

Belle nodded but didn't elaborate. 'You two got close while I was away.'

She *had* seen them kissing. Ellie's eyes lowered to their joined hands and lingered there. 'Past history already.'

'Why?'

'For one, he lives in Sydney. And secondly, he's not the settling down, one-woman type.'

Belle was silent a moment. 'He's been working in Sydney for several months but his base is Melbourne, and where he works doesn't matter. As for the second...I need to know, what are your feelings for him, Ellie?'

Ellie bit her lip but tears sprang to her eyes anyway. 'He's the most...' She shook her head, unable to express the gamut of emotions he invoked in her—joy and love and pain and frustration. 'He'd do anything for you, Belle. I've learned that about him. He's loyal.'

'And once you've earned his loyalty you have it for ever, but you've not answered my question.'

Ellie's breath soughed out along with the emotions she'd just discovered. 'I love him—and, oh...I tried so hard not to.' She swiped her eyes and willed herself to toughen up. Take control. Smile. 'But I'll get over it.'

'Why would you want to?' Belle said softly.

'Because he doesn't want more than temporary.'

'If he gave that impression it's because he's been hurt before and worse, by people he loved that he should have been able to trust.'

'It wasn't an impression, Belle. He spelled it out loudly and clearly in capital letters and I was the fool who thought I was sophisticated enough to handle it.'

'I've never seen the look in Matt's eyes that I saw this morning when he looked at you,' Belle said.

Oh... If Ellie didn't get out of here right now she was going to blubber, so she stood, still watching Belle. *Her grandmother.* 'Matt. You... This is all so overwhelming. I want to stay and talk and ask questions. There are so many things I want to know, but I have to get home and change for an appointment at Healesville.'

Ellie explained about the employment prospect but reassured Belle she intended finishing the herb garden. That it was a good career opportunity but out of the city which was now not so appealing since they'd just found each other. Belle offered her the use of her car for the month if she took the job so that Ellie could remain in Melbourne with her.

They both rose and sealed the deal with a hug. A family hug of warmth and trust and welcome.

'I have to get the job first,' Ellie said, not wanting to end the embrace but finally pulling away. 'The bus leaves the city at one o'clock, which doesn't leave me much time.'

Belle squeezed Ellie's shoulder. 'Of course, darling. You do what you have to do.'

'But I can come back tonight and we'll talk some more...'

'Yes. Stay the night.'

Under the same roof as Matt? 'Oh, I—'

Belle hugged Ellie again before Ellie could say that wasn't going to happen, her grandmother's eyes glinting with purpose as she stepped back to look at her. 'I insist. And you'll come live here with me. However, I don't think Matthew has to know about any of this yet. But he and I do need to have a conversation.'

He should be packing. The aircraft would be ready for take-off at 2:00 p.m. Instead, swinging the spade, Matt vented his frustration on a patch of soursobs. He stopped a moment, scowled at the lounge room windows, but all he saw was the sky's reflection. No way of telling what was happening beyond those sparkling clean panes of glass.

The spade sliced through the soft earth. *Dig, lift, toss. Dig, lift, toss.* He concentrated on the fresh smell of soil-rich air, the repetitive sounds of his own grunts and the soft *plop* of mud building up beside him. Not allowing his mind to stray to a pair of soft eyes clouded with hurt.

Dig, lift, toss.

Throwing the spade aside, he swiped the sweat from his forehead, blew out a long laboured breath and stared back at the faceless window.

'Matthew. Are you digging your way to China?'

'Maybe I'm just digging my way into a big black hole,' he replied before turning. So focused on his own inner turmoil, he hadn't heard Belle approach. 'Is that what I'm doing, Belle?'

She folded her arms across her chest and looked him straight in the eye. 'I'd say that's highly likely.'

'Where's Ellie?' He was painfully aware that her name rasped up his throat like sandpaper and came out dry, scratchy. Parched.

'She left ten minutes ago.' Belle turned back and picked her way over the damp grass and towards the house. 'Come inside, we need to talk.'

* * *

'Talk to me about Ellie,' she said when they were seated in the lounge room.

He could still smell her sweet berry fragrance in the room. 'Not until I know what's going on, Belle. What did you talk to her about?'

'That's between me and Ellie for the moment.'

'I thought you—'

She held up a hand, the flash in her eyes daring him to continue. He shut his mouth. Belle was the only person who could cut him off with a look.

'I promised, I know,' she said, 'and I'll get to that. Right now I'm more interested in what's going on between the two of you.' She shook her head when he opened his mouth. 'And don't even think of denying it.'

Okay. Where to start? 'We…she…' He trailed off, unwilling, unable, to put his thoughts and feelings into words he wasn't sure he wanted to acknowledge to himself, let alone voice to another. 'Ah, Belle, since the age of ten, you're the one person I've always been able to come to for guidance and advice.…'

'So what's changed?'

'This is different.' So different he'd never had to deal with anything remotely like it.

'There's something I've never told you, Matthew,' she said quietly. 'When I was nineteen, that man I told you about, the man I loved… We made a baby together.'

A baby… His gaze arrested on the woman who'd given him everything a child could want, and read the lingering sadness in her eyes. 'Belle…'

She shook her head and her eyes glinted with moisture. 'I listened to what others were telling me instead of my heart. I gave her up for adoption…and I've regretted it every day of my life since.'

Oh, Belle. Knowing Belle's gentle and loving nature, it

must have killed her to have been forced to do such a thing. He leaned out, caught her hands. 'I'm sorry.'

She tightened her fingers around his and looked deep into his eyes. 'What I'm trying to say here, Matthew, is that sometimes you have to make hard decisions, life-altering decisions, even when you don't have all the facts, knowledge or experience. Sometimes they're the right decisions, sometimes they're not. But you have to do what your inner voice tells you, not what others say is the right choice...or you may regret it the way I have.

'So, the question here is, what are *you* going to do about Ellie? If you love her, the decision will be easy.'

Love. Was that what this gut-wrenching pain and heartache and soul searching was all about? Love?

He didn't believe in love—not the foolish whimsical romantic kind. But he loved Belle. His love for her was rock-solid and abiding. He loved the honest, open, beautiful person she was both inside and out.

And when it came right down to it, wasn't that what he admired about Ellie? *Admit it, Matt.* It was *what he loved* about Ellie. The kind of love that wasn't going to fade. The kind that lasted for ever.

Without family support, Belle had made all her decisions by trusting her inner voice. Years ago she'd taken a chance on a kid called Matt with a murky background and a sullen attitude.

Now she expected the same of him. To take a chance, go with that gut feeling. He took a deep steadying breath to calm the hailstorm roiling within him. 'I take it you're not going to tell me why I've been here this past week as you promised you would.'

She shook her head. 'There's something you need to do first.'

Resigned, he acknowledged that.

'So I'll tell you only what you need to know. Ellie's leaving for Healesville this afternoon. The bus leaves at one o'clock.'

'Healesville? Why?'

But Belle only shook her head.

'Okay, go ahead and be stubborn.' There was no sting in his reply as he checked his watch. It didn't leave him much time. He kissed her on his way out. 'Thanks, Belle.'

The Southern Cross Station, a Mecca for travellers with its undulating steel roof floating above the vast cavernous space, usually fascinated Ellie. Today she didn't give it a second glance.

Her mind was still spinning with this morning's events. Belle. Matt. She felt as if she'd been forced through a meat mincer, dragged through a cyclone, then hurled onto a rollercoaster.

She presented her ticket and climbed aboard with moments to spare. The bus was crowded and already overly warm. She took a seat near the front beside a plump middle-aged woman who smelled of butterscotch. Ellie smiled at her then closed her eyes to forestall conversation. The engine's grumble vibrated through her bottom, passengers talked. The vent above her seat blew a refreshing draught over her face, letting her relax for the first time since she'd climbed out of bed.

It seemed like a lifetime ago. And in so many ways it was. Somehow she had to get her mind to focus on the afternoon ahead, if that was possible. For her own self-esteem as much as an income, she needed this job. She needed to get as far away from Matt as possible…except now she had a grandmother to consider.

Family.

Miracles did happen. A warm tide of emotion swamped her. She wanted to shout it to the world, to forget this job prospect and rush back to Belle. To throw her arms around her neck and tell her things she'd wanted to say to her mum all these lonely years, to tell her all about the daughter she'd given up.

Except her grandmother came with a nephew called Matt—who wasn't a nephew at all… That roller-coaster ride again.

She wanted to be near her grandmother, wanted to accept her offer to live there, and *damn it*, she *deserved* that. So how was it going to work because Matt would visit Belle and Ellie might be there and how was she ever going to get over him if that possibility was always lurking in the back of her mind?

'…need to speak with her.'

'…can't let you on without a ticket, sir.'

The familiar and impatient tone and commotion at the front of the bus had her pulse kicking up. Craning her head sideways she peered around the seat in front of her.

'I just need a minute.' Matt's voice rumbled over the sound of the engine.

His tall broad form blocked the entrance. His flattened hair stuck to his brow and he gripped the neck straps of a couple of bike helmets in one fist, brandished a bunch of dark windblown irises in the other.

Her heart swelled, then squeezed so tight she wondered that it didn't stop. Did he know irises meant faith and hope? How could he know they were her most favourite flowers in the whole world?

'Someone's about to get lucky,' murmured the woman beside her.

Then those dark eyes locked on Ellie's. Eyes that reminded her of storms and wild rides on motorbikes and all manner of risks. And pain. 'Don't be so sure,' Ellie murmured back. Just because she loved him didn't mean she was going to fall into those swirling depths because he willed it so. Definitely not. No way.

In two long quick strides he was towering over her and looking as confused—and determined—as she. 'Ellie. Please get off the bus. I want to talk to you.'

'No. And nor will I tolerate your stand-over tactics. Anything you have to say you can say here.'

If it were possible, his brow lowered further, and while passengers held a collective breath, she swore she heard the distant rumble of thunder.

He dropped the flowers onto her lap, then raked his free hand through his hair and lowered his voice. 'Come with me and let's sort this out.'

'There's nothing to sort out. You said it all this morning.'

His lips flattened, his white-knuckled hand gripped the seat in front of her. 'Is this you running off and being irresponsible again? Because I—'

'*Excuse me?*' She felt her vocal chords strain and stretch skyward. 'You were the one "running off" as I recall. To Sydney. As fast as you could.'

He acknowledged that with a barely-there shift in his posture, as if he had an itch between his shoulderblades he couldn't reach. Then, as if he was grasping at the last vine of summer, 'You can't leave—you haven't finished Belle's garden.'

'As of this morning that's no longer your concern.'

He leaned closer, his eyes dark windows to the roiling turmoil within. 'Another chance, Ellie.'

While her heart leapt at his words, a frown pulled at her brow. 'I'm confused. Are you giving me that next chance or asking for one?'

Hesitation. 'Both. Either. Whatever it takes.'

'And if I refuse…are you going to drag me off against my will like you did last time?'

A restless murmur of voices behind them. 'Not while I'm here.' The woman beside Ellie seemed to morph to monstrous proportions and placed a protective hand on Ellie's.

'Sir, buy a ticket or get off the bus.' She heard the driver's voice in the background.

'Damn it, Ellie... I...want you.'

The plea in his eyes almost undid her. But he'd brought this to a head this morning. Simple *want* was no longer anywhere near what she needed from Matt. She needed everything— total commitment, a lifetime, or nothing.

Either prospect terrified her.

She'd sworn never to surrender herself to another man again, yet trying to imagine a life without this particular man was a long, lonely road without end.

She looked away, down. At her hands twisting around the flower stems. Unless he offered her what she needed she had an appointment and she didn't intend to break it.

'Mate...*now*, or I'll have the transit police escort you off.' The driver's voice boomed down the aisle.

For two breathless seconds Matt stood his ground, then said, 'I'll be back.' His jacket creaked as he turned and made his way to the front of the bus, leaving the scent of leather wafting down the aisle behind him.

Ellie let her head loll back against the headrest and stared sightlessly at the seat in front of her. The sensation of numerous eyes boring into her transmitted a prickly heat up her neck.

'I'm Flo,' said her erstwhile protector, pulling a slim romance novel and cellophane packet from her bag. 'Persistent young man, isn't he?' She offered the packet. 'Butterscotch?'

Ellie shook her head. 'No, thanks. Not unless it comes without the butter.'

Flo chuckled. 'Men. Still, that one's got the looks. And

the potential, I suspect. I'd give it some thought if I was you.' She unwrapped a sweet and popped it into her mouth before opening her book.

One glance at the line-up snaking from the ticket office and Matt knew he'd never make it. He turned back to see the bus already reversing out of its bay. *Damn it all to hell.* Frustration tied his belly up in knots as he jogged to the parking station adjacent.

He was on his bike and into Melbourne's lunchtime traffic and dodging trams along Spencer Street in less than three minutes.

An hour later he cooled his boots while he waited for the bus to pull in at Lilydale, the last stop before Healesville. He had no idea whether Ellie was leaving town for good; Belle hadn't exactly been forthcoming with information. Except he'd noticed Ellie was dressed in smart black trousers and her jacket—not what he'd have expected her to be wearing.

Either way, he wasn't going home without her.

He paced one way, then the other. It might be easier to walk away from the best thing that had ever happened to him, easier to deny what he felt than to lay his heart on the line. *To love.* But Ellie… He gritted his teeth. Ellie made the whole risky attempt worthwhile.

He was sweating up a lather inside his jacket as the bus pulled up. His stomach took a dive as a few passengers disembarked, giving him sideways or lingering looks as they passed.

When the last passenger had cleared the steps, he hauled himself up and straight into the disbelieving gaze of the bus driver. 'I know,' Matt muttered. 'Give a guy a chance.'

The driver shook his head, a half-grin on his lips. 'Okay, mate. Thirty seconds.'

His heart jumped into his mouth when he saw Ellie's head poking into the aisle. Big dark eyes, the exact same shade as the irises on her lap. Porcelain cheeks. She was torturing her lower lip.

Ignoring the gaggle of onlookers, he fisted his hands at his sides to stop himself from going to her and dragging her off the bus and into his arms. Where she belonged.

Where she'd always belonged. His heart seemed to open up and swallow him whole. She'd belonged with him from the first time he'd seen her, he'd just been too blind to see it. Too damn stubborn to admit it, even to himself.

And now...was she leaving him? 'Ellie.'

She shook her head and implored, 'Get off the bus, Matt. *Please.*'

He wanted to tell her what was in his heart, right now, right here, in front of this busload of strangers, but he'd wait. There was something he had to explain first and it had to be done in private. 'I'll be waiting when the bus pulls in again, Ellie, and you *will* listen to what I have to say.' He meshed his gaze with hers, brief, blazing, intense. 'Think about that for the next twenty-five minutes.'

He nodded to the driver, his boots clattering on the metal step as he stepped off into the chilly wind.

From her position in the bus, Ellie couldn't see Matt as the vehicle pulled away, but a moment later she heard the roar of a motorbike and got a glimpse as he overtook them.

Her heart was jumping hurdles at a million miles an hour. Little chills were racing up and down her arms.

'I think he's serious,' Flo said around a mouthful of butterscotch, then sighed. 'Like Richard Gere in *Pretty Woman.*'

Oh, no, she'd had her share of *Pretty Woman.*

Flo resumed reading when Ellie didn't answer, too preoccupied with the way her world was spinning out of its orbit. For half her life she'd been afraid to open her heart for fear of the inevitable consequences, afraid to get close for fear of what *might* happen. But she wasn't the only one afraid today—for the first time she'd seen that same fear in Matt's eyes.

Belle had known her own share of fears and heartache but she'd worked through them. She thought of Belle's wise words of advice. Her grandmother loved them both. It was a starting point for new beginnings for the three of them.

She caressed the velvet petals on her lap with one finger and studied the rich purple shade and delicate yellow tongues. Hope and faith. Whether Matt knew the meaning of the iris or not, there was a message in there somewhere.

CHAPTER FIFTEEN

As THE bus rolled down Healesville's leafy main street and pulled into the depot, Ellie saw Matt's bike parked in front of the little shops next door and her heart picked up speed again.

The door opened with a hiss of compressed air. Passengers began disembarking. Ellie waited till most had left, then rose and let Flo pass by first.

It was a bit of a squeeze while the woman manoeuvred her wide girth out of the tight space. She gave Ellie a quick smile. 'Give that nice man a chance, now, won't you?'

Ellie replied with a vague, 'Uh-huh.' Finally, armed with her flowers, bag and business satchel hitched on her shoulder, Ellie made her way to the door. A few passengers lingered, waiting to be picked up. Or waiting for a final showdown? Ellie wondered, noticing a couple of discreet sidelong glances at her as she alighted onto the bitumen.

The wind whipped at her legs, her hair and the flowers she clutched. It also brought the aroma of onions and hamburgers from the shop nearby, reminding her she hadn't eaten lunch. Not that she could eat a thing what with her stomach twisting with all these nerves.

She saw Matt at the side of the bus, shoulders hunched, hands inside his jacket pockets. When he saw her, he picked up the helmets beside his booted feet and started towards her.

She watched him while her love wept from her heart. The emotion in his eyes was so naked, so raw, that she wanted to run to him and wrap her arms around him and never let go, but she stayed where she was.

A few hours ago he'd hurt her to the marrow in her bones.

When he was within arm's reach, he said, 'What are you doing here, Ellie?'

'Checking out a landscaping job.'

'A job.' His shoulders visibly relaxed, then he frowned. 'Way out here? You'll spend half the day travelling. I'll help you find you something in town.' Spoken as if the matter was already resolved. As if *everything* was resolved.

'No, Matt, *I* find me something, and right now I'm here to see if I like the look of this job and they like the look of me. It's only a four week contract.'

Matt judged the determined jut of Ellie's chin and decided that this was not the time to argue the point. 'Okay. Where is this job?'

'I have a map,' she said, hunting in her bag. 'I was informed it's only a ten-minute walk. This way.' She pointed down the Maroondah Highway. 'It's a bed and breakfast.'

'Maybe we can come here sometime and try it out, what do you say?'

'You're going back to Sydney,' she said, not looking at him. Not acknowledging the meaning he'd infused into those words *in any way.* She hugged her satchel and flowers as they turned off the main road and onto a quiet street bordered by winter grass.

'Only for a couple more weeks,' he said into the silence broken only by the wind. 'I'm not into long-distance relationships.'

She flicked him a brief sideways look, as if to say he wasn't into relationships of any kind.

And she'd be right. Barring the occasional fleeting acquaintance that lasted less than a few weeks, he hadn't had any meaningful kind of relationship with a woman in a long, long time.

But with Ellie it was different. It was right. With Ellie he wouldn't want it any other way. Yet looking at her now, every inch the professional in her business attire, hair tamed and sleek today, would she still be interested in what he had to say if she won this contract?

Or would she want to put all her time and effort into building a career? The way he had—until he'd discovered a career was no longer enough. The first night they'd met she'd told him she didn't want a family, that she loved being single. *Untrue.* Ellie craved love. But would she still insist she felt that way? After this morning, he couldn't blame her if she wanted nothing more between them. He had to convince her otherwise.

She checked her map, stopping in front of a little cottage. Primrose walls with china-blue trim. A large black pottery cat guarded the front door. Lichen-crusted stones overrun with ground cover flanked either side of the little path. No doubt about it, the garden needed attention, but Matt could see the potential. And the hours of work involved.

'Wait here,' she said at the gate and passed him the flowers. It squeaked on rusty hinges as she pushed it open. She walked up the path and he heard her speak to someone, then the door opened, closed.

A few moments later she reappeared with a middle-aged couple. They wandered the garden while Ellie made notes. Then he saw them shake hands. The couple went back inside and Ellie hurried up the path to meet him.

'I can't believe it.' She was breathless as he opened the gate for her. 'I start in two days. This is the biggest project I've worked on and they thought it would need two people but they're letting me do it on my own and if it takes longer they don't mind because—'

He put a finger on her lips. 'Ellie.'

'I'm rambling, aren't I? I can't help it. Today has been…' She trailed off and looked into the distance.

Matt saw his opportunity and took it. He pointed to an old wrought-iron seat by a clump of straggling bushes and headed for it. 'Let's sit down.'

Ellie's nerves did a double jolt. She knew she had to listen to whatever he wanted to say. But would what he said be enough? And what would her response be?

She walked with him, set her bags on the seat. 'I don't want to sit. Too nervous.' She rubbed her hands together in front of her face. 'I want to run.…'

'Later. Ellie…' He stood too, with his heart in his eyes, the scent of warm leather and man wafting towards her. 'I don't know what's between you and Belle,' he said slowly. 'She wouldn't tell me. But it doesn't matter. You're what matters. You and me.'

His hands were cold as he reached out and cradled her face between his palms. His eyes searched hers, so deep it was as if he were looking into her soul. 'Is there a you and me, Ellie?'

There could be. If she was brave enough. Could she risk it? Could she take that chance? For however long it lasted— because last week he'd put a time frame on their relationship. Even here, now, he'd not mentioned anything permanent. And if he left, she'd never get over it. She'd never be whole, ever again.

And yet she had a grandmother who'd been through more than her share of heartache and loss. A woman of strength and courage and determination. And love. Love enough for both of them. For all of them.

What could Ellie be with those same genes flowing through her own veins?

Today Belle had shown her that she had a choice. Ellie could let love's hurts and disappointments twist her up inside and turn her into a bitter and lonely old woman. Or she could refuse that option and live in the light.

Matt saw the conflicting emotions behind her gaze and bent his head, brushed his lips over hers. A touch. A promise. Knowing, knowing deep in his bones, that it was a promise of for ever.

'I think I'll sit down now,' she said and collapsed onto the seat.

But rather than following her down, he remained standing and shrugged out of his jacket. The stiff breeze cut across his T-shirt, his nipples pebbled against the chill.

'What on earth are you doing? It's freezing.'

'Giving you the shirt off my back?' His half-grin faded and he gestured to the front of his T-shirt. 'Read it.'

His heart thundered beneath his ribs as she leaned forward. 'I didn't have paper with me,' he explained. 'It's a promissory note signing over half the house in Lorne to you.'

'I can read,' she said slowly, the colour dropping from her face. 'What I want to know is why?'

Squatting in front of her, he tugged her restless hands to his chest. 'Isn't it obvious?' He lifted her arms, kissed her wrists. 'Because I love you.' The words spilled from his lips as easy as water. Not so difficult, was it? Not when you meant it with all your heart.

He saw her jaw drop open. He saw that same love reflected back. But he saw pain there too, in those violet eyes, and he squeezed her hands. 'I shouldn't have left you the way I did last night, nor acted like a dumb-ass idiot this morning. But when Belle told me you'd gone, I knew I couldn't let you go.

'And before you say anything more, I've got something

else to say. I've not been honest with you and it's time I was.
I want to tell you about Zena.'

'It's okay, you don't need to—'

'She was my mother, and I do need. She was the only
family I had. The one person any kid should be able to count
on. She was also Belle's housekeeper. She gave Belle one of
the sob stories she was so good at and Belle, being the kind
and trusting soul she is, gave us a room. One night she disappeared. Walked out on her own kid.'

He could remember it like it was yesterday. The bewilder-
ment, the fear, the feeling that he wasn't good enough to love.
The moody, unsociable kid it had turned him into.

'When she left, it was like a part of me shrivelled up and
died. The part that trusted and let others in.' He closed his
eyes briefly. 'Died, Ellie. I cut it out of me because I never
wanted to risk feeling that kind of pain again.'

He felt Ellie's hands tighten in his but he didn't look at
her. He looked at the tall thistle waving in the air beside his
left boot. 'Luckily Belle took me in, but it took her countless
hours of perseverance and dedication and unconditional love
to break through to me. Eventually the courts granted her
custody. We're not related but I love her and we're family.'

'That's what matters,' she said quietly. 'And that's what
makes a family. The love.'

'I was in a long-term relationship only once. Her name was
Angela and she wanted everything I couldn't give her. In the
end it was she who left. And in many ways I was relieved to
let her go.' He turned to look at Ellie then, searched her moist
eyes and let his heart say the words. 'She wasn't the one I
needed, the one I want. The one I love. You are.'

She gently tugged her hands from his grasp. 'Matt…I—'

'I know you said you didn't want a home and family.
Neither did I. Until I met you. I want you to have a home you
feel you belong in and I want to share it with you.' He kissed

her chin, her brow. 'Because I want to marry you and spend the rest of my life with you.'

She was silent for so long, he didn't think she was going to answer and his heart dived to his boots.

Then she sighed. 'Ah, Matt…I want that too. I've been living scared. Every time I get close to someone I lose them, or they lose me.' Hugging her shoulders, she rocked back and forth on the seat, staring at the garden. 'Everyone I love always leaves. But you know what?' She turned her gaze to him, and light and determination shone in their depths, turning her beautiful face radiant. 'I'm through with living that way. I'm through being afraid of the past repeating itself, afraid to reach out and find happiness.'

'I promise you, Ellie, I'll never leave as long as there's breath in my body. And I want to put that promise in writing on a marriage certificate.' Grabbing her shoulders, he turned her to face him. His fingers tightened on her arms. 'I'll even let you eat the whole damn cheesecake whenever you want.'

The smile on her lips was the sweetest one he'd ever seen. 'The whole cheesecake, huh?'

'Every last crumb. Oh, Ellie, sweetheart, I love you so much.'

'I love you too, Matt McGregor. I love that you're loyal and kind and generous. You're honest and hardworking and care about people, and—'

He put a finger against her mouth. 'Right back at you, Ellie. And one day I want you to have my babies.'

'Babies?' Her eyes widened, darkened. 'You want babies?'

'Only with you. And when the time's right.' Then he kissed her. A long, lingering kiss that filled the empty spaces inside him with light and life and hope.

'I still want to work,' she said when he let her come up for air. 'It's important to me. At least, until those babies come.'

'You can work for as long as you want. I'll help you any way I can—study, business, whatever you decide. As a matter of fact, I need a landscaper to do something with my front yard.'

'A landscaper.' She grinned, her apple cheeks pink with the chill of winter and the warmth of happiness. 'I might be able to help you out there.'

He rose, tugging her up with him, hauling her close, and whispered, 'Let's go home and tell Belle.'

'Belle… Yes.' Ellie wound her arms around Matt's neck and kissed him again. 'And then she and I have some other news to share with you.…'

EPILOGUE

Two months later

THE wedding was held in Belle's spacious home. Ellie wore a strapless cream gown shimmering with pearls, and a coronet of fresh spring flowers. She carried a bouquet she'd designed herself, a fragrant selection of freesias and irises tied with a wide purple ribbon.

Belle, in an ice-blue ensemble, gave Ellie away, and Yasmine, stunning in an emerald sheath, was her only bridesmaid. Yasmine's partner had flown in from Queensland the day before for the best man's duties.

Then Matt's colleagues and friends, now her friends too, shared the lavish buffet meal that followed.

No expense had been spared. Crystal and silver, caviar and champagne. And flowers—bowls of them on every available surface. A three-tiered cake towered in the centre of the room while a violinist, flautist and harpist performed one classical number after another.

'Mrs McGregor.' The voice behind Ellie was dark, sensual and husky as a large hand slipped around her waist.

She smiled and tilted her head to expose her neck. 'Yes, Mr McGregor?'

He nibbled at her earlobe, careful to avoid the new diamond stud earrings he'd presented her with yesterday. 'I have something for you.'

'Ah… Mmm, yes, so you do,' she murmured with a private grin. She could feel its hardness pressed intimately against her bottom. 'But it'll have to wait a while. We have guests and I don't think Belle would approve of us doing a disappearing act before the first dance, do you?'

'Probably not.' He chuckled. 'But that's not what I was referring to.' He turned her around and placed a tall cylinder in her hand. 'These are the final plans for the kid's centre's renovations. Work starts next week.'

'Oh, yes, yes, yes!' Holding it aloft, she did a quick pirouette. 'Thank you.' Her smile faded as she looked into his eyes and her love spilled over. 'Matt McGregor, you're the best husband in the whole world. And I love you. For ever.'

'For ever.'

Then he kissed her. Slowly, cleverly, meltingly…hot.

For ever.

INTERVIEW WITH A PLAYBOY

BY
KATHRYN ROSS

Kathryn Ross was born in Zambia, where her parents happened to live at that time. Educated in Ireland and England, she now lives in a village near Blackpool. Kathryn is a professional beauty therapist, but writing is her first love. As a child she wrote adventure stories, and at thirteen was editor of her school magazine. Happily, ten writing years later, *Designed With Love* was accepted by Mills & Boon. A romantic Sagittarian, she loves travelling to exotic locations.

CHAPTER ONE

'WELL, look who has just walked into the reception area,' Marco Lombardi murmured with a gleam of pleasure in his voice.

They'd been in the middle of studying an intensely intricate set of financial records, but his accountant looked up from the sheets of paper and curiously followed his boss's gaze towards the security monitors on the wall.

'Isn't that the reporter who has been hanging around the Sienna building for the last couple of days?' he said with a frown.

'Indeed it is.' Marco smiled. 'But don't worry, John, she's here by invitation.'

'Invitation? You mean you are *allowing* her in to see you?'

'You could say that,' Marco replied, somewhat amused by the other man's astonished tone.

'But you hate the press—you never give interviews!'

'Very true, but I've had a rethink.'

John stared at him in disbelief. The Italian multi-millionaire had always fiercely guarded his privacy, and since his divorce two years ago his attitude towards the press had toughened even further.

And yet here he was, inviting in the one journalist who in his opinion was trouble with a capital T. She always seemed to be nosing around at the moment; everywhere he went

Ms Keyes was there, asking questions about their takeover of the Sienna confectionery company. A deal that was supposed to be secret and was in the last sensitive stages of negotiation. It was a perfectly legitimate deal, but the woman somehow made him feel they were doing something wrong.

'So…why…?' John asked finally, as his thoughts crystallised and he remembered that this was Marco Lombardi he was talking to—a man renowned for being astute.

'There's an old saying, John, about keeping your friends close and your enemies closer. Let's just say I'm putting it into practice.'

John glanced back towards the monitor again. But he didn't really understand. He noticed Isobel Keyes was glancing impatiently at her watch. 'So what time is her appointment? Do you want me to take this paperwork away and work on it in the other office?'

'No.' Marco returned to the figures in front of him. 'Ms Keyes can wait; she's very lucky to have been invited here in the first place. So we will start as we mean to go on.'

'Ah!' Suddenly John understood. 'You're giving her the runaround until the deal is signed.'

'Not exactly. Keeping her occupied might be the more correct terminology.' Marco smiled. 'Now, let's concentrate on what's important, shall we?'

As John opened the top file he couldn't help but feel a dart of sympathy for the young woman waiting outside in her prim business suit. Right now she was probably feeling pretty pleased with herself for gaining an interview with the elusive multi-millionaire. But she didn't stand a chance in hell if she was thinking of pitting her wits against Marco Lombardi.

Isobel was not in any way pleased about this situation. An hour ago she'd been on the verge of finding out exactly what was going on within the Sienna company. She'd been granted an interview with one of the Sienna shareholders, and then at the last minute the interview had been cancelled and out of the blue her editor had ordered her to drop the story.

'I've got something better for you,' Claudia had gushed with excitement. 'I've just had a phone call from our editorial director. Can you believe it? Marco Lombardi has agreed to give the *Daily Banner* an exclusive interview!'

Isobel had indeed been stunned. She'd tried to get an interview with Marco on a few occasions and had never got past his secretary. 'Is he going to talk to me about his plans for taking over the Sienna confectionery company?' she'd asked hopefully.

'Isobel, forget about pursuing the business side of the story. What we want is a personal insight into Marco's life, and the real facts behind his divorce. That's the story readers really want, and it will be like gold dust for the paper.'

The word smokescreen came to mind.

Isobel clenched and unclenched her hands. She knew most journalists would have been ecstatic to get an interview with the handsome Italian. But she was a serious reporter, not a tattler of gossip. She didn't want to do an in-depth interview about Marco's love-life! She wanted to write a real story about people's jobs being on the line.

As far as she was concerned her paper had struck a deal with the devil—but, as usual, commercial considerations ruled the day, she reminded herself angrily.

'You can go up now, Ms Keyes.' The receptionist smiled over at her. 'Mr Lombardi's office is on the top floor.'

Hallelujah, Isobel thought sardonically as she glanced at her watch. He'd only been keeping her waiting for over an hour. And of course he had done that on purpose too.

As the lift swept her upwards, Isobel tried to compose herself. She had no choice now but to swallow her principles and give the paper the article they wanted, but it really did infuriate her. Because Marco was the type of man she despised. The type of man who did exactly as he pleased, regardless of the consequences, regardless of who he might hurt. And she had reason to know that more than most—because this was the man who had bought out her grandfather's firm eleven years ago, and had then systematically torn it apart, breaking her grandfather's heart in the process.

As far as she was concerned, Marco was a ruthless charlatan. And frankly she couldn't understand why there was so much speculation over his divorce. The reason he'd split with his wife seemed blindingly obvious to Isobel—he'd always been a womaniser. So much so that people had been stunned when he had announced he was getting married. And since his divorce he'd been pictured in the press with a different woman every week. Some sections of the press had even dubbed him a heartbreaker, for heaven's sake!

As the lift doors swished open Isobel took a deep breath and reminded herself—as she always did when working on a story—that she couldn't allow preconceived ideas to cloud her judgement.

'This way, Ms Keyes.' A secretary stepped forward to open a door into an office with sweeping panoramic views out across London. But it wasn't the view that held Isobel's attention. It was the man seated behind the large desk

She had heard so much about him over the years that now, suddenly face to face with her nemesis, she felt slightly unnerved.

Marco was absorbed in some paperwork and didn't look up as she approached slowly. 'Ah, Ms Keyes, I presume.' He murmured the words absently, as if he were only half aware of her presence. His English pronunciation was perfect, but more disturbingly she noticed that his velvet Italian accent sizzled with sex appeal.

He was wearing a white shirt left casually open at the strong column of his neck. Isobel noticed how the colour contrasted with the olive tones of his skin and the dark silky thickness of his hair.

She stopped next to the desk, and at the same time he looked up and their eyes locked. Inexplicably, her heart seemed to do a very peculiar flip.

He was incredibly good-looking, she thought hazily. His bone structure was strong, giving him an aura of determination and power, but it was his eyes that held her spellbound: they were the most amazing eyes she had ever seen—dark, smouldering, and extraordinarily intense.

She didn't know why she was so taken aback by him—it wasn't as if she hadn't already known he was attractive. There were snatched photographs of the thirty-five-year-old in the press all the time. And women were always raving about how handsome he was. But Isobel had always maintained that she couldn't quite see what all the fuss was about—she didn't like the guy, and as far as she was concerned a lack of moral substance overshadowed mere good-looks any day. It was therefore a total shock to find herself so….mesmerised.

'Sit down and make yourself comfortable.' He waved her towards the chair opposite him, and she had to shake herself mentally.

What the hell was wrong with her? She was staring at him like an idiot! And meanwhile she was well aware that his eyes had moved over her with a look that could only at best be described as quizzically indifferent. No surprise there.

Isobel knew there was no way she could match up to the women Marco would be drawn to—for a start his ex-wife was a film star, rated as one of the world's most beautiful women. By comparison Isobel was nothing—just a Plain Jane. Her clothes were businesslike, her figure bordered on being too curvaceous, and her long dark hair—although shiny and well cut—was held back from her face in a manner that was purely practical.

But that was her style. She didn't want to be overtly feminine or glamorous. She wanted to get on with her work and to be treated seriously. And she certainly didn't want to attract

men like Marco Lombardi, she reminded herself fiercely. Her
father had been a womaniser, and she knew how someone like
that could devastate lives.

The reminder helped to snap her back to reality.

'So, Mr Lombardi, it seems you have succeeded in diverting attention away from your proposed bid to buy Sienna,' she
remarked crisply as she took the seat opposite.

Marco had been about to finish his paperwork and keep
her waiting a little longer, but he found himself looking over
at her again. 'Have I, indeed?' he countered wryly. Her cool,
businesslike tones surprised him. Most women flirted with
him. Even when they were being businesslike they softened
their questions with a fluttering of eyelashes and a surfeit of
smiles. Isobel Keyes, it seemed, wasn't going to conform on
either front.

'You know very well that you have,' she retaliated. 'And
we both know it's the only reason I've been granted this
interview.'

Interesting, he thought as he gave her demure appearance
another quick glance.

His first assessment of her, when he'd seen her on the security monitors, had been that she was a staid little mouse—
someone who would probably be easily fobbed off with an
interview. Now he was busy reassessing her.

'You seem very certain about your facts.'

'I am certain.' She angled her chin up a little. 'I saw your
accountant at the Sienna offices this morning.'

'You probably did. He's a free agent—he can go where he
wants.'

'He goes where you send him,' she countered quickly.

He hadn't noticed her eyes until now. The feisty sparkle in
them made them glow a deep emerald-green.

His gaze swept slowly over her face again. He'd originally
thought that she was in her late twenties—probably because
he hadn't looked at her that closely. But now he realised that

it was just the way she was dressed that made her seem older, and that she was possibly nearer to twenty-one. Nice skin too. She might have been passably attractive if she made more of an effort with herself. The hairstyle did nothing for her, and she was wearing little or no make-up. As for the clothes… His eyes swept downwards. They were verging on boring.

No Italian woman would be caught dead in a blouse like that…especially with it buttoned right up to the neck! Her waist was small, and she appeared well endowed. That blouse would definitely benefit from being unbuttoned a few notches, he thought distractedly.

Isobel suddenly noticed his sweeping assessment of her appearance, and as his dark eyes moved boldly back to her face she found herself heating up inside with consternation. Why was he looking at her like that? It was almost as if he were weighing up her desirability.

The thought made her heat up even more.

Hell, she was blushing! How embarrassing was that, when she disliked Marco so intensely? She wouldn't be interested in him if he was the last man left in the universe, and she knew damn well that Marco would never be interested in her!

Maybe he looked at every woman like that—or maybe he was trying to distract her from their conversation. Now, that was a possibility.

'So, are you trying to tell me that you have no interest in buying Sienna Confectionery?' She sat up a little straighter in her chair.

Marco smiled slowly. He had to admire her tenacity, but it was time he reined her in. 'I take it you want to make this a business interview?' he murmured smoothly.

'No!' Her skin flared with even more heat as she imagined the hullabaloo at the paper if she ignored the brief they'd given her. 'I was just saying that…I know what is going on.'

His lips curved in an almost derogatory smile. Then he

reached for the phone on his desk. 'Deirdre, arrange for my limousine to pick me up outside in ten minutes.'

Isobel could feel her heart thudding nervously against her chest. 'Are you going to bail out on me because I dared question you on a subject you don't want to discuss?' She forced herself to hold his gaze, but inside she was suddenly terrified. Hell, if she mucked up with this interview she could find herself out of a job! The paper was desperate for an exclusive—in fact every paper in the land was desperate for an interview with Marco. Her kudos as a reporter would be out of the window if she messed this up.

Marco didn't answer her straight away, and her nerves stretched as she thought about the hefty mortgage she had taken on when she had moved apartments last year. She needed this job.

'Look, Mr Lombardi, I'll be honest with you. I'd rather do a business interview—because that's what I do. I'm a business correspondent. But the *Daily Banner*, in its wisdom, has sent me here because you've done a deal with them. You said you'd give the paper an exclusive glimpse into your life. So how about it? Because if I don't get this story... Well...'

'You're in trouble.' He finished her sentence for her and smiled. 'Why, Ms Keyes, are you throwing yourself on my mercy?'

He knew damn well that she was in a predicament—because *he'd* placed her in it, she thought furiously. With difficulty, she tried to remain calm. 'Yes, I suppose I am.'

He noticed how the husky admission almost stuck in her throat, and one dark eyebrow lifted mockingly.

'Did you bring your passport?'

'My passport?' The question caught her off guard, and she stared at him in apprehension. 'Why would I need that?'

'I offered your paper an exclusive glimpse into my life, Ms Keyes—and I travel quite extensively.' As he was talking to her Marco was packing away his papers into a briefcase. 'I have meetings in Italy and in Nice tomorrow, and I'm leaving in just under an hour. So if you want your story you're going to have to tag along with me.'

'Nobody told me that! I was told you were inviting me into your home—'

'I am. My home is in the South of France.'

'But you have a place here—in Kensington!' Her voice rose slightly. 'Don't you?'

Marco closed his case and looked over at her. 'I also have houses in Paris, Rome and Barbados, but I'm based on the Riviera.'

'I see.' She swallowed hard on a tight knot of panic. 'Well, unfortunately I haven't packed for a trip to France, and I have no passport with me.'

Marco almost felt sorry for her—almost, but not quite. Because she was a journalist, and as far as he was concerned journalists were the piranhas of this world, feeding off other people's lives. 'Seems like you are in a bit of a bind, then, doesn't it? Your editor will be disappointed.' He noticed impassively that she seemed to lose all colour from her face at that.

'Look, if you could drive to the airport via my apartment it would take me fifteen—maybe twenty minutes tops to throw my stuff together,' she suggested in desperation.

'I don't have twenty minutes to spare,' Marco told her tersely as he rose to his feet and reached for the jacket of his suit. 'But in the interests of goodwill I'll give you five.'

As Isobel looked up at him she saw the gleam of amusement in the darkness of his eyes, and she realised that he'd never had any intention of leaving her behind. He was playing with her as a cat would play with a mouse before pouncing for the kill.

She suddenly wanted to run a million miles from him—because this didn't bode well for her interview.

'When you're ready,' he grated impatiently as she made no move to stand up.

Hurriedly she got to her feet. What else could she do but go along with this?

CHAPTER TWO

As ISOBEL followed Marco out of the Lombardi offices, a group of waiting paparazzi across the road sprang into life. There were insistent shouts for them to look over towards the cameras, and calls for Marco to answer questions. They wanted to know where he was going, who Isobel was, if he had spoken to his ex-wife recently.

Marco seemed unfazed by the situation and made no comment, but the intrusion took Isobel by surprise. She wasn't used to being on this side of press attention, and the flash photography and the unrelenting questions felt aggressive. She was almost glad to reach the seclusion of Marco's limousine, with its smoked glass windows.

'Friends of yours?' Marco asked sardonically as he climbed in behind her and took a seat opposite.

'No, of course not!' The question startled her. 'I have absolutely nothing to do with them! They're like a pack of hyenas.'

'Your point being…?'

She was starting to get used to that derisive dry edge to his voice. 'My point being that is not *my* style of journalism.'

'Ah, yes, I forgot—you are a serious reporter, only interested in business.'

She raised her chin slightly. 'And I'm good at my job—well, I must be, mustn't I? It's the only reason you've agreed to give my paper an exclusive.'

'I hate to burst your bubble,' he drawled, 'but the main reason I've decided to give the press an exclusive is because of incidents like the one you have just witnessed, where I'm constantly pestered by reporters who want to know everything about me down to what I've had for my breakfast.'

Isobel had to agree that the situation had been unpleasant. She glanced out of the window and noticed that even though the chauffeur had pulled the limousine out into traffic the paparazzi were following on motorbikes.

'And then there are the important business deals that have been wholly jeopardised by unwarranted press attention and ill-timed sensationalistic reporting,' Marco continued sardonically. 'Ring any bells?'

She frowned. 'I hope you're not suggesting—'

'I'm not suggesting anything.' He cut across her firmly. 'I'm telling you why I've taken the decision to give a one-off in-depth interview—I'm hoping it's going to be an interview to end all interviews. And that I shall get some peace and quiet after it.'

'And you just happened to offer this opportunity to the *Daily Banner*?' she asked archly.

'I did my homework. And surprisingly your name has cropped up quite a few times over the last say…eighteen months. There was your report about my deal with the Alexia retail group…a few less than flattering columns about my takeover of a supermarket chain, and a very scathing article about my—I quote—"domination of the Rolands Group". Shall I go on?'

'No, you have no need to go on, I get the picture,' Isobel muttered hastily. OK, she *had* singled his business out for some in-depth coverage last year, but only because he had done a lot of buying and selling, and she had always done her research. 'I never said you had done anything wrong or illegal. Nothing I've written has been untrue.'

'But it has verged on scaremongering.'

'I'm a business correspondent. It's my job to report to the public about what is going on.'

He nodded. 'And now it is your job to follow me around and report on that.'

She stared at him. 'Like a kind of punishment?' The words fell from her lips before she could stop them.

Marco stared at her, and then he laughed. 'I feel I should remind you at this point that every journalist in the land would probably love to change places with you right now.'

His arrogance was extremely infuriating—and so was the fact that he was probably right. 'Yes, I do realise that.' She glared at him. 'And I'm not complaining. I'm just saying—'

'That you are a serious journalist who would rather write about my business ventures than my dietary requirements?' he finished for her, his eyes glinting with amusement.

'Yes, exactly. I mean, let's face it, the world hardly needs another celeb interview, does it?' She spoke impulsively. and then hastily tried to correct the mistake. 'That doesn't mean I don't *want* to interview you—because of course I do!'

'Relax—I know exactly what you mean. And I'm more than happy to talk about my businesses and my rise to the top of the financial markets. In fact, that is what I would like to focus on.'

Isobel was sure any business information he gave her would be very one-sided, and she wanted to say, *Yeah, right* in a very derogatory tone, but she didn't dare.

'Well, I wouldn't worry about it,' she said instead. 'Because it turns out that most people are only interested in your love-life.'

'Is that so?' His dark eyes held with hers.

'Yes… Bizarre, but there it is.'

Marco smiled. He was starting to like Ms Isobel Keyes. Had he hit the jackpot and engaged the one journalist who wasn't interested in digging the dirt on his marriage?

'So what exactly *is* the story with your divorce?' she

asked suddenly, her green eyes narrowing. 'Because everyone thought that you and Lucinda did seem like the perfect couple.'

No—he hadn't hit the jackpot, he berated himself. Like every other journalist she was a breed apart—a sub-species for whom no subject was too personal to have a good dig around in.

'Let's not get ahead of ourselves, Ms Keyes,' he said coolly.

Was it her imagination, or was his expression suddenly shuttered? Certainly the gleam of amusement in his voice had disappeared. Strange... She had expected that reaction when she talked about his business dealings, not his relationships.

Maybe he just didn't like the fact that the press knew he was a womaniser? Maybe that was another reason he had agreed to this interview—to try and reinvent himself?

Well, if he thought she was going to fall for that he had a shock coming, she thought fiercely.

The limousine was slowing down. And as she looked out she realised they were pulling up outside her flat.

'OK, I won't be long,' she murmured as the chauffeur got out and opened the passenger door for her.

One of her neighbours was walking past, and the woman almost fell over in surprise when she saw Isobel getting out of a limousine, closely followed by Marco Lombardi.

'Don't you think it might be better if you waited in the limousine?' Isobel said nervously as he walked with her towards the front door.

'No, I don't. What's the matter? Are you frightened there might be gossip about us?'

'Of course not!' She slanted a look up at him and noticed that the amusement was back in the darkness of his gaze. Yes, he probably thought that was oh-so-funny. As if anyone would seriously think that he would be interested in her when he had his pick of the world's most glamorous women.

The paparazzi had roared into the road now, and the usually quiet cul-de-sac was suddenly chaotic as once again they started to take photographs, shouting for Marco to look over.

Isobel was so flustered that she could hardly get her key in the lock fast enough, and calmly Marco reached to take it from her. The touch of his hand against hers was a shock to the system, and she jerked away from him abruptly.

'There you go.' He pushed the door open for her and looked over at her with a raised eyebrow. 'Are the press rattling you?'

'No, of course not.' The truth of the matter was that the paparazzi weren't bothering her half as much as he was.

'After you, then.'

'Thanks.' What on earth was wrong with her? Isobel wondered angrily as she stepped past him into the hallway. It was as if her senses were all on heightened alert around him.

And she had never felt more nervous in all her life as he followed her up the stairs to her first-floor flat.

She supposed it was just the strangeness of the situation. She'd disliked this man for so long from a distance, and now here he was stepping into her sitting room, acting as if he had every right to be here. In fact, his presence seemed to dominate the small flat.

Isobel watched as his gaze moved slowly over his surroundings, and for some reason she found herself looking at the place through his eyes.

The rooms weren't what you would call spacious, and her second-hand furniture looked shabby in the cold grey light of the afternoon. She was willing to bet that Marco's designer Italian suit had cost more money than all her possessions lumped together.

The thought brought her back to reality. OK, she didn't have a lot of money, but that was no reason to feel embarrassed or ashamed. She'd had no helping hand in life—she'd come from a poverty-stricken background and worked hard to get to where she was now. What was more, she had always treated people fairly along the way—which was more than Marco could say.

He'd practically bankrupted her grandfather's business, until the old man had been forced to sell out to him because he just couldn't afford to compete with him. And then as soon as Marco had taken over the firm he'd lost no time in restructuring—which had basically meant firing most of the staff. Isobel's father had been amongst the people in the first wave of redundancies.

She could still remember the shock in her father's eyes when he'd come home to tell them. She remembered how he'd sat at the kitchen table and buried his head in his hands. He'd kept saying that there had been no need to make people redundant—that the company was very profitable. And her grandfather had said the same.

'It's greed, Isobel,' he had said. 'Some people aren't content with making a healthy profit. They're only happy when they are making an obscene profit.'

Isobel remembered those words as she looked over at Marco. He'd been a couple of years older than she was now— about twenty-four—when he'd bought her grandfather's firm and sacked half the workforce. And then he'd gone on to sell the business twelve months later for a *very* obscene profit, as far as Isobel was concerned.

And it seemed Marco had repeated this move in other businesses time and time again, making him a multi-millionaire before the age of thirty.

She wondered if he ever had pangs of conscience about the way he made his money.

As soon as the thought crossed her mind she dismissed it as absurd. Marco wasn't the type to think deeply about other people's feelings. As demonstrated by the way he'd walked out on his wife after just eighteen months of marriage, and the way he changed the women in his life faster than some people changed the sheets on the bed.

Something he had in common with her father, as it turned out.

She turned away from him. 'I'll just throw a few things in a bag, I won't be long.'

'See that you're not,' he said laconically. 'I meant it when I said you'd got five minutes.'

Hurriedly she moved through to her bedroom and opened the wardrobe. What on earth should she pack for a night in the South of France? she wondered. She didn't have a lot of summer gear, but then it probably wouldn't be that hot as it was only May.

She glanced around as there was a knock on the door and it opened behind her. 'Four minutes and counting,' Marco told her as he leaned against the doorframe.

'For heaven's sake, I'm going as fast as I can.' She flung a pair of jeans and a T-shirt into an overnight case, and then moved to rifle through her nightwear and her underwear drawer. 'Do you think you could give me a moment's privacy?' she asked through gritted teeth as she looked around at him.

'Don't mind me.' He smiled, but instead of moving out of her room he came further in, and walked over towards the window to look out.

At least he had his back to her, but the guy had an unmitigated gall, she thought furiously. She selected a nightshirt and some underwear and threw it in the case.

'Don't forget your passport,' he reminded her nonchalantly. 'That's all that really matters.'

'Of course I won't.'

'Good.' He adjusted the blinds a little, so that he could look down to the road. And she realised that he had only come in here because it was the one room with a clear view out over the front of the property.

'Are the paparazzi still there?' she asked curiously.

'Unfortunately, yes.' He snapped the blinds closed and turned to look at her again. 'So you'd better get a move on—because otherwise you could be splashed all over the front page tomorrow and dubbed my new lover,' he added lazily.

He watched with amusement as her cheeks flushed bright red.

'I very much doubt that, Mr Lombardi,' she told him stiffly, wondering if this was his feeble attempt at trying to dissociate himself from the many women he'd been pictured with since his divorce.

'Do you? Why is that?'

'Because...' *What kind of question was that to ask her?* she wondered in annoyance. 'Well...because I am very obviously not your type.'

'Aren't you?' He looked across at her teasingly.

'No, I'm not!' She was starting to think he enjoyed winding her up. 'Everyone knows that you go for very glamorous blondes,' she added snappily, and tried to return her attention to her suitcase. But she was finding it really hard to concentrate on packing now; she was far too distracted by the way he was watching her. 'And just for the record you're not my type either,' she added for good measure as she glanced up at him.

He didn't look in the least bit bothered. In fact one dark eyebrow was raised mockingly, as if he didn't believe that for one moment. The guy was far too sure of himself, she thought heatedly. Probably because no woman had ever said no to him.

'And do you think that it matters for one moment that you are not my usual type?' he asked.

'Matters—in what way?' She was confused for a moment.

'Well, the press sensationalise everything. You could be my

maiden aunt and they would still think there was something going on between us.'

'That is not true!'

His dark eyes gleamed. 'Spoken like a loyal member of the press.'

'Well, maybe I am.' She shrugged. 'But I know we are not that easily bamboozled.'

'Bamboozled enough to think I only go for blondes,' he said with a smile. 'When in actual fact I have a penchant for the odd brunette.'

She felt her body burn as his dark gaze swept slowly over her. She knew he was only joking, but she found the intensity of his gaze wholly unnerving,

He was a total wind-up merchant, she thought uncomfortably as she turned away. There was no way on God's earth that he would ever be interested in her—nor her in him, she reminded herself fiercely. She knew it—he knew it—and pretending anything else even for a bit of fun was just hideously embarrassing. They were at different ends of a very wide spectrum.

She closed her case with a thud. 'I'll just go and get my toiletries, and then I'm ready.'

Marco watched as she hurried away from him. He didn't think he had ever met a woman so determined not to flirt with him, he thought with a smile. The strange thing was that the more she backed away from him the more intrigued he became.

He glanced idly around at her possessions. From what he could judge she seemed to live here alone. The place was almost minimalist in design, plainly furnished and yet striking. A bit like its owner, he thought with amusement. His gaze moved over to her workstation in the corner. The desk was tidy, but a huge stack of paper and notebooks led him to believe she probably did a lot of work from home. There were a few reference books—huge, serious tomes on economics. Was that her bedtime reading? he wondered with a grin.

There were also a couple of photographs in frames, and he glanced at them. One was of a woman in her fifties and the other was of an older guy of about seventy. Were they her parents? Her father looked much older than her mother. Marco looked more closely. Actually, the guy looked familiar.

Isobel came back into the room, and Marco turned his attention to more important things. He had a lot of paperwork to do, and a flight to catch. 'Time is marching on,' he reminded her, glancing at his watch.

'Yes, I do realise that—and I'm ready when you are.' She put the cosmetics bag into her case and zipped it up.

'Really? Well, I'm impressed,' he said with a smile. 'You have half a minute to spare and…' his gaze moved to the case in her hand '…probably the smallest amount of luggage of any woman I've ever taken away for the weekend.'

Did he have to make everything sound so damn intimate? she wondered uncomfortably. 'Well, that's because you're not taking me away for the *weekend*.'

'I think you'll find that I am,' he countered with a smile.

'We are going away on a business trip for one night,' she maintained firmly. 'And as today is only Thursday, that hardly qualifies even marginally as going away for the weekend.'

She really was an enigma, Marco thought with amusement. Most women fell over themselves to spend time with him, and yet she seemed almost horrorstruck by the thought.

'You can make your own way home tomorrow, if you wish,' he said easily. 'But I doubt your in-depth interview will be complete.'

As she looked over at him her eyes seemed to be impossibly wide and too large for her face. 'Well, we shall just have to try and move things along faster,' she said with determination.

'You can try.' He grinned. 'But I have a lot of business to attend to over the next forty-eight hours, so you will have to fit in around me. I think it would probably be more realistic to say that you will be in France until at least Monday.'

'You've got to be joking!'

'Not at all.'

Their eyes seemed to clash across the small dividing space between them.

She didn't want to spend a few days with him. The very thought of it made her blood pressure go into hyper-drive.

'I really don't think I will be able to stay that long,' she murmured uncomfortably.

'Well, as I said, it's up to you.' He shrugged.

But it wasn't up to her, was it? she thought nervously. And he knew that—knew that she would be forced to hang around until she got the story that her paper expected. A story that would be superficial at best.

And meanwhile he would finalise his deal for Sienna and start to take the company apart at the seams. Because that was what he did.

Isobel glanced away from him.

She hated that he could get away with it. Hated the fact that he was cocooned by his wealth—the type who seemed to glide though life unaffected by other people's problems.

But she didn't have to let him get away with it, she thought suddenly. Just because she could no longer write about his business dealings in depth, it didn't mean she couldn't expose him in her article for the uncaring, arrogant womaniser that he was.

Feeling a little bit better at the thought, she reached for her suitcase.

Marco thought that he was being oh-so-clever, but she would have the last laugh, she told herself firmly.

CHAPTER THREE

USUALLY when Isobel travelled through airports she had to wait in queues to check in, and then there would be more queues to get through Security and onto the plane. Travelling with Marco, however, was a whole new experience. There was to be no mundane waiting around for Marco. He breezed through everything at VIP level, and people couldn't do enough for him. It was *Yes, Mr Lombardi—No, Mr Lombardi—Nothing is too much trouble, Mr Lombardi*.

Isobel was absolutely amazed by the speed of the whole process—from check-in to getting aboard the aircraft. And then when they did step on board she was even more astounded to find it was his company jet and that they were the only passengers.

Just another little glimpse into the excesses of Marco Lombardi's world, she thought as she looked around.

They were soon travelling at thirty thousand feet, seated opposite each other in comfortable black leather seats that were larger than her sofa at home. Marco had swivelled his chair slightly, so that he could take advantage of the conference facilities aboard, and since take-off he'd been in a meeting with his corporate strategist in Rome, to discuss a project they were working on in Italy.

Isobel would have loved to know more details, but unfortunately that was all Marco had told her, and she couldn't understand anything he was saying because he was speaking in Italian. For a while she'd tried to pass the time by reading one of the newspapers the cabin crew had handed out to them earlier, but she'd found it hard to concentrate because she had been drawn to listening to Marco as he talked, mesmerised by the attractive, deep tones.

There was something deeply passionate about the Italian language. Marco sounded fiercely intent one moment and almost lyrically provocative the next. So much so that she found herself not only listening, but also covertly watching him. The accent combined with his good looks was a powerfully compelling combination…hard to pull away from.

No man had a right to be so sexually attractive, she thought distractedly. Especially a man who was so completely ruthless. But…hell, he really was gorgeous.

He glanced over at that moment and caught her watching him, and as their eyes met she felt a surge of heat so intense it made her feel dizzy.

How pathetic was that? she thought angrily, looking swiftly away. She should be focusing her mind on structuring the article she wanted to write about him, on revealing the true Marco Lombardi—not on idly admiring his looks!

Being handsome didn't mean a thing. Her father had been a good-looking man, suave, sophisticated, a definite hit with women. Even as a young child Isobel had noticed the way women smiled at him. She had been fiercely proud of her handsome dad—had hero-worshiped him.

And she had been naively unaware that the only reason he'd stayed around was the lure of her grandfather's money.

When his father-in-law had sold the business and he had been made redundant Martin Keyes had been self-pitying at first. But two months down the line, when her grandfather had died and it had been revealed that all his fortune had gone on death duties and taxes, he had been furious. Isobel had heard the arguments raging into the night. Had heard his parting shots to her mother—that the lure of the family business had been all that had kept him in the marriage, and that he felt as if he had wasted twelve years of his life. Then she had heard the slam of the door.

When she'd gone downstairs her mother had been sitting on the floor, sobbing. 'He said he never loved us, Isobel,' she had cried.

She could still remember that moment vividly—her mother's heart-rending sobs, the shock and the feeling of fear and helplessness, and also the knowledge that she had to be strong for her mum's sake.

Life had been tough after that. Her mother had struggled to cope, both financially and emotionally, and for the first year Isobel had found it hard to believe that her dad had truly abandoned them completely. She'd dreamed he would come back, that he hadn't meant those cruel words. Her birthday and Christmas had come and gone without any contact. Then one day quite suddenly, without warning, she'd seen him again outside her school gates. She'd thought he was waiting for her and her heart had leapt. But he hadn't been waiting for her. He'd been with another woman, and as Isobel had watched from a distance she'd seen a child from one of the junior classes running towards them. As Isobel had slowly approached they'd all got into a Mercedes parked at the kerb and driven away.

The really awful thing was that her father had seen her— but he hadn't even acknowledged her with so much as a smile. It was as if she had ceased to exist and was just a stranger.

She'd grown up that day. There had been no more daydreams of a happy-ever-after. And she supposed it had made her into the person she was today—independent and a realist. Certainly not the type to be drawn to a man just because of his looks.

Marco had finished his conversation and was packing some of his papers away.

'We have about twenty minutes before we land,' he said to her suddenly. 'Would you like a drink?'

Even before she answered him he was summoning one of the cabin crew.

'I'll have a whisky, please, Michelle,' he said easily as a member of staff appeared instantly beside him. Then he looked over at Isobel enquiringly.

'Just an orange juice, please.'

Marco turned his chair around to face her and she felt as if she was in a sophisticated bar somewhere—not on an aircraft heading out to the Mediterranean.

'We seem to be ahead of schedule,' Marco said as he looked at his watch. 'Which means we will be arriving before it gets dark. That's good. It will give you a chance to catch a little of the spectacular scenery along the coastline.'

'That would be nice. I can add a description of arriving at your house to my article. Do you live far from Nice Airport?'

'My residence is nearer to the Italian border—about half an hour's drive away. But we will be flying into my private airstrip just ten minutes away from the house.'

'You have your own airstrip?'

'Yes. Sometimes the roads are very busy getting in and out of Nice, so it frees up a little time—makes life easier.' He shrugged in that Latin way of his.

'You are a man in a hurry,' she reflected wryly, and he laughed.

'It's certainly true that there are never enough hours in the day.'

He had a very attractive laugh, and his eyes were warm as they fell on her—so warm, in fact, that for a moment she found herself forgetting what she wanted to say next.

The stewardess brought their drinks. Isobel noticed how she smiled at Marco when he thanked her.

He probably had that affect on every woman he looked at, she thought.

She was about to pour some orange juice into her glass,

but he did it for her. 'I take it you don't drink?' he asked conversationally as he passed her glass over to her.

'Thanks. I do, but not when I'm working.' She forced herself to sound businesslike. OK, jetting into the South of France with this man was probably every woman's dream, but she had to stay focused. Marco Lombardi wasn't the type of man to relax with. He was too smooth…too practised at getting exactly what he wanted. And what he wanted from her was probably to lull her into a false sense of alliance so that she would write about how wonderful he was. Well, that wasn't going to happen. She wasn't that easily fooled.

She just wished he wouldn't look at her with such close attention. She sat up rigidly in her seat, ramrod-straight, and tried to cultivate a definite no-nonsense look in her eyes. 'So, do you travel around the world a lot in your private jet?'

'You sound like you are going to shine a light in my eyes and cross-examine me on my carbon footprint,' he murmured in amusement.

'Do I…? Well, that wasn't my intention.' She shifted a little uncomfortably in her chair. 'I'm just trying to gather a few facts about you for my readers, that's all.'

'Hmm…' He lounged back and looked at her for a long moment, and she could feel her heart suddenly starting to speed up.

'Tell me, do you ever relax?' he asked.

The suddenly personal question took her aback. 'Yes, of course I do, Mr Lombardi. But as I said, not—'

'When you are working.' He finished the sentence for her, a gleam of amusement in his expression. 'OK, that's fine. But I've got a suggestion to make. I think, as we are about to spend a few days and nights together at my home, that we should drop the formalities—don't you?'

The words combined with that sexy Italian accent made alarm bells start to ring inside her. Did he have to make the situation sound quite so…intimate? she wondered apprehensively.

'So you can call me Marco,' he continued without waiting for a reply, 'and I'll call you Izzy. '

'Actually, nobody calls me Izzy,' she interrupted.

'Good. I like to be different.'

He smiled as he noticed the fire in her eyes, the flare of heightened colour in her cheeks. It was strange, but he found himself enjoying rattling that cool edge of reserve that she seemed determined to hide behind. 'We'll be starting our descent into the sunny Côte d'Azur in a few minutes, and it is not the continental way to be so uptight,' he added.

'I'm not uptight, Mr Lombardi—'

'Marco,' he corrected her softly. 'Go on you can say it… *Marco*…' He enunciated the name playfully, his Italian accent rolling attractively over it.

'OK…Marco.' She shrugged, and then for good measure added, 'Now you try *ISOBEL*…' She rolled her tongue over her name with the same emphasis, and then slanted him a defiant look that made him laugh.

'You see? You are getting into the continental spirit of things already,' he teased.

Their eyes held for a moment, then he smiled at her.

It was the oddest thing, but she suddenly felt a most disturbing jolt in the pit of her stomach—as if she had stepped off a cliff and was plummeting fast to the ground.

'Anyway, I…I think we are getting a bit off track,' she murmured, trying desperately to gather her senses again.

'Are we?'

'Yes, it's best…you know…to keep things strictly businesslike.'

There was a defensive, almost fierce glitter in her eyes now as she looked at him, but there was also an underlying glimmer of vulnerability. It was almost as if she was scared of lowering her guard around him, he thought suddenly.

The notion intrigued him, and for a moment his gaze moved over the creamy perfection of her skin, the cupid's bow of her mouth, then lower to the full soft curves of her figure hidden beneath that buttoned up blouse.

Their eyes met again, and she looked even more self-conscious.

Was it an act or not? There was something very alluring about that mix of wide-eyed innocence and hostile attitude. As if she could give as good as she could get—a wary kitten that might purr most agreeably if handled correctly.

As soon as the thought crossed his mind it irritated him! She was a member of the press—and there was nothing vulnerable about a journalist who was hungry for a story, he reminded himself firmly.

'Don't worry, Izzy, I won't allow us to get too far off track,' he grated mockingly.

The pilot's voice interrupted them, to say they were starting their final descent and would be touching down in precisely fifteen minutes.

Isobel watched as Marco reached to pick up the rest of the papers he'd been working on earlier.

When his eyes had slipped down over her body she'd felt so hot inside that she could hardly breathe. And she felt foolish now...foolish for imagining for one moment that he was flirting with her.

In reality he was probably laughing at her. The little plain mouse who melted when he smiled at her.

The thought made her burn with embarrassment—because she *had* melted.

Acknowledging that fact even for a moment made her feel very ill at ease, and angrily she tried to dismiss it.

She was here to get a story, and she was totally focused.

As Marco put his work away into his briefcase the plane hit an air pocket, and a few sheets from a report slid across the polished surface of the table and fell onto the floor at her feet.

She bent to pick them up for him, and couldn't resist glancing at the pages as she did. Unfortunately they were all in Italian, but she managed to catch the printed heading: *'Porzione'*.

She looked over at Marco as she handed it back to him. 'What is that?'

'Nothing that needs to concern you,' he said, tucking it safely away into his briefcase.

Which almost certainly meant it *would* concern her, she thought sardonically. It was probably some poor unfortunate company that he was about to gobble up and spit out.

'Don't forget to fasten your safety belt,' he said as he settled back into his seat.

'No, I won't. Thanks.' She buckled up, and then glanced away from him out of the window.

Sitting opposite him like this was completely unnerving; there was just something about him that put all of her sensory nerve-endings on high alert.

Porzione—she tried to focus on practicalities, telling herself that she should remember the name and look it up on the internet later. OK, she wasn't supposed to write about his business dealings, but that didn't stop her doing a little research and maybe adding a line here and there about his ruthless takeover deals.

She tried to focus on that, and on the bright blue of the sky, on the sound of the engines as the powerful jet geared up for landing—on anything except that moment of attraction she had felt for Marco a little while ago.

It was her imagination, she told herself fiercely. She would never fall under the spell of a man who was a known heart-breaker. And she didn't buy all that stuff that people spouted about desire overruling common sense. Maybe that happened to other people, but it wasn't going to happen to her. She was far too practical for that; she always weighed everything up logically. Probably because she'd seen from her own childhood just what could happen if you fell for the wrong man.

Isobel's mother had never really recovered from her divorce. She'd suffered from depression for a long time afterwards, with Isobel taking on the role of carer at some points. Once in a weak moment she'd even confessed to Isobel that she was still in love with her ex-husband.

How could you love someone who had treated you so badly? That confession had shocked Isobel beyond words. And she had always vowed that *she* would never allow a man to get her into that state, and that she would always be in control of her emotions.

She had pretty much kept to that vow. As a student at university she'd had a few boyfriends, but she'd always kept them at a distance—never allowing anyone to get too close and never getting into the whole casual sex scene. Instead she had thrown herself into her work. Coming from a single parent family, money had been tight. She'd had just one shot at getting her degree, and she'd been determined not to mess it up by getting sidetracked by a man.

After graduating she'd met Rob, and even though she'd liked him straight away she'd still kept her heart in reserve. Building her career had seemed more important. The thing about Rob was that he had seemed so safe and uncomplicated. He'd stayed around in the background, and little by little he had worked his way into her life. He'd gently told her that he didn't mind waiting until she was ready to make love, and that he respected her and admired her. He had even said that he held the same moral codes as her. That he knew all about heartbreak as his mother had walked out on him when he was young.

She'd felt sympathy for him when he told her that. And she'd started to trust him. Looking back, she supposed he'd become almost like a best friend. When he'd kissed her there had been no explosions of passion, but he'd made her laugh and he'd made her feel safe. And when he'd proposed to her it had seemed like the most natural thing in the world to say yes.

But Rob hadn't been the safe, reliable guy she had believed him to be. All those things he'd told her about fidelity being important had been lies. And when she'd caught him in his lies he had turned nasty—had told her that she'd driven him to it, that she was frigid.

Just thinking about it now brought a fresh dart of pain. It only went to show that no matter how careful you were there were no guarantees against heartache.

She closed her eyes for a few moments. At least she had found out her mistake before she had married him.

They were slowly starting to lose altitude, and the plane was juddering as currents of air hit it.

She'd been right all along: the best thing was to concentrate on a career, on being independent.

She opened her eyes and to her consternation found herself looking directly into Marco's dark, steady gaze. Immediately she felt the tug of some unfamiliar emotion twisting and turning deep inside her.

What was that? she wondered angrily. Because it wasn't desire. *Even if he did have the sexiest eyes of any man she had ever met.*

Hastily she looked away from him. Thoughts like that did not help this situation, she told herself angrily.

They were going through light, swirling clouds now. Then suddenly she could see the vivid sparkle of the Mediterranean beneath her, and ahead the shadowy outlines of the coast.

There were mountains rising sharply, and large swathes of forest.

Lower and lower they came, the engines whining softly, until Isobel thought that they might land in the sea. But just as she was starting to panic they skimmed in over a white beach and she saw a runway ahead.

A few minutes later they had touched down smoothly. And with a roar of the brakes they taxied to a halt.

'We are a bit early, but there should be a car outside to pick us up in five minutes,' Marco said casually as he unfastened his seat belt and stood up.

Isobel also got to her feet, and then wished she hadn't as she suddenly found herself too close to him in the confined space.

As he reached for his briefcase she sidestepped him so that she could open the overhead compartment and get her bag.

'Wait—I'll do that for you,' he offered, glancing around.

'No need. I've got it.' Hurriedly she opened the compartment, but the next moment a case slid out smacking into her shoulder.

'Are you OK?' Marco caught it before it could do any further damage, and swung it to the floor.

'Yes...' She grimaced and put a hand to her shoulder. 'I think so.'

'Let me look at you.' To her consternation, Marco put a hand on her arm and turned her to face him.

'No, really—I'm fine!' It was the weirdest thing, but the touch of his hand against her other arm made it throb more violently than her shoulder.

'It's torn your blouse.' Marco said as he looked at her. 'And you're bleeding.'

She glanced down and saw that he was right; there was a small crimson stain on the pristine white of her linen blouse. 'It's OK—it's only a scratch. I'll be fine.'

'It seems to be a bit more than a scratch. Do you want me to look at it for you?'

The mere suggestion was enough to make her temperature shoot through the roof of the plane. 'I most certainly do not!'

Her prim refusal amused him somewhat. 'Izzy, the cut is just fractionally below your collarbone. You will only have to unfasten the top three buttons of your blouse—it's hardly a striptease.'

The words made her skin flare with heat. 'It's fine... Really... I...'

He completely ignored her. 'Michelle, will you bring the first aid kit, please?' he called over his shoulder to the woman who had served them their drinks. Immediately she disappeared down to the bottom of the plane to comply. 'Now, let's have a look.' He turned his attention firmly back to her.

'Marco, I said I was fine—' She froze as he reached for the top button on her blouse and started to undo it.

Her heart was beating so loudly now that she felt it was filling the whole aircraft.

'Marco, I can do it myself!'

'At least you don't have any difficulty saying my name any more.' His dark eyes locked with hers and his lips twisted into a lazily attractive smile. For a panic-stricken moment she thought he was going to move on to the next button, but thankfully he didn't. He dropped his hands. 'Go ahead, then... You unfasten the buttons.'

'I'll do it later.'

'It's two little buttons, Izzy... Are you scared of me?' His eyebrow rose mockingly.

'No! Why would I be scared of you?' Angrily she reached up to comply—she was damned if she was going to let him think she was scared of him!

He noticed that her hands were trembling. He'd never had this effect on a woman before. He frowned as he saw the shadows in her eyes as she looked up at him... What was she so scared of? he wondered curiously.

'There! Happy?' She glared at him.

'I wouldn't go that far.' He said the words derisively, and noticed how she blushed even more, but this time she looked more humiliated than shy. He frowned and wished for some reason that he hadn't said that.

OK, she was a bit of a Plain Jane, and nowhere in the league of the women he usually dated, but there was also something…interesting about her.

Curiously he reached out and lightly stroked his hand over her collarbone, pushing the blouse back further until he could see the wound.

She wasn't prepared for the touch of his fingers against her skin; it sent a dart of sensual pleasure racing through her unlike anything she had ever experienced before. Horrified by her reaction to him, she could only stare up at him in consternation.

In the stillness of the cabin it was almost as if time stood still.

Marco smiled as he saw the flare of desire deep in the depths of her green eyes. *Now* he knew why she looked so scared…she definitely wasn't as immune to him as she'd been pretending all afternoon. That amused him…and for some strange reason even pleased him.

He noticed how she moistened her lips nervously, could see her breathing quickening by the rise and fall of her chest.

He wondered how it would feel to kiss her…

As soon as the thought crossed his mind he dismissed it. She was a journalist, for heaven's sake…one of a breed he despised! They were hard-bitten, uncaring, trouble-stirring… He could go on for ever listing the reasons he hated the press.

His gaze moved away from her lips and back to the cut on her collarbone. 'It's not deep—so that's good.'

The stewardess arrived with the first aid box and handed it over to him.

'Thanks, Michelle. Are the steps down yet?'

'Yes, sir. We are ready to disembark.'

Marco found a tube of antiseptic cream and some cotton

wool and handed it over to Isobel. 'That should fix you up until you get to the house.'

'Thanks.' Isobel was still trying to pull herself together.

What on earth had just happened? she wondered anxiously. Her heart was pounding as if she had run a long-distance marathon, and she felt shaky and hot inside.

And the worst thing was that feeling of pleasure that had blazed inside her just from the lightest brush of his fingertips. That had never happened to her before with anyone. And the fact that it had happened so easily, with such a casual touch, *with Marco* was horrifying.

That *had* to be in her imagination…

Numbly Isobel followed Marco from the plane. They seemed to be in the depths of the countryside. There was a vineyard to her left, and the regimented rows of vines stretched up as far as the purple haze of the mountains. Straight ahead of them there was an aircraft hangar, which was the only building in the vicinity.

Heat shimmered in a misty, watery illusion—like a stream running across the Tarmac.

That heat haze was like her attraction to Marco, Isobel told herself firmly. It looked real, but it was just an illusion—non-existent. Just because you thought you could see something it didn't mean it was really there.

She glanced over towards him. He was holding the jacket of his suit casually over one shoulder, and he looked extremely relaxed—every inch the Mediterranean millionaire, completely at home amidst the rugged terrain. She would have liked to describe him as pretentious, with his company jet behind him and his staff bringing the luggage out for him, but in all honesty he looked too casually indifferent for that.

She remembered the gentle touch of his fingers against her skin, remembered the heat in his eyes, and her stomach flipped.

What the hell was the matter with her? Hastily she looked

away again. He was Marco Lombardi, one of the most notorious womanisers on the planet, and she couldn't afford to forget that even for a minute.

There was a car approaching. She could hear the low, throaty murmur before she saw it, and then a limousine pulled up from around the side of the aircraft hangar and a chauffeur jumped out to open the passenger doors for them.

CHAPTER FOUR

THE road from the airstrip out to Marco's villa was a narrow, winding path that seemed to hug the side of the mountain, and every now and then as they rounded a corner there were sheer perpendicular drops down towards the Mediterranean. It was so spectacular that Isobel found herself holding tight to the edge of the seat as vertigo started to set in.

She didn't know what was more nerve-racking—the drive, or the fact that as they rounded corners her body seemed to keep sliding against Marco's. She wished she'd sat opposite to him now, but he'd advised against it, saying that she would see the view better facing forward and also that it helped to ward off any feelings of travel sickness.

Isobel didn't usually get travel sick, but she had to admit that these roads would test the strongest constitution.

'You were right about the coastline being dramatic,' she said as they rounded another corner and she took in an even more amazing view. They were winding their way downwards now, and she could see glimpses of golden beaches and villas tucked away behind lush tropical greenery.

'Yes, it's a lovely part of the world.' He flicked a glance over at her, noticing with amusement how she was desperately trying not to allow her body to fall against his as the car rounded a particularly narrow bend. For a moment his gaze moved lower. She'd left the top buttons of her blouse unfastened and had folded the collar over—probably so that it hid the stain and the tear in the material. But the small change made all the difference to her appearance; her curves were shown to better advantage and she looked less staid…almost sexy.

His phone rang, and impatiently he reached to answer it. He really had more important things to think about than a pesky reporter.

Marco was speaking in French, Isobel realised distractedly, and he was completely fluent, by the sounds of it. 'How many languages do you speak?' she asked him as soon as he had ended the call.

'Five. It helps in business.'

'Really? Wow!' She couldn't help but be impressed. 'I wish I could speak a second language, never mind a fifth! I did French for years at school, but I still struggle to have a conversation in it.'

'You'll have to practise while you are here,' he said with a shrug. 'It's just a matter of usage. When you have to speak it every day it starts to get easier.'

The limousine turned off the road, and Isobel tried to turn her attention away from him and back to what was happening. But it was hard. Because—she hated to admit it—she found him quite fascinating.

Electric gates folded back, allowing them to enter, and they drove along a wide sweeping driveway lined with giant palm trees. The gardens were very well tended. It was probably a full-time job for a team of gardeners, she thought as she looked out at the tropical shrubs and flowers blazing amidst lawns as smooth as a bowling green. They rounded a corner and suddenly a huge sprawling white mansion opened up before them.

It was built on two levels, and encircled by open verandas that looked out over an Olympic-size infinity pool, its blue waters seeming to merge perfectly with the colour of the Mediterranean.

'Nice house,' Isobel remarked. 'Are you sure it's big enough for you?'

Amusement glinted in the darkness of his eyes. 'You know, now you come to mention it, I suppose it is a bit on the small side.'

They pulled to a halt by the front door, and she reached for the door handle and got out before the chauffeur could come around to open it for her.

The heat of the late afternoon was heavy and silent; the only sound was the swish of waves against the shore beneath them. Isobel turned her head and saw a path leading down to a private beach. She also noticed the oceangoing yacht moored at the end of a long jetty.

'Is that another of your toys?' she asked Marco as he stepped out from the vehicle behind her.

He followed her gaze down towards the sea. 'It's a working toy. I use her for business, but also for pleasure. Sometimes it's good to unwind out at sea, away from everything and everyone.'

For a moment as she looked up at him she thought she saw a glimpse of sadness in the darkness of his eyes, as if at times he needed the solace of being alone out at sea. Then he turned and smiled at her, and she realised that the idea was ludicrous. Marco, international jet-set playboy, would never need solace! What was she thinking?

'Come on—I'll show you up to your room.' He turned away from her and led her into the house.

The entrance hall was palatial; it had a huge, sweeping circular staircase, and vast windows that towered above her like the windows of a cathedral. It was all very modern and new in design. 'How long have you lived here?' she asked curiously as she followed him upstairs.

'About two years now.'

'So you bought the house just after your divorce?' She

was finding it difficult to keep up with him because he was striding along the corridor at quite a pace.

'Around that time, yes.' He opened a door and then waited for her to catch up with him, so that she could precede him into the room.

Her eyes widened. It was decorated in shades of cream and turquoise, and was probably the largest and most luxurious bedroom she had ever been in. The bed alone looked as if it would sleep about twelve people, and there was a walk-in closet that was as big as her entire bedroom at home. The skirt, jeans and the few tops that she'd brought with her were going to look very lonely in there, she thought wryly.

'If this is supposed to be the spare bedroom, the master bedroom must be awesome,' she said as she glanced out of the folding glass doors at the veranda and the spectacular view of the sea.

'Come and have a look, if you want,' he invited. 'I'm right next door.'

She looked over and caught the gleam of mischief in the darkness of his eyes. She found herself blushing. 'Eh…no, thanks. I think my article can do without that particular piece of information.'

'Well, don't say I didn't offer.' He laughed. 'OK, I'll leave you to settle in and I'll see you downstairs for dinner in shall we say…?' He glanced at his watch. 'About an hour?'

'Yes…an hour is fine by me.' Isobel tried to sound confidently upbeat about the prospect of dining with him but her nerves were jangling. She really didn't want to have dinner with him, in fact she'd rather have hidden away from him up here until morning—but that was ridiculous. She had to spend time with him in order to get to know him and gather all the information she needed for her article. What on earth was wrong with her? It was just work, she reminded herself sternly.

As Marco left the room the chauffeur brought her suitcase in. Then she was left alone.

For a while she wandered around, investigating her surroundings. The *en suite* bathroom was completely mirrored, and it had a Jacuzzi hot tub positioned so that you could lie and look out on the veranda and the view of the sea. Maybe she'd do that later. Her shoulder was still a little sore, so it might help. But for the time being she decided to make do with bathing the wound and putting on some more antiseptic. As she pulled her blouse back to examine the damage in the mirror, the memory of Marco's hand touching her skin suddenly flared from nowhere. Hurriedly she blanked the memory out. Why did she keep thinking about that?

What she should be concentrating on was her article.

Deciding to busy herself before dinner, she got her pen and notebook and went to sit outside on the veranda.

It was about six in the evening, but the day was still warm and a delicious little breeze rustled through the palm trees. For a while she just sat there admiring the view, thinking back over the day.

Let's see, what do I already know about Marco? she mused. Apart from the fact that he's a ruthless wheeler-dealer.

On impulse, she took out her phone and decided to look on the internet for the name of the company that she had seen on his papers today. What was it…? Porzione…

She typed the name into a search engine and waited, but there was nothing except a charity for disabled children. She glanced at it briefly. It also supported families with premature babies, and did some very good work counselling couples dealing with the death of a child, but it was clearly nothing to do with Marco. Maybe she'd spelt it wrong. She was about to close the box, but before she did so something made her type Marco's name into the mix.

Immediately his name flashed up on screen as the founder

and director of Porzione, and she sat back in her chair. Why would Marco have founded a children's charity?

Curiously she typed in Marco's name followed by just the word *charity*, to see what else came up. To her surprise his name was associated with a very long list of charitable organisations.

Strange how that was never mentioned in the media—but then judging by the way she'd had to search for his name it seemed he liked to keep a low profile. And of course, stories about charities probably didn't sell as well as stories about his love-life.

A curl of guilt stirred inside her. Why hadn't she discovered this before? She drummed her fingers against the arm of the chair as she thought about her findings. A lot of big businessmen donated to charity, she told herself sensibly. And just because Marco donated money to good causes it didn't make him a good person. It was probably some kind of tax dodge, anyway.

She returned her attention to the internet and impulsively typed in the name of his ex-wife—Lucinda White. A lot of information came up about the films she had starred in, but there was also a lot of material about her marriage to Marco.

Isobel glanced through some of the old articles and photographs.

As the couple had always fiercely guarded their privacy, almost everything that was written was pure conjecture. The only fact that couldn't be denied was that they had once loved each other, as evidenced in some of the snatched photographs of them together.

They had made a very glamorous couple, and it was no wonder the press had been obsessed with them. A picture of Marco and Lucinda together at a party or even out for an afternoon stroll had sold newspapers and magazines by the ton. There had been a greedy appetite to know everything there was to know about their whirlwind love affair—where they shopped, where they went on holiday, how they decorated their home in Beverly Hills. In fairness, Isobel could see why Marco disliked the press. It had all got a bit out of hand.

Although the couple had studiously avoided giving the media any intimate details about their lives, people had thought they knew them—thought their relationship was the real thing. They had been depicted as the perfect couple.

Then suddenly, eighteen months later, the marriage had ended without any explanation.

Irreconcilable differences, they'd said. But they hadn't said what those differences were. The divorce had been quick and yet dignified. There had been no war over money, no trading of recriminations or insults—in fact they had stated that they would always be friends.

That had been almost two years ago now, and since the split neither one of them had been involved with anyone else. There had been rumours every time Marco was seen out with a woman—which was frequently. But there seemed to be no one serious in his life, and the same for Lucinda.

Some people said that they still loved each other. But if that were the case they would still be together. It wasn't as if the press interest had diminished because they were divorced. In fact it had sparked a whole new direction of spin.

There were lots of articles on the internet now with various theories about what had happened. Some said Marco had just reverted to type and got bored—once a womaniser always a womaniser, they said. Some alleged that Lucinda had wanted children and Marco hadn't. A few suspected that Lucinda had been the one to have an affair.

So what was the truth? Isobel wondered.

If she had to guess, her money would be on Marco having an affair—possibly the thought of committing to a family had sent him running scared for the hills. You only had to look at the articles and the lists of women he had dated both before and after his marriage to realise he liked playing the field. There were even kiss-and-tell articles by women he had unceremoniously dumped after just a few dates. He was a player. It wasn't rocket science.

But of course she could be wrong, she reminded herself, because she was just guessing. Lucinda was a very beautiful woman and a very successful actress; she *could* have been the one who'd had a fling.

Isobel paused to look at one of her publicity pictures. The actress was wearing a white bikini that left little to the imagination. She had a fabulous body, glorious long blonde hair and big blue eyes.

Maybe one of her leading men had made a play for her and she hadn't been able to resist. Things like that happened all the time in Hollywood.

But if she'd been the one to have an affair wouldn't it have been splashed all over the papers? Since the divorce there had been no rumours about Lucinda, no cosy photographs of her out having dinner at restaurants and then returning to someone's apartment late at night, leaving early in the morning. Not like Marco.

Marco seemed to have sailed through his divorce without giving it a second thought. Although there was one shot of him just after the decree nisi where he looked as if the whole thing had suddenly got to him.

She flicked back to that photograph and studied it. They'd caught him leaving his offices, and there was a bleak look in his eyes, a troubled air about him.

Perhaps he wasn't unfeeling. Perhaps Lucinda had been unfaithful and he had been devastated.

As soon as the thought crossed her mind Isobel frowned. Why was she suddenly looking for excuses for him? He'd probably looked shattered that day because he'd been out all night, or because he hadn't made as many millions that week as he'd expected—not because his divorce was final.

Nevertheless she was supposed to be keeping an open mind,

she reminded herself. If she had to write a celebrity interview, the least she could do was to make it the best interview she could, and that meant being accurate with details.

Isobel sighed and disconnected from the internet. She would find out the truth, she told herself with determination, and she would start by putting some questions to Marco tonight over dinner.

With that thought in mind, she got to her feet and went inside to get ready.

It was strange... She was usually so eager to get a story, and not at all nervous. But as she headed downstairs a little while later her confident business mood felt as if it was evaporating—a fact that wasn't helped when she rounded a corner and caught sight of her reflection in the hallway mirror. The black skirt and blouse she was wearing were OK for the office, but for dinner with Marco they seemed suddenly lamentably dull.

Isobel frowned. She had interviewed a lot of different people over the years, and this was the first time she had ever worried about what she was wearing! Usually she was totally focused on getting the story. And that was how she should be now, she told herself firmly. It wasn't as if she was out to impress Marco—which was just as well, considering his usual dinner companions were movie stars and models. This was just work.

Trying to forget the stupid undercurrents that were whirring around inside her, she held her head high and moved down the corridor in search of her quarry.

A door was open a little further along, and as she looked in she saw Marco sitting behind a desk in a large book-lined study. He was immersed in paperwork and didn't hear her until she knocked on the door. Then he sat back and smiled.

Something about that lazy, casual smile and the way his gaze drifted over her appearance made her senses start to spin. 'Sorry, I didn't mean to interrupt...'

'That's OK—I'm just finished. Come on in,' he invited.

It entertained him to watch her reactions to him—she was so cautious, like a gazelle poised for flight. And even her dress sense seemed to verge on the side of caution. She looked smart, but in a very efficient, non-sexual way. The black top she was wearing was loose and completely hid her curves. Anyone would think she was scared of allowing a man to look at her body, he thought. And why did she insist on scraping her hair back into a ponytail like that?

Isobel tried to pretend that she didn't notice the analytical way he was dissecting her appearance, but she could feel herself tensing even more. OK, she knew she was not model material, but he had no right to look at her like that!

'So, what are you working on?'

Her voice was deliberately cool and businesslike, and he laughed. 'With a question like that, I take it you're still working as well?'

'Well…that *is* why I'm here.' She tried to angle her head up in a way that told him that she didn't care what he thought about her—that there might be a million women in France who would give anything to be here in his company and would probably dress up for him, but she wasn't one of them. She was totally work-orientated.

To her consternation he just kept looking at her, with that gleam in the darkness of his eyes, as if she were a very interesting sub-species and as if to say, *I know you're not immune to me*.

But that was in her imagination, she warned herself hastily. Maybe he looked at every woman with that same provocative gleam in his eye.

'So, you were telling me what you are working on?' She tried to jog him lightly into continuing.

'I wasn't, actually,' he replied with amusement. 'But seeing as you are enquiring so…nicely…I'll tell you. I'm putting a deal together to buy a French company called Cheri Bon.'

'The name rings a bell...' She frowned. 'Oh, yes—I read about them last year. It's a confectionery company that started out as a small family-run concern and made it big very quickly. Didn't they get into financial trouble because they'd overstretched themselves?'

'Well done.' He looked impressed. 'Obviously all that reading material next to your bed on the financial markets isn't just for show.'

'There is no need to sound quite so surprised. I am a journalist, you know, and we like to keep abreast of what's going on.'

'Ah, yes... So you are...' He smiled. It was strange but every now and then he found himself forgetting that.

'Anyway, I thought you were buying the Sienna confectionery company.' She got the point in quickly.

She was very much the journalist now, he noted as he pushed his chair back from the table to stand up. 'Come on— let's go and have dinner. I've had enough of business.'

'So...are you buying both companies?' Even though she knew she probably shouldn't be asking, she couldn't leave the subject.

He just laughed. 'You're tenacious, aren't you?'

'Just interested.' She shrugged.

'Well, how about I tell you all about Cheri Bon tomorrow?' he suggested nonchalantly. 'They have their main factory in Nice. You can accompany me down there and I will fill you in on my visionary plans for a very sweet future.'

'Really? That would be great!' Her eyes widened with interest. 'So I take it you're hoping to merge the two companies?'

'As I said, I've had enough of business for now. That's tomorrow's subject, Izzy.' He put a hand on her arm and steered her towards the door. 'Now, let's see what Stella has prepared for us to eat.'

The light touch of his hand sent weird little darts of

awareness through her body, and she quickly moved away from him, hoping he wouldn't notice.

But Marco did notice. He also noticed how she deliberately gave him as wide a berth as possible as he stood back to allow her to go ahead of him out of the door. It was as if she was terrified of accidentally brushing against him—in fact of having any bodily contact with him at all. And maybe that unleashed something of the hunting instinct in him, because as he watched her walk past he found himself deliberately wanting to step into her path, hem her in, just so that he could see the light of consternation in her eyes, the pulse beating at the creamy base of her throat.

He forced himself to do no such thing. But as he followed her out and along the corridor, he found his eyes drawn to her hips. He suspected that she had a nice figure beneath those staid clothes, and the more he was around her the more his curiosity was building.

'We're dining outside, Izzy,' he told her as he opened a door into the warmth of the evening.

Isobel found herself out on the terrace. A table had been laid for two, and candlelight flickered and reflected over crystal wine goblets and silver cutlery. There was even an ice bucket that contained a chilled bottle of wine, open and ready for them. The scene looked impossibly romantic against the backdrop of the Mediterranean Sea, now tinged with the oyster-pink of the setting sun.

'You seem to have gone to a lot of trouble,' she murmured apprehensively.

He smiled. 'I haven't gone to any trouble at all, I assure you; this is all the work of my cook, Stella. She always…how is it you English say?…pushes the boat when I have company for dinner.'

'Pushes the boat *out*,' she corrected him absently. 'She does know that I'm not one of your girlfriends, doesn't she?' she added impulsively. 'And that this is a working dinner?'

'No, I don't think she does know that.' She could see a teasing gleam in the darkness of his eyes now. 'Stella is my chef, Izzy. I've never felt the need to furnish her with the personal details regarding my dinner arrangements. Apart from anything else, I don't think she would be remotely interested. However, if you feel it's important I will of course call her out here and bring her up to speed for you.'

'No—no, obviously it's not important.' Isobel could feel herself starting to blush. Why had she said that? Why did she keep feeling the need to assert businesslike boundaries? It wasn't as if Marco would be interested in her in a million years! No wonder he was looking so amused.

In desperation, she tried to salvage her pride. 'It's just that I might need to make notes as we talk, that's all, and if you'd told her she might have laid the table with a bit more practicality. It's a little dark out here...don't you think? With just the candlelight?'

'Ah! I understand.' He pulled out one of the chairs for her and watched as she walked hesitantly over to sit down. 'Well, I'll just have to see what I can do about that for you. There are some extra lights out here somewhere.'

'Thank you.' Why did she feel so unbearably self-conscious? she wondered angrily. Why was she aware of every nuance in his voice, every flicker from his dark eyes as they moved over her?

She watched as he walked across to a light switch and switched it on.

'So how is that?' he asked.

Isobel had expected a bright overhead light to come on, but instead garden lights flickered on, glittering like icicles around the palm trees and the edges of the veranda, giving the gathering dusk an even more romantic feel.

'As you probably know, that isn't any help at all,' she muttered, and he smiled.

'Really? I think it's much better.' ' He strolled back and sat down opposite. 'Best I can do, I'm afraid.'

Somehow Isobel didn't believe him. In fact she got the distinct impression he was enjoying her feeling of discomfiture. 'Well, never mind. I'll just have to use my Dictaphone,' she said as she reached to get it out of her bag. 'You don't mind, do you?' Without waiting for an answer she turned it on and put it down in the centre of the table.

'Actually, yes, I *do* mind.' Calmly he leaned over, picked the machine up and talked into it. 'Note to Ms Izzy Keyes… You need to relax a little, unwind and switch off.' As he spoke his eyes held hers. 'And by the way—has anyone ever told you that you look quite extraordinarily attractive when you are angry?'

Then he switched the machine off, and watched as her green eyes blazed with fire.

'Marco, stop making fun of me! I really need to start assimilating information for my article,' she told him in consternation.

'I wasn't making fun. I was being serious.' And he really was, he realised suddenly. There was something exciting about the way her intelligent green eyes could blaze like that—the way her smooth, pale skin could warm up to boiling point.

'Let's assimilate information the old-fashioned way… hmm?' He murmured huskily. 'Let's have a conversation and get to know each other.' He watched as her eyes narrowed warily on him. 'Anyone would think I'd suggested something scandalous,' he said humorously.

'No, you haven't, but I think you are missing the point.' Her heart was thudding uncomfortably hard against her chest as she strove to sound in control. 'I'm interviewing you, and—'

'No, I think *you* are missing the point Izzy. We are sitting on a terrace overlooking the Mediterranean, about to have dinner. Life is too short for rigid rules. You can assimilate your information, as you like to put it, but let's do it my way.'

'Yes, but—'

'*My* way Izzy…or no way.' He cut across her firmly.

'Well, what can I say…?' She shrugged helplessly. She wasn't at all happy about the way this conversation was going, and she was totally out of her comfort zone now. 'I was just trying to be organized, so I don't forget anything.'

It was strange, but the more she tried to put up her business-like barriers the more Marco felt inclined to tear them down. 'You won't forget anything,' he told her softly. 'And here's a radical idea—if you do, you can ask me in the morning and I'll remind you.'

He leaned across and filled both of their wine glasses.

'Now, what shall we drink to?' he asked nonchalantly.

She wanted to tell him again that she didn't drink while she was working, but as she saw the humour glittering in the darkness of his gaze she realised he expected her to say that. So she changed her mind.

'How about the truth?' she said quietly instead. 'Let's drink to that.'

The suggestion jarred a little with Marco. 'Since when has a journalist ever been interested in the truth?'

'Since right now.' Her eyes held with his, and something about his derisive remark made her lean forward earnestly. 'Not all journalists are the same. We are not all out to sensationalise a story, or get the story at any cost.'

'Nice try, Izzy.' He laughed, but this time there was little humour in the sound. 'But that's not my experience.'

'Well…you obviously just haven't met the right journalists.'

'Is that a fact?' Marco's eyes drifted over her lazily. He couldn't quite work out if she was just the most practised liar in the world, or if that really was sincerity in her voice.

Not that he particularly cared—because, no matter how

much sincerity shone from her, she would not be getting the inside track on his marriage breakdown. There were some things that he would never discuss with anyone, never mind a journalist.

'Well...we'll see.' He shrugged. 'So, why don't you set the conversation rolling and tell me a little about yourself?'

'I think you've just stolen my line.' She cast him a fulminating glare from wide eyes, and he laughed.

'Izzy, if I'm going to tell you about myself, the least you can do is give me a brief summary of your life.' He reached and took a sip of his wine. 'That's the thing I hate about the paparazzi—total strangers shouting questions. What gives them the right...hmm?'

The softly asked question made her look over at him. She supposed he had a point. But even so she was loath to open up to him even on a superficial level. 'I'm really not that interesting,' she murmured.

'I don't believe that for a moment.'

Oh, he was far too smooth, she thought nervously.

Marco noted the shadows in the depths of her eyes. He still couldn't fathom why he found her so fascinating, but he did. Perhaps it was nothing more than idle curiosity...because she certainly wasn't his type. Maybe she just stirred the hunter instinct in him, or maybe it was that air of fragility that gave her a certain mystery.

Whatever it was, he found himself remembering that moment when he had unfastened the top button on her blouse. The intensity of the sensual heat that had flared between them had been quite a surprise.

And as his gaze flicked down over her again he found himself thinking that he would like to unbutton her a little more and then take her to bed—just for the hell of it.

CHAPTER FIVE

DARKNESS had fallen quickly, and there was a full moon shimmering in the inky blackness of the sky, its light reflecting over the stillness of the sea like a wide silver pathway to heaven. There was something very surreal and tranquil about the scene, but there was nothing tranquil about the way Isobel was feeling.

Every time she met Marco's dark gaze across the table she could hear her heart thundering, as if she were running fast across difficult terrain pursued by the devil himself.

Why was that? she wondered distractedly. Was it just the fact that he was undeniably handsome?

The white shirt unbuttoned at the neck seemed to emphasise the smooth olive tones of his skin. His thick dark hair was immaculately groomed. Even the hint of stubble on his square jaw made him look more…enticing…if that was the word she was looking for. She frowned…. Maybe not! She certainly couldn't use that adjective when she wrote about him!

'So, you were about to tell me about yourself?' He smiled, as if her hesitation totally amused him.

'Marco, I really don't see the point—'

'Well, you will just have to humour me, won't you?' He cut across her easily. 'Tell me about your parents and your childhood—that kind of thing.'

She shrugged. 'I was brought up in London,' she began hesitantly. 'And my mother lives in Brighton now.'

'And your father?'

'I don't know where he is. He left when I was eleven and he didn't come back.'

'Not even to see you?' Marco frowned.

'My dad was a bit of a complex character,' she murmured non-committally.

'Which is code for the fact that he was a dreadful parent, I take it?'

It was really strange, but she found she didn't want to tell Marco that he was right. Why was that? she wondered. Was it because she remembered that Marco was the man who had sacked her father from the job he'd loved at the factory? Did she still feel some kind of loyalty towards her dad? The discovery surprised her, because her dad certainly didn't deserve any kind of loyalty after the way he'd behaved... Maybe that old saying about blood being thicker than water was true!

'Let's just say he had problems. Everyone can't get a best parent award, I suppose.' She reached and took a sip of her wine. He was looking at her with that close attention that unnerved her so much—as if he were interested in her—as if he cared about what she was telling him.

He was just practised in that kind of concerned attitude, she told herself quickly. It came under the heading of charm.

But even so, those dark eyes were incredibly warm as they held hers...

They were interrupted by Marco's cook, who came to put some plates of prosciutto on the table, accompanied by ciabatta bread. She was a large lady in her fifties, and obviously couldn't speak much English—because Marco introduced her in French, and the conversation stayed in that language for a few minutes as the woman put some bowls of olives on the table. There was a lot of laughter and what sounded like light-hearted banter, and Isobel was glad of the interlude.

Glad to switch her thoughts away from old memories and the new challenge of not getting drawn in by Marco's smooth charisma.

'Stella says that our starter for this evening is Italian, in my honour, and that our main course is British, in your honour,' Marco told her as they were left alone again. 'But apparently the dessert is French, in honour of the fact that French food is the best—not that she is biased at all.' He laughed.

'No, obviously not.' She smiled. 'She seems a nice lady.'

'Yes, she is—and as a rule she is very reliable... However, all is not as it seems.'

'Oh?' She looked over at him intrigued, thinking he was serious. But then she saw the gleam of humour in his eyes.

'I have a feeling these olives are not truly Italian,' he said seriously. 'I believe they come from a grove down the road.'

'No!' She played along with him and looked suitable horrified. 'That's very underhand of her, isn't it?'

'Absolutely. You can't trust anyone nowadays.' He reached and took one of the plump green olives from the bowl to examine it closely. Then he put it into his mouth.

'So what's the verdict?' she asked with a smile.

'Not so sure I can tell you...' He looked at her with a raised eyebrow. 'I don't want my views splashed all over the papers tomorrow. The olive world in Italy could be in uproar.'

She giggled.

'You may laugh, but we take our food very seriously in Italy.'

'Don't worry—you'll find I am the soul of discretion. Sensitive, responsible journalism is my speciality.'

'Hmm...well, as I said earlier I'll reserve judgement on that for a while.' Their eyes held for a moment. Then he smiled at her and slid the bowl a little closer to her. 'Try one—they are very good.'

They *were* good she thought, as was the warm bread and the prosciutto. She hadn't realised how hungry she was until now. But when she thought about it she hadn't eaten since breakfast.

'So, moving on from your childhood, tell me about the guy who broke your heart?' Marco asked suddenly.

The question took her completely aback. 'What makes you think someone has broken my heart?'

'I don't know. Call it a wild guess.' He shrugged. 'Sometimes I imagine I catch a vulnerable look in your eyes.'

'Sorry to disappoint you, but I'm more your practical, pragmatic type.' She raised her chin.

'The tough journalist, coolly aloof from emotional ties—that kind of thing?' He looked vaguely amused.

'Yes…that kind of thing.'

As their eyes held across the table Marco wasn't sure what he believed about her. There was something about the hesitation in her reply, that expression in her eye…

'And, you know, my love-life really isn't any of your business,' she continued fiercely.

'Ah! But in a few moments you will be asking me about *my* love-life won't you?' he countered. 'You'll be traipsing out all the old tired questions.'

'I don't have any old or tired questions; mine are all fresh and full of zing.'

He laughed at that.

'But actually we *should* move on to that—'

'So you've never been married?' Marco continued lazily, as if she hadn't even spoken. 'Never lived with anyone?'

Why did he keep asking her these personal questions? He was driving her mad. 'I was engaged for a while. But it didn't work out and we called it off.' She slanted him a warning look. 'I'm over it. There's no underlying vulnerability to me whatsoever.'

'And did this happen fairly recently?'

'About six months ago. Now, can we move on?' There was an unconsciously pleading look in her eyes.

'OK, I won't say another word on the subject.' He held up his hands.

'Good—because we are supposed to be talking about you.'

Stella interrupted them to clear away their plates and put out some serving dishes between them.

'I hope you are not going to be disappointed,' Marco said as they were left alone again.

'Why?' She looked over at him with a frown, thinking he was talking about their interview.

'Because your British dish…' he lifted the lid off one of the casserole dishes '…is not roast beef.' He flicked her a teasing look and she couldn't help but smile.

For a while there was silence between them as he put some food onto her plate. 'I think it is beef casserole with herbs of Provence,' he said as he tasted it. 'Which *I* would think is a French dish.'

'Whatever it is, it's very good. I wish I could cook like this.'

She could hear the sound of the sea against the shore beneath them; there was something very relaxing about it, and about the warmth of the air.

She looked down over the garden towards the sea. 'I can understand why you bought this house. The setting is spectacular. But I'm surprised that you have your main home here in France. I would have thought, being Italian, your home would be in Italy.'

'Italy will always be my first love, but I have to admit that I'm torn. France is like a very beautiful mistress—compelling and provocative, hard to get out of the system.'

There was a honeyed edge to his voice that made little darts of adrenalin shoot through her.

'Well, you'd know all about mistresses, I suppose,' she murmured, trying to ignore the sensations.

'I know about passion,' he corrected softly. 'How it can fire the senses, take you over.'

Something about the way he was looking at her made her feel hot inside…made her wonder what it would be like to be kissed by him, to be held in those strong arms. As soon as the thought crossed her mind she was shaken. She had more sense than to ever be attracted to him, she reminded herself furiously.

'So, is that what happened with your marriage?' Desperately she tried to bring herself back to reality by asking the question. 'Did you go out one night and meet someone, and allow passion to take you over to the point where you allowed yourself to forget that you were married?'

'Same old tired questions…' He shook his head. 'And I thought you said you could do better.'

The mocking words made her skin flush with colour. 'It's the question people are interested in.'

'It's two years since my divorce, Izzy. You'd think people would have moved on.'

There was an undercurrent to the words that she couldn't work out. Was it anger? Sadness? Or just plain irritation?

Their eyes held. 'Are you going to give me an answer?' she asked hesitantly, and he shook his head.

'Not right now…no.'

The reply took her by surprise. 'But you invited me here specifically to interview you about your life—'

'My life is more than my divorce, surely?' He fixed her with that mocking look that completely unnerved her. 'I think you should work up to that question.'

'Do you?' She looked at him archly. 'Is this let's-make-the-journalist-jump-through-hoops time?'

He laughed. 'You know, I like the sound of that!'

Stella interrupted them again as she came to clear the table and serve the desert—a *crème brulée* with a thick, creamy crust that Isobel would have enjoyed if she hadn't completely lost her appetite now.

'So, what questions am I allowed to ask you, Marco?' she murmured as they were left alone again. 'I suppose it's OK to dwell on your life in the fast lane, with your planes and your yachts?'

'I thought you said you didn't exaggerate? It's one plane and one yacht,' he corrected her with a smile, and then sat back in his chair to regard her steadily. 'And am I to gather from that note in your voice that you disapprove of my—as you call it—life in the fast lane?'

'It's not my place to disapprove or approve. I'm just making an observation.' She shrugged.

'Oh, is that all it is?' He laughed. 'And your *observation* is that I have no idea what real life is like? Is that it? That I don't know how poverty can bite to the bone?'

She shrugged. 'Well, now you come to mention it—'

'Izzy, I spent the first eight years of my life living in the back streets of Naples. We had nothing.'

She frowned. 'But I thought you came from a wealthy family.'

'My mother was from a wealthy family, but she was cut off without a penny when she married my father because he had committed the ultimate sin of being born poor. It was only when my father died that we were received back into the fold.'

'I didn't know that,' Isobel said in surprise. 'The blurb on your background always says that you are from a wealthy dynasty.'

'Well, there you are, you see—you don't know everything.' Marco's mobile phone started to ring, and he lifted it up to look at the screen. 'Excuse me, I'll have to take this. It's a business call.'

Isobel watched as he leaned back in his chair, noticing how his Italian tones blended attractively into the warmth of the night. His revelations about his family background had surprised her—how was it that no one had found out this information before? she wondered. And what else didn't she know about him?

Stella came over to the table to see if they were finished and to ask if they wanted coffee. Isobel tried to communicate with her in her stumbling French, thanking her for the meal and declining coffee as she was still enjoying the delicious wine.

'Ah, the wine is from Marco's vineyard in Provence,' Stella said in broken English. 'It is good, yes?'

'*Très bon,*' Isobel replied and then tried to say that she hadn't realised that Marco owned a vineyard.

Unfortunately Stella replied in such rapid French that Isobel couldn't understand a word, so she just nodded as she watched her clearing the table, and then said a quick thank-you in French before she disappeared.

She caught Marco glancing over at her with that amused look in the darkness of his eyes. Probably laughing at her lamentable attempt to communicate. But not everyone was bilingual. Really, the guy was perfectly impossible!

There was also more to him than she had first realised. He'd obviously been through some tough times in his youth, and he was a bit more…*human* than she'd thought he would be. He had quite a good sense of humour, and—

Suddenly Isobel caught herself. What on earth was she thinking? Even if he'd had a harsh upbringing in Italy, he was still the same ruthless man who had practically stolen her grandfather's firm. Not to mention the fact that he was a womaniser—all good reasons for not being drawn in by that playful gleam in the darkness of his eyes.

On impulse she got up from the table and walked to the edge of the terrace. She could see the pool from here, and the shimmering turquoise water looked cool and inviting in the tropical heat.

She listened to Marco's smooth flow of Italian and wondered what he was saying. She needed to find out more about his ruthless side, she reminded herself—needed to keep her senses firmly grounded.

'You were right about one thing, Izzy,' he observed suddenly, and she turned around to see that he had finished his call and was getting up from the table.

'And what is that?'

'Your conversational French needs work.' He smiled at her.

'Thanks for that. I knew you were amused!'

'No, actually I was impressed that you made an attempt. And amused by the fact that you sounded quite cute as you did so.'

'Thanks,' she murmured with embarrassment. 'What you really mean is that I sounded silly.'

'No, that's not what I meant at all. Don't be so hard on yourself.' He strolled back towards her, and something about the way he was watching her with such intensity made her emotions spin.

'Anyway, we should get back to where we were before we got interrupted by your phone call,' she continued swiftly, her mind racing to try and get back into the safety of work mode. 'You were telling me about your childhood.'

'Was I?' He shrugged. 'I think we should move on from that. Maybe you should tell me a little more about yourself.'

'Is this another of your let's-make-the-journalist-jump through-hoops moments?' she asked.

'No, it's more of a let's relax moment.' He came to a halt beside her. 'It is ten o'clock, Izzy—don't you ever switch off from work?'

'Says the guy who has just taken a business phone call,' she retorted swiftly.

He laughed. 'You're right. Maybe we are both guilty of burying ourselves in work.' His gaze suddenly turned serious.

'My excuse is that I have a lot of people depending on me to get things done, a lot of jobs riding on my decisions. What's your excuse?'

'I don't need an excuse. And I don't know why you keep asking me these questions.'

'Because I'm interested. In fact I'd say I'm as curious about you as you are about me.'

For a few dangerous seconds she could feel his eyes moving over her face and down to the graze along her collarbone.

She remembered how he'd made her feel when he'd reached to unfasten that one little button at the top of her blouse earlier, and as their eyes connected again she could feel the same heat swirling almost violently inside her. Hastily she took a step away from him.

'Izzy, why are you so frightened of letting your guard down?'

The husky way he asked that question made her heart start to thud nervously. 'I'm not frightened of anything!' He was too damn alert; like a heat-seeking missile he seemed to be able to zone in on her vulnerability...on the fact that she found him far too attractive. Desperately she tried to remind herself that she shouldn't be thinking like this... 'And as for your being worried about people's jobs! Frankly, I find that hard to believe.'

He smiled. 'You could win an award for that defence system of yours, do you know that?'

'I don't know what you are talking about!' She would have backed further away from him, but there was nowhere to go. She was penned in now against the wooden rail.

'I'm talking about the fact that you seem to need to hide behind a businesslike attitude at all times. And it seems to be a pretty negative one as well where I'm concerned. Tell me, are you like this with all men, or is it just me?'

The lazily amused question made her temperature soar. 'I just know the truth about you, that's all.' As soon as the words slipped out she desperately wanted to recall them. She didn't want to make this personal.

'Do you care to explain what you mean by "the truth"?'

There was a tense stillness about him, and as Isobel stared up at him she felt her nerves twisting.

'Not really.' Her voice was a mere whisper. 'Marco, I think we should leave things as they are—I think we should call it a night.'

She tried to move past him but he just reached out a hand and caught hold of her arm.

'On the contrary—you are not going anywhere until you enlighten me.'

The touch of his hand against her arm made her heart thud heavily against her chest.

Their eyes clashed, and she knew he wasn't going to let her go until she said something. 'OK, I just…think you are arrogant and…and ruthless in business.' He was looking at her with that impassive look that fired her blood—as if he was not taking anything on board and as if she were just an irksome little reporter talking rubbish. 'You buy companies and strip them of their assets,' she continued, a little more forcefully. 'You play God as you fire people and tear their lives apart.'

'You certainly hold very biased views about me, don't you?' He shook his head lazily.

The observation made her blush. 'The truth is important to me, Marco—I wouldn't say those things without first-hand knowledge to back up the accusations. And I know that when it comes to business you are in for the kill.'

'I'm a businessman. I have to make tough decisions sometimes when I take over a company.' He shrugged. 'But as for your accusations that I fire people without thought and tear companies apart—I don't know where you are getting that from.' His eyes were hard for a moment. 'Where possible I try to move people around within my organisation. I'm in the business of building up strong companies, and I employ a hell of a lot of people.'

'You make it sound so reasonable.' She tipped her head up angrily. 'But I know how you use your power, Marco. I know how you can force small companies into selling to you.' The charge fell from her lips with raw emphasis.

He stared into the blaze of her green eyes. 'Izzy, I have never forced anyone into selling to me.'

'Well, now I *know* you are lying.' With determination she held his gaze. 'And I know that because you forced my grand-father into selling his company to you.'

There—she'd said it! She'd confronted him. But even as the words tumbled out she was regretting them.

Her job was on the line here—she needed to get him on side, get her stupid gossipy interview and just leave. And here she was, raking up stuff that no one except her cared a damn about!

'Your grandfather?' Marco frowned. 'What company would that be?'

She shook her head. 'Look, Marco, I've said too much already. We should leave this subject—because you and I will never agree on your business practices.'

But Marco wasn't even listening to her; instead he was looking at her with that intensity that she found so unnerving. 'Keyes…' He murmured her name as he ran it through his memory banks and then shook his head. 'I don't know what you are talking about…' Suddenly his voice trailed away as he remembered the photo on the shelf in her bedroom. He'd rec-ognised the guy. Like a piece in a jigsaw puzzle the name sud-denly flashed into his mind. 'Hayes…David Hayes—that was the man in your photograph. Was he your grandfather?'

He watched the telltale flush of colour on her cheek-bones.

'Well, well…' He shook his head. 'I bought that company over ten years ago.'

'There are some things you never forget,' she said stiffly. 'He was a decent honest man and you broke him.'

'Is that what you think?' Marco frowned.

'It's what I *know*,' she told him firmly. 'You squeezed him out...the big guy bullying the small trader...until you got the business for next to nothing.'

'That's not how it happened, Izzy,' he said calmly. 'Yes, once I'd ironed out the problems I did get a good deal with that business. It was a very profitable venture. But it was bad management that was your grandfather's undoing, not me.'

She shook her head. 'He told me—'

'I don't care what he told you. I'm telling you the truth.' Marco cut across her briskly. 'For some reason your grandfather trusted a man he'd put in control of the factory, and he ran the place into the ground. My first job when I took over was to sack him.'

Isobel stared at Marco, and for a moment the earth seemed to tilt to a very strange angle.

'He'd been running up debts, not paying bills. The guy was—' Marco stopped as he saw the colour starting to fade from her cheeks. 'Are you OK?'

'Yes.' She tried to hold her head high.

But she wasn't OK, because suddenly she'd realised that for all these years she had blamed Marco for what he had done to her grandfather...and the real culprit had been her father. *Her father had been in charge of that factory!*

Why hadn't her grandfather told her the truth? Why had he backed up all the lies her father had told about the ruthless Marco Lombardi? Even as she asked herself the question she knew the answer. Because in those days she had adored her father, had hero-worshipped him, and her grandfather probably hadn't been able to face disillusioning her. He'd been old school: gentle, courteous. And he had loved her very much. In fact he was probably the only person who had ever truly wanted to protect her.

But the fact remained that he had still lied to her, and that hurt. She'd always thought he was the one man in her life that she'd been able to believe in.

The truth was important to her—no matter how painful, she believed it was always best faced.

Silence seemed to shimmer uneasily as she tried to pull herself together.

'My father ran that factory,' she told Marco quietly.

He nodded. 'I've just made the connection. And I'm telling you the truth, Izzy. The guy was a rogue—and that's putting it politely, for your sake.'

'Don't pretend to do me any favours!' Her eyes held angrily with his for a long moment. Then she looked away helplessly. It had been so much easier to believe that Marco was to blame. Part of her still wanted to believe that he was lying to her now. That maybe her father had done nothing wrong. But even as she said the words to herself they didn't ring true.

Her father wasn't the reliable type... *She knew what he was.*

All those years of looking at the situation from the wrong perspective made her feel foolish. She felt as if someone had just opened a window into her life and an arctic breeze was sweeping all her orderly thoughts into chaos.

Marco put a hand under her chin and tipped her face upwards, so that she was forced to look at him. 'You can apologise any time you like,' he murmured softly.

The touch of his hand made her senses swim.

She didn't want to lower her barriers and apologise to him, because it felt far...far too dangerous.

'Yes, well... I might have got it wrong.' She wrenched herself away from his touch.

'There is no *might* about it. You *did* get it wrong.'

'But the fact still remains that you got a damn good deal when you bought that business,' she maintained stubbornly.

'And since when has that been a crime?' The quietly asked

question sent ripples of consternation though her. 'Izzy, it was over ten years ago, I was just starting out. I saw a business opportunity and I took it.'

Isobel swallowed hard, appalled that she had made such an error. 'OK, I...I made a mistake.'

His gaze raked over her with almost ruthless strength as he took in the fierce glitter in her green eyes.

'And I'm sorry.' The words broke from her lips with trembling force.

She didn't even realise that she was crying until he reached and wiped a tear from her cheek.

'Don't!' She flinched away from the light, disturbing touch of his fingers. 'I feel enough of a fool as it is. And I'm not crying...' She glared at him defensively. 'I'm just angry with myself for getting things so wrong.' She bit down on her lip. 'It all happened before my dad left us, and I still believed in him. I guess my grandfather didn't want to break that.'

'I can understand that,' Marco said quietly.

'Can you? I'm not so sure I can right now.' She brushed a hand impatiently over her face. 'I think he should have told me the truth. Because a few months after his death, when it was apparent there was nothing of value in his will, my father left.'

'And hindsight is a wonderful thing...' Marco said with a shrug. 'Everyone makes mistakes, Izzy. Your grandfather did what he thought was right at the time. He must have loved you a lot.'

The words made her eyes brim with tears again. 'Sorry.' Furiously she tried to wipe them away. 'I'm being stupid.'

'No, you're not.' He looked at her with that teasing gleam in the darkness of his eyes. 'Maybe earlier, but not now.'

The fact that he was being so understanding made her stomach tie into knots as she looked up at him.

And then suddenly his gaze moved towards her lips, and the

atmosphere between them altered subtly, becoming charged with electricity.

'Sorry… Anyway, I suppose we should call it a night, shouldn't we…?' She looked away from him in confusion. She could almost feel the tension crackling between them like a living entity—could feel her heart thundering against her chest as she fought with herself not to sway closer.

What was the matter with her? she wondered frantically.

'Running away, Izzy?' he taunted.

'No! Why should I run away?' Her eyes flicked back towards his and he smiled.

'Good question.' He reached out and idly stroked a finger along the side of her face. The feeling made little darts of awareness shoot through her, and she felt almost drugged by desire as his gaze raked over her lips again.

She wanted him to kiss her, she realised suddenly as he leaned closer…wanted it so much that her whole body ached. The knowledge shocked her, and she told herself to move away from him, but for some reason she couldn't make herself.

'Marco…' She murmured his name softly, and almost as if he were responding to an invitation his lips captured hers.

But this was no ordinary caress. His mouth was skilled, hungry and demanding, and yet so provocative that she was held immobilised by it for seconds.

And then to her consternation she kissed him back, with equal passion. She could taste the salt of her tears against the power of his lips, and she was conscious of thinking that the taste was probably very apt—because she was kissing a man who was experienced in seduction and heartbreak, and she was asking for trouble if she didn't pull away right now and put a stop to the madness.

But it felt so good that she didn't want it to stop. She could feel the warmth from his caress sweeping all the way through her, stirring up a deep longing to be even closer.

If this was how pleasurable it was to be kissed by him, how

would it feel to be even closer? she wondered recklessly. To have his hands against her naked body, holding her, stroking her?

The thought brought fire thrusting through her, and the jolt of it helped her to pull away.

'What are we doing?' She stared up at him in consternation, her breathing ragged as she strove for control.

'I think it's called kissing, Izzy.' He smiled, and unlike her he sounded totally at ease.

'And I think it's called madness. I'm not your type, Marco, and you certainly aren't mine.'

'And yet we seem curiously drawn to each other. '

The matter-of-fact words were like an incendiary device as far as Isobel was concerned, and she shook her head angrily. 'I'm not drawn to you at all!'

'Izzy...Izzy, what am I going to do about you? You are such a bad liar.' The taunting words made her blood boil.

But as their eyes held she knew he was right. She *was* drawn to him. She knew for Marco this was probably just idle curiosity, because she was so far removed from his usual type, but she wasn't sure what it was for her. All she knew was that if he kissed her again the same thing would probably happen—only the next time she might not have the strength to pull away.

The knowledge made panic spin through her.

'Marco, I think under the circumstances I should leave tomorrow and some other reporter from the *Daily Banner* should take my place.'

She really hadn't planned to say the words, they'd just spilled out, and Marco gave a long low whistle. 'You really are scared of me, aren't you?' he reflected softly.

'No! I'm not scared of anything!' She glared at him. 'I'm just trying to be sensible. Everything is getting too personal— and I'm not talking about the...kiss, I'm talking about the link to my past—everything.'

Marco shrugged and moved away from her. 'OK, if you want to leave that's fine. I'll get my chauffeur to drop you at the airport in the morning, But once you leave here, Izzy, my deal with the *Banner* is done.'

'You don't mean that,' she countered.

He met her eyes steadily. 'I always mean what I say, Izzy,' he assured her quietly. 'Always.'

CHAPTER SIX

ISOBEL couldn't sleep. The night was hot, and her thoughts were racing around in circles, causing her to toss and turn in the huge double bed.

She couldn't understand why she had felt the way she had when Marco had kissed her.

He might not have torn her grandfather's business apart, but he was still a ruthless womaniser, she reminded herself fiercely. He was still the type of predator who could sense weakness and turn it to his own advantage…both in business and in his private life.

So the sooner she got out of here in the morning and returned home to sanity the better.

Isobel turned her pillow around, searching for some cool cotton against her skin and some sleep.

And yet…her brain wouldn't switch off. Because how would she know these facts about Marco were true if she didn't stick around to find out? She'd made a mistake about him once—she didn't want to do it again.

The only thing that she was sure of about Marco was that he was a far more complicated character than she had ever imagined.

That and the fact that he turned her on more than any other man she had ever met.

The knowledge made her temperature shoot through the ceiling, and she tried desperately to block the thought out.

But as she closed her eyes the memory of that kiss returned with powerful intensity, and the fact remained that no man had ever made her feel so alive...or so scared.

Certainly Rob had never set her heart racing like that; in fact he had never unleashed *any* wild feelings of desire. She'd told herself that was what she wanted. That she didn't want to lose control—that she wanted a safe, steady relationship where she could settle down and start a family.

Little had she known that all the time Rob had been pursuing her he'd had another woman in the background. She might never have found out either, if she hadn't called round to his flat late one night after finishing work.

He'd tried to tell her that the scantily clad blonde in his living room didn't mean anything to him—that it was a one-time-only mistake and that it was Isobel's fault for not sleeping with him.

For a while she'd started to wonder if that was true. She'd even started to think that there might be something wrong with her. Because it had always been far too easy for her to pull away from a kiss and to put work first... Easy until now.

The knowledge blazed with unwelcome intensity as she remembered just how difficult she had found it to pull away from Marco.

And she supposed she'd put her job on the line by telling him she wasn't going to continue with their interview. If she went back to the *Daily Banner* without the story they wanted, her reputation would be in tatters.

Her stomach lurched crazily at the thought.

Of all the people in the world to have this effect on her! Why Marco? She couldn't understand it, because he was everything she'd always said she didn't like in a man.

She wondered what he would say if he knew that she was still a virgin. For a moment she imagined his lips twisting in that mocking smile of his. He'd probably tell her she was emotionally scarred from her childhood. He'd been trying to tell her something like that earlier, at dinner.

Angrily she closed her eyes and tried to concentrate on something else. It didn't matter what Marco would say. She didn't care what he thought. And she wasn't scarred from her childhood—if anything, what had happened to her had made her stronger, had taught her to be wary. And there was nothing wrong with that. Especially around someone like Marco Lombardi.

Isobel was just drifting off to sleep when she heard a noise that sounded like a door closing. Frowning, she sat up and listened. But the night was silent.

On impulse she threw the covers back and went over to look out of the window.

The full moon was clear and bright in the sky, and it shone over the curve of the bay, highlighting Marco's yacht moored by the jetty as if someone was shining a spotlight on it.

Isobel glanced at her watch. It was four in the morning. She'd probably just imagined the noise; it was far too early for anyone to be up and about. She was about to go back to bed when she saw Marco, walking away from the house. He was dressed in a suit and he was walking down the path towards his yacht, his steps purposeful.

You didn't dress like that to go for an early-morning sail! Was he taking her at her word and leaving her here to pack up her stuff while he sailed off on business?

It seemed very likely. He'd probably left his chauffeur instructions to drive her to the airport.

The idea sent a wave of panic rushing through her, and she realised suddenly that she wasn't ready to walk away from Marco yet. Not when there was so much more that she needed to find out.

Without even stopping to think about it, she snatched up her dressing gown and went running after him.

When she reflected on the moment afterwards she realised

she hadn't really been thinking straight. All she'd wanted to do was catch up with him and tell him she had changed her mind. Even when she'd stepped outside the front door into the early-morning darkness and realised she hadn't got anything on her feet, it still hadn't made her stop.

It wasn't until she reached the end of the garden path and the start of the long wooden jetty that she paused for breath. The yacht looked much larger and more impressive up close. Giant masts towered above her into the bright starlit sky. This was more like a cruise liner than a private vessel; it was the luxurious toy of a man who only had the best of everything. The kind of pleasure craft where Marco probably entertained sophisticated women-friends—women who would wear cock-tail dresses and diamonds—and here she was just in a robe.

For the first time she wondered if this was a good idea. Maybe she should go back to the house, wait for daylight, and then tell the chauffeur that she had changed her mind about leaving.

But say he insisted on following Marco's instructions. Or told her Marco wouldn't be back for a few days.

The thought made her step onto the gangplank and then down onto the polished deck. Apart from the moonlight she was completely in the dark, and it felt slightly eerie. The only sound was the gentle whisper of the breeze in the rigging, and the creak of the ropes that held the ship securely to her mooring.

Isobel stood for a moment, indecisively wondering which way to go, and then to her relief a light flicked on from a window further down.

She headed towards it and peeked cautiously in.

Modern chandeliers blazed over a large lounge area, with white leather sofas and glass tables. But there was no sign of Marco.

Cautiously she walked further down the deck, looking for a doorway, and then suddenly as she rounded a corner there he was—leaning against the rail of the ship, staring out to sea. She didn't realise that he was on the phone until he spoke to someone.

'So, you'll need to prepare those figures for me,' he was saying decisively. 'And I'll head out to New York to deal with it when I can.'

As she moved forward he turned and saw her. 'Anyway, I'll leave it with you, Nick, and phone you later,' he said as he hung up.

For a second there was silence between them as his eyes swept over her, taking in everything about her from her bare feet to the way the black satin dressing gown was tightly belted at her waist.

'Well, now, look what the tide has washed in,' he murmured, and something about that husky tone made her senses plunge into freefall. 'What are you doing out here, Izzy?'

What *was* she doing here? she wondered. She felt suddenly as if she had walked straight into a danger zone. 'I…I couldn't sleep, and then I saw you leaving the house.' She shrugged helplessly.

'You couldn't sleep?' One dark eyebrow lifted.

'No, and I thought I'd better come after you to tell you that I'd changed my mind.'

He moved closer to her. 'Changed your mind about what?'

Her heart seemed to bounce unsteadily against her chest. 'About…our interview, of course.' To her annoyance her voice came out as little more than a whisper. 'I've…I've decided to stay.'

'Ah.' He smiled at that. 'Of course you've decided to stay. You're a journalist—you want your story. I never had any doubts about that. But why are you out here now?'

'I told you…I just thought I'd better come after you in case you'd taken me literally and were going off on business somewhere.' She tried to sound practical, but it was a bit difficult when she was standing in front of him just wearing a dressing gown.

'I *am* going off on business. I've got an early-morning meeting over in Italy. But I was planning on returning to take you down to Nice afterwards.' His eyes narrowed on her. 'You thought I was leaving without saying goodbye?'

'No! Well…yes.' Her voice shook a little. 'As I said, I just wanted to check things were still OK between us after our conversation last night.'

'Yes, things are still OK.' The quiet way he said that, combined with the way his eyes were moving over her face, made her temperature sizzle.

And she realised that her interview wasn't the main reason she'd come running after him. In fact her motivations were somehow much more personal…and for the first time in her life work was on a very low flame by comparison.

The knowledge scared her. 'Anyway, I'll get back on dry land now we have that sorted out…'

'Bit late for that.'

'How do you mean?' Even as she waited for his answer she felt the ship swaying, and her eyes widened.

'The crew have cast off. We are moving out to sea,' he informed her nonchalantly.

'You *are* joking!' In consternation she sidestepped him and headed towards the rail.

But Marco wasn't joking. As soon as she walked out from the sheltered section where they had been standing a warm salt breeze swept her hair around her face. And as she looked out she could see they were a few miles out from land and starting to gather pace.

'Marco, we need to turn back!' she wailed in agitation.

'I haven't got the time to go back, *cara*.'

'But…I can't go to Italy with you!' She turned to face him and then wished she hadn't—because he was standing very close to her…perhaps too close.

'Why not?' he asked with a smile.

'Because…I'm just wearing a dressing gown! Because…'
She trailed off helplessly. 'There are a million reasons why
not.'

He looked at her quizzically. 'And yet you came running
out here without a second thought for any one of those million
reasons.'

His gaze drifted slowly over her. She looked totally different with her dark hair loose and tousled by the sea breeze,
and he couldn't help comparing her appearance now with the
buttoned-up way she usually dressed.

Her black satin dressing gown had slipped down, so that he
could see the creamy line of her shoulder and the dark bruise
where she had hurt herself on the flight.

He remembered how he'd felt when he'd unbuttoned her
blouse. He'd suspected that underneath all that prim clothing
she would be a very sexy woman, and the more he was around
her the more he realised he was right. That kiss last night, for
instance, had been filled with smouldering passion. But for
some reason she was afraid of stepping out from behind that
cool pretence and letting go.

'You don't understand, Marco. I…I really need to go back.'
She tilted her chin and looked up at him with eyes that shone
bright and clear in the moonlight.

He couldn't help thinking there was something very touching about the picture she presented.

'I do understand, Izzy,' he told her softly. 'But you've got
to understand it's too late to go back.'

The ship rolled and pitched suddenly, and he put a hand
out to steady her, catching her around the waist.

She tried to pull away, but the touch of his hand was like
fuel to the fire that was suddenly smouldering inside her.

'There is a chemistry between us that can't be denied, Izzy,
and you can't keep fighting it.'

'I don't know what you mean.' She raised her eyes towards

his and then immediately wished she hadn't, because he was looking at her with that teasing warmth that made her emotions stretch as if they were made of elastic and were being pulled...pulled to breaking point.

'You know exactly what I mean.' His gaze rested on her lips and she moistened them nervously. 'And I don't think these feelings are going to go away, Izzy, do you? Not unless we address them.'

The calm question rebounded inside her like some instrument of torture.

'You know, I think you are probably *the* most arrogant person I've ever met—and the most infuriating.'

He smiled, liking the fire in her voice, in her eyes. He wondered if she would be as fiery in bed.

Maybe it was time he found out. Because this swirling need that was building between them couldn't be ignored for much longer. It was like an elephant in the room—they both knew it was there, and they both knew exactly what was going on.

And the more she tried to fight against it, the more intrigued he became.

His gaze moved slowly down over her body as he remembered how good it had felt to kiss her last night.

OK, she was a reporter and not his type, but the more he was around her the less it seemed to matter. Well...it didn't matter now, for a few hours, he corrected himself quickly.

He had some time to pass...*why not while it away pleasurably?*

'And do you know *why* I infuriate you so much, Izzy?' he asked softly.

Her heart-rate was starting to increase. Of all the men in the world, why did it have to be Marco who had this effect on her? Why, as soon as he got too close, as soon as he looked at her in a certain way, did she start losing her sanity? She didn't want to lose control...she mustn't lose control, she told herself angrily.

With difficulty she tried to focus. 'The reasons why you annoy me are so...so many, I couldn't possibly begin to list them.'

'Well, let me help you, *cara*... The fact is, I drive you mad because I turn you on.'

The husky matter-of-fact words merged with the surge of the ocean and the hissing of the seaspray as it hit the ship.

She stared up at him, wide-eyed. 'That's...not true...' She tried desperately to insert some fierceness into the denial, but her voice sounded as frail as she suddenly felt. She couldn't believe he had just said that to her!

'You want me to kiss you... And you want me to make love to you... And it scares the hell out of you,' he continued evenly.

She shook her head. 'You are so damn sure of yourself, aren't you?' Her voice trembled alarmingly.

He put one hand on her arm and pulled her closer. 'I'm sure of this.'

Desperately she tried to resist, but he pulled her into his arms with ease, and the impact of his powerful body against hers sent her senses reeling.

She told herself that she needed to pull away, but somehow she couldn't find the strength, and as she looked up at him she was completely terrified by the feelings that were flowing through her.

'Please...Marco...' She whispered the words unsteadily.

'Please...what?' he asked teasingly. 'Please kiss me? Please show me what I've been missing?'

She could feel her heart pounding hard against her chest as he bent closer.

He said something in Italian, and then his mouth captured hers.

For a moment she tried very hard not to kiss him back, but it was like trying to hold a tidal wave at bay. The sensations that were spiralling through her just swept her away. One instant her hands were flat against his powerful chest, and the next they were curling up and around his shoulders as she hungrily kissed him back.

She could taste the salt of the sea on his lips, and the thundering, pounding sound of the ocean seemed to match the pounding of her emotions. *She wanted him so much!*

Just when she thought she couldn't stand it any more, when she thought she would just die from need, she felt his hands untying the belt that held her robe in place.

Her eyes moved to lock with his.

She was naked beneath, and she knew she should reach out and stop him, but she couldn't make herself. Because she wanted him to touch her more intimately—wanted to give herself to him completely.

At first his hands just rested at her waist as he brought her even closer against him, then they smoothed down over her slender hips.

'So, was I right,' he murmured provocatively against her ear. 'You want me so badly it hurts, doesn't it?'

Under ordinary circumstances the words would have infuriated her. She would have slapped him, she would have pulled back, she would have told him to go to hell. But she couldn't do anything rational because a devil seemed to have possessed her senses. She was totally incapable of anything except kissing him, luxuriating in his caresses.

His hand moved from her hips to between her legs. There was nothing tentative about his caress. It was boldly assertive...and the contact of his fingers against such a sensitive area shocked her so much she gasped.

But she liked it... And as he started to caress her *she liked it too much*. She shuddered with need as his mouth captured hers again, his tongue mimicking his fingers, invading her senses and taking over her mind, until she couldn't think about anything except here and now and wanting him.

Then suddenly he pulled away from her. Her breathing was

ragged and uneven and she couldn't get it under control—just as she couldn't stop the pounding need that was still flowing through her body.

'I think we should take this somewhere a little more comfortable, don't you?' he said softly.

She felt dizzy as she looked up at him, and she wasn't sure if that was due to the need he had stirred up in her, or if it was the tilt and flow of the ship as the vessel skimmed through the darkness.

From somewhere a little voice of reason tried to tell her to say no, to walk away. But it was like a voice trying to whisper down a tropical storm—a voice drowned out by the fierce elements of Mother Nature.

He bent and kissed her again, and hunger lanced through her. OK, this was madness, but maybe if she slept with him these feelings would leave her…maybe she would be free of needing him for evermore?

Marco didn't even wait for her acquiescence. He swept her up into his arms and carried her along the deck.

Her heart was thundering out of control as he opened the door into a cabin and placed her down.

She stared up at him, her eyes wide, her silky hair dishevelled around her shoulders, and Marco thought that he had never seen a woman as lovely.

Shyly her eyes moved away from him and around their luxurious surroundings, to linger on the massive double bed.

How many other women had Marco seduced in here? The thought flicked through her mind in a moment of sanity, like a glimpse of clear sky in the midst of a storm. It wasn't too late to say no—to tell him that this wasn't what she wanted.

Except that it was what she wanted. Had been from almost the first moment she'd seen him. He was right.

Marco had taken his jacket off and was unbuttoning his shirt now. He had the most incredible body, she thought hazily.

Powerful, wide shoulders, a hard flat stomach and lean hips. The body of an athlete.

He looked over and caught her watching him, and smiled. 'Come here,' he demanded.

For a moment she hesitated and stood where she was by the door.

'Come.' He stretched over and playfully pulled her closer. Then he sat down on the end of the bed and slid the robe she was wearing down from her shoulders, so that it crumpled to the floor by their feet and she stood before him naked.

'I've been wanting to do that from the first moment I saw you out there on the deck,' he told her huskily.

She felt her body burn as his eyes moved slowly and provocatively over her figure, assessing her with a passionate intensity that made her shyly discomfited whilst at the same time alive with desire.

'Now, wasn't this a good idea?' He whispered the words as he pulled her down onto his knee.

'I don't know…I think I've taken leave of my senses,' she murmured softly as she wrapped her arms around his shoulders. She loved the feel of her breasts pressing against his chest, naked skin against naked skin… 'But I suppose you are used to that…I suppose that is the effect you have on every woman you take to bed…'

He laughed. 'A gentleman doesn't talk about his previous conquests…you should know that.'

'Hmm… Yes, I should know that…' She raked her hands through the thick darkness of his hair and then drew her breath in on a gasp as he kissed her neck, then moved lower to kiss her breasts. 'I also know that you are no gentleman.' She breathed the words out in a wave of pleasure as his lips nuzzled against her nipple. She'd never experienced such breathtaking sensations; she wanted more—was greedy for more. How come no one had ever made her feel like this before? It was as if she were coming alive for the first time.

She bent and kissed his neck, biting him gently.

'And I knew for all that buttoned-up pretence that you'd be a wildcat.' He laughed and rolled her over, straddling her.

She was hardly even listening to him. All she could think about was how much she wanted him. And as his kisses became fiercer, more demanding, she met them gladly, giving herself to him and to the moment totally. They rolled over again, play-fighting as he pretended to try and hold her still.

'Ow!' She winced slightly as he caught her sore shoulder, and instantly his touch gentled and he leaned down to kiss the bruising.

Something about that moment made her want to cry.

She wrapped her arms around him. She liked his superior strength, liked the way he'd placed her, the way he knew exactly how to turn her on, exactly how to tease and torment her. But most of all she liked his tenderness.

For the first time in her life she felt like a woman—could feel the power she had over him. And at the same time she loved the overwhelming control he had over her. It still scared her…but she wasn't going to fight it….couldn't fight it.

Marco reached for the packet of condoms in his bedside cabinet.

'Better safe than sorry…hmm?' he murmured light-heartedly as he rejoined her on the bed.

His lips covered hers, and hungrily she returned his kisses.

It was only when he started to enter her that she froze and gave an involuntary exclamation of pain. Instantly he stopped, and looked into her eyes. 'Am I hurting you?'

'No!' she lied fervently, wanting him to continue, wanting the moment to pass.

He moved against her again, and she bit down on her lip. He *couldn't* find out that she was a virgin—that would be too embarrassing.

Marco pulled away from her with a frown. 'What's the matter?'

'Nothing. Why are you stopping?'

'I'm stopping because I'm obviously hurting you. Anyone would think you hadn't done this before...' His voice trailed away, and she could almost hear his mind ticking over.

'Don't be silly.' She reached up and stroked her hand along the broad contour of his shoulder, willing him to continue, but she couldn't look him in the eye.

He frowned.

No, she couldn't be a virgin, he thought derisively as he remembered the fire and the passion of her earlier responses. But then he found himself remembering other things...the way the chemistry between them had so obviously freaked her out. The way she'd tried to fight against it. The way she had sometimes looked at him as if she were scared of him.

'Isobel, are you a virgin?'

He sounded so incredulous that she felt her whole body suddenly turn cold with indignity. 'No!'

He knew in that one instant that she was lying. He sat up, and as she tried to wriggle away from him pulled her back.

'Isobel, stop it.' He pinned her down easily against the bed with just one hand. The other he used to turn her face, so that she was forced to look at him.

He asked the question again. 'Are you a virgin?'

'What difference does that make?' she blazed, her eyes on fire as they met with his.

'It makes a big difference.' He breathed the words softly. 'Believe me. If you'd told me, I'd have...' He hesitated for a moment.

'You'd have what? Had a good laugh at my expense? Taken pleasure in notching a virgin onto your crowded bedpost?' She cut across him fiercely, his hesitation hurting.

'I'd have taken more care of you,' he said quietly.

'Well, I don't want you to take care of me. This is just sex—no big deal.' Her eyes glittered, over-bright.

Was she trying to convince herself of that, or him? Marco wondered. He stroked her hair tenderly back from her face.

Sex obviously *was* a big deal for her. And someone had obviously hurt her a lot in the past. Who? he wondered. Her father? Or the guy she'd been engaged to? Maybe both?

He told himself that it was none of his business, that he only wanted a light-hearted roll in the sack. But he found himself cradling her against his chest. Then he kissed her again—kissed the tears away from her cheeks.

Hell, but she was so gorgeous…so feminine, so soft…so desirable. Amazing to think that such a body was completely innocent.

But how could he take her now, knowing what he knew?

'Sex *is* a big deal, Isobel.' He whispered the words against her ear. 'And I don't want to hurt you.'

'You won't hurt me,' she murmured, just wanting him to continue.

He drew back from her and looked into her eyes. 'I mean I don't want to hurt you emotionally…'

She frowned, the words causing a curl of sensation inside her that she couldn't even begin to understand.

He stroked a hand tenderly through her hair. 'The thing is I can't make you any promises, *cara*.'

The husky words made her frown, and there was an expression in his eyes that she couldn't begin to fathom.

'You're a player, I know…' Her voice sounded unsteady even to her own ears.

For a second he seemed lost in his own thoughts.

She had the opportunity to pull away, and she told herself that she should. But the fact that he was being honest with her somehow meant something. She'd rather that than lies.

'I don't need any promises, Marco.' She whispered the words softly. 'I just want honesty, and if tonight is all we have then that's fine.'

CHAPTER SEVEN

ISOBEL stretched languorously in the large double bed. Her body felt strange…achy…tired… And yet alive with feelings that just made her want to smile. Why was that? In the moments between waking and sleeping she couldn't think clearly—she wasn't even sure where she was as she rolled over in the bed and reached out into the space next to hers. It was only when she heard herself murmur Marco's name that her eyes jolted open.

What had she done? Even as she was asking herself the question memories were falling in on her—memories that caused such complete and utter panic that she hardly dared look across at the space next to hers.

She held her breath and quickly glanced, but Marco wasn't there. Holding the sheet firmly across her body, she forced herself to sit up and look around the room. He wasn't in the cabin either—she was quite alone.

Relief mixed with overwhelming consternation as she fell back against the pillow. She could hardly believe what had happened, or how easily she'd fallen into Marco's arms last night. She remembered kissing him as they'd stood together out on the deck—she remembered the wild pleasurable sensations, the feeling that it had all seemed somehow to be right, as if she had found a place that she belonged.

She stared up at the ceiling, trying to get her thoughts and her emotions under control. Every woman Marco kissed probably felt like that, she told herself angrily. The man was a master at seduction!

How had she allowed herself to fall for him? The question pounded through her, but as much as she searched there was no rational answer. It was as if she had been somehow bewitched—as if she didn't even know the person she had turned into. One moment she had been trying to cling on to sane and sensible thoughts, and the next...

Memories flooded back—memories of Marco sweeping her off her feet and carrying her down to this cabin—memories of him discovering that she was a virgin.

She groaned and rolled over, burying her face in the pillow. That should have been her wake-up call; she should have called a halt to things right there and then. But she hadn't wanted to!

And even now, as she thought about what had happened next, she felt a strange melting sensation deep inside. At first he had been so gentle with her, easing her through the moment of pain until she'd found enjoyment, and after that he'd seemed to glorify in awakening her body, sending her senses spinning, making her beg for more as he took her to dizzying heights of pleasure over and over again.

Her total lack of control horrified her. She'd always been so adamant that it wouldn't happen to her, but it had—and with Marco Lombardi of all people!

She'd even told him that it was OK if their night together was a one-off. And the strange thing was that she had meant it. She had wanted him so much that the only thing that had mattered was the moment.

A wave of red-hot heat enveloped her body, and hastily she flung the covers back and got out of bed.

It was best not to dwell on it, she told herself fiercely. OK, it was one night of madness. But people did that in today's modern world. It was no big deal because it would never happen again.

Somehow the words didn't make her feel any better.

But it was best forgotten, she told herself again. She was sure Marco had forgotten it already, moved on to something more important. The ship didn't seem to be moving, so they were probably at anchor somewhere in Italy and he was probably in some boardroom somewhere, his mind totally focused on his work. Sex, to a man like Marco, was just recreation— business was all-important. She should be the same.

Isobel headed for the *en-suite* bathroom, turned on the shower and stepped under its full forceful jet. She would concentrate on work now too, she told herself sensibly, and hopefully this time when she sat opposite Marco and tried to question him about his life all those undercurrents of sensual tension would be gone—played out—exhausted.

It was the modern way.

Desperately Isobel tried to ignore the little tremor of consternation at the thought of sitting opposite him again—at the thought of trying to behave as if nothing had happened between them.

She could do it, she told herself sternly—she *had* to do it. Because last night had been just meaningless sex, and to think of it in any other way would be a grave mistake.

Stepping out of the shower, she reached for a towel and wrapped it around her body. Marco's shaving gear was on the side of the hand basin, and she remembered suddenly how roughly abrasive his skin had been against hers last night— how somehow the feeling had been incredibly erotic.

She remembered how his kisses had moved lower down over her abdomen, then lower still, until her body had seemed to liquefy into pleasure.

Swiftly she shut the thoughts away and headed back to the bedroom. She couldn't afford to think about how much she'd enjoyed last night—not when she had to face Marco in a professional capacity today. Things were difficult enough—

especially as she had no clothes to wear except the robe from last night.

Reluctantly she picked the dressing gown up from the floor and put it on. As she did so she glanced at the clock on the bedside table.

It was a shock to find that it was almost midday!

She wondered if Marco was still at his meeting or if she would find him up on deck casually having lunch. The very thought made her nerves twist unbearably, and she glanced in the mirror to check her appearance.

She didn't look her best. Her skin was flushed, and her lips were slightly swollen from Marco's kisses, plus her hair was starting to dry in curls around her face. But who cared? she told herself firmly. She wasn't trying to impress. Marco meant nothing to her. *Nothing.* And she wasn't going to be one of those women who imagined she could change him—or that one night with him somehow meant something. That would be taking the stupidity of what she had done to the absolute limit.

Gathering her courage, she opened the door and headed up towards the deck to investigate.

The day was bright and warm, and the sky was a clear azure blue. Taking deep breaths of the sea air, she looked around. They were anchored in tranquil waters a little way out from the coastline, and she could see the colourful blaze of a busy harbour in the distance against a backdrop of mountains.

As she walked further along the deck she came to a dining area with a table set for one. The white linen tablecloth and silver cutlery gleamed in the sunlight.

'Good morning, *mademoiselle*.' A man of about her own age dressed in a smart black uniform came up from the galley. 'Are you ready for breakfast?' he asked as he walked over to pull out the chair for her.

The polite request took her aback somewhat—this was like being in a five-star hotel, she thought.

'Just coffee would be good, thank you.'

'Are you sure I can't get you something more? Scrambled egg…cereal…croissants? Monsieur Lombardi said you were to make yourself completely at home.'

'That's very kind, but just coffee, thank you.' She sat down at the table and watched as he went to pick up a silver coffee pot that was sitting on a side table. 'Where is Mr Lombardi this morning?' she asked, trying to sound casual, as if she didn't really care.

'He is attending a business meeting in Nice, *mademoiselle*.'

'Nice?' Isobel glanced towards the coast. 'I thought we were in Italy.'

'We were in Italy earlier this morning, *mademoiselle*, but now we are back in France.'

At least Marco wasn't on the ship. She relaxed a little at the knowledge. You see, she told herself firmly. Business came first with Marco, and that was exactly how *she* should be.

The rich aroma of coffee mingled with the warmth of the sea air as the waiter poured her coffee. 'The morning papers have been delivered, *mademoiselle*,' he said as he replaced the pot back down on the table beside her. 'And also a parcel for you. Would you like me to bring them to the table?'

'Yes, please.' She watched, intrigued as he disappeared down to a lower deck. The parcel probably wasn't for her at all—it was probably for another one of Marco's girlfriends. After all, nobody knew she was here so it couldn't be for her!

The waiter returned with a stack of papers and two gold boxes wrapped with red ribbon.

'So, were these delivered by boat this morning?' she asked, as she watched him spread the selection of papers out for her perusal.

'Yes, *mademoiselle*. No matter where we are in the world,

Monsieur Lombardi likes his papers delivered out to the yacht.'

Of course, Isobel thought wryly—everyone should have the morning post and papers delivered direct to their yacht. She smiled as she flicked her eye over them, deciding that this was a piece of information she would definitely include in her article. The papers were mostly in French and Italian, but she noticed a couple of English ones amongst the mix. They were all financial papers—no *Daily Banner,* of course.

She took a sip of her coffee before returning her attention to the boxes. There was a letter attached to the top one, and with a jolt of surprise she saw it had her name on it.

Quickly she slit the envelope open, and pulled out the crisp sheet of white paper.

Izzy, hope you slept well. Meet me for lunch at the flower market in Nice. Restaurant Chez Henri, one o'clock, and don't be late, Marco.

It was more of a summons than an invitation, Isobel thought as her eyes flicked over the bold, clear handwriting.

Hope you slept well, indeed! And how could she meet him for lunch when she had no clothes? Unless...

She looked at the boxes underneath, and quickly unloosened the red ribbon and lifted the first lid.

Nestled in amongst folds of tissue lay a silk dress in the most exquisite shades of green and purple. Even before she looked at the label she knew it was an expensive designer dress. It was in her size too!

She opened the next box and found a pair of gold Jimmy Choo high-heeled shoes with a matching clutch bag.

Isobel swallowed hard. Never in her entire life had she owned an outfit so beautiful or so expensive.

But somehow it didn't seem right, accepting such gifts from

a man she had just slept with. She felt a bit like a mistress or a kept woman or something.

With a frown, she put the lid back on the boxes.

She had to think sensibly. If she didn't accept the clothes she wouldn't be able to meet Marco for lunch. And maybe... just maybe...he would give her an interview today. Then she'd be able to put this episode behind her, go back to London and forget all about Marco Lombardi.

At exactly twelve-forty-five Isobel was skimming across the sea in a speedboat that was taking her from Marco's yacht into Nice Harbour.

As the boat slowed and entered the port she smoothed back her hair with a feeling of apprehension. She hoped she was going to be able to deal with this lunch in a purely professional way—that she could look at Marco and forget what had happened between them.

The boat pulled alongside the quay and a man in the same uniform as the man who was piloting her came hurrying to help her step out onto dry land.

Marco seemed to have a lot of staff; whilst she'd been lazing aboard his yacht this morning she'd counted at least five people wearing that uniform.

There was a limousine waiting for her next to the dock. And Isobel was aware of a few curious glances being thrown her way as a chauffeur got out to open the passenger door for her.

She wasn't used to so much attention, and she had to admit she felt good; the dress she was wearing was fabulous. It was perfectly cut, skimming over her curves in a very flattering way, and it even had short, feathery little straps that covered the bruise on her shoulder. It seemed Marco had thought of everything. All she lacked was some make-up—not that her appearance was important, she reminded herself firmly. Really she should be focusing on work.

Isobel looked out of the limousine with interest as they drove around the quayside. She loved the colourful buildings and the quaint old-world charm about the place. They passed pavement cafés and restaurants, and then swept past a huge memorial to the fallen of World Wars. Further around the headland she could see the Bay of Angels glittering in the sun, and the long sweep of the Promenade des Anglais.

The limousine turned off the main road at that point, through an archway into what looked like an old medieval part of the town, before pulling to a stop.

'Monsieur Lombardi is waiting for you,' the chauffeur told her as he opened the door for her and pointed towards a cobbled street lined with pavement restaurants.

She felt a bit like a nervous teenager on a first date as she walked in the direction the chauffeur had indicated. With determination, she held her head up high. This was just a business lunch, she told herself over and over again. It would be madness to think of it in any other way. She tried to concentrate on the beauty of her surroundings, the lovely old buildings in rich shades of yellow and umber, the profusion of flowers on the stalls in the centre of the street, the scent of carnations and lilies and roses merging in the warmth of the day with the French buzz of the market.

She saw Marco before he saw her. He was sitting at one of the pavement cafés, studying the menu, and he looked so relaxed and sophisticated in his dark suit and white shirt that she felt all her sensible thoughts immediately start to desert her.

Was this gorgeous man really waiting for her? she wondered dreamily. Had last night really happened, or had it been some kind of crazy hallucination? None of this felt real, somehow.

He looked up, and her senses flipped even more as she saw the look of surprise in his eyes as he took in her appearance. 'Izzy, you look great,' he said as he got to his feet.

'Thank you.' She felt suddenly unbearably self-conscious. She wished she was wearing make-up—she wished that she were as beautiful as the women he usually dated. A dart of anger rushed through her at the absurdity of that thought.

This wasn't a real date, she reminded herself firmly. And even if it were, she knew what type of man he was—knew that even if she were the most beautiful woman in the world, his interest in her would probably go no deeper than last night's sex. And he'd most likely even forgotten *that*.

'The dress suits you.' He took his seat again as she sat down.

'Yes…thank you. I take it you have a secretary who is good at shopping in her coffee break?'

He laughed. 'Actually, I saw it in a boutique window as I walked up to the office. But you are right—I have a very obliging secretary who ran out for it in her coffee break.'

And was probably used to doing such things, Isobel reminded herself matter-of-factly. 'Well, thanks anyway. I was a bit unsure about accepting it, but I thought arriving for lunch wearing a dressing gown might cause a bit of a stir.'

'I'm sure it would have done. Because you looked very sexy in that as well,' he told her with a gleam in his eye.

Maybe he hadn't forgotten last night.

She tried desperately not to look in any way uncomfortable about the remark, but she could feel herself heating up as she remembered how he had untied that robe last night—how he had moved his hands boldly over her naked body.

'So, how are you today?' he asked nonchalantly as he put up a hand to summon the waiter.

'Absolutely fine.' Isobel forced herself to hold her head high and maintain eye contact. She could do this, she told herself firmly. She could be just as casual as he—could forget all about what had happened between them.

'Good.' His gaze moved slowly over her. He'd thought that she would look good with her hair down and the right clothes, but he hadn't realised she would be this striking. Her long dark hair lay in glossy curls around her shoulders, and although she wasn't wearing any make-up her skin was smoothly perfect and her lips had a natural apricot glow. She really was naturally stunning, he thought absently.

But it was her eyes that held him—she looked so determined and yet at the same time so…defenceless. The combination intrigued him, made him remember how sweetly and innocently she had responded to him in bed.

'I enjoyed last night,' he told her lazily.

He watched with interest as the skin over her high cheekbones seemed to flare with a wild rose colour. He couldn't remember the last time he'd made a woman blush like that.

'Yes…it was…OK.' It took every ounce of Isobel's self-control to make the nonchalant reply. What she really wanted to do was to get up from the table and run as far away as she possibly could. She couldn't handle this. She was mortified… absolutely mortified.

He laughed. 'Yes, it was definitely OK,' he told her, and the husky, teasing warmth in his tone made her skin flush even more.

She looked over at him from beneath the long dark sweep of her eyelashes and he smiled. Yesterday he had wondered if that shy look was for real…now he knew that it was.

And she was obviously struggling to cope with this situation.

'So, how was your business meeting this morning?' She tried to change the subject.

'To be honest, it was an extreme inconvenience,' he told her softly.

'Was it…?' From nowhere she suddenly remembered how at one point last night she'd sleepily suggested that he forgot about business today.

'Absolutely.' His lips twisted in a half-smile. 'Another few hours in bed would have been most welcome.'

'Marco, I think you should know that I wasn't thinking very clearly last night…or this morning, for that matter.' She cut across him breathlessly. 'So if you don't mind I'd rather we didn't spend time analysing what happened.'

He smiled. 'Isobel, I kind of gathered that. Neither of us planned for last night. It was one of those things—chemistry, Karma…call it what you want.'

She nodded, and tried to tell herself that she was glad they'd had that conversation and cleared the air. Except as she looked over at him things didn't feel any less complicated.

'Now, shall we order some lunch?' he suggested matter-of-factly as the waiter stopped beside their table.

'Yes, of course.' She grabbed the menu and tried to study it. But she wasn't in any way interested in anything that was on it, and she was so wound up she didn't think she could eat anything.

'The seafood is good here,' Marco told her. 'Also the Salade Niçoise is a speciality of the region.'

Isobel grabbed on to the suggestion gratefully. 'I'll have the salad, then, thank you.'

Marco nodded and gave the order in perfect French.

She tried not to think about how sexy he sounded—tried not to think about anything connected with last night. But as he turned his attention lazily back to her she could feel herself heating up even more.

He seemed so perfectly at ease. But then she supposed he was used to going to bed with a woman without thinking deeply about it.

By contrast, as she looked at his hands all she could re-member was the way he had caressed her. When she looked at his lips she was remembering the way they had possessed hers. And as their eyes held across the table she wanted him all over again.

The knowledge twisted painfully inside her. So much for hoping he was out of her system! So much for being able to act as if last night had never happened! Her reassurances to herself about getting with the modern programme now felt hollow and foolish—like a very bad joke.

She didn't want to feel like this.

Marco's gaze drifted over her, taking in the vulnerable gleam in her eyes, the pallor of her skin. The chemistry was still swirling between them, and he knew he only had to reach for her to break down the flimsy defences that she was so desperate to construct around herself.

He was tempted to do that right now—because for the last few hours of his business meetings he had been distractedly thinking about possessing her body again.

But something in her eyes held him back, told him to bide his time, take this slowly.

She was his for the taking...but he found himself in the un-usual position of wanting to take things at a leisurely pace—of wanting to explore her mind as well as her body. He was inter-ested by the fact that he had taken her virginity—fascinated about why even now she was so scared of letting go and open-ing up to him.

Most women fell over themselves for so much as a smile from him...but she was different.

OK, since his divorce he hadn't wanted to get involved with any woman, especially a journalist, but he did have a little time on his hands before he took a business flight to New York in a few days, and she was...very appealing.

'Actually, I have some news for you. My deal with Cheri Bon was finalised this morning,' he told her.

'Really?' She sat up a little straighter. 'Are you going to tell me all about it?'

He smiled at her. 'I just might.'

For now he'd play along with her need to be businesslike—but after lunch things were going to change, he told himself determinedly.

CHAPTER EIGHT

THE sun was warm on Isobel's back. The food was good and the conversation stimulating. Marco was giving her the inside details of his takeover deal with the French confectionery company, and it was completely absorbing.

'When you make up your mind that you want something, you really go for it, don't you?' she murmured with a shake of her head.

'Don't you?' He looked at her humorously. 'Aren't you the young woman who hung around the Sienna offices for weeks to get the inside track on what was happening there?'

'I was convinced you were about to take the place apart...' She looked over at him guiltily. 'Sorry—but there was a factory last year in London that you *did* close.'

'Henshaws...' Marco shook his head. 'That company was dead in the water when I bought it, Izzy. It was the land that was valuable.'

'Yeah, well, I thought it was similar to what had happened at my grandfather's firm...and, yes, I realise I got it wrong.'

He shook his head and watched as she looked away from him. 'It still hurts you to think about what happened with your family's firm, doesn't it?'

She shrugged self-consciously. 'I just feel like an idiot for being shocked. I honestly didn't think my dad could hurt me any more than he had...'

Marco's dark eyes moved over her slowly.

'Anyway, let's not talk about that,' she said hurriedly.

'No, let's not. Have I told you that you are the first reporter that I've actually wanted to spend time with?' He leaned forward and reached to tuck a stray strand of her hair behind her ear. 'It's very curious,' he murmured huskily.

The words and the touch of his hand made her emotions flip.

She wanted to tell him that she liked spending time with him too. But she forced herself not to because that would be madness…emotional suicide. He was a player, she told herself for the hundredth time…and he was playing her right now.

His phone rang and he reached lazily to answer it, his eyes still on her face.

He was speaking in Italian now. She remembered how he'd spoken to her in Italian last night, and how she'd asked him to translate words in between kisses. The memory sent little butterflies dancing around in her stomach. They hadn't been loving words, they had been sexy, tantalising…provoking words, and just thinking about them made her feel hot all over again.

Frantically she tried to bury the memory—it didn't help.

Marco hung up and put his phone back on the table. 'Unfortunately I'm going to have to call by the office before we head back to the yacht. You don't mind, do you?'

'No, of course not.' The thought of going back to the yacht with him made her very apprehensive anyway. It was all very well keeping up a pretence here, while they were surrounded by people, but once they were alone…how would she deal with her feelings for him then?

'You know, I do believe there is a storm coming in,' he observed suddenly as he summoned the waiter to ask for the bill.

Isobel hadn't even noticed the weather until he'd pointed it out, but now that she looked around she saw dark clouds were sweeping in from the direction of the sea.

They left the table, and Marco reached to take hold of her arm as they walked through the square and then turned up a narrow side street.

Isobel told herself she should pull away from him, but somehow she couldn't make herself. There was something enchanting about strolling along beside him through the atmospheric streets. It was a little like stepping back in time, the houses were so old and picturesque, and some had windowsills packed with bright flowerboxes or canaries in cages.

'Is this your first time in Nice?' Marco asked as he noticed how she was taking in the surroundings.

'Yes…I've never been to the South of France before.'

'Really? Well, if we get some time I'll have to show you around.'

'That would be fun…' She glanced up at him, not sure if that was a serious offer or not. 'Although I'm not supposed to be on holiday.'

'Me neither.' He smiled. 'But we could play hooky a little.'

The teasing suggestion sounded good, but before she got a chance to answer it started to rain. Huge fat drops splattered down—slowly at first.

'Come on—we'd better hurry.' Marco's hand tightened on her arm as he picked up the pace.

The afternoon was growing strangely dark, and a low growl of thunder tore through the air, reverberating through the narrow streets.

People were scattering for cover now, and the rain suddenly started to lash with torrential force—as if someone was tipping buckets down from the heavens.

One moment Isobel was a little wet, and the next she was soaked.

Marco pulled her into the shelter of the first doorway. There wasn't much room, and they huddled closely under the small awning, watching the rain bounce and people running.

'Wow! What's happened to the day?' she laughed.

'When it rains here it really rains—that's why the countryside is so lush and green.' Marco turned his attention from the weather to her, his dark eyes moving over her in concern. 'Are you OK?'

'I'm fine.'

He brushed a wet strand of hair back from her face. 'You're completely soaked.'

'So are you.' For a moment all she could do was look up at him. And suddenly the rain was forgotten as she noticed how his gaze had moved to her lips.

She wanted him to kiss her, she realised…wanted it so much…

As he lowered his head and his mouth captured hers she surrendered immediately to the warmth of his lips, kissing him back hungrily.

Marco released her after a few moments. 'It's a long time since I kissed someone in a shop doorway,' he said with a grin.

'Yes, me too. I think I was sixteen.'

'I think I would have liked to know you at sixteen,' he said teasingly. 'However, I think the age difference might have been a bit much back then.'

For some reason Isobel wished she'd known him at sixteen too…and that she had been a different sixteen-year-old—one who could have been carefree…one who could have kissed him and had time to while away an afternoon without care instead of rushing to get home, frightened by what she might find…

He looked past her. 'The rain seems to be abating. Shall we make a dash for my office? It's not far from here.'

She nodded. 'I can't get much wetter anyway.'

As they stepped back out into the street Isobel tried not to analyse what was happening between them. It felt too real… too good. She'd spent her life trying to be sensible and careful, trying to avoid heartbreak, and where had it got her? she asked herself fiercely.

Marco cut across to another road.

They were at the back of a large building now, which had electric gates. Marco tapped in a security code on the brass box on the post, and the gates swung open into lush gardens.

'Welcome to the Lombardi headquarters.'

The old mansion house was painted yellow, its white shutters thrown open to the day.

'I didn't expect an office to be quite this beautiful,' Isobel said in surprise.

'It was my mother's home when she was a child. It dates from the early nineteenth century.'

'What a shame to have turned it into offices.'

'I know, but it's conveniently located, and as I'm usually short of time, that's what counts these days.'

Marco led her into a grand entrance hall with a sweeping staircase. At one side there were doors leading through to the offices. The building had obviously been very sympathetically converted, so as not to take away from the natural beauty of the place, and from the glimpse Isobel had the results seemed to have led to a very pleasant working environment.

A secretary came hurrying out with a pile of post in her arms and spoke to Marco in French. Isobel wondered if she was the one who had been sent out to buy her dress. She was blonde and probably about eighteen or nineteen, wearing a black T-shirt and mini skirt with ankle boots.

She was very attractive, and Isobel couldn't help noticing how she smiled at Marco before she handed him the post and headed back to her office. Probably half his workforce was in love with him, Isobel thought idly. Even with his dark hair wet and slicked back from his face he looked too damn handsome.

'Right, Isobel, we may as well go and try to dry off and

have some coffee upstairs,' Marco said as he led the way towards a lift. 'I'll phone the chauffeur to come pick us up.'

Isobel thought that when they stepped from the elevator upstairs they were just going to be in another office, but when the doors slid back on the top floor she found herself in a very elegant apartment, with tiled black and white floors.

'This is lovely,' she murmured as Marco showed her through to the drawing room.

'Yes, I had the interior decoration done by someone who is an expert on the period. They've restored it almost exactly as it would have looked when it was first built.'

'It's very stylish.' She ran her hand over a piece of antique French furniture that looked as if it was worth a small fortune, then moved to the doors that led to the balcony. On a good day the view over the Mediterranean was probably spectacular, but today the sea was almost obliterated by dark clouds and lashing rain.

As Isobel looked out a vivid gash of lightning lit the sky.

'This storm doesn't seem to be going away,' she murmured. 'I'm almost glad we're not back on the yacht.'

'You would be perfectly safe out there. In fact it's very exhilarating to be out at sea in an electrical storm.' Marco had been flicking through his post, but as he glanced up the outline of her body distracted him. The damp dress was clinging very provocatively to her curves, highlighting just how fabulous her figure really was.

And as she turned to look at him he realised he wanted her right here...*right now.*

'But we don't need to go back to the yacht tonight. We can just stay here,' he told her huskily.

Isobel knew exactly what he was saying to her. There was no mistaking his tone, or the sudden predatory gleam in the darkness of his gaze as he looked at her.

The really scary thing was that she felt an answering

surge of need straight away, and she didn't want to fight it any more.

'That sounds…like a plan,' she murmured, her heart suddenly starting to thunder against her chest as he moved closer.

Her eyes were wide and jewel-bright as she looked up at him. How had he ever thought for one moment that she was plain? Marco wondered. How had he not noticed how lovely her bone structure was, how soft and inviting her lips were?

And as for her body… His eyes raked down over the firm thrust of her breasts against the silk fabric. Just looking at her made him grow hard with desire.

'You know, you looked great in this outfit over lunch, *cara…*' he murmured. 'But I have to say I like the wet look even better.' As he spoke he smoothed the straps of her dress down and bent to kiss her shoulder. At the same time he ran his fingertips over the wet silk, caressing the hard thrust of her nipples. 'In fact I think you should dress like this all the time.'

Isobel discovered she was so turned on she couldn't find her breath to answer him.

'I like being able to see the gorgeous thrust of your nipples…the pert shape of your *derrière.*'

'Marco!' She blushed fiercely, and he laughed as he gently tugged the silky material down a little further and kissed the exposed creamy curve of her breast.

'Have I told you how much I like that librarian-type streak you have?' he asked throatily.

'You mean…used to have…' she murmured unsteadily, and then gasped with pleasure as his head moved lower and his mouth found her nipple, the warmth of his tongue licking over her, tormenting her with wild pleasure.

There was a loud roar of thunder outside, and it seemed to echo the feelings that were blazing through her entire body.

She moaned softly, desire eating her away, and then his lips were on hers, silencing her, dominating her senses, until she felt she would go out of her mind if she didn't get closer.

'I want you right now, Izzy,' he breathed. 'I want to possess your body over and over again…until I'm completely sated.'

The words were a command, and they made her temperature soar. She wanted him right now as well. Her body was demanding fulfilment with an urgency that was taking her over, leaving no room for embarrassment or shame or any kind of rational thought.

He kissed her with a fire that seemed to sizzle through her entire body, and then he lifted her up to place her onto the table, sweeping the letters and packages there onto the floor with complete impatience.

He pushed up her dress, his fingers stroking up along the naked length of her thighs, and then roughly pulled at her panties, tearing the flimsy silk away from her.

She pressed herself closer, her legs wrapped around him. Then shuddered with pleasure as she felt the hardness of his body against the warm, sweet sensitive core of her.

'Where has my shy, sweet librarian-type gone now?' he teased. 'Come—let me hear how much you want me.'

'Don't torment me, Marco…' she replied, running her hands up over his shirt, trying to unbutton it and failing miserably because she was so impatient for him. 'You know I want you.'

He reached and unzipped her dress. It fell down, leaving her completely naked from the waist up. 'But I find I *want* to torment you, *cara*,' he murmured. 'I want to hear how much you want me.'

He said something in Italian…something that sounded hot and steamy and made her senses pound. Then his lips moved to nuzzle against her breast.

'I ache for you…' She closed her eyes on a wave of ecstasy.

'And I thought you just wanted to forget all of this and

be practical…' He looked up at her and watched how she blushed.

'I do… I mean, I did… But not now…'

He laughed.

'Marco, I…need you…right now…please!' Her eyes opened and met with his and he smiled. He knew he could make her beg for him…knew that all her sensible words over lunch meant nothing, that this chemistry between them was a long way from being over.

'Patience…*cara*.' He reached for some condoms that he had placed in his jacket pocket earlier. 'I need to put some protection on…'

'I don't want to be patient!' She sat further up. Her hair had started to dry and it looked glossy and gypsy-like, and her eyes were wide with need as they met with his.

He had never seen her look more beautiful than she did in that moment, and he felt his stomach clenching as he fought to keep control.

She slid slightly back and then boldly brought her hand down to stroke him. She wanted to be in control for a little while, she thought fiercely, and she wanted him now.

She saw the flare of heat in the darkness of his eyes, and then he kissed her lips hungrily and suddenly other forces took over. It was as if a wildfire had swiftly broken through the flimsy barriers they had tried to set up, and now it raged out of control, consuming them both totally. Neither of them was in control any more. Neither of them could think clearly any more. All they could do was fiercely try to get closer to each other, to devour each other, to try somehow to quench the flames burning so urgently inside them.

Contraception was completely forgotten. And when release finally gripped Isobel it was so pleasurable that she found herself almost dizzy with the wild sensations.

At that point it took every ounce of Marco's restraint to

try and pull back. They clung to each other breathlessly, and it took a while for any reality to return.

Her head was pressed close against Marco's chest and his arms were tightly around her. She could hear the heavy beat of his heart and it seemed to echo her own—as if their bodies were still in unison for those seconds. A clock chimed somewhere, the melodic silvery tones resounding through the emptiness of the apartment and merging with the heaviness of their breathing.

'What just happened?' She was the first to speak, her voice shaky with incredulity, and he found himself laughing, his hand moving to stroke tenderly over her dark silky hair.

'I think the South of France was just rocked by a major earthquake.'

She smiled sleepily; she didn't understand why she was behaving so wildly, so rashly. All she knew was that she liked being held like this and she didn't want to move away from him—because when she did she knew that she would start to question herself, and she didn't want to think that deeply right now. 'Well, I think we just about survived.'

'Just about,' he agreed lazily.

He'd never lost control like that before in his life—was always so careful about using contraception. It was as if a mist had come down over him and he'd only just managed to draw back at the very last moment after sating her.

He hoped it was enough.

It *had* to be enough he told himself, angry with himself.

'Marco, are you OK?' she murmured suddenly as the hazy mists of pleasure started to lift and she realised he was looking at her with a different blaze in his eyes now.

'We were playing with fire, *cara*…'

Isobel knew what he was talking about straight away—and that was amazing, because up until that minute she hadn't even stopped to think about it.

He saw the realisation dawning in her eyes, saw the sudden fear there. 'Marco, what on earth was I thinking?'

The panic-stricken question almost made him smile.

'Probably the same as me—only about pleasure.'

Her skin flared with heat. It seemed there was no limit to her stupidity around him. Horrified, she drew away from him and started to pull up her dress, cover herself up.

'Hey!' He put a hand under her chin before she could pull away from him. 'What just happened between us was incredible…and neither of us were thinking particularly clearly. Don't beat yourself up about this, *cara*…we are in it together.'

The gentle words and the touch of his hand made her want to melt back into his arms.

'Besides, I did manage to exercise restraint, so it's probably fine.' He pulled her closer and kissed her.

And when he released her her heart was beating in a different mode. There was something about the way he touched her that could turn her on so quickly…

She looked away from him hurriedly, not wanting him to know how he was affecting her—again!

'Maybe I should go and have a shower, or a bath or something.'

He smiled. 'Make yourself at home. The bathroom is down the hall to the right,' he told her easily, and watched as she smoothed down her dress before she slid from the table.

He should have taken more care of her, he told himself angrily as he watched her walk away from him. The door closed behind her and he moved to the window to look out.

What the hell had he been thinking? He'd been so careful since his divorce to keep an emotional distance from the women he dated. He didn't want to get involved with *anyone* on a deep level.

Which made the risk he had just taken with Isobel totally unacceptable!

It was still raining outside—hard, unforgiving rain that bounced and hissed against the tiles on the patio.

For a second he found himself remembering a day in California when the weather had been exactly like this. The day Lucinda had lost their baby.

He swept a hand through his hair as he tried to block the memory out. They had wanted their child so much, and he had never felt so helpless...so wretched.

But it was done...it was over. Lucy was getting on with her life putting it behind her, and he was doing the same. For him life now revolved around work, with the occasional casual interlude with a woman—and that was all he wanted.

He turned away from the window and noticed the letters he had swept onto the floor earlier. He found himself remembering how much he had wanted Isobel...how fiercely he had needed her.

He frowned and went to pick the envelopes up.

She was a journalist, he reminded himself tersely, so it was never going to be more than a casual fling.

OK, there was something different about her and even thinking about her now made him want her again. But some women just took a little longer to get out of the system, he told himself swiftly. That was all it was.

CHAPTER NINE

ISOBEL tore the dress from over her head and stepped under the pounding jet of the shower. Was it only this morning that she had sworn to herself that this wasn't going to happen again? What was wrong with her? Why was she being so weak?

She raised her head to the jet of water and allowed it to pummel down over her face as she tried to clear her mind. But nothing made sense—certainly not the fact that she hadn't even thought about something as vital as contraception. The very thought made her temperature rise with panic.

How had she gone from being so sensible and so determined not to make a mistake to the other side of the scale so quickly?

Marco was completely wrong for her...the antithesis, in fact, of everything she'd told herself she wanted in a man. She knew the relationship wasn't going anywhere—knew that when she flew home to London she wouldn't see him again.

And yet when he touched her, when he looked at her in that certain way, none of that seemed to matter. She still wanted him.

She got out of the shower and wrapped herself in one of the large fluffy towels. There was a hairdryer next to the dressing table unit and she gave her hair a quick blast with it, teasing her fingers through the long dark strands until it dried into glossy curls.

It was a few moments before she realised she wasn't alone.

Marco was standing behind her, leaning indolently against the open doorway, watching her.

She flicked the hairdryer off and their eyes met in the mirror.

'I made you a coffee.' He came in and put the china mug down on the countertop.

'Thanks.' Her heart started to pound as, instead of leaving, he leaned against the wall beside her. She noticed he'd changed out of his suit and was wearing jeans and a white T-shirt. She'd never seen him dressed so casually, and the look suited him.

'My clothes were a bit rain-washed,' he said as he saw her looking at him.

'Yes, my dress is the same.'

'You look good in the towel,' he said huskily.

She tried not to feel self-conscious as his gaze drifted down over her—after all, he'd seen her without any clothes, so being wrapped in a towel was an improvement in the modesty stakes. However, she still felt shy, and the situation felt far too intimate.

'Is it still raining out there?' she asked—more for something to say than anything else.

'Yes, it is… What is it you English say…? Throwing it down in cats?'

'Raining cats and dogs,' she corrected him, and smiled. Most of the time his English was absolutely perfect, but he sounded so…so *sexy* when he got it slightly wrong.

She put her coffee down again and tried not to think too deeply about that.

'So I gave the chauffeur the night off,' he said quietly. 'I thought we might as well stay here.'

Her heart seemed to do a crazy skip, and she tried very hard to ignore it and be sensible. 'Marco, do you think that's a good idea…? I mean, maybe we should be getting back to reality.'

'Maybe we should,' he agreed lazily.

'I should be focusing on my article and—'

'And you keep getting distracted,' he finished for her with a smile.

'Yes.'

'If it makes you feel any better I have a pile of paperwork I should be doing, and I feel equally distracted.' His glance moved to her curves, so provocatively concealed under the white fluffy towel.

'It doesn't make me feel that much better,' she whispered hoarsely.

'Well, let's see if I *can* make you feel better.' Marco reached and traced a playful finger over the edge of the towel. 'We will just have to make time count now…'

He didn't even wait for her to answer—just tugged at the material so that it loosened and fell to the floor.

One more night wouldn't hurt, he told himself as he reached to pull her into his arms.

When Isobel woke she was lying in Marco's large double bed, cradled in his arms. She loved being here with him like this, she thought drowsily, loved the feeling of her body held close against his powerful physique.

Somewhere outside church bells were ringing, and daylight was slanting in through a chink in the curtains.

She turned her head slightly and glanced up at him. His eyes were closed and his handsome features were relaxed, but she wasn't sure if he was asleep or not. For a little while she allowed herself to drink him in, her gaze resting on the sensual line of his lips, the square jaw, the dark thickness of his hair. No man had a right to be so good-looking or so good in bed, she thought hazily.

Last night had been incredible.

She wanted to reach up and trace her fingers over the smooth olive tones of his skin. But if she did she would probably wake him up—and if she woke him up he would discover that the sky outside the bedroom window had turned an oyster-pink and the sun was slowly starting to rise over the city.

And once he discovered that, their time together in this apartment would be over. He'd probably want to get back to work. She remembered last night he'd said he had a pile of paperwork waiting for him. Maybe he would even throw a few facts at her for her article and have her packed off back to London by nightfall.

She frowned, cross with herself for feeling down about it. She should be keen to get her interview and leave, and she shouldn't for one moment expect anything more. Because, according to the newspapers, since his divorce his relationships had lasted no more than two days max. And this was no relationship… She wasn't even his type… She didn't know what this was. She supposed her old sensible self would say it was some kind of madness…and she'd probably be right. But right now Isobel didn't want to acknowledge that.

Marco opened his eyes suddenly and caught her watching him. She blushed.

'Morning, sleepyhead.'

'Actually, I think you are the sleepy one. I've been awake for ages,' she retorted, trying to sound as if she was totally indifferent about waking up with him. 'I just didn't want to disturb you by disentangling myself.'

'Is that right?' He didn't sound in the slightest bit fooled. 'So how come you were snoring ten minutes ago?'

'I was not!' She looked at him in consternation. 'For one thing, I don't snore!'

'How do you know if you haven't slept with anyone before?' He laughed as he rolled her over so that he was pinning her to the bed.

His hands were linked through hers, holding them back

against the pillows behind her head. She wriggled a little to get free, but he didn't release her.

For a moment he just looked at her, hardly able to believe how beautiful she was with her hair spread out around her on the pillows, her skin all flushed from his teasing, her lips slightly pouted. She really didn't look like the same woman who had stormed into his office in her starchy buttoned-up blouse, that was for sure.

He frowned. 'And how come you *haven't* slept with anyone before?' he asked softly. 'When you are so…deliciously good at it?'

The husky question made her deeply uncomfortable. She really didn't want to discuss her sex-life—or lack of it—with him. 'Let's not waste time on my past, Marco.'

'Why not?' One dark eyebrow rose.

'Because I told you I'm not that interesting.' She tried to look away from him, but he nibbled on the side of her neck, making her laugh breathlessly, making her look back at him.

'Now, come on… As I introduced you to the sport in question, why don't you humour me with the truth?'

'A sport…? Is that how you see it?' She looked into his eyes and saw a flicker of emotion there that she couldn't quite work out.

'Well, maybe since my divorce I haven't taken it as seriously as I should…' His dark eyes moved over her solemnly for a moment.

The husky admission made her still. 'Because you've been so cut up?'

He hesitated. '*Sì*… Cut up, as you put it…' He added something else in Italian, and she would have given anything to be able to understand him.

'Marco, I don't know what you are saying.'

For a second he hesitated, and she wondered if he was

going to explain further, but then the expression in his eyes became veiled.

'Good, because what I said was not important,' he told her lightly.

She didn't believe him—because she had understood the bleak look she had glimpsed for just a moment. She wondered if he would have opened up more to her if she wasn't a journalist.

The thought made her frown. 'Marco, I—'

'Hey, what is important right at this moment is you…' He cut across her gently and released her hands to trail one finger slowly over the little frown marks between her eyes, smoothing them away and sending little shivers of desire through her. 'I don't think it is any secret that I enjoy making love—that I think it is one of life's great pleasures.'

The words made the shivers of need inside her escalate.

'But I was asking about you…and how you see things,' he finished firmly.

She wanted to be so much closer to him… She felt a dart of anger at herself for wanting it so much…for wanting to get inside his skin and know exactly what he was feeling.

If she did she might not like what she saw, she reminded herself fiercely. He was a master of evasiveness and a heartbreaker. And yet… There was something about him that made her just want to trust him. And she was starting to think that he wasn't as cavalier about his marriage break-up as she had first believed.

'Izzy, we are talking about *you*,' he reminded her firmly.

'Believe me, Marco, there is nothing mystical about my lack of experience. I just never got around to that…particular sport.' She hoped he would leave it like that.

But he was continuing to look at her, as if fascinated by her reply.

'It was just circumstances,' she whispered helplessly. 'My

mother was ill for a long time after her marriage broke up, and she went through a series of disastrous relationships…'

For a moment she was quiet as she remembered all the times she had hurried home from school, worried about what she would find.

'And someone had to be the sensible one…hmm?'

She shrugged. 'As soon as I was old enough I got a job in the evenings to try and support my studies—as I said, it was just circumstances.'

'But then you met someone and got engaged?'

'Yes…big mistake.' As he released his hold on her she managed to slide away from under him. 'Rob just caught me at a point in my life when I was feeling lonely. It was never a passionate relationship. In fact I think I thought of him more as a friend than anything else, and I was busy building my career.'

She sat with her back to him at the edge of the bed. 'When he suggested we get married and said that he was OK about waiting to consummate our relationship until our wedding night it sounded…romantic.' She bit down on the softness of her lip. 'Anyway, to cut a long story short, I called round to his apartment one night and found him otherwise occupied with another woman. We'd only been engaged a week.' She flicked a look over her shoulder at Marco. 'Silly me.'

'The guy sounds like an idiot,' Marco said brusquely.

She smiled. 'Thanks, but I think I was the idiot for agreeing to marry him.'

Marco's shirt was hanging over the side of the chair beside the bed, and she reached to put it on rather than walk naked across the bedroom. 'You know, we should be talking about you…not me,' she told him as she pulled it across her body and turned to look at him.

'We should… But despite what you say you are so much more interesting—especially dressed in my shirt.' There was a gleam in his eye that made her senses quicken.

Hastily she moved away from the bed, trying to think sensibly. 'You could get a degree in being evasive, you know.'

'Could I, indeed?' He leaned back against the pillows and watched as she walked around the end of the bed to draw the curtains back, admiring the long length of her legs, the sway of her hips.

'How's the day looking?' he asked.

She stood for a moment, admiring the view. 'It's perfect,' she murmured, gazing out over the red roofs and the clear blue sky towards the glitter of the sea. 'It's as if the storm has washed everything clean and it's all shiny and new.'

She turned to look at him, noticing the way he was watching her.

He was so vital, so extremely masculine and attractive, that it was difficult to drag her eyes away from him—but she did.

'Right, I'm going to see if my dress is dry. Do you want a coffee or something while I'm in the kitchen?' She headed to move past him out of the door, but he reached and caught hold of her arm and drew her back onto the bed beside him with ease.

'What I want is an early-morning kiss…' he murmured huskily as his lips claimed hers.

She kissed him back. She couldn't help herself. It just felt so wonderful.

'That's better…' He released her, and for a moment they just stared into each other's eyes. 'Now, I suggest you get dressed and then I'll take you out for breakfast and we'll make the most of this brand-new day together…hmm?'

She nodded. 'I'd like that, Marco,' she said softly.

When Marco had suggested breakfast she'd thought they would just wander through the city streets and find a pavement café, but instead when they stepped outside there was a shiny red convertible sports car waiting for them on the drive.

'Wow…this is a fabulous car,' she murmured as he opened the passenger door for her and she settled herself into the luxurious leather interior. 'I didn't see this when we arrived yesterday. How has it just appeared as if by magic outside your front door?'

Marco laughed as he went around to the driving seat. 'Sorry, *cara*, there is no magic involved, I just phoned down and asked a member of staff to take it out of the garage for me.'

'I'm still pretty impressed. Everything seems to run so smoothly and effortlessly around you.'

'Not always, Izzy…believe me, not always.' He found a pair of sunglasses on the dashboard and put them on. Then he flicked the ignition switch and the powerful car flared into life with a low, throaty growl.

It was a good feeling, driving down the Promenade des Anglais beside Marco. It was still early, but already the sun was beating down with some power, and the warm breeze that drifted in over them was deliciously refreshing.

She admired the scenery, and Marco told her a little of the town's history. He pointed out the Hotel Negresco, with its impressive Belle Époque architecture—probably one of the most elite of hotels, built with only the rich and famous in mind.

As they stopped at traffic lights Isobel noticed how women glanced over at Marco. The Italian car and the Italian driver were a head-turning combination, she thought wryly. Yet Marco seemed totally unaware of the interest.

'I thought we should take breakfast along one of the most scenic coastal roads in the world, the Corniche d'Or, and then head out to St Tropez.'

'Sounds great,' Isobel said happily. 'What time have you got to be back?'

He laughed at that. 'Izzy, I don't have to be back at all,'

he said with a shake of his head. 'There is no point being the boss if you can't take a day off when you want.'

She glanced over at him in surprise. 'Oh, right—I just thought you had lots of paperwork to do.'

'I have, but it can wait. Finalising the deal yesterday with Cheri Bon has freed me up a bit.' Marco found himself lying. He was supposed to be in a meeting this morning with his board of directors, but he'd rung to postpone it when Isobel had been taking her shower.

He still couldn't work out why. It was a long time since he'd put work on the back burner in order to spend time with a woman. But it was just a one-off, he told himself firmly. He deserved a day playing tourist—he'd been working too hard recently. And Izzy was remarkably good company...*for a journalist*. And good on the eye too, he thought, his gaze flicking over her curvaceous body. That dress looked great on her...although he had to admit he still preferred the wet look.

He shifted up a gear as they headed out of town. 'I think I'll ring and get the yacht to pick us up from somewhere around Cannes. We could sail the rest of the way down to St Tropez, or go over to the Îles de Lérins, if you'd prefer?'

'I'm happy to place myself in your hands...' She flushed as she realised what she had just said. 'If you know what I mean.'

'Yes, I know what you mean.' He smiled. 'And that's fine with me, *cara*,' he assured her softly. 'Let's just enjoy the day...hmm?'

It was amazing how one minute she could feel tense around him and the next blissfully relaxed. It was like being on some kind of rollercoaster. Best just not to think too deeply and go with the flow, she told herself as she looked out at the spectacular views.

They drove along the highway out of Nice, and through some little villages until they reached Cannes, with its glitzy hotels and palm-lined promenade. There were giant placards up everywhere, advertising the film festival, and Isobel read them with interest, recognising famous names with excitement. 'I forgot the Film Festival was on, I suppose the place will be awash with famous stars right now?'

'Yes, it will be pretty busy.' Marco nodded towards a building on the left. 'That is the convention centre, where the film festival is held.'

Isobel glanced over and saw the impressive red-carpeted steps where all the stars had their photos taken, and she remembered suddenly that Marco and Lucinda had been photographed there. Marco had been wearing a tuxedo and Lucinda a long white dress.

She remembered how stunning the actress had looked, and how everyone had commented on the fact that they made such an attractive couple.

She probably should question Marco about it now, but strangely as she looked over at him the words seemed to stick in her throat. She was loath to break the relaxed mood of the day. Or was the reason verging on something deeper...? By Marco's own admission he had been cut up by the divorce—was she worried about delving more for fear that she would find he was still in love with his ex-wife? Because she was starting to get the feeling he was hiding something like that from her.

The knowledge swirled inside her uncomfortably. If she didn't get her act together she was heading for a fall both professionally *and* personally, she told herself furiously.

It would make no difference to her if he were still in love with Lucinda, because her affair with Marco was a two-day interlude at most, she reminded herself sharply. She needed to get her story...needed to have something at the end of their time together.

'You've gone very quiet.' Marco looked over at her.

She shrugged. 'Actually, I was just remembering that you and Lucinda attended the Film Festival together a few years ago.'

'Yes…Lucy was in a film that was nominated for an award.'

The way he said her name sounded warm.

'That was a long time ago,' he said quietly.

Hell, in some ways it felt like a lifetime ago. They'd been happy when they'd been here, he remembered. Happy making plans for the future because Lucinda had just found out she was pregnant…

They stopped at traffic lights. Isobel watched as he adjusted the controls to increase the cold air blowing on them.

There it was again—that grim expression on his face. As if he was remembering something…something that really hurt.

Her heart thudded uncomfortably as she prepared to ask him what had happened. But she just couldn't… The time wasn't right now, she told herself fiercely.

Marco had been expecting her to follow through with the usual questions, but to his surprise she fell silent. He frowned. He really couldn't make up his mind about her at all; just when he thought she was reverting to type she became once more the rather vulnerable young woman who for some reason intrigued him.

'I thought we'd stop and have breakfast out of town. There's a lovely restaurant just a few miles out with great views,' he suggested casually.

She nodded. 'Anyway, the paparazzi will probably be out in force around here, so I suppose a retreat out into the country is a better idea.'

He laughed. 'Yes, there is that.'

Isobel leaned her head back. She wasn't losing sight of reality, she reassured herself. She would ask all the questions she needed to ask later. Why spoil the day by broaching them now? Why not just enjoy these moments with a handsome man?

The Corniche d'Or was one of the most spectacular roads Isobel had even travelled along. The dramatic cliffs were a red-gold colour that seemed to blaze against a backdrop of blue sea and sky and the road snaked around between them, hugging hairpin bends and giving amazing views down over sheer drops to the sea.

Isobel felt a bit dizzy at some parts, and was glad that Marco was such a good driver. A little further on they pulled in at the restaurant Marco had mentioned.

The views over the sea were breathtaking and they lingered on the sunny terrace, drinking coffee and eating *pain au chocolat*, laughing and talking about nothing in particular.

'I would never usually eat chocolate for breakfast,' Isobel told him a little later as they strolled along a white sandy beach. 'I feel a bit like I'm on holiday.'

Marco had to admit for the last few hours he'd felt more relaxed than he had done in a long time.

He smiled, and turned her around so that he could look at her. The breeze was blowing her hair around her shoulders in silken waves, and she looked young and carefree.

'So let's *be* on holiday,' he suggested suddenly. 'Let's call the yacht and sail along the coastline for a few days—making love at lunchtime, eating and drinking, doing *absolutely* what we want.'

The suggestion sent little thrills racing through her.

'And what about work?'

'What about it?' There was a gleam of devilment in his gaze. 'I have a meeting in New York in three days...I can give work a miss until then.'

'And what do I tell my editor? Because she will be asking for an update soon...'

'Turn your phone off,' Marco told her with a grin. 'Or tell her that things just got complicated.'

CHAPTER TEN

THE sun was beating down from an uncompromising clear blue sky, and the temperatures were spiralling into the mid-thirties.

Isobel walked to the rail of the yacht to try and find a cooling sea breeze, but there was hardly a breath of air stirring.

They were anchored out in the bay of St Tropez and, gazing out across the bright silver glitter of the sea, she could see the town nestling at the foot of green hills, with dusky purple mountains rising behind in the distance. The town seemed to sparkle in the sunlight, its terracotta roofs and bell tower like something from an Impressionist painting.

Isobel thought that it was probably the most perfect view, and she tried to store it away in her memory banks so that she could remember it on grey winter days to gladden her heart. She was storing up a lot of perfect memories, she thought with a smile. Because these last few days with Marco had been nothing short of idyllic.

On the first day they had sailed down the coast to Juan-les-Pins, where they had taken lunch and window-shopped around the most exclusive of boutiques.

Later, when Isobel had got back to the yacht, she had found all the clothes and the swimwear she had admired had been delivered to their cabin.

She had been mortified—and still was—but Marco had insisted that she needed a 'holiday wardrobe', and as she had nothing to wear other than the clothes she stood up in, she really hadn't been in a position to argue.

Isobel had never possessed such a wonderful wardrobe: linen dresses that flowed coolly around her body in the heat of the sun, silk evening dresses for dinner on deck, and the most sensuous of underwear and night attire.

For the first time in her life she felt desirable and glamorous... OK, not in the same league as Marco's usual womenfriends, but attractive just the same. And that wasn't just down to the clothes Marco had bought for her, but also to the way Marco made her feel. He'd been treating her as if she was special to him—had wined and dined her under the stars, had taken her out for meals and for picnics. They'd visited the island of St Honorat and walked through fields of wild poppies and olive trees, had sipped champagne in the shade of eucalyptus trees. Made love on the deck of the ship in the heat of the day and under the cool blaze of the stars at night.

It had been the most perfect three days of her life, and she didn't want their time together to end. But she knew it had to. Knew that tomorrow Marco had to fly to New York.

They hadn't talked about it, but the knowledge had lain heavily between them ever since they'd got up this morning. She'd tried very hard not to let it spoil their remaining time together, but there was a sadness inside her that was hard to ignore.

Marco was in his office now, taking his first business phone call in three days. And over dinner tonight she was going to have to broach the subject of their interview.

She'd got to know him during their time together, and she would now be able to write about his phenomenal rise to become one of the most successful businessmen of their times, would be able to discuss his wicked sense of humour, his poverty-stricken background in Naples, the fierce sense of pride that had made him want to make his own fortune rather than rely on his mother's family for backing.

But she still didn't know the real reason behind his divorce. All she knew was that when he mentioned Lucinda's name he sometimes looked unbearably sad, and it made a mockery of her previous suspicions that he hadn't cared about his marriage.

They were pulling up anchor, Isobel noticed, and the masts were being hoisted up. Suddenly she wished that Marco was beside her—that he would put his arms around her and tell her that everything was going to be all right, that this wasn't the beginning of the end. But there was no sign of him, and she knew she was being unrealistic—because although they'd shared a wonderful time together there had been no false promises. She knew exactly where she stood.

And this was the end.

When Marco stepped up onto the deck a little while later she was standing at the back of the ship, watching the white frothy wake they left in the water as they forged forward with some speed.

She seemed lost in thought, and whilst she was unaware of his presence he allowed his eyes to move over her, taking in every little detail of her appearance.

The long green halterneck dress that she was wearing was very sexy; it was cut low at the back, showing her honey-gold tan and her long straight spine to perfection. Her hair was twisted up on top of her head, leaving a few tendrils to spill down appealingly onto her shoulder.

Over the last few days he had watched as she had transformed before his eyes into a sophisticated and beautiful woman. Even now when he looked at her he had to do a double-take to remind himself that she was that little mouse journalist.

He moved forward, and she turned and saw him.

'I thought you'd got lost down in that office,' she said with a smile.

'Yes—unfortunately having a few days off has resulted

in an in-box jammed with e-mails and a hundred voicemail messages.'

'I haven't dared turned my phone back on yet,' she admitted with a shrug.

He noticed how she tried to smile, how she looked away from him so that he wouldn't see the spark of sadness in her eyes.

'No regrets, though…hmm?' He put a hand under her chin and turned her so that he could look into her eyes.

'No…no regrets,' she admitted huskily. 'I've enjoyed playing hooky with you.' She made her voice deliberately light. And it was true. She didn't regret a minute of the time they'd had together, and she knew the score.

'Me too…' He leaned closer and kissed her—a long, lingering, passionate kiss that made her melt with desire. 'Unfortunately I've had to move my flight to New York forward, due to a problem in the office over there. Which is the reason we're heading back to my villa now.'

'I see…' She suddenly felt very cold, despite the heat of the day.

'But we've still got tonight. I won't have to leave until about midnight.'

'Well…that's good.' She tried desperately to keep the tremor out of her voice.

For a while his eyes held hers. 'I've bought you a little something.' She hadn't noticed the long narrow box in his hand until he brought it forward with a flourish and handed it to her.

'What is it?' she asked with a frown.

'Well, open it up and see.'

With shaking fingers she did as he asked, and then gasped as she saw the emerald and diamond necklace that lay inside.

'It's beautiful Marco…but I can't possibly accept it.'

'Of course you can.'

She shook her head. 'You've bought me too much already.

I shall be leaving France with a large suitcase when I only arrived with an overnight bag!'

'And your problem is…?'

Her problem was that she would trade everything just for one more day with him, she thought, swallowing hard.

'My problem is that it's too much.'

'Nonsense. It's just a trinket—a token of how much I have valued our time together.'

He reached for the box and took the necklace out to put it on for her. Just the lightest brush of his fingertips made her ache.

'There…perfect.' He stepped back to admire the jewellery. 'I thought the stones would match your eyes and they do.' He smiled. 'You have the most incredible green eyes I have ever seen.'

'And you have the smoothest and most charming lines,' she said archly, and he laughed.

'That's what I like about you, Izzy—you always try to be oh-so-sensible.'

But not always with success, she thought wryly. In fact sometimes she felt monumentally stupid—because right at this moment she was starting to believe that she was falling in love with him, and that would be the most foolish thing ever.

The thought made her heart race with fear and she quickly dismissed the idea. She wasn't that stupid! This had only ever been a fling for Marco—she was so out of his league that she might as well have been from another galaxy.

'And while we are on the subject of being sensible, I have a few loose-end questions for my article.' She tried desperately to make herself sound businesslike.

'Well, we can't have any loose ends,' he said with that roguish gleam in his eyes that she knew so well.

'I mean it, Marco,' she said quickly.

'And so do I.' Marco reached for her and pulled her into

his arms. 'And we'd better tidy all those loose ends away...
later.'

'Marco...' She tried to be strong, but as usual his touch
was too hard to resist and she couldn't pull away.

'You know what I'd like?' he murmured, his hand moving
to the tie of her halterneck. 'I'd like to see you wearing nothing
other than that necklace.'

When Isobel woke up she was lying in Marco's arms and the
cabin was in darkness.

She wondered what time it was, and a rush of panic went
through her as she remembered that Marco was leaving tonight. She couldn't believe that she had fallen asleep when
they had so little time left together! But their passion had been
so intense, their lovemaking so frantic, that it had just wiped
her out.

'Marco? Are you awake?' She sat up a little, looking for
the clock.

'Yes...relax.' He drew her back down to him and kissed
her forehead.

'What time is it? she whispered, cuddling in against him.

'Time I was getting up. I was just trying to gather the
energy and the willpower to drag myself away from you.'

'Were you?' She hardly dared to believe that.

He rolled over, pinning her beneath him. 'Yes, I was,' he
murmured huskily. 'Something very strange seems to have
happened over these last couple of days. I think you have
placed some sort of weird spell over me with your journalistic
voodoo, because I can't seem to get enough of you.'

She smiled. 'Journalists don't do voodoo.'

'Yes, they do. They also speak with forked tongues.' He
kissed her on the lips. 'But, hell...it's some tongue...some
voodoo...'

'So why don't you stay and sample some more?'

As soon as the words left her lips she couldn't believe

that she had said them. She told herself to make some sort of joke and withdraw the suggestion, but as their eyes held she realised it was too late for that.

So she took a deep breath and continued. 'It's just a passing thought…but you could always miss your flight and spend one more night with me.'

He moved up onto one elbow, and for a moment she thought he was considering the option, but then he shook his head. 'I can't, *cara*. I have an important deal that needs signing.'

'Yes…of course.' She felt her skin stinging with colour as humiliation washed through her. She shouldn't have asked. What the hell was the matter with her? she asked herself angrily. 'You're right—we've played truant long enough. I have to get back to London.'

For a moment Marco wondered if he was doing the right thing. She really did look very enticing, he thought idly. He would have enjoyed another night with her… But then he reminded himself firmly that he really was behind with work, and really did need to get to New York as soon as possible. And maybe it was for the best that they drew a line under these last few days, because in the short space of time he'd known her she had started to become addictive—and that was never a good thing. He knew himself well enough to know that it wouldn't work. He wasn't cut out for cosy relationships—he'd already proved that to the world.

He looked into her dark green sparkling eyes and remembered how new she was to all of this. He really didn't want to hurt her. 'Izzy, you knew I couldn't make you any promises, and—'

'Marco, I can assure you I don't want any promises.' She pulled away from him, the humiliation inside her intensifying. 'I was just enjoying being in holiday mode—nothing more.'

She was sitting on the side of the bed, putting on a T-shirt.

'Have we got time for a coffee, do you think?' she asked lightly. 'I don't know about you, but I really could use one.'

'Yeah, that would be good.' He switched on the bedside light as she pulled on a pair of white-cropped trousers. She was still wearing the emerald necklace, he noticed, and it glinted with the same depth of fire as her eyes as she glanced over at him.

He wanted to reach for her but he forced himself not to. Instead he made himself get out of bed. 'I'll have a shower and see you up on deck.'

It was a relief to get out of the cabin—to stand on the deck and take deep shuddering breaths of the night air. What was wrong with her? she asked herself fiercely. She knew the score—why was she making a fool of herself by wanting more?

Marco was never going to be serious about her...they were a total mismatch. He went for beautiful models or famous actresses, and he detested journalists.

She wondered if he would have opened up to her more if it hadn't been for her job, and for the first time in her life she wished she did something else...

Trying to pull herself together, she made her way over towards the galley. She noticed they were moored by Marco's villa, and she couldn't help but remember the first night, when she had come running down here in her dressing gown. That seemed like a lifetime ago. She felt like a different person now—and certainly not one driven by her career any more, she thought wryly. In fact she had hardly given her interview a second thought over these last few days.

Surely Marco realised that...didn't he?

But whether he did or not it seemed to have made little difference. The only difference was that when she got back to London without her in-depth story she might find herself out of a job, she told herself angrily. And she really, *really* should care more about that.

There was no one in the galley—in fact, looking around,

it seemed that most of the staff had left the yacht. So Isobel made coffee herself and carried it up on deck.

Marco appeared a few minutes later. He was wearing a dark business suit with a blue shirt, and he looked so handsome she felt her senses flip.

'I bet you haven't really got time for coffee, have you?' she said huskily, noticing how he glanced at his watch as he walked over to join her.

'I do need to be leaving soon.' He took a sip of the drink and then put it down. 'I've arranged for a member of staff to pack your clothes and bring them up to the house for you. I think it would be better if you slept up there tonight.'

He sounded so crisp and businesslike. A million miles away from the way he'd been with her over these last few days. She'd thought she'd been gradually getting closer to him, but that had just been an illusion, she told herself fiercely. This was reality.

'Fine…' She shrugged, not really caring where she spent the night now. 'I'll arrange a flight home first thing tomorrow.'

'I've taken care of that for you. My chauffeur will pick you up at ten.'

'You've thought of everything.'

Everything except how difficult it was to leave her, Marco thought suddenly. With a frown, he glanced again at his watch. 'Come…walk up to the house with me. *cara*.'

He reached and took hold of her hand, and she wanted to pull away from him, to angrily tell him not to touch her. But she didn't…because she just didn't have the willpower.

They walked in silence for a while through the darkness of the gardens, following a winding path up through the lemon trees. She could smell their fresh scent mingling with rosemary and the wild honeysuckle that climbed over the arbour leading to the patio.

'There are some photos in the top drawer of my bureau

in the study,' Marco told her suddenly. 'They might help you with your article, so I want you to take them.'

'OK…what are they of?' she asked curiously.

'There are some wedding snaps of Lucy and I in the Caribbean. We managed to escape the glare of the press, so no one has seen them before. There are also some photos of my parents on their wedding day.' As they reached the top of the path he turned to look at her. 'And just for the record, Izzy, I *did* love Lucy very much.'

'Yes…I kind of gathered that.' She shrugged, and something made her add softly, 'So couldn't you forgive her?'

'Forgive her for what?'

'For…' She paused and wished she could see the expression on his face, but the patio was in darkness and he was standing in the shadow of the trees. 'I assumed she was the one who had an affair…' Isobel shrugged. 'She was an actress, and—'

'And therefore it follows that she had to be unfaithful?' He cut across her fiercely. 'You journalists are all the same, aren't you? Jumping to conclusions to the last.'

'I don't deserve that, Marco!' she snapped. 'I've gone out of my way not to judge—not to ask painful question, and not to intrude! Is that how you think of me? As—as just another journalist?'

The question lingered between them in the darkness, and when he didn't answer immediately she turned away, running up the steps, wanting to get as far away from him as possible.

He caught her by the arm just as she reached the front door.

'Izzy, wait.' He swung her around. 'That's not how I think of you.'

'Well, you could have fooled me. You haven't answered any of my questions about your marriage and I haven't pushed you.'

'It wouldn't have made any difference if you had,' he said

softly. 'I never had any intention of telling you anything about my marriage. At first because you were a journalist, and then because…because we were having too good a time, and I found myself switching off from the past.' He frowned. 'Not something I do very easily, if the truth be told.'

She swallowed hard. 'So what happened, Marco?' she murmured.

Marco was silent for a long time before he finally answered. 'Lucy was pregnant—eight months, to be precise—when she lost our baby.'

'God, Marco—I'm so sorry!' She looked at him in horror. 'Why didn't you tell me? I thought…'

'You thought like everyone else that our break-up had to be about infidelity.' His eyes were harsh as they met hers. 'But you don't have to be unfaithful for a marriage to break apart. Our divorce was about loss—the loss of a baby—and our complete inability to deal with it.'

'I'm so sorry, Marco! I'd no idea! There was never even any hint or rumour about the pregnancy.'

'Yes, well…as you know we both worked very hard to have our privacy. And Lucy had a big part lined up in a movie twelve months down the line. She didn't want any adverse publicity to ruin it for her, so she was waiting to sign the contract before breaking the news. She was small anyway, and carried quite neatly, so it wasn't too hard for her to hide behind loose tops. And as the months went by she didn't go out as much—became quite the homemaker. I think she was even starting to reconsider taking the part when it was offered to her.'

'So what happened?' Isobel murmured as he fell silent.

'What happened was a car crash.' Marco raked a hand through his hair. 'One moment we were driving through the rain, making plans for the future, and the next I was swerving to avoid a vehicle on the wrong side of the road.'

Isobel looked at him in horror.

'The strange thing was we were both unharmed...or so we thought. But I insisted on taking Lucy into the private clinic we were using—just to get her checked out. They thought everything was OK at first, and then she went into labour. Our son was stillborn three hours later. He was beautiful, Isobel...a beautiful little boy who looked so perfect...'

Isobel felt a cold shiver run through her as she saw the bleak expression in Marco's eyes.

'Marco, that's so awful... There's no words to say how—'

'Words don't help, Izzy... Believe me...nothing really helps. Because I will always feel guilty...always.'

'Why?' Isobel frowned. 'It wasn't your fault!'

He shook his head. 'Wasn't it? How do you know that? I was the one who was driving...'

'Marco, you can't think like that! It was just one of life's cruel twists of fate!'

He shook his head. 'Well, we will never really know that for sure, will we? The only thing I do know for sure is that it was the catalyst for our divorce. And I could have handled it better. We were both so devastated, both so driven to do anything to forget, that we started burying ourselves into our work. Things fell apart pretty quickly after that. But there was no affair, Izzy. Sometimes I wish there had been—it might have been easier. We could at least have hated each other.'

'And instead you still love her...?'

She didn't know if Marco didn't hear that question, because her voice was so low, so tremulous, or whether it he didn't want to answer it. But he made no reply, and at that same moment the limousine pulled into the drive behind him.

'That's my lift to the airport. I'd better go.'

She frowned. 'Marco, is this the first time you've talked about this to anyone?'

'Yes...and I picked a journalist...on my own front doorstep!' He looked at her with a raised eyebrow. 'Life can really throw some unexpected curveballs, can't it?'

'You know I won't say anything,' she whispered unsteadily.

'Well, I'm in your hands now, aren't I?' He shrugged. 'Izzy, I suddenly don't care what you write…just so long as you go easy on it for Lucy's sake…OK?'

'You don't even need to say that.'

For a moment neither of them moved. They just looked into each other's eyes.

'You're a pretty special person, *cara*.' He stroked a hand along the side of her face. 'And if I had to tell anyone about my marriage, I'm glad it was you.' Then he turned towards the car and was gone.

Isobel stood where she was until the red lights of the car disappeared into the darkness.

CHAPTER ELEVEN

'WHAT was Marco Lombardi really like?'

Isobel was starting to wish she hadn't come into the office today. Because if she'd had a pound for every time she'd been asked that she would have been able to fly first-class to the Caribbean tonight—or maybe New York. Not that she *wanted* to go to New York, she told herself categorically. It was just a passing thought.

'He was very charming, as you would expect, Joyce.' She answered the secretary's question cheerfully, and then gave a sigh of relief as the woman nodded her head and seemed to accept the set turn of phrase.

'I thought he would be. I really enjoyed your article about him, by the way. He sounds as if he's a genuinely good man... all those charities that he has supported for years in secret... how lovely is that? And he seems to have been genuinely cut up by his divorce. And of course he's gorgeous; you're *so* lucky to have met him.'

The woman walked away before Isobel had a chance to comment on that. She wasn't so sure about that last observation at all. Sometimes, as she lay alone in her double bed and thought back to those few days with Marco, she wished she had never met him...because she missed him too much. Other times she wouldn't have changed a thing.

It was seven weeks ago now. Of course she hadn't heard

from him, and she didn't expect to. *Nor did she want to*, she reminded herself heatedly, because it was just a fling.

Best to chalk it up as an experience and forget it.

Trouble was, it was hard to forget Marco when everyone kept mentioning him. She had written quite a sensitive piece on him, focusing on his achievements and underlying it with his sense of loss about his marriage break-up. She hadn't mentioned the child he had lost—had just said that pressures of work and the constant intrusion of the press had all contributed to put pressure on his relationship. And then she had talked about his tough upbringing and his early years in Naples.

Everyone had been fascinated as it had shown a totally different side to him—well away from his womanising image. The sales of the paper that weekend had gone through the roof, and her editor had been so pleased that she now wanted Isobel to do another article.

'Let's ring him up and see if we can do an informal "at home with Marco" item,' she'd suggested excitedly earlier that day. 'This time maybe he will allow us to send a photographer with you.'

Isobel had tried to tell her that Marco was a very busy man and probably wouldn't take her call. 'He doesn't like the press,' she'd reiterated over and over. 'He said this was a one-off interview to put an end to all the speculation about him.'

But her editor hadn't wanted to hear that, and she'd been summoned into the office today to discuss it.

Well, she was damned if she was going to contact Marco again, Isobel thought angrily as she gathered her notes together. She'd told her editor that she'd go with what she already knew. Maybe she could write about his house—describe the décor? Or write about his yacht or something? But nothing had been finalised.

As she put everything away into her briefcase Isobel was aware that she hadn't used the photos Marco had given her in

France. Instead she'd gone with old ones from the newspaper's archives for her article.

Which meant that she could have offered them to her editor today and taken some of the pressure off.

But for some reason she hadn't been able to bring herself to do it.

They were too poignant. They opened up all sorts of questions in Isobel's mind about Marco's feelings for his ex-wife.

Did he still love her?

She needed to switch off from the subject—go home and get some rest. Because she was tired—really tired. Probably due to the fact that she hadn't been sleeping too well. Her nights as well as her days seemed to have been haunted by thoughts of Marco Lombardi lately. Well, no more, she told herself firmly.

The rain was bouncing off the pavements outside, and Isobel lingered in the shelter of the lobby for a moment, wondering if she should ring for a taxi.

'Evening, Isobel.' Elaine, one of the receptionists, waved over at her. 'Loved your piece on Marco Lombardi—hell, but that man is good-looking.'

'Yes…isn't he?' Isobel tried to smile. If one more person mentioned Marco to her she thought she would scream—she was glad she'd been doing most of her work from home recently, because she couldn't have stood seven weeks of this.

'Are you writing another article about him? I believe he's back in London at the moment.'

'I think he's still in New York,' Isobel corrected her quickly.

'No, he's back in London. There were pictures of him in one of my gossip magazines a few days ago at JFK—it said he was heading back to London.'

Isobel turned slowly. She hadn't seen anything about that! But then she hadn't been as efficient with things as she usually was. Normally she bought a range of papers and magazines to keep abreast of current affairs, but she'd been feeling so tired that most of them were still unopened back at her flat.

'There are rumours that he will still be here to attend his ex-wife's film premiere. It shows in Leicester Square next month.'

'That will be a good photo opportunity, I wonder if Lucinda's coming over for it.' It took all of Isobel's willpower to try and keep businesslike.

'I don't know—I was going to ask *you* that.' Elaine laughed.

'Afraid I don't know anything more than you. I hardly know the man.' Isobel turned up the collar on her raincoat. She really needed to get out of here.

'Hey, do you want me to ring for a cab for you? It's a horrid night.'

'No, it's OK, Elaine. Some fresh air will do me good.'

Isobel stepped out onto the street. It was a relief to get out of the building and away from the awful, never-ending reminders.

The rain was icy cold, and it was more like winter than summer. She couldn't help comparing it to the warm rain in France. She remembered running hand in hand with Marco through it, laughing with him, kissing him… The memories made tears merge with the rain on her face.

Marco was back in London and he hadn't contacted her. She didn't know why she felt so hurt. It was hardly a surprise. He hadn't phoned her whilst he'd been in the States, so obviously he'd no intention of keeping in contact.

She was drenched by the time she reached the underground station and joined the throngs of people hurrying down the steps. It was the usual Friday night mayhem, and the platforms were packed.

Isobel hated the underground when it was like this. She tried to keep back, so that the crowds didn't hem her in, but as soon as the train pulled in she found herself swept along with everyone else and jammed into a small standing space in one of the compartments. She closed her eyes as the doors closed, and tried to imagine that she was somewhere else.

She only had three stops before she could get off, and usually the visualisation trick helped to make her feel less claustrophobic. Only today all she could visualise was Marco—and that definitely didn't make her feel any better.

Was he here for his ex-wife's premiere? she wondered.

Not that she cared.

The train stopped and more people got on. There was a smell of damp clothing and wet hair. Isobel started to feel a bit queasy.

Maybe next stop she'd get out, she thought frantically. Because she'd rather walk in torrential rain than feel like this.

Come to think of it she'd been feeling a bit queasy on and off all day.

Isobel's eyes snapped open.

In fact she'd been feeling tired and queasy and a bit tearful for a few days.

Weren't they the symptoms of pregnancy?

It was raining so heavily that Marco could hardly see out of the windows of the limousine. He was parked across the road from Isobel's address…and he'd been there for the last twenty minutes.

Where had she got to? he wondered impatiently as he glanced at his wristwatch. She surely should be home by now; the receptionist at her office had told him that he'd only just missed her, and her offices weren't so far away.

He was just wondering if he should come back later when he saw her rounding the corner—her head down against the rain, a bag of shopping in her hand.

'OK, thanks, Henry. I'll ring you when I want you,' he told his chauffeur as he climbed out from the warmth of the car.

Isobel had just opened her front door when Marco reached her side. 'Hello, Izzy.'

The familiar Italian tones made her whirl around in surprise.

'Marco!' She was so surprised that she could only stand and stare at him as the rain lashed down over her. Was he a figment of her imagination? she wondered hazily. 'What are you doing here?'

'Getting as wet as you.' He reached and took the shopping bag from her, noticing how cold her fingers were, how pale her skin was. 'Come on—let's get you inside, out of this.'

Isobel's apartment was on the first floor, and as she went up the stairs ahead of him she still felt as if she was dreaming—that he wasn't really here. It was only when he followed her in through her front door and carried her shopping bag over towards the kitchen that reality seemed to set in.

He was wearing a dark raincoat over the top of his suit, and he looked as incredibly attractive as ever. By comparison she felt like a total mess. Her hair was soaked through, and the grey trousers that she had felt so smart in earlier were sticking to her like a second skin.

'What are you doing here, Marco?' she asked again, her voice sounding strained even to her own ears.

'I thought that was obvious. I've come to see you.' He watched as she peeled off her raincoat and put her briefcase down on the kitchen table. She'd lost weight, he noticed suddenly; in fact she looked quite frail.

Isobel was well aware of that deliberate measured assessment of her figure, and it made her body flare with heat. How dared he look her over as if he owned her? She hadn't heard from him or seen him in weeks, and suddenly here he was, with his bold, sensual attitude... Well, to hell with that.

He didn't own her; in fact he had no claim on her at all—no right to be here at all.

'You know, I'm a bit busy right now. I've got a pile of work to do. So if there isn't something specific that you've dropped by for, I think maybe you should leave.' She tipped her chin up defiantly. OK, he thought he was God's gift to women, and most women would probably have agreed with that, but she was leaving the fan club, she told herself fervently.

Marco smiled. He'd almost forgotten how fiery she was, and how much he enjoyed that about her. 'Well, it's a good job I *have* called about something specific, then,' he told her, his gaze resting on the softness of her lips. Then he reached for her, pulled her into his arms, and kissed her.

Instinctively she kissed him back, her senses pounding in sudden chaos.

'There—that's better,' he said lazily as he let go of her.

She couldn't talk for a moment because she felt so shaken up. She hated the way he could do this, she thought hazily. One moment she was promising herself that she wasn't interested in him, and the next she was feeling hot inside and falling back under his spell.

'You shouldn't have done that,' she told him breathlessly.

'Probably not.' His gaze was still resting on her lips. 'But I'm glad I did. Now, I suggest you run along and get changed out of those wet clothes.'

'Marco, I'm not going to sleep with you.' She raised her chin firmly. 'We had a fling and it's over.' It took all her strength to say the words. 'If you think you can just turn up here and—'

He laughed. '*Cara,* relax—if I wanted to sleep with you we'd be in bed right now.'

'I don't think so!'

He was looking at her in that bold Italian way that made her body start to melt. And suddenly she realised it was prob-ably best not to try and argue that point. Because whatever chemistry had once been between them was definitely still there.

'Go and get changed, Izzy,' he told her again softly.

She hesitated for a moment. Then with a shrug moved away from him towards the bedroom door.

He really had a nerve, turning up here unannounced— and on a Friday night too, she thought as she opened up her wardrobe and rummaged through it for something suitable to wear. She might have had plans of her own…a date.

And serve him right if she had, she thought as she remembered he'd been back in London for a few days. How dared he come waltzing back in here, kissing her as if he had some God-given right to kiss her?

What was he doing here? The question sizzled through her.

And what was she going to put on? She didn't want to look as if she was making too much of an effort for him—but then again she wanted to look her best just to give her confidence a boost.

Her hands shook as she pulled out a plain black dress from the wardrobe.

You couldn't go wrong with a black dress, she told herself reassuringly. You could dress it up or down accordingly. Quickly she took off her wet clothes, dried herself, and then gave her hair a quick blast from her hairdryer.

'Have you eaten yet?' Marco called from the other room. 'We could go out and have a light supper somewhere, if you'd like?'

The invitation gave her butterflies of anticipation. Part of her would have liked to accept. But jumping when Marco clicked his fingers wasn't a good idea. She needed to be sensible. He was already arrogant enough. She didn't want to be some stopgap in his diary.

She took a deep breath. 'No, I've had a busy day—I don't want to go out, Marco.'

Probably just as well, seeing as she still felt queasy. The knowledge swirled inside her, making her nerves increase even more.

She slipped into the black dress and put some lipstick on. That was better, she thought as she gave her reflection a quick check-over in the dressing table mirror. At least she felt human again, and could hold her own with Marco now.

Taking a deep breath, she went back out to face him.

'So, if you don't want to go out, have you got anything in these cupboards that's edible?' He was in the kitchen, assessing the contents of her cupboards, and she didn't think she could have been any more surprised if she'd tried.

She hated to admit it, but he looked good in her kitchen. He'd taken off the jacket of his suit and rolled up his sleeves.

'Marco, what are you doing?' she asked, leaning against the doorframe to watch him.

'I'm raiding your cupboards—because I've just come directly from a meeting and I'm starving.'

'Don't tell me the mighty Marco Lombardi can *cook*?' She looked at him teasingly.

'Of course I can cook. I'm Italian. But I do draw the line at this.' He pulled out a packet of dried pasta from her cupboard and looked at her accusingly. 'What *is* this disgusting stuff?'

She laughed. 'Sorry, Marco, but you're talking to someone who never has much time.'

'Hmm… And someone who has stopped eating, by the looks of it.' He cast a glance over at her. 'You're fading away, Izzy.'

'No, I'm not!' Even as she denied the claim she knew he was right. She had lost a lot of her curves recently.

'Well, we shall just have to put up with this dried pasta…' He was scrutinising her olive oil now.

The oven was on and the kitchen felt cosy. There was

something nice about having him here like this, she thought dreamily.

But that was the crazy part of her talking. She'd liked spending time with Marco in France, and since she'd come back she'd missed him—had felt lonely. But that was most likely because she was ready for a new relationship. A relationship with the right man, she reminded herself firmly. And that wasn't Marco.

She needed to tread very warily.

He was starting to put away her shopping from the bag she'd brought home. *The bag that contained the pregnancy testing kit she'd just bought!*

The memory made her pounce and take the bag from him. 'It's OK—I'll do that!' she told him hastily.

He smiled at her. 'OK—and then you can pour us a glass of wine and watch a master at work.'

'There is no end to your arrogance, is there?' she said with a shake of her head.

'No point being falsely modest, Izzy. It gets you nowhere in life.'

She emptied the shopping and then, when she was sure his back was turned towards her, took the bag with the kit in it into the bathroom.

What would she do if she found she were pregnant?

The question burned through her.

OK, Marco was here now, and this display of domesticity was all very well—but it wasn't real. This situation wasn't real. He was doubtless just here on a whim. And deep down she knew that the last thing he would want was for her to tell him she was pregnant... He wasn't over Lucinda, and he wasn't over the child they had lost.

The reminder made her heart thump uneasily, and she hid the kit at the back of the bathroom cabinet.

She *wasn't* pregnant, she told herself soothingly. She'd had a period since she'd come back from France...hadn't she? The awful thing was she couldn't remember.

She closed the bathroom cabinet and leaned her forehead against the cool of the glass.

Everything would be OK, she told herself firmly.

It had to be.

As Isobel's only table was in the kitchen, they ate in there. Isobel dimmed the overhead light and lit some candles. Then as she sat opposite him she wished she hadn't—because it suddenly felt too intimate.

'So, what are you really doing here, Marco?' She forced herself to ask the question as he reached to pour her a glass of wine.

'I've called to see how you are. Is that really so surprising?' He looked at her with a raised eyebrow. 'We had fun in France, didn't we?'

'Yes, but...that's all it was—a bit of fun. I didn't expect to see you again.'

What she said was true. And he hadn't planned on seeing her again. He didn't want anything serious. But the strange thing was he hadn't been able to get her out of his mind since they'd said goodbye—and that wasn't like him.

He'd tried to tell himself that she was just a journalist, and that very soon he'd probably read about his marriage break-up in detail in the *Daily Banner*—which would make a mockery of those deeply sincere green eyes of hers. But that hadn't happened; instead she'd kept her promise, and her remarks about his marriage had been restrained...even insightful. And that had made him think about her even more. He'd found himself in video conferences, trying to focus on important deals, only to be sidetracked by the memory of her passionate kisses. Or in boardrooms about to clinch a vital deal when he'd remember making love to her on the polished table, their passion so strong, so impatient, he hadn't even been able to think coherently enough to wear protection.

By coming here this evening maybe he was hoping for some sort of closure on all of that.

'Well, I thought we had some unfinished business,' he murmured slowly. 'For one thing I wanted to tell you I read your article.'

'Oh!' She sat up a little straighter in her chair. 'That must be the first time you've ever opened up the *Daily Banner*! I'm honoured.'

'Yes, you are.' He smiled, but his eyes held steadily with hers. 'I don't know what I was expecting, but it wasn't the article I read.'

'Wasn't it?' She looked at him in puzzlement.

'You kept my secret.'

'Did you think I wouldn't?' Her heart thudded painfully.

'I never take anything for granted, Izzy.'

'Especially with a journalist?' She looked over at him with a raised eyebrow.

'OK.' He nodded. 'I should have trusted my instincts more with you. Sometimes I'm too wary. But I appreciate your discretion.'

The words were huskily sincere, but Isobel didn't really want his thanks—and if that was the only reason he'd come then she'd rather he hadn't.

'You don't need to thank me, Marco,' she said quietly. 'But you're welcome anyway.'

'I know I don't need to thank you…I just wanted to.' He looked at her quizzically. 'And something else puzzled me. You didn't print the pictures I said you could take.'

She shrugged uncomfortably. If anyone at the paper found out she had those photos and hadn't volunteered them her name would be damned for all time. 'When it came down to it I didn't need them. You can have them back if you want—I have them safe.'

He took a sip of his wine and let his eyes drift over her thoughtfully, but he made no reply. Something about the way he was looking at her made her senses stir. Hastily she glanced away, trying to remain focused on reality.

'I believe you are going to attend Lucinda's premiere next week?'

'You've been reading the gossip rags,' he accused sardonically.

'Well, actually the receptionist at work has. She told me you'd been back in London a few days and that that was the reason you were here.'

'Amazing, isn't it, how a receptionist somewhere can know so much about my life? More, in fact, than I do.' He shook his head. 'The truth is that I only touched down at Heathrow this morning. We had to stop off in Dublin on the way back from New York, due to some problems with a company I own there.'

'Oh…' Why did she feel pleased? she asked crossly. OK, he'd only just arrived back in the country—but he still hadn't made any attempt to get in contact with her in the weeks since they'd parted. 'And is it true about the premiere?'

'Ah…more complicated. Lucinda has asked me to attend. But it's not the reason I'm here.'

'Let me guess—you had other pressing business to take care of?' she said lightly.

'Yes, some very important business…'

The candlelight flickered between them, throwing his face into shadow. She noticed how his gaze moved towards her lips, and a shiver of need ran through her, twisting into an ache as their eyes held.

How was it that he could make her want him so much that it hurt?

It scared her.

Isobel looked down at the plates in front of them. They'd both finished eating a while ago.

'I should make us some coffee…' She tried to focus on being practical, to snap out of that kind of thinking.

'Izzy…?'

She looked back at him, her eyes shadowed.

'Are you OK?' he asked.

'Of course I'm OK.'

She remembered him asking her that the day they'd sat having lunch in Nice.

She remembered going back to his apartment—remembered how they hadn't even managed to make it into the bedroom in those first few moments because they'd wanted each other so badly.

She pushed the thoughts fiercely away. 'Why wouldn't I be?'

'Just checking.' He shrugged. 'We took a few risks in Nice didn't we…?'

Was that the important business he was talking about? Had he come to make sure there were going to be no unwelcome surprises a few months down the line? She stared at him and wondered what he'd say if she told him she thought she was pregnant. The words hovered on the edge of her lips…

But she wasn't pregnant, she told herself fiercely—and if she was she needed to come to terms with it before she discussed it with him.

'Yes, it was a bit crazy…' She shrugged. 'But you don't need to worry about me—I'm fine.'

She got up to clear their plates away to the sink.

'Maybe you should go, Marco,' she said suddenly.

'Maybe I should.' He stood up and walked over to stand beside her, his eyes moving slowly over her. 'But the thing is I don't want to go.'

'Yes, but it's getting late, and I'm a bit jaded. You know what it's like when you're working hard.' She wished he wouldn't look at her so closely.

'Maybe you should take some time off.' He stroked a hand

absently down over her arm, and it made memories of France
stir, made her heart start to race in a way she really wanted
to control.

'Well, it's the weekend, so I will.' Their eyes met, and she
saw that gleam in his gaze. 'Marco, we shouldn't...' The rest
of her words were drowned out as his lips captured hers.

'I know we shouldn't...' He pulled her closer. 'And I told
myself that we wouldn't. But, hell, anything that feels so right
can't be wrong—can it?'

She tried very hard to be strong. 'Not necessarily true...'

But they were the last coherent words she spoke.

Isobel woke in the early hours of the morning and cuddled
closer to Marco's warm body. She loved being with him like
this. She pressed her lips against his shoulder and closed her
eyes again. Dawn was breaking outside and rain was still
pounding against the windows. It might be a good idea just to
stay in bed today, she thought groggily. She felt a bit queasy
again. In fact she felt *very* queasy. She tried to fight down the
feeling, tried to think about something else, but it wouldn't
go away.

Hastily she got out of bed and hurried down to the bathroom. She just made it.

It was the first time she'd actually been sick, and she sat
on the side of the bath afterwards trying to gather herself
together again.

Was she pregnant?

She told herself that she should do the test now, but the
thought of it scared her to death.

Just say she was.

Could she go through with it? Could she be a single mother
and inflict an absentee father onto her child? And what if she
was like her own mother and found it hard to cope?

The painful thoughts made it hard for her to breathe. She
needed to do the test. She needed to do it *now*.

CHAPTER TWELVE

MARCO rolled over in bed and glanced at the clock on the bedside table. It was six in the morning, and he told himself that he should make a move back to his own apartment. He was playing with fire with Izzy.

He'd been so careful since his divorce about the women he chose to get involved with. He didn't want anyone serious in his life, and he'd made sure that his nights of pleasure had all been with sophisticated and experienced women who knew the score.

Then Izzy had come along, and she'd fitted nowhere into his scheme of things. There was a dangerous kind of magic about her...a magic that had made him forget the rules he'd laid down for himself since his divorce.

He should have called a halt to things when he'd found out that she was a virgin. He glared up at the ceiling. He should have walked away. But he just hadn't been able to resist her.

Just as he hadn't been able to resist coming back to her.

He swore under his breath and threw the bedcovers back. He had to get out of here.

He was almost fully dressed when he realised that Isobel had been gone from the bedroom for a long time. Leaving his shirt unbuttoned, he wandered out into the corridor to look for her.

He half expected to find her making a drink in the kitchen, but she was standing at the window, staring out at the morning.

'Izzy?'

She didn't look around immediately—didn't seem to have heard him.

She was wearing a bright blue dressing gown and she had nothing on her feet.

'You'll catch cold standing there,' he said softly. 'It's not warm in here.'

Isobel wanted to say that catching cold was the least of her worries. She turned and looked at him then, quietly taking in the fact that he was dressed. 'Are you leaving?'

He nodded, and started to button his shirt up as he walked closer to her. 'How come you're up so early?'

She looked about seventeen as she raised her eyes towards his—young and vulnerable, and far too beautiful for any man's peace of mind.

'I couldn't sleep.' She tried to smile. 'What's your excuse?'

'I always wake at six. And I have things to be getting on with.'

'Yes, me too.' Pride came to her defence. She really needed him to go because suddenly she just wanted to cry.

'Hey, you're supposed to be having a lazy weekend.' He put a finger under her chin and tipped her face upwards, so that he could scrutinise her properly.

Her skin was so pale it was almost translucent, and her eyes seemed much too large for her face. 'I think you've been working way too hard over these last few weeks.'

He sounded as if he cared. But of course he didn't, she reminded herself forcefully. 'Maybe I'm more like you than you think.' She found it suddenly hard to keep her voice nonchalant. 'My career tends to come first.'

Marco ran his fingers up along the side of her face, and as he caressed her he could feel her body trembling with reaction.

She wasn't thinking about work now, he thought with satisfaction. And neither was he.

God, he wanted her. Wanted to take her into his arms... take her back to bed.

She was the type of woman who could get under a man's skin very easily, he thought broodingly. Which was exactly the reason why he needed to leave...but weakness was setting in.

Isobel pulled away from him. She couldn't think straight... couldn't function when he touched her and looked at her like that.

And yet this was all just a game to him, she told herself angrily. He could have her right here and now in this kitchen, then go back to his apartment or hotel, or wherever he was staying in London, and just forget about her.

The thought was a sobering shot of reality, and as she stared up at him she found herself trying to imagine his reaction if she told him right now that she was pregnant. There was no doubt in her mind that he would be horrified.

'Anyway, Marco, you really need to go now.' She forced herself to keep her head held high and to sound as if she really meant it. 'I'm going to make myself a drink and turn on my laptop. I like to work early in the morning, when everything is quiet. I'm sure you are the same.'

He looked a bit surprised by her words, and she tried to take comfort from that as she moved past him and flicked on the kettle. It was good to take back a little bit of control. Marco was a man who had too much of his own way where women were concerned.

The last thing she wanted was tea or coffee—but at least it gave her an excuse to turn her back on him. Because if she looked at him she might weaken.

Marco leaned back against the windowsill and watched her for a few moments. He'd told himself he was leaving... but suddenly he was hesitating.

It was as if she'd woven some kind of spell in the air around her.

Well, if he had any sense he'd just get out of here now—because she spelt *danger* with a capital D.

'You're right—I do need to go.' He watched as she took a china cup from the cupboard. She wasn't even looking around at him.

'Just close the door behind you on the way out,' she said lightly.

The cool words made Marco glare at her ramrod straight back.

If he reached out and pulled her back against him she would change her mind—he knew that for a fact! She wanted him as much as he wanted her.

But would it be fair of him to do that when he knew he didn't want a serious relationship with her—*with anyone*?

He only had to think back to that day when he'd got his divorce papers to remember how he felt about commitment.

And Isobel Keyes was different from the women he usually slept with—she would want much more than he could give.

He watched as she made a pretence of opening a packet of tea. 'I do believe the rain has stopped now—if you hurry you won't get wet.'

Marco had been about to walk to the door, but that was his breaking point—because now he found himself catching hold of her arm to turn her firmly around to face him. 'So... no farewell kiss?' He looked at her mockingly.

She seemed almost to flinch away from him. 'Do you mean farewell or goodbye?' she asked softly, and he realised as he looked into her clear green eyes that he should never have gone that far. 'Don't make this any harder, Marco.' She whispered the words pleadingly as she looked up at him. 'Let's just leave things as they are, shall we? Before we irrevocably spoil everything. We both know this isn't going anywhere.'

He frowned. He'd said something like that the last time he'd wanted to finish with someone.

This wasn't right—he was the one who decided.

But he already *had* decided, he reminded himself firmly. As soon as he'd woken up this morning he'd known he should leave.

'OK, *cara*…' His voice held a husky tone. 'If that's how you want things.'

'It is…' She glared at him. 'It really is.'

For a moment his gaze held hers. Then he let go of her arm and nodded.

The door closed behind him quietly.

Isobel could hear his footsteps through the flat, and then the door closing behind him with a resounding thud.

There—she should be glad he'd gone, she told herself angrily.

So why didn't she feel glad? Why did she feel as if the world was caving in on her?

She felt sick again, and suddenly she was rushing for the bathroom.

Marco had reached the front door out onto the street when he stopped. What the hell was he doing? he asked himself suddenly. Did he really want to end things this way?

He remembered how she'd told him that her career came first. But if that were the case she would have told the truth about his divorce, and she would have published those photos he'd let her take from his house.

He remembered how sweetly she had returned his kisses last night, how passionately she had responded to him.

Then he remembered that gleam of hurt in her eyes as she'd turned towards him just now and told him to go—told him that it was for the best.

Somehow he didn't think it *was* for the best. In fact he was unexpectedly sure of it. He suddenly found himself turning around and making his way back upstairs.

Her door was unlocked, and he went back inside and headed through towards the kitchen. But she wasn't there. She was in the bathroom. He could hear her being sick, then the sound of taps running, and then silence.

He paused outside the door. 'Izzy—are you OK?' His voice boomed out in the silence of the apartment.

A stunned kind of stillness greeted the question, and then she whispered gruffly, 'I thought I told you to go away.'

'Are you ill?' He didn't wait for her to reply, but pushed the bathroom door open and strode in. She was sitting on the edge of the bath and she had just rinsed her face, and was drying it with a white bath towel.

'What the hell are you doing, Marco?' She looked up, horrified by his intrusion.

But he didn't pay the slightest bit of attention to her; instead he strode over and crouched down beside her, so that he could see her properly.

'Why didn't you tell me that you were feeling ill?'

The gentle concern in his voice and in the darkness of his gaze was almost her undoing.

'Please, just go away, Marco!'

He reached to touch her, but she flinched from him. 'I don't want you here!' She glared at him. 'I told you to leave.'

'I know what you told me!' He frowned.

'Well, then—go!' She was starting to feel hysterical—especially as he glanced towards the sink and saw the empty box from the pregnancy testing kit.

'Isobel, are you pregnant?' He asked the question in a stunned kind of way, as if he couldn't quite take in what was happening.

She wanted to laugh—except that it wasn't funny. And she couldn't find her voice to answer him—could hardly even look at him.

'Isobel, I asked you a question!' His voice was rigid with anger, and it made her gather herself together.

She raised her eyes to his then, and he could see the truth shimmering in them even before she answered. 'Yes, Marco, I'm pregnant.'

He stared at her for a few minutes, as if not quite digesting the information. 'I asked you last night if there were any… repercussions from our time together, and you said no—'

'I didn't know for sure last night. I'd only just bought the testing kit.'

'So you waited until this morning—found out you were pregnant and then calmly asked me to leave without saying anything!' His eyes seemed to lance through her like daggers they were so sharply furious.

And suddenly she snapped. How dared he be angry with her? How dared he rant and rave like this? 'And what would you have said if I'd told you last night or this morning?' Her eyes blazed into his. 'Would you have said, *Oh, darling, how wonderful. Let's get married and live happily ever after*?' She held up a hand as he looked set to interrupt. 'I was being ironic, by the way—I don't want a proposal. I don't want to marry you.'

'Well, that's OK, then—because I certainly have no intention of proposing.'

Their eyes held angrily for a moment before she hurriedly looked away. 'Well, at least we understand each other.'

'Do we?' He shook his head. 'I still don't understand how you could let me walk out of here this morning without telling me the truth.'

'For heaven's sake, Marco—let's face it: you could hardly wait to get out of here this morning!' She raked a hand unsteadily through her hair. 'And quite frankly I'm in shock. I don't even know how I feel about this…so I'm certainly in no fit state to deal with how *you* feel.'

There was silence for a moment as Marco digested her words. 'I guess we're both in shock.'

'Yes, I guess we are.' She buried her head in her hands.

'We had one moment of carelessness... It's so unfair when people try for months and years sometimes to have a baby.'

The words trickled through him, their reality pulling him up, making him think.

There was silence between them for a long time as he went over and over the situation.

'Maybe we should be looking at this in a different way.'

'What kind of a different way?' She stood up. 'Do you mean like an inconvenience that can be got rid of?' The words tore out of her breathlessly.

'No, I don't mean that.' He caught hold of her arm before she could push past him. 'I was thinking more along the lines of a child being a gift.'

'A gift?' Her voice wobbled precariously on the edge of tears.

'Yes—a gift that is precious...more precious than anything in life.'

As she looked at him she knew he was thinking about his son...probably remembering how he had felt when his wife had told him she was pregnant...remembering how he had felt when their child was lost. Her heart slammed painfully against her chest.

'You need to think very carefully about what you want, Isobel.' He took hold of her hand. 'I can afford to support a child.' He looked at her with a raised eyebrow. 'I can afford to support you both in a more than comfortable lifestyle.'

Why did those words hurt so much? she wondered as she looked into his eyes. Why had her heart lurched with hope just now...? What did she expect? she asked herself fiercely.

'So in other words you think this is a problem that you can just throw money at and it will go away?' She pulled her hands away from his, her eyes shimmering. 'We're talking about a child here, Marco—not a horse that you can shove into stables and forget about.'

'I know that.' His voice was dangerously quiet.

'Do you? Money isn't going to fix this, Marco. A child needs to feel loved and wanted.'

'And you think I'm incapable of loving a child?'

'No—I don't think that!' She stared at him. It was obvious that this pregnancy was stirring up all kinds of memories for him. That he was revisiting the loss of his son. She wanted to say that she thought he wasn't over the death of his child, the break-up of his marriage—*that he was still in love with his ex-wife...*

The words hovered precariously on the edge of her lips, but she didn't let them drop and pushed angrily past him into the lounge. She couldn't say any of those things to him because there was a small part of her that was scared to hear the answer.

'I don't know what I want right now,' she told him unsteadily as he followed her.

'You're thinking of terminating the pregnancy?' He sounded so deeply shocked that she spun to face him.

'No, I'm not saying that! I just...' She bit down on her lip. 'I always promised myself that I wouldn't have a child unless I could bring it into a settled environment. ' Her voice broke slightly. 'My childhood was so chaotic, Marco—I don't want that for my baby.'

She didn't realise she was crying until he came closer—until he reached and wiped the tears from her eyes with a gentle hand.

'I'll look after you, Izzy. I can't say any fairer than that.'

She supposed he couldn't—and she supposed that she should feel grateful.

But she didn't want to feel grateful. Because all she felt was sad and angry. She wanted so much more.

She loved him, she realised helplessly. Like an idiot she had gone and fallen in love with him. Even though she'd known it would never work.

She took a deep shuddering breath. 'I don't want your false promises, Marco—I'd rather be on my own.'

'I'm not giving you any false promises, Izzy. I can't...' He shook his head and then reached for her, pulling her into his arms.

For a moment she allowed herself to be held by him, tried to draw strength from him.

'I can't do the marriage thing again,' he said quietly, almost to himself. 'I have never failed at anything in my life—but I failed at that. So you understand why I will not be repeating the experience?'

'Yes, I understand, Marco.' She raised her head proudly then, and moved back from him. 'And I told you I don't *want* marriage. I don't want anything from you.'

'I'll set you up in a flat here in London,' he said decisively, as if she hadn't spoken.

'I beg your pardon?' Isobel took another step back from him. 'What the hell are you talking about? I *have* a flat! I don't need you or your charity!' She was glaring furiously at him now.

'This has nothing to do with charity! It's practicalities. You can't live here—'

'Marco, I want you to go!' She cut across him furiously. 'I don't want to hear about your practicalities, thank you very much.'

'You're not thinking straight—'

'Yes, I am.' She raised her chin and stared at him calmly. 'In fact I'm suddenly thinking more clearly than I have in weeks. Thank you for your offer, but I will not be accepting your help. I will not be leaving this flat, and I can take care of myself. Now, I want you to go.'

Marco would have argued with her, but for all her fire and determination she suddenly looked exhausted.

'I'll go, Izzy. But only for now. We will discuss this when we are both feeling calmer.'

'There is nothing more to discuss!' she told him heatedly.

'On the contrary—there's everything to discuss. Now, go and get some rest and I'll call you later.'

CHAPTER THIRTEEN

'I THINK your ideas for the follow-up article on Marco are good, Isobel. People will be very interested to read about his lifestyle in France and his lovely home. But you need a little more personal information.'

The more her editor said that to her, the more Isobel felt her blood pressure rising. They had been over and over this a hundred times, and the walls of the small office felt as if they were starting to close in on her. She should have made an excuse to get out of coming in to the newspaper today, she told herself angrily. Because she really wasn't up to discussing Marco.

It was a week since she'd discovered that she was pregnant—a week of feeling as if she was on an emotional rollercoaster. And as time passed the only thing she knew for sure was how much she wanted her baby.

'You really need to contact Marco again and discuss a few things,' Claudia was saying briskly.

She wondered what Claudia would say if she knew the truth—knew that Marco had been on the phone to her several times this week, demanding to see her. The whole situation was tearing her apart. Because she wasn't ready to see him— wasn't strong enough to discuss the situation with him, as he was demanding.

He'd come round to the flat a couple of times too, but she hadn't answered the door. She'd wanted to. And maybe that was the problem—maybe that was why she couldn't face him just yet. Because she was so scared of needing him—scared of being just like her mother, unable to cope without a man by her side no matter how wrong that man was for her. But she *wasn't* like that, she reassured herself fiercely. She didn't need anyone. And she would prove that to herself and to her child.

With determination she reached and took a sip from the glass of water on the desk and tried to concentrate. She really needed to wrap this meeting up.

'I know Marco Lombardi doesn't like the press, Isobel, but you've already managed to get one interview,' Claudia reasoned. 'If you could ring him and get a second that would be wonderful. Perhaps you could even ask him about all these rumours that are flying around regarding his ex-wife's premiere—is he going to be attending with Lucinda, and is there a chance they might get back together? That kind of thing.'

How was she going to extricate herself from this? Isobel wondered frantically. If she didn't agree she might never get out of the office, but she didn't want to cave in. She didn't want to ask those questions.

'I don't think that's a good idea, Claudia. My first interview was closure on the past for…Mr Lombardi.' She carefully avoided using his first name. 'He is totally sick of the press asking questions about him and his ex-wife, and he feels he's answered them now. If I start to ask more questions he'll probably just get so mad he won't even want me to write the piece on his homes.'

'I'm sure you can tread diplomatically around that—' Claudia was distracted by a commotion in the outer office, and she broke off to look out through the partition window.

'Gosh, there is a very good-looking man standing at Rachael's desk, and he's causing quite a stir of excitement amongst the staff,' she observed. Then she frowned. 'How strange! If I didn't know better I'd swear that Marco Lombardi had just walked into the *Daily Banner* offices! That guy is so like him it's uncanny!'

Isobel could feel her heart starting to slam hard against her chest.

Marco would never come here...would he? No, he hated the press, she reasoned calmly. This was the last place he would come. Even so, she leaned forward to look through the window, just to check, and to her utter consternation her eyes connected with Marco's.

'Do you know, I think that *is* Marco Lombardi!' Claudia stood up, her eyes alight with excitement. 'Good heavens, Isobel—how fantastic is this? Quick—ring down to the desk and get the photographers up here. Quick, Isobel!'

But Isobel couldn't move. She was frozen with trepidation as she watched him moving decisively in her direction. What did he want? What was he going to say?

The next moment the door swung open and he strode in. The atmosphere in the room was almost electric.

'Mr Lombardi!' Claudia approached him, and she looked and sounded completely awestruck. 'This is such an unexpected surprise!'

But Marco wasn't looking at her; his dark eyes were riveted on Isobel.

'Well, I was just passing,' he said coolly. 'And I thought I'd call in to see you, Isobel—seeing as you never seem to be in when I call by your apartment.'

Isobel was vaguely aware that Claudia's eyebrows had risen so high they'd almost disappeared into her hairline.

How the hell should she answer that? she wondered furiously. He was going to get her sacked!

So she took a deep breath, tilted her head up, and said the first thing that came into her head. 'Gosh—you've called by the apartment? That was very good of you, Mr Lombardi. I...I just left that message on your answer-machine in the hope we could…eh…talk about a follow-up article. I never expected you to call round in person!'

For a second there was a flare of anger in the darkness of his eyes. 'Well, you should have expected that, Izzy… you really should.'

'Wow—this is absolutely fantastic!' Claudia was fluttering around as if her numbers had just come up on the lottery. 'I didn't know Isobel had already left a message for you! The thing is, we are most eager to do a section on your home in the South of France.'

'Is that so?' Marco grated the words sardonically, his eyes never leaving Isobel's face.

'Yes, we were just discussing it now, as a matter of fact. We were hoping to persuade you to allow us to send some photographers—and Isobel has lots of questions to put to you about your trip to London and your ex-wife's premiere.'

'Well, perhaps I could have a word with your employee alone for a moment, Ms…?' Marco suddenly transferred his attention from Isobel to the other woman and smiled. She practically swooned.

'Miss Jones—but please call me Claudia.'

'Claudia.' He took her hand and shook it. 'I think we might just have some crossed wires here, so if you would give us a moment…?'

'Of course… Take all the time you want. I'll… Um… I'll be outside, in my secretary's office…'

'Lovely.' Marco was opening the door for her, and before Claudia could gather her breath she was on the other side of it.

'What the hell do you think you're playing at?' Isobel asked shakily as soon as they were alone.

'Strange—I was just about to ask you the same question,' he drawled. He regarded her steadily for a few moments, and then took a step closer. 'Why have you been avoiding me when we have important things to talk about?'

'I'm not avoiding you. I told you I needed time to come to terms with…this situation.' She got to her feet and took a step away from him.

'Take all the time you want, but in the meantime we should be working this out together.'

'Look, you don't need to worry about me—'

'Tough. I *am* worried about you—and about my baby. We need to talk.'

'Shh!' Isobel flicked an agitated glance towards the door. 'Keep your voice down, for heaven's sake. Remember where you are!'

'I don't care where I am, Isobel,' he told her calmly.

'Well, you might when tomorrow's paper comes out and our…our business is broadcast all over the country,' she reminded him shakily. 'Marco, I work here! Please… I don't want my life turned upside down by people asking me questions right now—*questions that I really can't answer.* I thought you of all people would understand that.'

'So talk to me now,' he said steadily, his eyes holding hers.

'I can't.'

Her senses felt as if they were in freefall. He was so handsome, so achingly familiar. And he was the person she wanted to open up to most in the world. She wanted to tell him how scared she was—how determined she was to be a good mother and not repeat the mistakes that had been made in her own childhood. How much she wanted this baby… *How much she loved him…*

But there was the problem. He didn't love her. So how could she say any of those things to him? The last thing she wanted was for him to feel obligated to stay around. She'd rather be on her own. She knew she could manage.

She took a deep breath. 'Look, Marco, now isn't the time or the place to talk about this.'

'So get your bag and leave with me, and we'll discuss it over dinner.'

'I can't.' She shook her head and glanced past him to the window. Her work colleagues were all pretending to be busy, but she knew that they were all watching through the glass window. 'Marco, we can't leave here together—think about it. It's going to cause too much of a stir.'

'So what?'

'I told you—I have to work with these people. They are going to want to know every detail of what you're saying to me now as it is. Look, I've got a scan booked in two weeks. Come with me to that, if you want.'

'Date and time?'

The abrupt question flustered her. 'Um…twenty-fifth, at nine-thirty.'

He nodded.

'Now, please just go.' She lowered her voice to a husky whisper. 'I don't want anyone to know about my pregnancy—it's too early. And I can hardly think straight, let alone make any decisions.'

'OK, I'll go—but you've got ten minutes to follow me out to the car.'

'Marco!'

'Ten minutes,' he warned her brusquely. 'Otherwise I shall come back in.'

Without another word he turned and left the room. She watched as Claudia tried to waylay him, without much success, and the next moment her editor was back in the room.

'Wow—what did he say to you, Isobel? Is he going to allow us to send photographers over to his house in France?'

'I'm not quite sure.' Isobel picked up her bag and her coat. 'He said he'd think about it.'

'And did you get a chance to ask about this premiere and his ex-wife?'

'No, not yet. Look Claudia, I have to go. I'll ring you tomorrow.'

It was an effort to get out of the building, and when she did, and saw Marco's stretch limousine waiting for her directly outside, her temperature soared.

'You could have waited around the corner, or something,' she told him in agitation as she got in and sat opposite.

'Nice to see you too,' he said with a smile. 'What took you so long?'

For a moment his gaze moved over her, from the tip of her high heels to the smart black business suit. The look made her go hot inside. 'I…I wasn't long. I was less than ten minutes.'

'Ten minutes and one week.' He fixed her with that steady look that so unnerved her. 'Why are you avoiding me?'

'I'm not avoiding you. I've spoken to you on the phone. I told you that the doctor has confirmed my pregnancy, and I've just told you about my scan. You're up to date. And I really don't appreciate being hauled out of work like this—my job is important to me. I need it.'

'Actually, you don't,' he corrected her softly. 'I told you I'd support you.'

'And I told *you* I don't want that. I want my independence, Marco—I need that too.' She looked away from him as the limousine pulled out into traffic. 'Can't you see that I'm doing us both a favour here?' she whispered the words unsteadily.

'No, I can't see that, Izzy.' He frowned and leaned forward. 'How do you work that out?'

'We don't love each other.' She whispered the words huskily. 'We had a fling and…and this wasn't supposed to happen.'

'No, it wasn't supposed to happen—but it has, and now we need to deal with it.'

The cool, pragmatic words just made the hurt inside of her escalate. 'And I am dealing with it. I'm facing facts. I want this baby, Marco, but you really don't. You're just trying to do the decent thing. And to be honest I'd rather you didn't. Because I know what it's like to have a father who pretends to want you when really he can't wait to get away—'

'Hold on a moment—you think I don't want this child?' He cut across her forcibly.

'I know you don't, Marco. I know you're not over losing your first child and I know how devastated you were—'

'Yes, I was devastated when my son died…and, yes, it's taken me a long time to come to terms with that.' He stared at her. 'But I *want* this baby, Izzy…I want it more than you can ever know.'

The honesty in those words made her eyes start to sting with tears. Furiously she blinked them away before he could see them.

'If you really genuinely feel like that, then I'm sorry… I shouldn't have tried to close you out.'

'Apology accepted—'

'But that doesn't mean I'm going to let you set me up in a flat or anything,' she added hastily. 'I still want to be independent.'

'Well, maybe I was a bit hasty with that suggestion…' He shrugged. 'How about we take it a day at a time from here?'

She nodded. 'But we should be honest with each other. If you're going to get back with your ex-wife then I want you to tell me up-front—'

'Izzy, I'm not going to get back with Lucy.' He reached forward and took hold of her hand. 'Yes, I loved her once—but we've both moved on.'

She wasn't sure how much she believed that. But for now it would have to do, she told herself firmly.

CHAPTER FOURTEEN

ISOBEL turned over the page on her desk calendar and smiled to herself. She was going for her first ultrasound scan today. And she was so excited that she felt like shouting it from the rooftops—she probably would have done too, except that she and Marco had agreed to keep the pregnancy a secret.

For one thing she felt as if it was tempting fate, telling everyone about it too early. And for another she didn't want her photo splashed across every magazine in the land, with all the speculation that would entail. She'd already been snapped by the paparazzi as she'd got out of his limousine that day he'd picked her up from the office, and then again the following week, having dinner with him. But she'd covered it by telling everyone that she was just interviewing him for the follow-up article. And everyone seemed to believe it.

Probably because she was nowhere near as glamorous as his usual girlfriends.

For a moment the notion made her frown, but she pushed it away fiercely. The important thing for now was that their secret was safe—and she didn't have to answer any awkward questions about the future because the truth was she didn't know where her relationship with Marco was going.

They hadn't slept together since the night before she'd discovered she was pregnant, and there was a swirling tension between them all the time. Sometimes Isobel ached for him to take her into her arms… And other times she told herself sensibly that it was best that he didn't. Because she knew that in reality he was only around because she was expecting his baby.

And she suspected that despite his protestations to the contrary he *did* still love Lucinda.

The actress was now in London, for the premiere of her latest film, and she and Marco had been caught on camera having coffee together in Covent Garden yesterday. The press had gone wild with speculation, saying that they were probably going to get back together.

Just thinking about it now filled her with pain. Annoyed with herself, she pushed her chair back from her desk. There was no point sitting here brooding—she needed to get herself ready for her hospital appointment. She'd said she would meet Marco there fifteen minutes before the appointed time.

Isobel had just changed out of her jeans and into a skirt and blouse when the front doorbell rang. For a moment she considered not answering it. She wasn't expecting anyone, and she was busy applying her make-up, but when she didn't go down immediately the bell rang again—loud and insistently.

'All right, all right—keep you hair on,' she muttered as she hurried downstairs and opened the door.

Marco was outside, and just the sight of him in his dark suit made her senses instantly spin into chaos. 'I hope you didn't just run down those stairs?' he enquired lazily, one dark eyebrow raised.

'Well, as you just rang the bell in a very insistent way, what did you expect?' she replied snappily, and he smiled.

'I expect you to think about that child you are carrying and resist rushing around,' he replied, and his gaze moved over her lazily. She looked lovely. Her long dark hair was loose around her face and her skin was radiant, her eyes bright. 'You look really well today, Izzy… No morning sickness?'

'No, it seems to have passed. What are you doing here, Marco?' She glanced at her watch. 'I thought we were meeting at the hospital?' For a moment she wondered if he was here to tell her he wasn't coming—that he had a business meeting to attend or a flight to catch.

She didn't like the cold feeling that thought stirred up inside her, so she raised her head defiantly. 'If you can't come that's perfectly OK,' she added hastily. 'I will be fine on my own.'

Marco noticed the way she held her head, the spark in her eyes. 'Of course I can come,' he said gently. 'I'm here to pick you up.'

'Oh, right…' She shrugged. 'I thought we'd agreed that it was best to meet there because the press might catch us going into the hospital together?'

'No—as you know, Izzy, *you* said that, not me.'

'Did I?' She tried to feign ignorance, knowing full well that he was right—she *had* said that. 'You'd better come in, then. I just need to drink another couple of glasses of water, so that the sonographer can get a good look at Junior.'

'OK.' He smiled at her. There was a part of him that wanted to pull her into his arms, break down that standoffish independent streak of hers… But he held back—just as he had been holding back since he'd discovered she was pregnant. He needed to tread warily, he told himself fiercely as he followed her upstairs and into the kitchen. She was so vulnerable right now. 'You've got ten minutes and then we need to leave.'

He noticed her hand wasn't quite steady as she reached to pick up her glass.

'Nervous?'

'No, not really.' She tried to lie, and then as she caught his eye had to smile and admit, 'Maybe just a bit.'

'It will be OK.'

'Yes, I know that.' She tried to keep her tone blasé. But something about his reassuring tone made her heart twist. 'Let's just get out of here, shall we?'

They didn't talk much on the way to the hospital, and as they walked into the antenatal clinic Isobel felt acutely conscious of the space between them. She wished so much that things were different, that they were a real couple—but that was weak and stupid, she told herself.

She needed to keep strong, and as independent as possible. Because this was obviously how things were going to be from now on—they'd be together for their child but that was it.

The knowledge made the ache inside her grow deeper.

She gave her name at Reception, and couldn't help noticing how the staff smiled at Marco. They all recognised him, of course, and all looked at her with curious eyes.

'Maybe it wasn't such a good idea for you to come here,' she said as they sat down to wait. 'It will probably be all over the papers tomorrow.'

'Do you care?' Marco's eyes held with hers.

'Yes, in some ways I do—because we are going to be bombarded with questions.'

He shrugged. 'Tell everyone to mind their own business.' He smiled at her. 'Like I did with you when we first met.'

She found herself smiling back.

'Ms Keyes?' A door opened and someone called her name, and a few minutes later she was lying on a couch.

This was it, she thought anxiously. Why was she so frightened?

Was it because she'd realised how much this baby meant to her?

She'd always wanted a family—even as a teenager she'd found herself dreaming about the kind of family she wanted. And her dream had always been the same: two girls and a boy, and a husband who adored her…and loved the children so much that he just lived for his family.

She must have watched too many Walt Disney films as a child, she chastised herself angrily. The adoring husband bit wasn't going to happen. She glanced over at Marco's face as he watched the sonographer put jelly on her stomach. He looked stern.

'So, is this your first child?' the woman was asking conversationally.

'Yes…' She looked over at Marco and wondered if he was thinking about his son. She wanted to reach over and take his hand. But she forced herself not to.

'Right—let's have a look.' The woman started to run the probe over her skin. It was a strange, slippery feeling, and the gel was cold. 'You can see your baby now, if you want to look at the screen,' the woman said in soothing tones.

There was silence for a moment, and suddenly the woman was frowning.

'Is everything OK?' Isobel was aware that her voice was strained.

'There's something irregular about the heartbeat.' The woman moved the dials and ran the probe over her stomach again. 'Try not to worry…'

Isobel's eyes met Marco's. Suddenly he reached and took her hand.

'I think I'll just nip out and get a second opinion.' The woman took the probe away. 'I won't be a minute.'

Isobel felt as if her heart was beating so hard in her chest it was going to implode. 'Marco, do you think something is wrong?'

'I think you should try not to get agitated—it's not good for you.' He moved closer.

'You mean it's not good for the baby!'

The minutes ticked by, and they felt like hours…weeks… years.

'I bet you wish you weren't here with me now!'

'Hey, of course I don't.' His eyes met hers again.

'Marco, if I wasn't pregnant you would probably be with your ex-wife right now, making up with her—you wouldn't be with me.'

'Isobel, I want to be with you.'

She shook her head. 'No, you don't. You're still in love with Lucinda...your photo was all over the papers today.'

'Hey, I told you we are still friends. I wanted to tell her about you...she deserved to hear it from me first. You're not starting to believe what you read in the papers, are you?'

'No...' She glared at him. 'Well, maybe!' she admitted reluctantly. 'I'm scared, Marco.' The words were squeezed out of her, her pride deserting her totally. 'I want this baby so much...'

'I know...and it's going to be OK.'

'I'm not so sure! But if the worst does happen at least you won't feel you have to stick around for me any more.' A tear rolled down the pallor of her cheek.

Marco felt the sharp pain of loss as she said those words. He wanted to 'stick around', as she put it. He wanted her so much—wanted to make everything right for her. Dear God, this couldn't happen... They couldn't lose this baby!

He said something in Italian under his breath, then, '*Cara*... you're not going to lose this baby! But if the worst happens I will still be here for you. We will work through this!'

She shook her head, all pretence at being strong gone now.

'*Cara*, I love you...' The words were wrenched from him, and there was an anguished look in the darkness of his eyes. 'I never wanted to feel like this again. I wanted to close myself off from emotions, bury myself in work—and then I met you, and little by little you made your way into my heart, into my soul... Now I feel like you are a part of me. I don't know how it happened. *I didn't want it to happen.* But it has.'

Silence swirled between them, and she wondered if she had imagined those words because she wanted to hear them so much.

'I've been fooling myself where you are concerned,' he continued huskily, 'right from the very beginning...'

'You really love me?' She stared at him, still too stunned to take it in.

'Yes. I was just too…stupid to realise it. Too scared of making another mistake.' He squeezed her hand 'I want this baby, Izzy…but I want you too. I've just been too wary of mucking up your life to tell you. Because I've mucked up before…I'm not a safe bet. And you look at me with such vulnerability in your eyes sometimes that I ache to take it away…to make everything OK… But I'm just so wary of making promises.'

'Marco, I told you I don't need promises,' she told him huskily. 'But I *do* need you to tell me you love me again.'

'I love you with all of my heart, darling Izzy…'

'And if there is something wrong with the baby?' The question tore through her fearfully.

'We'll deal with it together.'

He sounded so sure. Was she going to wake up and find this was all some kind of strange dream? she wondered suddenly.

The door opened and the sonographer came back into the room with a doctor. 'I just need a second opinion on something,' she murmured.

Once more the roller was placed on Isobel's stomach, and everyone was looking at the screen.

'Ah, yes…' The doctor nodded and pointed at the screen. 'You're expecting twins, Ms Keyes,' he said with a smile. 'And everything is looking good.'

Isobel felt dazed as they made their way out of the hospital and across to where Marco had parked the car.

'Did they just say that I'm expecting twins?' she murmured, and Marco laughed.

'Unless we are both suffering from the same defective hearing…yes—twins!'

They got into the car and just sat there for a few moments.

'Twins,' Isobel said again as she looked across at him, a look of wonderment in her eyes. 'And did you just say that you loved me?'

Marco smiled. 'Yes—all true.'

'So it's not some extraordinary dream?'

He shook his head.

'And you are not still in love with your ex-wife?'

'Oh, Izzy, no—most definitely no. We both let go of those feelings a long time ago. Lucy is very happy these days, and so am I—because for the first time ever I believe in second chances...'

Their eyes held.

'I love you, Isobel Keyes.' He said the words softly. 'You will give me that second chance, won't you? You will let me break down those wary barriers of yours and prove that I can be trusted...that I am good husband material?'

'Husband material?' She looked at him with wide eyes. 'I thought you couldn't do that again?'

He reached and stroked her hair back from her face. 'Back in that hospital, when I thought for a moment that we might have lost the baby, I suddenly woke up to the fact that I could lose you too...that you might just walk away. And suddenly taking a risk with love again was nothing...*nothing* compared to the agony of not having you in my life.'

'Are you *sure* this isn't a dream?' she asked shakily.

He shook his head. 'So how about it, Izzy? Will you let me take care of you, protect you...love you for all time?'

She started to cry.

'*Cara*...don't cry. I know you have trust issues, but I promise I won't let you down.'

'Oh, God, Marco—I love you so much.' She went into his arms then, and they kissed, and a kiss had never felt so good... so blissful...like coming home, she thought dreamily.

It wasn't until they broke apart that they realised the car

was surrounded by paparazzi, frantically capturing every minute of their embrace.

'Time to take this somewhere more private, I think,' Marco said as he looked into her eyes. 'Back to my place?'

'That sounds good to me.'

THE SHAMELESS LIFE OF RUIZ ACOSTA

BY
SUSAN STEPHENS

Susan Stephens was a professional singer before meeting her husband on the tiny Mediterranean island of Malta. In true Modern™ romance style they met on Monday, became engaged on Friday, and were married three months after that. Almost thirty years and three children later, they are still in love. (Susan does not advise her children to return home one day with a similar story, as she may not take the news with the same fortitude as her own mother!)

Susan had written several non-fiction books when fate took a hand. At a charity costume ball there was an after-dinner auction. One of the lots, 'Spend a Day with an Author', had been donated by Mills & Boon® author Penny Jordan. Susan's husband bought this lot, and Penny was to become not just a great friend but a wonderful mentor, who encouraged Susan to write romance.

Susan loves her family, her pets, her friends, and her writing. She enjoys entertaining, travel, and going to the theatre. She reads, cooks, and plays the piano to relax, and can occasionally be found throwing herself off mountains on a pair of skis or galloping through the countryside. Visit Susan's website: www.susanstephens. net—she loves to hear from her readers all around the world!

PROLOGUE

STRETCHING out his powerful limbs, Ruiz Acosta took the call from his brother Nacho in Argentina. Gazing out across the sophisticated cityscape through the elegant window of his town house, Ruiz knew he had come to love London as much as the wild reaches of the pampas, if not more. The contrast was extreme and the challenges different, but just as stimulating.

And the women?

Pale, harried, and bundled up in so many clothes it was impossible to imagine them freeing themselves from the many wrappings long enough to make love—

'Will I be home in time for the annual polo match?' he asked, refocusing in order to reply to his older brother Nacho's question. 'Wild horses wouldn't keep me from that brawl. Just make sure I have a stallion that can out-run Nero's fire-breathing monster and I'll be back in time to watch your flank, Nacho—'

'And the business?' the hard male voice interrupted.

'We're in pretty good shape. I've completed the reorganisation. I just have to approve one or two new members of staff. I'll be splitting my time between Argentina and London in future, but—'

'So long as you don't forget your family on the other

side of the world, Ruiz,' Nacho interrupted. 'You're the glue that holds us together—'

'Glue can stretch,' Ruiz pointed out wryly.

Not liking this challenge to his authority, Nacho changed tack. 'Have you heard from Lucia, recently?'

'Lucia? No. Why?' Ruiz sat up, hearing the change in his brother's voice. 'Is there a problem?'

'Our sister's gone off radar again—changed her number—'

'Lucia was always tricky.' And who could blame her with four older brothers looking over her shoulder? Ruiz reflected. But his sister's safety was paramount. 'I'm on it. I'll drop by Lucia's flat later to see if she's back, or if she left any clues behind.'

Nacho seemed satisfied now he knew Ruiz was picking up the latest family problem; his voice mellowed into a dark-chocolate drawl. 'Have you found yourself a woman yet?'

Ruiz laughed as someone, or rather something, nuzzled its way between his knees. 'No, but a dog found me.' There was a curse on the other end of the line, which Ruiz ignored. 'This great black mutt wandered in from the street while I was having some furniture delivered and made himself comfortable in front of the fire. Didn't you, Bouncer?'

'You've given the dog a name?' Nacho interrupted sharply.

'Not just a name—a home. Bouncer is part of the furniture now.' Ruiz ruffled the big dog's ears.

'This is so typical of you, Ruiz,' Nacho rapped, reverting to elder brother mode. 'You always were a sucker for waifs and strays. If anyone needs TLC, you're there before they know they need help. *Dios!* Get rid of the mongrel!' Nacho thundered.

'Butt out!' Ruiz fired back. They weren't boys now for Nacho to push him around. His brother should know that where animals were concerned Ruiz cut no corners.

'See you at the polo match,' Nacho growled, 'without the mutt!'

'Goodbye to you too, brother,' Ruiz murmured, staring at the silent receiver in his hand.

Nacho had issues. Having taken responsibility for his siblings when their parents died, Nacho sometimes forgot they were all adults now and that, having made his home in London rather than the pampas, Ruiz was independently successful.

Sensing his irritation, Bouncer whined. He stroked the dog to reassure him. 'I should make allowances for Nacho?' Ruiz queried as Bouncer's expressive eyes invited him to take a walk. His brother ran an *estancia* in Argentina the size of a small country and Ruiz supposed Nacho was entitled to have his off days. 'Okay, boy, you're right. Let's go,' he said, standing up.

A big dog like Bouncer needed hours of exercise. Not unlike his master, Ruiz reflected, catching sight of his swarthy, unshaven face in the mirror. It had been another long and ultimately disappointing night. None of the women he'd met in London appealed to him with their bony figures, heavy make-up, and uniformly dyed blonde hair. It would be fair to say he had become more than a little jaded. Perhaps Nacho was right and he should return to Argentina to find some sophisticated, black-eyed siren, full of the fire and passion of South America who could not only match him in the bedroom but who would share his zest for life.

That was the type of woman his brother Nacho could do with, to shake him out of permanent warrior mode,

Ruiz reflected wryly as he locked the front door. It didn't occur to Ruiz that a similar wake-up call might be waiting for him just around the corner...

CHAPTER ONE

I've always kept a diary. I'm a compulsive writer some might say. I've heard that in the absence of anyone else to confide in people often record their thoughts.

This is day one of my new life in London and my train is just pulling into the station, so I have to keep this short. To make sure everything is in line with the K.I.S.S. principle—which, just in case my journal is discovered a thousand years from now, stands for Keep It Simple Stupid, there are only two rules:

Rely on no one but yourself.

No men—at least, not until you are established as a journalist and can call the shots!

THERE was sleet dripping down her neck and a really old man had just decided Holly was the one who needed help. Was she trying to work out which bus would take her to the station? 'No, but thank you for asking—I just got here,' she explained. Chin up. Jaw firm. Smile big. Stop tapping diary notes into your phone and put it away. 'I'm waiting for a friend,' Holly added to reassure the elderly Samaritan. Well, it was almost true. She was waiting to get hold of a friend on the phone.

The old man wished her well and went on his way but with the brief moment of human contact snatched away again she felt doubly lost. It was the noise in London, the constant traffic and the mobs of people that took some getting used to when you had just arrived in the capital from a small market town. It didn't help that her winter coat was soaked right through, she was frozen, and her long red hair hung in sodden straggles down her back.

How could things go so wrong?

It wasn't as if she hadn't made the most meticulous plans before coming to London to take up the job at *ROCK!* magazine, carefully tallying her start date with an amazing offer from her best friend from school to stay in her central London garden flat until Holly could sort out her own accommodation. So how was it that the black cab that had brought her from the station to this faceless part of town had left her in front of a door that should have been flung wide in welcome but had instead been opened by a stranger who didn't even know her name?

Wiping the rain from her face, Holly pulled out her phone and tried to call her friend Lucia again.

'Lucia?' Holly exclaimed excitedly, forced to execute a little unplanned dance as she dodged spray from the traffic. 'Lucia— Can you hear me?' Holly yelled over a deafening soundtrack of horns tooting, grinding gears, and steel drums—

Steel drums?

'Holly!' Lucia shrieked with equal excitement. 'Is that really you?'

'Where are you, Lucia?'

'St Barts. Can't you hear the sea? Holly, it's incredible here. You'd love it—'

'St Barts in the Caribbean?' Holly interrupted, shivering as she bowed her head beneath a fresh onslaught of wind and icy sleet. Lucia was from a very wealthy Argentinian family, so anything was possible. 'Isn't it some unearthly hour there?'

'Dunno… Still partying!' Lucia shrieked as if to confirm this with a thousand friends.

'So…didn't you get my text?' Holly asked carefully.

'What text?' Lucia sounded bewildered.

'The one I wrote confirming I'd love to accept your invitation to stay with you this week until I find a place to live down here?'

'Breaking up…breaking up.' Lucia was shrieking with laughter now with her hand over the phone. 'This line is terrible, Holly,' she confided in a slurry voice. 'Why don't you just catch a plane and come over here?'

Er, zero cash? Zero bikinis? Zero desire to cop out of a life that had already been through the shredder…

Holly held back from explaining to Lucia that they might have attended the same school but, while Holly had been a full scholarship pupil, Lucia had been a new sports hall, an Olympic-sized swimming pool and a riding stables complete with indoor arena. Oh, yes, St Bede's School for Girls had had a very shrewd headmistress.

'So, where are you now, Holl?' Lucia demanded to the accompaniment of clinking glasses.

'Outside your flat. "Meet u apt 12/20th Nov",' Holly read the text from her phone, leaving out the bit about how Lucia 'cdnt wait', followed by ':-D' and a dozen exclamation marks.

'Did I send that?'

'Yes, but no problem,' Holly lied brightly.

Lucia groaned. 'I did! I said it would be okay for you to stay. I remember now. And it is okay. At least, it would be if I were there. And I sublet my part of the house. Oh, you poor darling, I completely forgot. Were they awful to you?'

'Actually—'

'But you can book into a hotel, right?' Lucia chirped before Holly could explain that the woman who had opened the door to her had been quite nice, if a little bewildered to find a stranger with a suitcase standing on her doorstep looking hopeful. 'Of course I can,' Holly soothed. 'I'm really sorry I interrupted your break, Luce—'

'No. Wait.'

'What?'

'The penthouse!'

'The penthouse?' Holly queried.

'The family's London penthouse is free! I'm sure it is.'

'The penthouse, where?' Holly said, frowning.

'Right there at the same address,' Lucia explained triumphantly. 'There's a spare key in the key box by the side door. Give me ten minutes to ring someone to make sure the penthouse is empty and find out what the code is.'

'Are you sure?'

'Is the sun shining in St Barts?' Lucia screamed with laughter. 'And there's a café right across the road,' she said. 'See it?' Lucia demanded, tense with excitement now she had identified a way out of the problem. 'Have a coffee and wait for me to call you—'

Holly stared at her silent phone. Only a member of the powerful Acosta clan could have a penthouse going spare in London, she thought wryly. Putting her phone away, she glanced across the road and saw the café Lucia had mentioned. The windows were all steamed up. It looked inviting, and also warm. But it also looked very smart,

Holly thought, losing confidence. The café was all black glass and bronze—the sort of place her boyfriend had frequented between those colossal deals he used to tell her he was brokering.

Her ex-boyfriend, Holly reminded herself as she started jiggling her cumbersome suitcase down the kerb. You didn't have to be middle-aged and weary to lose everything to a good-looking swindler, Holly had discovered. You could be young and ambitious, and think you knew it all too. But she wasn't going to let one mistake rule her life. She was going to forget Mr Crud-for-pants dipping his greedy little paws into her bank account, and start again. Right now her goal was reaching that café where she could have a hot drink and dry off while she waited for Lucia to call.

Choosing her moment, Holly launched herself across the road—only for her suitcase to get stuck at the opposite kerb long enough for a truck to drive past and soak her. She was still spluttering with shock when a huge black dog appeared out of nowhere and attempted to lick her dry. And now a hunk in jeans had joined the scrum. 'Here. Let me,' he insisted in a deep, husky voice with an intriguing accent. Lifting both dog and suitcase away, he tried to steer Holly off the road.

'Get off me!' She was spluttering with shock, her voice rising with each syllable as she attempted to push him away. But he was like a rock and what made it worse was that he was so incredibly good-looking—exotically dark, extremely clean, and very big—which made her feel correspondingly washed-out, mud-streaked, very clumsy, and annoyed.

'Sorry,' he exclaimed, turning away to comfort his over-excited dog.

'Can't you control your animal?' she flashed. 'Perhaps something smaller would be easier for you to handle?'

Holly's barb missed its mark by a mile. The man only seemed amused and succeeded in looking sexier than ever with his mouth pressed down as she ranted on. 'Bouncer is a rescue dog from the streets,' he explained, straightening up to his full, towering height. 'I still have to teach him manners. I hope you can find it in your heart to forgive him?'

The voice was as delicious as she had first thought, and she had stared for far too long into those dark, compelling eyes, Holly warned herself. But instead of standing on her dignity and ending this, she heard herself say, 'You could buy me a coffee and I'll think about it.'

'I could,' the man agreed.

Had she gone completely mad?

Was *Rule two: No men* out of the window already?

Hmm, maybe. The man was not only incredibly good-looking—tall, dark and handsome in the best possible way, which was to say a little rugged and not too contrived, with quite a thorough coating of sharp black stubble on his face and excellent teeth—but as well as an exotic accent he had an intriguing way of looking at her. His gaze didn't flicker away like some people she could mention, but remained steady on her face.

But was that a good enough reason to risk it?

'May I take your hesitation for acquiescence?' he prompted. 'You look frozen.'

She was. And the man's steady gaze was making her feel uncomfortable. She wasn't used to attracting interest from such good-looking men. Of course, it would have to happen when she looked more of a mess than usual. Typical. 'I suppose a coffee wouldn't hurt.'

'Strong, hot coffee is what you need,' he said firmly.

'But before we go inside, are you going to forgive my furry friend?'

How could she refuse a request like that? Her ex hadn't been able to get near a dog without it biting him, Holly remembered as the big dog stared back at her, panting hopefully. 'Forgiven,' she said, watching with interest as the man made a fuss of his dog, tempting him with a bowl of treats someone had laid out ready beneath the cafe's rain-proof canopy. He even pointed out the bowl of clean water—

'Bouncer's done a real number on your outfit,' he observed, turning round.

'Yes, he has,' Holly admitted ruefully. It wasn't so much an outfit as a motley collection of sale items she'd kept at the back of the wardrobe too long to take back to the store.

'How about I pay for dry-cleaning?'

'Oh, no. That's okay,' she insisted. 'The mud will wash off—'

'If you're sure? I'm happy to pay.'

A man offering to pay for anything was a first too, Holly thought. 'Really, I'm sure,' she said with a small smile, and then, embarrassed by so much concern and attention from a stranger, she turned away. 'Hey, Bouncer.' Predictably falling for the liquid brown sappy look, she started tickling the dog's ears, which Bouncer took as a cue to roll onto his back, waving his giant-sized paws in the air.

'You have a way with animals,' the man observed.

'When they're not trying to lick me to death,' Holly agreed wryly.

'Shall we?' he said, starting for the door.

In nothing more exciting than a pair of jeans, scuffed boots and a heavy jacket, he looked exactly like the type of man who could turn a girl's world upside down. Rebuilding herself after a devastating love affair meant stepping out and stepping up. It did not mean running away. And it was only a coffee.

The guy was so big he made Holly feel dainty as she walked past him, which was another first. She was built on a heroic scale, as her father always reminded her proudly before he gave her that second and rather concerned look—the one she was supposed to miss. But it wasn't every day a dog could coat her in mud and make her smile, or a man could hold her gaze for longer than two seconds. And at least he was polite, she reasoned as he held the door.

As the warm, coffee-scented air swept out to greet them Holly relaxed her guard enough to brush past him on the way in. The jolt to her senses woke her up and warned her to take more care in future. But it wasn't as if she was coming on to him, Holly reasoned. He was deeply tanned and film-star striking, while she was pale and not that interesting. But there was some common ground. She felt out of place in London and he looked about as much at home on a grey day in London as a polar bear on a beach—

And about as dangerous.

Once they were inside the café he reached behind the counter and grabbed a towel, which he tossed to her.

'Well caught,' he said as she gasped and snatched hold of the towel. 'May I suggest you wipe the worst of the mud off your clothes?'

'Won't they mind?' Holly said worriedly, throwing a guilty glance at the counter staff.

'They'll mind more if you don't wipe it off before you sit down,' the man observed, curving his attractive smile again.

Men as good-looking as he was could do as they liked, Holly concluded as she watched him return the towel with a few words of thanks to the staff. There wasn't one complaint. And why should there be? she thought as he shrugged off his jacket and everyone turned to look. Who wouldn't want a better view of that body? Holly mused as her gaze roved reluctantly past the well-packed jeans to the crisp white shirt with the sleeves rolled back to display a pair of massive forearms. Her day had definitely improved. Until the girls behind the counter started flirting with him and she felt a stab of something unexpected.

And a warning that drew a parallel between this man and her ex. The ex had been good-looking too, and had packed a certain degree of charisma—not pure, one hundred per cent gold star charisma like this man, but enough—until she had scratched the surface and found the base metal underneath—

'I'll get the coffee,' he said, distracting her, 'while you grab a table.'

She registered a shivery reflex when the man touched her shoulder and was powerless to hide the quiver of awareness that streaked through her. He must have felt it too. He had, Holly concluded, noticing how the steady gaze was now laced with humour. 'You might want to wipe some of the dirt off your backside before you sit down?' he murmured discreetly.

The fact that he'd noticed her backside was concerning. Craning her neck, Holly groaned.

'The ladies' room is just over there,' one of the waitresses supplied helpfully.

'Why don't you leave your suitcase with me?'

She looked at the man and evaluated her choices. She could leave her belongings with someone she didn't know, or struggle back through the crowded café with a large case in tow.

'You can trust me,' he said, reading her.

And you know what they say about people who tell you you can trust them, Holly thought.

'In my case it happens to be true,' he said evenly as if reading her mind were second nature to him.

She left the case.

Trying to ignore the amused glances of the up-market clientele, Holly retraced her steps through the café. As her face heated up under the critical scrutiny she realised that for the short time she'd been with him the man had made her feel good about herself. She didn't want to sit down in their fancy-pants café anyway. They probably charged twice as much here for a latte as they did at the popular chain down the road—

But rebuilding Holly meant never running away. And was she seriously going to make some pathetic excuse and leave an attractive man in the lurch?

Having cleaned herself up, she returned to find him reading the financial pages with her suitcase stowed safely at his feet. 'I had to guess what you'd like,' he said, setting the newspaper down.

'Skinny latte and a toasted cheese and tomato *ciabatta*? You're spoiling me—'

'No,' he said bluntly. 'I was ordering lunch, and I thought you might like some too.'

'Thank you.' An honest man was a refreshing change too. 'It looks delicious…?'

'Ruiz,' he supplied, reaching over the table to shake her hand.

'Holly.'

'Pleased to meet you, Holly.'

A lightning bolt shot up her arm when they shook

hands. And she shouldn't be staring at him like this. 'Ruiz?' she said. 'I love your name. It's so unusual.'

'My mother devoured romantic novels while she was pregnant. Mediterranean heroes?'

'I was born on Christmas day.'

They laughed.

And now it occurred to her that she couldn't remember the last time she had relaxed with a man. Laughing at the ex's jokes was expected, even demanded, but laughing because she was happy only brought accusations that she was braying like a donkey. So she didn't laugh.

'Is the coffee okay for you?' Ruiz said.

She looked at him. 'Delicious. Thank you.'

He held her gaze with eyes that were warm and interested. She wanted to know more about him. 'My guess is you're between seasons and that's why you're in London—'

'Between seasons?' Ruiz queried, frowning as he sat back. 'What do you mean by that?'

'Ski and surf? The tan, the build...' The confident swagger that came as standard equipment on a body when a man was in peak condition, she kept to herself.

'Am I so unusual?'

'Yes, you are.' Holly curbed her smile as Ruiz glanced around. He stood out like a very tanned and elegant thumb amongst a room full of stressed-out sore thumbs. 'But you've got a dog with you,' she said, frowning as she progressed her thoughts, 'so you must live close by.'

'Must I?' Ruiz queried with amusement. 'Do you always go into this sleuth-mode when you meet someone for the first time?'

'Sorry—it's really none of my business.'

'No harm done, Holly.'

She loved the way he said her name—and at least he

had remembered it—not that she was a troll, but if beauty was a matter of millimetres she could do with that extra inch.

Relaxing back in his seat, Ruiz tipped a toast towards her with his cup, which made Holly wonder if she was guilty of becoming too comfortable with a man she knew nothing about just because they were here in this safest of settings. The best thing to do was drink up and leave, she concluded.

'Hey, where's the fire?' Ruiz demanded as she gulped her coffee down.

How could anyone look so dangerous when they smiled? Ruiz's gaze was dark and experienced—with the emphasis on experienced. Heat curled deep inside her as he curved a sexy smile. 'I really should be going,' she said, coming to her senses. Why didn't her phone ring? What had happened to Lucia?

'Why the rush?'

'I thought you'd be pleased to be spared further investigation.'

'No, I like to hear your musings,' Ruiz argued. 'You've got a great imagination, Holly. Are you a creative, by any chance?'

'Advertising? No. I'm hoping to become a journalist,' she explained, though right now she wondered if she would make it to the first pay cheque. As far as interview technique went she was pants. She still didn't have a clue about Ruiz—where he came from, what he did—

'Do you have a job lined up?'

Holly brightened at the thought of it. 'Yes, I start as a lowly intern on *ROCK!* magazine on Monday—'

'*ROCK!* magazine.' Ruiz hummed, clearly impressed.

'Congratulations. It's not everyone who gets the chance to start their working life in London at the top of the tree.'

'It's not that much of a deal,' Holly admitted. 'You've heard of starting at the bottom? Well, this is the rung below that.'

Ruiz laughed and pushed his coffee cup away. 'Tell me more,' he encouraged.

'I've been hired to work as a gofer on the team who write the agony-aunt column. The post is so low-key it's practically invisible. I'm guessing that as long as my coffee-making technique is up to scratch, I'll be fine.'

'Well, at least you're doing your research,' Ruiz pointed out, adopting a mock-serious expression as he glanced at their empty cups.

Holly laughed. 'What about you?' She blushed as Ruiz angled his chin to stare at her. 'I'm sorry. I'm doing it again, aren't I?' she said. 'You must think I'm rude asking you all these questions when we've only just met.'

'No,' Ruiz argued. 'I think you're a cute kid.'

Ouch.

'I think you'll make an excellent journalist one day.'

'Is that a polite way of saying nosey's in my genes?'

'No. It means you're interested in the world and those around you,' Ruiz observed.

She wasn't going to argue with him—especially as Holly's world had just shrunk to the size of their table.

'So, Holly-would-be-journalist, just for the record, I do love skiing and riding the waves, so you were right as far as that goes, but bumming around the world is not what I do.'

'What is?'

Touching his nose, Ruiz grinned. 'Look at it this way. Your interview technique can only get better from here on in.'

It would have to, Holly thought wryly, or she'd have nothing to write about. 'Well, thank you for allowing me to try it out on you.'

'Don't mention it,' Ruiz said with amusement, sexy lips pressing down.

And just as Holly was wondering how she could ever bear to look away and bring this folly to an end the waitress handed them the bill.

The café was filling up, the girl explained with an apologetic shrug, and they needed the table.

'It's lunchtime and people are keen to get out of the rain,' Holly agreed, already on her feet. She had taken up enough of Ruiz's time. She made a grab for the bill, but he was too fast for her. 'My treat, remember?' he said. 'And if you change your mind about the dry-cleaning...'

'I won't.' And then finally, as she extended the handle on her suitcase, Holly's phone rang.

'Let me help you,' Ruiz suggested as she attempted to juggle her belongings and the phone.

Checking the number with relief, she answered and said quickly, 'Can you give me a minute?' Then holding the phone to her chest, she put Ruiz off as politely as she could. 'That's okay, honestly. I've got it. Sorry.'

'You're sorry again?' Ruiz murmured dryly, the attractive crease down his cheek reappearing as he smiled. 'You spend a lot of time being sorry, Holly...'

She didn't know what to say to that, and stared at him, hoping she would remember that dark, compelling stare as well as the last delicious punch to her senses that came with it. 'Bye, Ruiz. Thank you for lunch.'

'Goodbye, Holly,' he called after her as she raced outside to take Lucia's call.

Lucia rattled off five numbers. 'Got it?' Lucia demanded.

'Got it,' Holly confirmed, her heart still pounding from the last moments with Ruiz.

'You sound out of breath,' Lucia observed suspiciously. 'I didn't interrupt anything important, did I?'

'Not the sort of *anything* you've got in mind,' Holly protested, laughing. 'The café you recommended was just so noisy I had to run outside to take your call.'

'Just so long as you remember the numbers.'

'I will,' Holly promised, reciting the code Lucia had given her. So the great adventure begins, she thought, staring up at the impressive Palladian mansion across the street.

Nice. Very nice—if a little unsophisticated for his taste, but variety was the spice of life, Ruiz reminded himself as he strode back to his town house with Bouncer in tow. Would he see her again, or would Holly simply disappear into the great melting pot of the metropolis? He liked her a lot. In fact, he couldn't remember a woman making such a strong impression on him in so short a time. Perhaps it was because she made him laugh, or was it that clear green gaze he had found so open and expressive? He could even remember the scent she had used—fresh, citrusy, with just a hint of vanilla. He liked her mouth too—especially when she bit down on the swell of her bottom lip as if that would stop her asking him any more questions. And when she smiled—

'Hey, Bouncer, you liked her, didn't you?'

Soulful eyes turned his way, reminding him he had to find a solution for Bouncer before he returned to Argentina for the polo match...

No. Forget it. That would never work. The idea was ridiculous. He hardly knew Holly and the chances of ever seeing her again were remote. Though he couldn't help wishing he might, Ruiz realised.

Oblivious to the filthy weather, he turned in through the gates of the park. It wasn't the pampas but at least it was a big green space in the middle of the city where the big dog could enjoy some sort of freedom. When Bouncer had first wandered into his life he had intended to turn him over to the police, but when the moment had arrived he hadn't been able to bring himself to do it, and so he'd reported Bouncer missing and taken him home. They'd been together ever since. There had to be some sort of reward for a dog who had sensed an animal lover in a world of pet-free pavements, Ruiz reflected as he reached for the ball he'd stuffed in his pocket. Firing the ball across the park, he had to admit his brother Nacho was right—Ruiz shouldn't have taken the big dog on, only to keep him confined in London.

'Time is running out for us, boy,' he told Bouncer when the dog came bounding back. Ruiz shot the ball again, and felt his heart jag when Bouncer, having joyfully snatched it up, came racing back to him. Was it wrong to hope fate would smile on them? Ruiz reflected as the big dog dropped the ball at his feet. And then he remembered Holly and wondered if it already had.

CHAPTER TWO

London Diary:
If at first you don't succeed—
GIVE UP

No!
No. That wasn't what she meant to write at all.
So. Delete that and start again.
Okay…

You'd think it would be seventh heaven living in the
Acosta family penthouse with all that space, state-
of-the-art gizmos, and furnishings courtesy of a top
interior designer, but actually it means not using
anything in the kitchen in case you scratch, burn,
or break it. And don't get me started on the bath-
room. Basically, I'm fed up with tiptoeing around.
I might be living in the city, but I'm still a coun-
trygirl at heart. *Think* Bigfoot with ten carrier
bags on each arm blundering through the glass
department at Harrods—and you're still not even
close. And then there's the job at ROCK! Working
at the hottest magazine in town should be a dream
come true, right? Wrong. Things really couldn't get
any worse—until you come to my love life.

Love life still zero, though lustful thoughts are on the up, thanks to the man I met at the café called Ruiz, who looks like a sex god and who thinks I'm a 'cute kid'.

Oh, good. I am a twenty-three-year-old 'kid' with breasts and a Brazilian.

The wax?

I always was the glass-half-full type of girl, and judging by the pressure on the front of Ruiz's jeans he could fill that glass very nicely indeed.

Not that she was looking for a boyfriend, but her readers didn't need to know that where Holly was concerned it was a case of once bitten for ever shy. She had to light up the page not dwell on her mistakes, because it was all going wrong at *ROCK!* The job that should have been perfect for her, where she could be involved in things that mattered by working on the agony-aunt column, in however lowly a position, was on the line. She stared at the latest e-mail memo on her screen; it seemed she was about to be booted before she even got a chance to prove what she could do.

Latest figures dire. Agony column doomed unless reader numbers improve significantly. Need a diary feature to head the column—something juicy. Go, team! And remember: last in, first out. That means you, Holly.

Forcing her chin up, Holly flashed a promise-to-do-better smile at the staffer who had circulated the mail. What was Holly supposed to do to make things better—unless readers would be interested in the incredible-disappearing-sock story, or perhaps the find-a-white-bra-amidst-the-various-shades-of-grey scoop?

'I'm on it,' Holly assured the staffer on her way out of the office that night, adopting a seriously concerned expression. She was seriously concerned—for her job.

The staffer managed an even more seriously concerned expression. 'Don't want to lose you, Holly, but…'

The staffer was right. The column was dead unless someone came up with an idea fast.

Hiding behind other people's problems instead of risking another Holly-picks-the-wrong-man-again screw-up had been an attractive proposition when she'd first come down to London, Holly reflected as she walked briskly through the Christmas shopping crowds to the bus stop. But now all she wanted was to take her new life by the scruff of the neck and make a success of it. Her days of hiding behind anything were over. And with no reader letters to answer hiding behind other people's problems wasn't an option, anyway. The sticking point with the failing agony-aunt column was that no one cared any more—people just moved on to the next relationship. It was uncool to admit you needed advice. She had to come up with something novel. If she failed she'd be back at that door with the peeling paintwork and steel mesh security panel to prevent it being kicked in, otherwise known as her first job disaster.

She'd been straight out of college and green as a cabbage when she rocked up at *Frenzy*, a well known magazine. Well-ish known, Holly amended, hailing a bus. She had thought herself really lucky to have such an exciting opportunity straight out of college, in what had turned out to be a badly lit call centre. 'I'm supposed to be on the features desk?' she had explained to the old man in carpet slippers who'd shown her around. It had turned

out Holly's desk was a length of chipped and yellow-
ing plywood facing a peeling wall and she was to share
said desk with around twenty other girls. The girls had
been too busy speaking on the phone to notice Holly's
arrival, and at first she hadn't been able to figure out
why they were all working from dog-eared scripts and
panting into microphones—until her mind had flicked
rapidly through the pages of the magazine. *Frenzy* was
quite raunchy, though nothing out of the ordinary until
you came to the back pages where there were a lot of
ads for services like Personal Tarot Readings, Massage
By Britain's Strongest Woman, or Chat To Chantelle In
Perfect Confidence—

Oh…

'Erm…I'd like to see my supervisor, please.'

And that had been the end of that.

She definitely wasn't going back to some telephone
sex dungeon, Holly determined as she arrived at the penthouse—or Acosta heaven, as she had come to think of
her temporary lodgings. She was going to stay at *ROCK!*
and make a success of the job she had. Once through the
door, she carefully removed her shoes to preserve the
immaculate gleam of the highly polished wooden floor.
Shrugging her coat off, she draped it on a chair, shooting
her bag, briefcase, newspaper, magazines and scarf into
the mix. Just think. If she made a success of her career
as a journalist she could own something like this herself
one day…

Dream on, Holly thought, turning full circle in the
huge marble-tiled hall. A vaulted glass ceiling with a
fabulous view of the stars glittered overhead, while life-
sized Roman busts that might have been originals from
antiquity for all she knew stood on pedestals either side
of the huge double doors. Not only was the cost of a place

like this far beyond Holly's wildest dreams, she would also have to learn how not to be clumsy. A lesson too far, perhaps? No wonder she felt on edge amidst this splendour—one sneeze and she could be bankrupt for life. But for now the penthouse was home, so she might as well make the most of it. Tonight was green face mask night. She did all her best thinking in the bath, so this soak was set to be a long one.

Fate played strange tricks sometimes, Ruiz thought, frowning thoughtfully as he put the phone down and sat back. After he'd been searching high and low for his sister, Lucia had called him up out of the blue, unprompted. He might have known if it was a question of loyalty to a friend, Lucia would break cover immediately. There had been a swift exchange of information and a deal had been brokered between them. Like Nacho, Ruiz was keen for his kid sister to make use of her qualifications rather than to waste her time hanging around the party circuit. Lucia would return to the real world if he agreed to maintain his silence on her current whereabouts. 'But get home fast. On the next flight,' he stressed.

'So you don't mind my friend Holly staying at the penthouse?'

'Not at all.' Fate was definitely playing into his hands, Ruiz reflected while Bouncer murmured with contentment as he rearranged his massive furry body on Ruiz's feet. Apart from the dog's future looking a whole lot rosier, Ruiz had asked enough questions to establish that the Holly he had met at the café and had felt an instant connection with was the same friend his sister had forgotten she had invited to stay. Confirmation of this had elicited several squeals of excitement from Lucia when she realised he had already met her best friend, while he was more than looking forward to a return match with Holly. And as for making up for his sister's oversight—

'There's just one thing, Ruiz,' Lucia said, interrupting these thoughts.

'Which is?' he prompted.

'I gave Holly the impression that she would have the penthouse to herself.'

'How was I supposed to know my town house would flood?'

'Of course you couldn't know, but—'

'I need somewhere to stay,' he pointed out. 'My town house is within walking distance of the penthouse, so it makes perfect sense for me to stay there while the repairs are being carried out. I can keep an eye on the builders that way. Your friend Holly will just have to make room for me.' Lucia knew as well as he that the penthouse had more than enough bedrooms and could comfortably fit a medium-sized house within its walls.

'I'm sure she will,' Lucia insisted. 'I'm just asking you to be diplomatic, Ruiz.'

'Aren't I always?'

'Er, no,' his sister said.

'There's a first time for everything, Lucia.'

'Yeah, right.'

'Is that it?' he asked impatiently.

'Play nice, Ruiz.'

That was easy. 'I promise.'

'Not too nice,' Lucia added, concern returning to her voice. 'Please try to remember that Holly is a good friend of mine.'

'How could I forget?' he said dryly. 'Come on, Bouncer,' he prompted. 'I bet there's a brand-new sofa at the penthouse for you to chomp on.' There was certainly a female interest for Ruiz.

Scenting change in the air, Bouncer lifted his head to look at him. 'You're right,' Ruiz agreed. 'What are we waiting for? Let's get moved in.'

This was the first time she had relaxed properly since arriving in London, Holly realised as she settled back in the deliciously scented foam bath. It was the first time she had trialled a bright green face pack also. Attempting to move her mouth, she quickly forgot the idea in case the face pack cracked. She also had a gloopy oil treatment on her hair and cooling discs of cucumber balanced precariously on her face to soothe her resting eyes. All these preparations were essential for clearing her mind ready for the Great Idea to drop in. It was a little worrying that so far no idea, great or otherwise, had shown the slightest inclination to drop by—

What was that?

Shooting up in alarm when she heard the front door opening, she snatched the cucumber from her eyes, switched off the bubbles and remained still, listening.

When she recognised the voice of the intruder she cracked the face pack.

What the hell was *he* doing here?

And should she be in any doubt at all as to the identity of the intruder a big dog was barking excitedly.

He hammered on the bathroom door. What the hell was Holly doing? He had arrived at the penthouse with all sorts of images in his mind—Holly freshly showered and scented, with her hair clean and gleaming, falling in soft waves around her shoulders, Holly with rosy cheeks instead of frozen-to-the marrow cheeks, her green eyes in harmony with the big smile on her welcoming face. He had not expected to discover that Holly appeared to be holding a garage sale in the hall—or to trip over the handles of her briefcase. Having expended some of his irritation in a few, well-chosen words, he now discovered she was in the bath.

This wasn't going to plan. What was he supposed to do now?

'Open this door now,' he commanded.

What should she do? Holly wondered, still cowering in the bath. Ruiz from the café was threatening to break the door down. This didn't make any sense. Who was he? Some kind of crazy? Had he followed her? More importantly, was he dangerous? 'Where did you get the key?' she yelled out.

'From the key box,' he yelled back.

'And the code?' she said suspiciously.

'From my sister.'

'Your sister?' Holly's brain went into overdrive, and then crashed.

'My sister, Lucia Acosta,' Ruiz shouted through the door.

Yes, she'd got that far.

So Ruiz was one of the notorious Acosta brothers. Holly had never met Lucia's playboy brothers so couldn't claim to know much about them, but she did know they were polo-playing bad boys, who, according to Lucia, rode rampage through the world's women as well as their opponents on the field of play. 'And what are you doing here?' she demanded, swishing bubbles over her naked bits.

'More questions, Holly?'

He could laugh at a time like this?

'Why don't you come out of the bathroom and speak to me face to face?' Ruiz challenged.

Yes, she would, Holly determined, firming her jaw.

She wasn't going to cower in the bath. The house might belong to the Acosta family, but Lucia had been very clear when she had told Holly that the penthouse was empty and that Holly could have exclusive use of it until she found somewhere else to live. Lucia hadn't mentioned brothers barging in without warning. 'Shouldn't you be in Argentina playing polo?' she countered, playing for time as she turned the shower on to rinse the gunk out of her hair

'I live and work in London,' Ruiz called back. 'Will you be long?'

'As long as it takes.' Did her nipples have to respond with such a ridiculous amount of interest to Ruiz's shiver-inducing drawl?

Snagging a robe from the hook on the back of the door, she prepared to confront him. Belting it tightly, she reminded herself that new Holly didn't run away, and that new Holly stayed to fight her corner. Braced for battle, she swung the door wide. They stood confronting each other for a moment and then Ruiz began to laugh. 'What?' Holly demanded. It was only when her frown deepened and bits of green gunk started dropping onto the floor that she realised she had forgotten to rinse the face mask off. With an imperious tilt to her chin, she backed into the bathroom and closed the door.

'Would you like me to come back later?' Ruiz jibed through the door.

Holly responded with something unrepeatable that only made him laugh. She quickly washed the face mask off with ice-cold water. She needed a shock to get over seeing Ruiz again. He shouldn't be so stunning. It wasn't fair.

'Perhaps you'd like more time to compose yourself?' Ruiz growled through the door.

'I'm ready to see you any day of the week,' she assured him, flinging it open. Okay, but maybe not today, Holly conceded as Ruiz gave her a lazy twice-over.

'Something bothering you?' he enquired.

'I'm perfectly calm,' she said as her cheeks fired red.

Ruiz met this with a sceptical huff. 'Even when I tell you I'm planning to move in?'

'You can't move in!' Holly exclaimed.

'Can't?' Ruiz queried laconically.

'Of course not. I'm living here,' Holly protested indignantly.

'So...?' Ruiz shrugged.

'So Lucia said I could have sole use of the penthouse until I find somewhere else to live, and—'

'And do you have a contract to this effect?' He was beginning to feel more like the big, bad wolf than the brother of Holly's best friend. He was used to sophisticated women who knew the score, rather than girls like Holly, and was torn between indulging her and kissing the breath out of her lungs. Only Lucia's plea that he should be on his best behaviour stood between them.

'No, of course I don't have a contract,' she was protesting. 'How can I when Lucia's in—when Lucia's away,' she amended, clearly uncertain as to how much he knew about his sister's whereabouts. 'We have a verbal agreement.'

'My sister acts on impulse sometimes,' Ruiz agreed, easing confidently onto one hip.

He admired Holly's loyalty and could only imagine how it might be having Lucia as a friend. This felt like new territory to Ruiz. His strategy had already gone out of the window. Then he was distracted by something flimsy and pink on the floor and noticed Holly's face had turned a deeper shade of pink when she saw him looking at it. She quickly toed away the racy thong. 'Lucia must have warned you I was coming?' he pressed. 'I can't imagine my sister didn't call you.'

'Probably a thousand times,' Holly agreed, no doubt imagining her best friend's panic. 'But my phone is in the bedroom.'

She saw the tension in Ruiz's shoulders relax a little, but as he slowly looked her up and down Holly was sure that lazy gaze could easily penetrate anything as mundane as towelling.

'Well, I'm here now. So I advise you to get used to it, Holly. May I suggest you get dressed while I go and settle Bouncer in?'

'Bouncer?' Holly exclaimed. She couldn't hide the panic in her voice. 'Is it wise to bring Bouncer in here?' The damage the big dog could do to all the treasures in the penthouse didn't bear thinking about.

'Would you prefer me to leave him on the street?'

'No, of course not, but—'

'Or put him into kennels while my town house is being repaired?'

'That would only distress him. You told me he's a rescue dog.'

'Precisely,' Ruiz interrupted. He was serious for a moment, and then his expression changed to one Holly didn't like at all. 'I imagine Bouncer could have a field day in here unless he was properly supervised…'

'I agree,' she said. She didn't like Ruiz's tone, but it did seem as if he might have seen the light where the dangers of breakages were concerned.

'But with you to watch him while I'm away—'

'Me?' Holly exclaimed. 'You can't go away and leave Bouncer with me.'

Recognising his name, Bouncer, no doubt remember-

ing the fuss Holly had given him the first time they met,
padded over to the bathroom door and sat at her feet.
What was she supposed to do? Ignore him? Bending
down, she gave the dog a proper welcome, which
Bouncer took as his cue to clean her all over again.

'Look how pleased he is to see you,' Ruiz said in a
coaxing tone that set more alarm bells than ever ringing.
'How can you possibly turn him away?'

Holly sighed, but the look she reserved for Ruiz was
not at all kind-hearted. He got the special hard look she
was working on to deter those who thought they could
put one over on new Holly. Ruiz responded to this with
the lift of one ebony brow and a look that reminded Holly
that, unlike his dog, Ruiz was dangerous. The Acosta
brothers were notorious playboys with hair-raising rep-
utations, and like Lucia, they inhabited a very different
world from Holly.

So? Keep your nerve and fight fire with fire.

'Bouncer,' Holly murmured fondly, choosing to ignore the dog's master for now. 'Are you looking for a little mayhem?' Gazing up, she threw the gauntlet straight
back in Ruiz's face. 'You are? Good boy. There's a lot of
scope for you here.' Game on.

The look Ruiz gave her now made Holly's heart beat
a rapid tattoo. She should have remembered that Ruiz
Acosta was an international sportsman who liked nothing better than a challenge, and in spite of her tough
talk Holly's self-confidence was as fragile as a sugar
strand. Making her handsome parents proud of their un-
accountably plain daughter by winning a full scholarship
to a prestigious school had been one of the high spots of
Holly's life, until she'd discovered how the other, more
privileged girls had felt about it. It was only when Lucia,
easily the most envied girl in the school, had palled up

with her that Holly's confidence had slowly returned. Well, that sugar strand had just snapped and now she was steeped in self-doubt again.

'I'm going to have a beer and then I'm going to the gym,' Ruiz said. 'Make sure you've cleared up your mess by the time I get back.'

Yes, master. Holly's face burned red, but for once she remained sensibly silent.

Please don't hurry back, Holly thought, catching her breath against the bathroom door. She needed time to think. She could hear Ruiz moving about in the kitchen, but for a moment she did nothing, thought nothing, barely breathed, until, pulling herself round, she came to exactly the same conclusion: this wasn't going to work. Living with a playboy when she was still recovering from the most disastrous love affair of all time? How could she share the same space as a man as brazenly masculine and as unswervingly domineering as Ruiz Acosta? If Ruiz was moving in, she was moving out—

And that was exactly what she would have done had not sensible Holly chosen that moment to intervene and remind flustered Holly that she would still have to sort out alternative accommodation first, and that in the meantime she had no alternative other than to get along with Ruiz. Let's face it, she thought our paths don't even need to cross in a penthouse this size.

'Can we just get one thing straight?' she said to Ruiz, entering the kitchen after having thrown on her fat jeans, as opposed to her I've-lost-weight jeans, together with her oldest, most comfortable shirt. She had left her hair to dry naturally, and bother the make-up—she wasn't interested in men. She merely wanted to catch Ruiz before he left for the gym and set a few things straight.

He paused with the bottle of beer hovering close to his mouth.

Sexy mouth...

Concentrate, Holly told herself firmly. They had to get things out in the open if living together stood any chance of working.

'Yes?' Ruiz prompted.

Did he have to have such gorgeous eyes? Did he have to angle that stubble-shaded chin to stare at her? Did his mouth have to curve in that infectious and very dangerous smile? 'When you say you're going away,' she said, feeling her throat dry as she forced her gaze somewhere to the west of Ruiz's left ear, 'don't you mean going away as in flying to Argentina to play polo with your brothers?'

'That will be my next trip,' Ruiz confirmed, his dark eyes watchful.

'So this isn't just the occasional weekend we're talking about—this is full-on adoption of a huge, lollopy dog.'

'Temporary guardianship,' Ruiz corrected her, 'of my dog.'

He made it sound like a royal command—a privilege. And if there hadn't been such a lovely dog involved...

Ruiz showed no shame, Holly concluded. 'You're going to leave Bouncer at the penthouse I've been cautiously tiptoeing around. May I remind you that Bouncer has a huge fluffy tail and four big feet?'

'Your feet are lovely,' Ruiz observed, completely taking the wind out of her sails.

He wasn't supposed to say things like that and sound as if he meant it. Now all she could think about was the fact that she hadn't put shoes on because she'd been in too much of a hurry to speak to Ruiz before he went out.

Concentrate, Holly told herself fiercely as Ruiz

curved a questioning smile. There was no point giving him any more satisfaction than she already had. 'What you're suggesting,' she hissed in a low, urgent voice as if Bouncer could understand them, 'is a licence for carnage.' Couldn't she create enough of that on her own? Holly reasoned. She was just recoiling from the mental image of the type of carnage Bouncer could create when The Idea dropped in.

No one said it was going to arrive at the most convenient time, Holly reasoned as Ruiz began to frown. 'What now?' she prompted.

'I was just thinking that it's not like you to be silent for so long. You are feeling okay, aren't you?' Holly's warning look only succeeded in making Ruiz's eyes glow a little brighter. 'Anyway,' he added offhandedly, 'I'm going out.'

But she wanted to float her idea. 'No, wait.'

'Missing me already?' Ruiz suggested with maximum irony.

'Not one bit,' she snapped. 'In fact, please don't feel you must hurry back.'

This provoked a crooked smile that lodged attractively in Ruiz's stubble-darkened cheek. 'I love it when a plan comes together, don't you?' he said. And when Holly gritted her teeth in order not to say something she would regret, he added, 'I understand you'd probably like a little time to prepare yourself properly for my return.'

'Prepare myself properly?' Holly exploded. 'Who do you think you are? The Sheikh of Araby? I was merely pondering the possibility of doing some work without any further interruption,' she assured him primly.

'Oh, come on, Holly,' Ruiz murmured. 'You and I both know that too much work and no play will make you a very dull girl indeed. See you after the gym?' he said, his eyes dark and dangerous.

'I can't wait,' Holly called after him sarcastically. Living with a playboy wouldn't be easy, but at least Ruiz had given her The Idea.

Bravo! Holly-the-journalist!

Except…there was one small problem. She already knew Ruiz didn't like Holly poking her nose into his business.

But what was he going to do—refuse her offer to dog-sit in London while he was playing polo in Argentina? She didn't think so. She'd seen the glint in Ruiz's eyes. He'd gone in hard, thinking she would quickly fall into line. He had expected her to offer to help him in any way she could. Well, she might—on one condition that Ruiz helped her too. He must give her some titbits to write about. If he did, living with a playboy might not be so bad after all. In fact, it might just save her bacon. The column she had in mind would be an observational piece—meaning she could safely witness the life of a playboy while remaining at a prudent distance. This would be like confronting her demons from behind a screen. To save her career she would lift the lid on living with a playboy for her readers. Why shouldn't everyone else laugh at her trials and tribulations? She did.

Slinging his gym bag over his shoulder, he left his luggage in the hall and stormed out of the penthouse. The only solution, Ruiz had concluded, was to pound his way out of frustration. Having been knocked for six—or was that sex?—by the sight of Holly with her glorious red-gold hair streaming around her shoulders like a gleaming cape, Holly half naked with her creamy flesh just visible above the robe, he was painfully threatening to burst out of his jeans. In that respect, she had exceeded his expectations. Truthfully? He had never felt like this before. If Holly had been staying in Lucia's garden apartment he could have just about coped, but having her stay with him at the penthouse only yards from his bed?

Gritting his teeth, Ruiz lifted his own body weight above his head, but nothing helped to blank out the voluptuous woman waiting for him back at the penthouse. And hard as he tried he could find no solution to the problem. He wouldn't touch a friend of Lucia's. He couldn't eject a friend of Lucia's from the penthouse, either. So must he put his own life on hold? He could hardly entertain while Holly was in residence. Lowering the bar slowly back into its cups, he made a silent pledge not to go near her. He could only hope for Holly's sake that she found somewhere else to live as soon as she could.

He had left Bouncer with the girls on Reception where his faithful hound was sure to get a spoiling. The dog bounded up to him, seeming as excited as he was at the prospect of returning home.

Not excited, Ruiz told himself firmly. Certainly not excited to get back to the penthouse and find Holly waiting for him. It had been a long, hard day, and when he opened the door on what was supposed to be a luxurious hideaway in the best part of London, there would be girl stuff everywhere. No doubt the kitchen would be a mess, and, having seen the state of the hall, he had no doubt Holly would have trialled every bathroom by the time he got back, strewing damp towels all over the place. All he longed for was a good night's sleep, but with a big dog to care for checking into a hotel was out of the question. The penthouse, with its stunning views of London and seductive luxury, should have been perfect, and it might have been, had he not had an unexpected—and frustratingly unsettling—lodger to entertain.

Okay, so he'd set some ground rules.

'Come on, Bouncer,' Ruiz prompted, snapping the leash onto the dog's collar. 'Let's get this over with.'

CHAPTER THREE

Research. And that's all it would be. I wouldn't be breaking rule two—no men. I would simply be observing this man from a purely clinical point of view. My 'Living with a Playboy' idea would be like one of those fly-on-the-wall documentaries. I wouldn't be hands-on—I should be so lucky. More, all hands to the pump—gulp—as I try to do my bit to save the agony-aunt column. (Though I can't deny the thought of living so close to this particular playboy has done wonders for my metabolic rate. I've eaten a whole tub of double chocolate chip in anticipation of his return and I can still get into my jeans.)
(Imagine how slim I'd be if we lived together permanently.)
(Not that I'd ever consider living with anyone after my experience with the ex.)
Love life? Vicarious. Active. Very active indeed. Lustful thoughts? Are there any other kind?
And the playboy? This might all be over by tomorrow. He didn't exactly seem thrilled to see me, and I have yet to discover how he feels when he returns from the gym to find I'm still here.

HAVING finished her London diary entry, Holly was still tinkering with her first 'Living with a Playboy' feature when Ruiz arrived back. The new headline looked fabulous on the top of the agony-aunt column. If that didn't attract reader interest, nothing would.

She listened as Ruiz went into one of the bathrooms to take a shower and tried her hardest not to imagine him stripped naked. That proved a lot harder than she'd thought. The secret of successful cohabiting was not getting in Ruiz's way, Holly concluded, tensing as the shower turned off. If she was going to make a success of the 'Living with a Playboy' feature, she had to make sure Ruiz didn't think of her as a nuisance, always watching him and asking questions. She wasn't in any danger, she told herself repeatedly, counting the seconds until he entered the room, since she had vowed off men, and anyway there was no chance Ruiz would look at her that way. The main thing was not to give him an excuse to throw her out if she was going to make him the subject of her column.

Buttering-up time had arrived. While he'd been gone she had tidied away all her things and knocked up a tasty soup, using the fresh ingredients she had bought earlier. She'd also made sure there was plenty of ice for the large gin and tonic she guessed a sophisticated man like Ruiz might want, and had even put on some make-up—not very expertly, and certainly not enough to suggest she was after him. She hoped that assuming the role of un-threatening temporary lodger might work. She would even play housekeeper at a stretch. She'd do anything to salvage her career. She'd even iron a few shirts if she had to. She couldn't see any man objecting to that. Whatever it took for Ruiz to agree to become the subject of her column, Holly told herself tensely, flinging herself down in front of her laptop when she heard him advancing on the kitchen.

Living with a Playboy
Well, here I am, living the dream—or nightmare— not sure which it's going to be yet. I should know more if I survive these next few minutes.
I don't think I could have engineered living with a playboy. Who could, unless they wanted to be a rich man's plaything? And I can't say that's ever appealed to me. But I will do my best to keep a roof over my head until I can make alternative arrange- ments. I don't particularly like myself for being so cold-blooded about this, but it's the only solution I can see to keep my job right now.
To make up for my scheming I'm going to be the best housemate anyone could have—at least, that's what I keep telling myself. But the first time the playboy brings home a playmate I'm guessing I might show another side of myself altogether. It's not that I'm interested in him, and he certainly isn't interested in me. This is all in the line of duty, and—

Lowering the lid on her laptop, Holly arranged her face in a welcoming smile and stood up to greet Ruiz. Enter Ruiz: dark, glowering, massively powerful, and stunningly attractive. 'Hello,' Holly said brightly. 'I hope you had a good session at the gym?'

As Ruiz angled his head slightly to stare at her Holly realised she would never be able to keep this up. Faced by so much pumped and bulging muscle and with his thick black hair still damp from his shower, she knew she couldn't live with Ruiz as a passive observer without going completely off her head. 'Drink?' she enquired. Was that piping voice really hers? 'Gin and tonic, perhaps…?'

'A beer would be good.'

'Beer it is, then.'

'You're unusually compliant, Holly,' Ruiz observed, narrowing his eyes suspiciously.

She made a dismissive gesture. 'I'm just feeling a little guilty that I didn't make the connection between you and Lucia right away. When we first met at the café?' she prompted.

'I didn't make the connection either,' Ruiz pointed out. 'And Lucia told you what exactly about her brothers?'

Holly blushed. The thought of even the smallest part of what Lucia had told her about her brothers was enough to make the hair stand up on the back of her neck. 'You must be stressed out and tired,' she said to change the subject, 'and frustrated that you haven't got the private space you anticipated, but—'

'Breathe,' Ruiz suggested dryly.

Ruiz's dark gaze washed over her in a way that made her bones melt. She had dressed carefully—demurely—on purpose, Holly realised now, in a pair of baggy jeans and a shapeless old shirt, so as not to draw attention. She suspected Ruiz knew exactly what she'd done, and that he also knew she was suffering a very female response to his extremely masculine assessment.

'Where's that beer you promised me?'

Maybe this subservient domestic goddess role was going to be a little harder than she thought, Holly reflected, realising she was still gazing at Ruiz. 'Coming right up,' she said, forcing her feet to walk away.

Her hands were shaking by the time she got to the fridge and her heart was beating like Thor's hammer.

How on earth was this going to play out? Her bright idea of making a column out of living with a playboy didn't seem so clever now. Being sneaky didn't suit her, and a high-flyer like Ruiz would hardly want Holly sharing details of his private life with the general public. But she had to live somewhere. She had to earn a living. And this was the best, the only idea she had come up with to date.

'Thank you.' His gaze lingered on Holly as he took the beer. He'd run the shower on its lowest setting to try and knock some sense into his head, but innocence was a potent drug. He noticed her hands were shaking and guessed Holly was still reeling from the messy relationship Lucia had told him about and didn't trust her judgment where men were concerned. No problem for him. He could resist the lure of an unexpected visitor, however attractive she might be.

'Are you hungry, Ruiz?'

The punch to his solar plexus when she turned to look at him caught him by surprise. 'Starving.'

'You're in a better mood since you got back from the gym,' she observed as she vigorously stirred the soup.

'Yes, dear,' he mocked her lightly.

'And here was me thinking you might have knocked some of that frustration out of your system at the gym.' She blushed and stopped talking abruptly, but he knew she was referring to his ill-tempered arrival at the penthouse.

Lifting the bottle in a toast to her back, he drank it down. He had dressed casually after his shower in a pair of jeans and an old, faded blue sweatshirt, which he felt comfortable in around the house. Holly was barefoot in jeans and a pale blue shirt, which he found both casual and appealing. She was wearing hardly any make-up and had a tea towel tucked into the waistband of her jeans like someone who loved cooking and didn't care who knew it. She looked great. The pale blue shirt suited her, and he had to try very hard not to notice that it was straining over her breasts.

'Sure soup is going to be enough for you?' she asked, avoiding his gaze.

'For now.'

Opening the fridge, he found it stocked with fresh ingredients and a line of cold beer. 'Soup smells good,' he observed, joining Holly at the cooker. 'I usually call for take-away when I'm in London, unless I'm eating out—' He was staring at the back of her neck, longing to drop kisses on it. She had brushed her hair to one side, leaving the soft skin temptingly exposed, and he was standing close enough to see it had the texture of a peach. 'Are you sure you want to share your supper?' he murmured, thinking of anything but soup.

'I can't drink the whole pan full myself.' She turned to stare at him.

'I'll get some spoons,' he said, breaking away first, knowing that if he didn't he would have to take her to bed.

'I'm sorry for our rocky start this evening, Ruiz. I hope the soup makes up for it.'

'I'm sorry too,' he said. 'I was hardly Señor Charming earlier.' She was a friend of his sister's, he told himself sternly. It was his duty to be nice to her. Equally, it was his duty not to seduce her. 'Why don't we forget it and start over? Minestrone.' He hummed with appreciation. 'My favourite.'

'Really?' She seemed surprised. 'I had you down as more of a vichyssoise man.'

'Oh, please. Do you think I have my newspapers ironed before I read them too?'

'I'll be sure to be up early enough to do so, sir.'

'Be sure you are,' he teased, holding the emerald gaze until her cheeks flushed red.

A friend of his sister's? His good intentions where Holly was concerned weren't holding up too well, Ruiz concluded, registering the pressure in his jeans. 'Hurry up, I'm hungry,' he commanded mock-sternly, hoping that by adopting the role of master of the house he would distract them both.

Holly smiled and shook her head. 'Do you treat all your staff like this?'

'My staff?' he queried.

'The people you pay to do things for you,' she teased him.

'Was that supposed to be a joke?' he countered, finding he couldn't bring himself to avoid the extraordinary green gaze and that he really didn't want to.

'What do you think?' She laughed.

'I think you like living dangerously, Ms Valiant,' he said quietly.

Holly's smile died. He got the distinct impression that this brush with a man who really liked her was too much too soon for Holly. 'Do you think Bouncer would like some soup?' she asked him in a decidedly humourless tone.

'If you sprinkle cheese on it I doubt he could refuse,' he said, matching Holly for matter-of-factness. This was like trying to win the trust of a damaged pony. He couldn't lay his cards on the table—tell her she was beautiful and that he wanted her. He had to earn her trust and wait for Holly to come to him. She was graceful, he thought as she dipped low to feed the dog. She was kind and gentle and funny too. This was proving to be an unexpected distraction and he was enjoying tonight more than he could possibly have imagined.

'I realise this must be awkward for you,' she began as she straightened up.

'Awkward?' he queried.

'Living together like this,' she explained. 'I'm not exactly experienced when it comes to flatmates.'

He doubted she was experienced in any sense. 'Don't worry. You won't be seeing a lot of me.'

She laughed. 'Can I have that in writing, please?'

'And when I'm here I promise to keep out of your way,' he added.

'That's all I need to know,' she said, but her darkening eyes told a different story.

As they settled down to drink the soup together either side of the kitchen table it occurred to him that, as Lucia's friend, Holly was practically an honorary member of the family and so deserving of his protection, which was ironic when what she needed was protection from him.

'Soup okay, Ruiz?'

'It's delicious,' he said. It was. And when she smiled like that, looking so relieved and happy, he knew that Holly was as oblivious to her talents as she was to her beauty. It was when she cut a fresh slice from the crispy loaf, saying, 'I like a man with a healthy appetite,' that he had to reach for the butter and pretend he hadn't heard what she'd said. 'Hey, Bouncer.' He called the dog to draw the spotlight off her. 'Are you snoring?' he suggested as the big mutt grunted in his sleep.

'You're asking questions of a sleeping dog?' Holly enquired, watching him chin on hand.

'Is that permitted?' he teased, thinking how beautiful her eyes were.

Shaking her head, she smiled. 'I think you love that

dog. Don't worry, I'll clear up,' she said, pushing her chair back.

'Let me help you,' he offered, realising how much he wanted to be close to her.

One step at a time, Holly thought, feeling heat curl low inside her when Ruiz brushed past her at the sink. Now, if she could just control that heat and direct it into building a friendship with Ruiz everything might work out fine.

'Why don't you tell me something about the gap between school with my sister and now?' Ruiz suggested casually, taking her off guard as they loaded the dishwasher together. 'You can leave out anything you don't want to talk about.'

'That would mean leaving out most of it,' she said, trying to make a joke of things she really didn't want to remember. 'And I'd much rather talk about you.'

'I'm sure you would,' Ruiz agreed dryly, easing onto one hip.

'A playboy makes a much more interesting topic of conversation than the life of a would-be journalist,' Holly pointed out.

'A playboy?' Ruiz queried. 'Is that how you see me?'

'That's how the world sees you.'

'Really?' His lips pressed down. 'It seems a rather old-fashioned term for a man who works hard for a living.'

'A man who lives like this,' Holly interrupted him, glancing round the designer kitchen. 'Most people would find it fascinating.'

'That's only because they don't know the truth about the boring slog associated with getting to this point,' Ruiz assured her with amusement.

'And if they did?' she said carefully.

'What are you getting at, Holly?'

'Can I be honest with you?'

'I hope you're always honest.'

She braced herself. 'The column I'm working on is failing. If it has any chance of surviving it needs something different, something unique, to draw people in.'

He looked at her for a moment, and then he said, 'Oh, no.'

'Please let me finish,' she begged him. 'I'm proposing to write a fictional piece to head up the column and build reader numbers. I've always kept a personal diary,' Holly explained, 'and this would be a public extension of that—half serious, mostly poking fun at me, ordinary Holly Valiant, living with a glamorous playboy.'

'No,' Ruiz said flatly.

'It was just an idea—'

'You're not ordinary and I'm not glamorous.'

But Ruiz seemed glamorous to her with his wild, thick black hair and swarthy complexion. He was darkly dangerous and dangerously sexy. And readers would love him. He was standing very close—close enough to touch—close enough for her senses to pick up on his mood. It wasn't anger she sensed, but something a lot more worrying.

'And I'm certainly not a playboy,' he added, moving away.

'But who's to know that?' she pressed.

'I can see I'll have to watch what I say to you in future, Holly Valiant.'

So it wasn't a complete no, Holly thought, feeling excitement build inside her. 'I would never write anything derogatory about you.'

'I should think not…' And why was he even giving her this much of an opening? It might amuse him to read it, Ruiz reasoned. 'So is all this talk about a new column just a ruse to get out of telling me about your past?'

'If I tell you about my past you'll be asleep in five minutes,' Holly assured him. 'Why don't you start the ball rolling?' she suggested. 'Just make sure you leave out anything you don't want to see in print,' she added, tongue in cheek.

He stared at her for a moment, and then he laughed. 'Touché, Ms Valiant.'

'*En garde*, Señor Acosta.'

She made him laugh. She made him relax. She made him realise he could enjoy being with a woman without taking her to bed. Who knew? Ruiz mused wryly.

An hour into their chat and they were still going strong. It turned out she did have a talent for teasing out interesting facts, after all. Ruiz had relaxed enough to laugh when she told him about some of her more colourful teenage years. 'There was the home perm, the fake tan incident, and the gothic fright phase that almost got me thrown out of school. I tried to dye my red hair black, and it turned out green.'

When Ruiz pulled a face his sexy mouth pressed down in the most attractive way. 'So what did you get up to?' she pressed.

'Do you mean, what can I tell you about?' Ruiz shook his head as he accepted the challenge. 'I ran away to the pampas when I was about fifteen. When you live on an *estancia* the size of a small country there is only the pampas to run away to.'

'Lucky you.'

'I didn't think so, aged fifteen.'

It was just another form of isolation, Holly mused, thinking back to her own uncertain teenage years.

'I lived like a wild boy off the land.'

And she could picture him with limbs as brown as the parched earth he rode across, and his frame as lean as the predators that circled his campfire each night. 'Weren't you afraid?'

'I was too young to know fear. I was fit and strong, and thought myself invincible.'

She couldn't breathe for a moment, and then the dark eyes that had been dancing with laughter one moment stilled as Ruiz levelled a brooding stare on her face. Lifting one lock of her hair, he curled it around his finger. 'I can't believe you tried to dye your beautiful hair, or that you risked turning it into a frizz with a perm.'

'Risked?' Holly queried, pulling back, wishing she were ready for this and accepting she might never be. 'My hair not only frizzed, it fell out. I thought it would never grow back.'

'You thought no man would ever look at you again?' he suggested.

'It isn't easy being a teenager—for anyone. So, what were you like?' she pressed. 'I mean when you grew out of the running-away-to-the-pampas stage?

'In my early twenties I was insufferably arrogant.'

'No?' Holly mocked. 'I find that impossible to believe.'

He laughed. 'Believe,' he assured her. 'I was quite ridiculous. And rude.'

'But you're so polite now.'

'Why, thank you. I guess my manners managed somehow to survive those years. I have my older brother Nacho to thank for them. He was always very strict with us.'

'Tell me about him,' Holly pressed. 'Tell me about the band of brothers and your sister Lucia.'

'You probably know Lucia better than I do.' But he

told her how they all felt they owed everything they were and everything they had to Nacho, who had stayed to raise his siblings when their parents had died in a flood.

How could she not warm to this man? Holly wondered as Ruiz's massive shoulders eased in a regretful shrug while he tried and failed to recover memories of his parents from his early childhood. The more she learned about him, the harder it was going to be to live with him and keep things light—let alone write about him with any form of impartiality. Tugging her feet free from Bouncer's furry weight, she left the table for the relative security of the sink. 'I'll finish clearing up,' she offered. 'You can go and—'

'I can go and…what?' Ruiz murmured.

He was standing right behind her, Holly realised, quivering as she felt the caress of Ruiz's breath on her neck. She started to launch into some excuse to move away, but Ruiz was way ahead of her. 'Goodnight, Holly,' he said. 'And thanks for supper. It was great.'

CHAPTER FOUR

Reality bites.
Love life.
Lustful thoughts.

THE headings for her personal diary were as far as she got. She would have to change her way of working, Holly decided. She didn't want to think too closely about reality where her love life was concerned when the only love life she wanted was one she didn't have the courage to embrace and couldn't have anyway. She would confine her writing to her fictionalised column in *ROCK!* It didn't hurt so much. She couldn't bring herself to be flip or even name the deeper feelings Ruiz had stirred inside her.

'There's no hope for you, Holly Valiant,' she told her reflection in the bedroom mirror. 'You are a lost cause where men are concerned.' But with fair weather and a following wind she might still become a reasonable journalist one day. Opening the lid on her laptop, she began to write.

The playboy has just moved in, so now we are sharing the same living space courtesy of a humungous screw-up on the part of his sister, my best friend. It's a fabulous penthouse overlooking the River Thames, the Houses of Parliament, and every other iconic London building you can think of—I can see them all from my bedroom window as I write to you. One day in and I can already tell you that playboys are just like the rest of us...but I know that's not what you want to hear. You want to hear about the fabulous lifestyle, the sex, the drama, and all the extravagance—for that's how the playboy life appears to us mere mortals. Whereas owning several homes, a couple of private jets, and having the tailor come to call on you is commonplace for the playboy. The only thing I can't tell you about yet is the sex—it's too soon—but I have no doubt there will be women flocking round in no time. And I can't tell you about the tailor, because I made that bit up. But the playboy...that's another matter. He's no figment of my imagination. He's hard and tanned, and stands over six feet tall, with massive shoulders and impossibly strong forearms. His hair is thick, black and wild, like a man who answers to no one, and his eyes are dark and brooding. I've never seen his face without a coating of sharp black stubble and his teeth are perfect. You'll have to imagine my sigh of despondency here, for I am barely five foot three and I'm a redhead. The type you used to call gingers with a hard 'g' at school? Plus, I always know the answer to 'Does my bum look big in this?' If this rings a bell for you, join me, why don't you, on my journey of discovery? And I'll share everything I discover about him here with you.

She could only try, Holly thought, pressing Send. If the team didn't like the piece they didn't have to run it.

And she couldn't fight the compulsion to write—or, more truthfully, to write about Ruiz. It was probably going to be the only way she could express her feelings for him.

Since their chat she was seeing Ruiz in a completely new light, as a real man, rather than a fantasy figure. Hearing him go into his own room and close the door, she had crept back into the living room with her laptop. A change of scene usually made ideas flow, but it was hard to imagine she would write any more tonight when her head was stubbornly full of strong arms, and strong tanned hands with lean, elegant fingers. No wonder Ruiz was a world-class polo player. She could so easily imagine those powerful thighs wrapped around the sides of a horse, or those sensitive hands lightly fingering the reins.

How was she supposed to sleep when her head was full of that? Thank goodness she was a realist and could channel all her X-rated thoughts into the column. As far as real life was concerned she had done nothing risky other than sit down and have supper with Ruiz, Holly reassured herself, and where was the harm in that?

'What do you think, Bouncer?' she murmured, turning from the makeshift desk she'd created on a table to fluff the animal's massive ears. 'At least you've got the good sense to maintain a neutral silence,' she observed wryly as Bouncer adjusted his position on her feet with a contented sigh. 'I can't think of a better companion to keep me company through the night than you,' she told the big dog fondly.

Which was a pity, Ruiz reflected wryly, standing outside the door. Holly was too innocent and too bruised for someone like him to lead astray. Holly believed in love and happy ever after while his hunting instinct was firmly tuned to the here and now. So what now? Was he supposed to go to bed, close his eyes, forget Holly and drift away? Even his dog had changed allegiances.

He should be pleased about that, Ruiz reminded himself, shooting one last glance through the door at the homely tableau Holly had unwittingly created with Bouncer. If someone was going to take care of the dog while he was away, who better than Holly?

Holly almost fell off her chair when a hand touched her shoulder. 'Ruiz!' Who else could unfurl a starburst of sensation like that? Holly reasoned, swinging round. 'Did I wake you?' she said with concern. 'I'm sorry.'

'I saw the light on,' Ruiz explained.

He was wearing a robe that had fallen open at the front to reveal a torso that would defy her best attempts to describe it to her readers. 'Ripped, tanned, and shaded with just the right amount of dark hair,' would fail utterly to do justice to a body that was unique in Holly's experience. But then she glimpsed the black boxers beneath the loosely fastened belt and knew it was time to look away. 'I should have remembered to shut the door when I put the light on,' she said, blushing furiously.

'It's good you're keen about the job,' Ruiz observed, propping one hip against the end of the table where she was working, 'but don't you think you should get some sleep?'

'I work best at night—and I'm going to bed soon,' she added in response to his sceptical look.

'I suppose I should thank you,' he said.

Ignoring the danger signal that streaked down her spine, she asked him what he meant.

'I couldn't sleep either. I thought I might come in here and watch a game on TV. But if you're working...'

'You can watch TV. It won't disturb me.' And company would be nice, Holly thought, though in Ruiz's case she had yet to discover if she could concentrate while he was in the room.

'No, I think bed is better than dozing on the sofa,' he said, turning for the door. Stretching out a hand, he added casually, 'Are you coming?'

It was a moment before she realised he wasn't talking to Bouncer, but to her. 'Certainly not,' she exclaimed indignantly.

'I was only suggesting you should get some sleep—in your own bed,' Ruiz stressed, to Holly's hot, burning shame.

'In a minute,' she said, bending low over the laptop so that her hair concealed her face. 'I've got a couple of things I need to finish off here first.'

'Would you like me to read what you've written so far?'

'No, thank you.' All her yearning and insecurities written to amuse the reader were a little too close for comfort where Ruiz was concerned. She looked up to him standing over her, his eyes dancing with laughter. 'Have you been reading over my shoulder?'

'Me?' he drawled.

'Yes. You.' Closing the lid on her laptop, she stood to confront him, which involved some serious neck-craning. 'I prefer to finesse my work before I show it to anyone. I'd only be sharing bullet points with you at this juncture.'

'Oh, would you?' he asked, mocking her suddenly starchy English accent with a chocolaty South American drawl. 'Well, if you're quite sure?' The wicked mouth tugged in a sexy grin. 'My sister tells me I'm a very good listener…'

'I'm sure you are,' Holly agreed, then deflated instantly as Ruiz turned for the door. Why had she driven him away? What was wrong with her? 'Do you mind if I keep Bouncer with me tonight?' she said, hardly realising it was an attempt to keep him a moment longer.

'Be my guest,' he said with an expression in his dark, laughing eyes that said as far as attempts to stop him leaving her went, this was lame. 'I'm relieved you and Bouncer get along so well.'

Why were alarm bells ringing? She should have picked Ruiz up on that last remark, Holly realised. She hadn't agreed to dog-sit Bouncer for him, had she? She had a horrible suspicion that Ruiz had taken her agreement to do this for granted.

She handled relationships with animals better than she did with men, Holly reflected, kneeling down so she could cuddle up to some non-judgmental warmth. 'Oh, Bouncer, why am I such a clutz when it comes to men?' She sagged as the door clicked quietly shut.

There was better news for Holly the next morning. The team had not only accepted her first submission to the column, but was delighted and relieved she could deliver a follow-up so quickly. Holly couldn't help but smile when they showed her the first article in print, with her second article already up on the web site. Early signs suggested that hits on the web site had increased, and they had all gathered round to read what she had to say.

One failed relationship does not a lifetime of disastrous love affairs make. Don't let it rule your life. Don't let it dictate what you should expect from life, or restrict what you achieve, says the redhead who doesn't even register on the playboy's radar—but who would like to. As you may have suspected, liv-

ing with a playboy isn't as straightforward, or as glamorous as it sounds. The playboy may see me as a quirky nuisance, but I have all the same lusts and longings as the most beautiful playgirls we've ever featured in ROCK! My trouble is, I waste far too much time wondering how can a girl like me attract a man like that? When the simple answer is: I can't. And why would I want to, when you and I both know I'm looking for something more than a one-night stand—however memorable that one night stand might be. And it would be memorable. But please don't think I'm defeated, because after last night's surprisingly cosy supper chat back at the penthouse I think the playboy and me might have something going on in the friendship depart-ment. And friends are one of the most precious things in life, don't you agree?

There had been friendship between herself and Ruiz last night, hadn't there? Holly fretted as the team con-gratulated her. She couldn't help but keep running over everything Ruiz and she had said to each other, and had to drag herself back to the present so as not to offend her colleagues when they suggested a celebratory lunch at the local coffee bar.

After lunch, she worked until the end of the day on reader problems. Quite a few more had come in by e-mail. All the team had their heads down, and some-one suggested readers might have grown in confidence knowing they wouldn't receive a flip response from someone who was having her own battle with insecurity.

'Let's hope this isn't a flash in the pan,' Holly told the staffer on her way home that evening, when even he had

said well done. She could hardly believe it when the king
of the sceptics cracked a smile and winked back at her.

Ruiz had arranged a supper date with a woman who always made him laugh. He sat through it glancing at his
watch, wondering what Holly was doing at the penthouse.
She didn't have many friends in London yet, and with
the trouble she'd mentioned at work—the predicted early
demise of the agony-aunt column—he guessed she must
be feeling low. He made some polite mumble in response
to the woman sitting opposite him at the high-end restaurant, but they both knew his thoughts were elsewhere.

'Excuse me, Ruiz.'

He refocused as the woman across the supper table
from him touched his hand. 'Forgive me,' he responded.
'It's been one of those days.'

'I can see that,' his blonde companion murmured in
a suggestive purr.

'Do you mind if we cut this short?' Even the tone of
her voice set his teeth on edge, and they both knew the
answer to his question. Players in the field could read
each other like well-thumbed books and he was tired of
playing the field, or whatever this type of civilised prelude to sex was called. 'Please accept my apologies,' he
said, abruptly standing. 'I realise I've been lousy company tonight.'

His companion didn't argue.

Two weeks had passed since her first article for the column, and these days she was rising before dawn to start
work on her ideas. There didn't seem to be enough hours
in the day now her 'Living with a Playboy' feature had
been officially declared a success, but at least that made
it easier to live with Ruiz. Keeping busy gave Holly less

time to regret that she wasn't a five foot six blonde with more up front than behind, and meant she could channel her energies into the column. Since that night when Ruiz had come back and looked at Holly long and hard as if he were trying to work out what particular brand of sugar and spice she was made of, he had kept away. There had been no more cosy chats. And, of course, that suited her.

No, it didn't. She had spent most of last night wondering where he had spent the night. Plus, her thoughts on Ruiz's lady friends were not all worthy of the girl she used to be. She had become an evil shrew and felt an uncontrollable urge to share this with her readers, who were growing in number by the day. It turned out that even so-called nice girls could discover a very different side to their natures when there was a gorgeous man involved…

Glancing at the stack of newspapers piled neatly by the side of the desk she had improvised in the penthouse, Holly knew she must put Ruiz out of her mind for ten seconds, finish her work, and then study the Classified ad section and circle some rooms to let. She couldn't go on like this. She had to find somewhere to live where she could stand on her own two feet. Frowning as she bent her head over the keyboard again, she completed the advice section for the agony-aunt column and then turned to her next piece for 'Living with a Playboy'.

I would have stayed in the background as I had intended had it not been for a very expensive pair of designer shoes…
Don't believe anyone who tells you women are on the same side when there are shoes and a playboy at stake. In this situation it's a case of survival of

*the fittest—and I have discovered that I need to
have a serious rethink if I'm going to survive.
Honestly, I don't have a clue. How was I supposed
to know that the high-heeled shoes I found dumped
in the hallway when I got home from work would
lead to a pair of sexy hold-ups artfully draped
over the handle of the living room door? Or that
the woman reclining on the sofa in a bright pink
Basque and a rather scary translucent thong was
expecting our mutual friend to walk in rather than
me?*

*How was I supposed to know she had a key?
I don't know who was more surprised—me, or the
blonde. Anyway, I apologised, and, on my way out
of the room, managed to tumble over her shoes and
snap the heel off. Needless to say, all hell broke
loose. Quickly realising that neither my vocabu-
lary nor my stumpy, bitten nails were up to a cat
fight I took myself off to the bathroom and locked
the door, where I proceeded to sing tunelessly with
my hands over my ears until I heard our mutual
friend arrive. When I removed my hands from my
ears it was to hear him promise to do something
about the mad woman in the flat and replace the
shoes she had destroyed. Traitor, I thought.
But the promise of shoes made me think that here
was a man I might be able to do business with...
until I considered this more deeply and realised
that a playboy would never do it for me, because I
want to buy my own shoes and I'm pretty sure one
pair wouldn't be enough...*

Closing the computer, Holly sat back before turning to
her next task. Lifting the newspapers onto the table, she

sorted and stacked them, and then started methodically trawling through the ads. She had a reassuring number of opportunities circled when she heard the front door open and a familiar stride coming her way. Her heart began to thump. It was very early in the day to have any sort of confrontation, let alone be thrown out on the street with some bimbo cheering Ruiz on. It was with enormous relief that she realised he was alone. Opening her laptop again, she pretended to be working when he came into the room.

'Good morning, Holly.'

'Morning,' she said offhandedly. But she rather spoiled the effect by looking up to find Ruiz dressed immaculately in a sharp dark suit, with a crisp white shirt, and a pearl-grey tie. He looked amazing.

'I just got in from Paris,' he explained, dumping an exquisitely wrapped box of tiny rainbow-tinted macaroons on the table in front of her.

'What have I done to deserve this honour?' she enquired in the same cool tone, while hectic images of hysterical girlfriends re-enacting the 'off with her head' scene between the Red Queen and Alice leapt unbidden into her head. Did the Red Queen wear a translucent pink thong, perchance? 'What?' she said as Ruiz shrugged off his jacket, loosened his tie, freed a couple of buttons at the neck of his shirt, and stretched out on the sofa swinging a distinctive carrier bag from a well-known Parisian boutique above his head.

'What size feet have you got?' he asked.

'Isn't that a rather personal question?' There were some things a lady never divulged. Though, to be fair, the shoes she had trashed belonging to Miss Pink Basque had been the same size Holly wore.

'Well, if you don't want them.'

'If I knew what you were talking about...'

'Why don't you come over here and find out?' Ruiz suggested. 'If the shoes are the wrong size you can always take them back to the store and change them.'

'In Paris?'

'No need to sound so snippy,' he said, sitting up to bait her with a stare. 'Not jealous, are we?' And just like that the dark, dangerous eyes were laughing again.

But after the bimbo affair Holly refused to be won over quite so easily. 'I'm not at all jealous of you,' she said crisply. 'I've seen your friends.'

'You've seen a passing acquaintance,' Ruiz assured her, 'who has now passed.'

'Away? How unfortunate.'

'Into history, I was about to say. Don't be sarcastic, Holly,' Ruiz warned, pretending to be stern. 'It doesn't suit you.'

She turned back to the keyboard, hurting inside. Even a mistress who had passed into history was a mistress too far. 'I suppose I can use the story for the column,' she muttered.

'If you don't want the shoes...'

Holly stiffened. 'Are you saying you bought the shoes for me?'

'I bought the blonde shoes—'

'What a gentleman you are,' Holly interrupted acidly. 'How thoughtful of you.'

'Holly,' Ruiz droned good-humouredly, 'I bought the shoes to replace the ones you broke, but the blonde decided she'd prefer a cheque for a somewhat larger amount, so I took the shoes back to the store—'

'Do I need to hear this?'

'I just want to make it clear that I'm not giving you

anyone's leftovers. I bought them for you. Don't you want to see them?'

'For me?' she said suspiciously, hating the way her voice was trembling. 'You bought shoes…for me?' She turned to find Ruiz looking less confident than usual, or maybe she was delusional, which was entirely possible. In the end curiosity got the better of her. There was nothing wrong with taking a look. She could only hope Ruiz's taste in shoes was an improvement on his taste in women. She could fake it for the column, but she was pretty sure she couldn't fake anything for Ruiz, though he stood a serious risk of having the shoes land heavily on his head if this was another of his jokes!

'Before we came to the mutual decision that cash was king the blonde chose some trashy, sparkly things, like the ones you stomped on,' Ruiz explained, handing the box over. 'I thought they looked better in pieces, frankly, and so I chose these. What do you think?'

Did shoe heaven cover it? The leather was the softest she had ever felt, the heel was the highest, the colour was a beautiful pale dove grey. And the sole was scarlet. 'I think…' They're divine, Holly thought, feeling a quiver of excitement at the prospect of wearing them. She could never have afforded shoes like these… 'I think you should return them to the shop,' she said, remembering the advice she had given one of her readers in capital letters on this very subject: 'Never Accept Expensive Gifts From Men. Why? Because it puts you in their debt.' And the piece hadn't even gone to press yet, sensible Holly reminded drooling Holly sternly. 'As they haven't been worn I think you could get a full refund,' she said, placing the shoe back in its box.

'What's wrong with them?' Ruiz demanded, removing his crossed feet from the table and sitting up straight.

'I never accept gifts like this from men.'

'Well, that's a habit you should change right away,' Ruiz observed dryly. 'I suppose it also means I can't take you out to supper tonight—though if you feel badly about it, I can always let you pay…'

Ruiz was asking her out?

No. Ruiz was asking her to take him out, which gave Holly a problem. If this had been a straightforward invitation to supper she could refuse, but seeing as she was taking up half a penthouse that was rightfully his, the least she could do was stand Ruiz a meal…

'Perhaps if we go out I'll get a chance to talk to you about paying a fair rent to live here,' Holly murmured thoughtfully. To date, both Ruiz and Lucia had refused to take any money from her, while Holly's house-hunting efforts had swung disastrously between scratching sounds behind the skirting boards to smelly drains, and even, on one memorable viewing, an infestation of ants. 'Rent?' she prompted, seeing now that there was something very worrying in Ruiz's eyes.

'What a great idea,' he agreed mildly. 'Trust you to come up with something.'

The day improved when Holly arrived at *ROCK!* to find she had been given her own office with two assistants to help her, which she had to take as a sign that the agony-aunt column was on the up. 'But let's not get carried away,' she cautioned the two girls sent to help her. 'This is still early days, and—'

'You've worked a miracle so we can all keep our jobs?' Pixie suggested.

'I wouldn't put it quite like that,' Holly argued red-faced.

'You have to carry on living with the playboy now…

poor you,' Freya said, exchanging a wry look with Pixie. 'Not that we're jealous, or anything.'

What would Ruiz have to say about that? Holly wondered, feeling the buzz inside her ramp up a gear at the thought that she had to go out to supper tonight with him.

'Anyway, we're just glad to be here,' Freya added warmly as she plonked a thriving pot plant, her personalised mug, a budget-sized box of tissues and a generous supply of chocolate for them all to share on the desk.

'You're right,' Holly agreed, telling herself not to be so selfish and join in the celebration. She had to stop wishing and longing, and pretending she could steer her life to a happy-ever-after-ending in which a confident Holly Valiant won the hand of a prince instead of a frog. She could do what she liked through the column, but not that. The 'Living with a Playboy' feature was a fiction to boost reader numbers, which it had done, and that had to be enough for her. Except it wasn't, Holly admitted silently as she exchanged spirited high fives with the other girls.

But hang on a minute, Holly thought as the celebration subsided. Wasn't this expansion of the column and securing of their jobs the moment she'd been working towards? And wasn't it essential to immerse herself in that work if she was going to forget being anxious about supper with Signor Sexy tonight? Her gaze fired as the other girls looked to her expectantly. 'Chocolate?' she said.

'Tick!' the girls chorused.

'Bottle of fizz to celebrate?' She was less sure of this one and was already planning to slip out and buy something.

'Tick!' Pixie said triumphantly, producing a bottle from behind her back.

'I think we have everything we need,' Holly confirmed. 'Let's kick this column into shape!'

And let me have something I *can* control to think about, she prayed fervently, instead of a whole lot of man that I can't.

CHAPTER FIVE

'Mirror, mirror on the wall—' Will someone cover the damn mirror!

Tonight's the night. I am taking the playboy out to supper and I can't decide what to wear.

I realise that taking him out reverses the natural order of things—but then I am not the playboy's natural order, if you take my meaning. I am more of a meagre side dish—the type of thing you order to try, and more often than not leave untouched.

Me? Lacking in confidence? What makes you think that?

All right. I admit it. Every item of clothing I possess is on the bed, or on the floor. Carrier bags and sales tickets are scattered around like confetti, because, as it turns out, my wardrobe is full of nothing to wear. And, as I am constantly reminded by the playboy's long-legged basque-wearing friends, sex sells. Not exactly my area of expertise. Consequently, I have decided that my next article for you will be a helpful piece on the subject of staying out of debt. At least that's where my credit card provider told me I should be concentrating my thoughts.

I must admit the real crisis of confidence came

when I tried to decide what to underpin my modest outfit with tonight. As I don't possess a single bàsque, or hold-up stocking, should I chance a shocking-pink thong?

As my underwear is unlikely to receive an airing, that hardly matters, does it?

And the playboy? He's acting as cool and as sexy as ever. Accompanying me to supper is nothing more than a workaday chore for him in order to keep in his sister's good books. So at least I should be safe. And I should be glad about that—right?

TYPING up her column was a displacement activity Holly had hoped would take her mind off the fact that she would soon be sitting across a table from Ruiz—speaking to him, staring into his eyes—all the time pretending they were nothing more than friends. Her shopping had been more erratic than usual with her frantic purchases more suitable for a royal wedding than a casual supper in a local bistro and she was fast losing confidence in her ability to pull this off.

Closing the lid on her laptop, Holly glanced at the shoe box the unscrupulous Ruiz had left temptingly outside her door. It was on her bed now. She had been forced to bring it into the bedroom in case someone fell over it. But of course she couldn't wear the shoes unless Ruiz allowed her to pay for them. And as that would take a whole month's salary...

The dress she had finally chosen to wear was a sale-rail spectacular—A-line, with a flirty skirt and a high scooped neck. It wasn't black, which was about the best that could be said for it, but at least it was the same soft blue as her favourite shirt. With her hair neatly brushed, lip gloss present and correct, and just a suggestion of smudgy grey eye shadow to complement the flick of black mascara, she was ready. And nervous.

What did she have to be nervous about? Eating supper was a harmless activity.

Sharing food could be very sexy.

Fish and chips?

Mating rituals like eating supper together and how to avoid them was another good headline for her column, Holly concluded as she shifted anxiously from foot to foot in the hallway, waiting for Ruiz. But seeing as there was no escape from tonight, fish was out—ditto anything like spinach that might get stuck in her teeth. Thankfully, she had identified a healthy-food café where they could nibble on crudités and drink sparkling elder-flower water. Perfect. She would keep a clear head and as the café was brilliantly lit with sensible, hard-backed chairs Ruiz wouldn't want to stay for long—

And when they came home?

She'd plead tiredness and go to bed. Alone.

Just when she'd almost given up on him, Ruiz stormed back into the apartment like an avenging angel in a cloud of cold air and warm smiles with Bouncer panting vigorously at his heels. 'Ready?' he demanded.

'Ready,' Holly confirmed.

'Where are you taking me?' he said as he bent down to remove Bouncer's leash.

'I thought the little café down the road—'

'The one where we met?' Ruiz sounded upbeat as his lips pressed down with approval of her choice. 'Hang on while I fill Bouncer's water bowl—'

'No… No, that one's shut,' she called out.

Ruiz sauntered back into the hall. 'Tell me you're not taking me to that place where they serve lentil soup, and you have to sit round a communal table on hemp sacks?'

'What's wrong with that?' she said. 'They do have private booths.'

'Where you can sit on even bigger hemp sacks? No, thank you.'

'So where do you want to go?' she said irritably.

'You're letting me choose?' Ruiz's mouth curved in a grin.

Why couldn't she learn to keep her big mouth shut? She would never be able to afford Ruiz's preferred style of restaurant. 'I'm sure I can find somewhere else you would like,' she told him firmly.

'I know somewhere you'd like,' Ruiz countered. 'It's walking distance from here—and not expensive,' he added when Holly's eyes widened in panic. 'Mid-week is all about economy, Ms Valiant.'

'Are you mocking me, Señor Acosta?'

'Would I?' he said.

Holly's look said it all. And now her mind was swinging wildly between the safe café of her choice and somewhere of Ruiz's choosing—and how *economical* that would be in terms of their very different incomes. 'Am I dressed okay for this place of yours?'

'You'll do,' he said, holding her gaze with a raised eyebrow and a sexy grin.

'It's still my treat,' she insisted firmly, trying to hang onto her composure.

'Of course it is,' Ruiz agreed. 'Though I am prepared to make a deal with you.'

Why was he staring at her shoes? Her comfortable, clunky-heeled shoes? They were perfect if they were going to walk to the place Ruiz had mentioned. Did he need to look at them as if she had committed some terrible faux pas and make her even more nervous about stepping into Ruiz's world than she already was?

'This is the deal.' Ruiz angled his disreputably stubbled chin in Holly's direction. 'I'll pay for supper tonight if you wear the shoes I bought for you.'

The shoes he bought? Accept his gift? Take a totter on the wild side on five-inch heels instead of remaining safely corralled inside the magazine column on her clunkies? 'I can't walk in high heels. And, anyway, I already told you that I—'

'Don't accept gifts from men,' Ruiz supplied. 'I do remember.'

'So, how does this work?' Holly demanded. 'I get the shoes and you pay for supper. Do you seriously think I'm going to go for that?'

'I think you should,' he said evenly. 'I think if you had any sense you would.'

'Well, clearly I don't have any sense,' Holly fired back, 'because—' Because what? Come on, come on '—because tonight is supposed to be my treat for you.' Ah, yes, sweet relief. 'Because you have to let me do something in return for allowing me to stay in the Acosta penthouse.' *Yes!* 'And as for wearing a pair of brand-new shoes that you could easily take back to the store and get a refund for—'

'Oh, get over yourself,' Ruiz flashed, raising the emotional temperature by a few thousand degrees. 'You're my sister's best friend. If my friends were in London and needed accommodation I would expect Lucia to show them hospitality. This is a courtesy to my sister.'

As she had thought. Okay, she'd asked for that, Holly accepted as Ruiz and his storm-face reached the door. 'Okay?' he questioned, banging it open.

'Okay,' she fired back. Stepping out of the fictional world she had created for Ruiz and into reality with him might be a little more combative and complex than she

had first imagined, Holly realised. And as for the effect
on her senses, she could only trust that the keeper of her
moral code was on duty tonight.

'I thought we might go dancing,' Ruiz dropped in casually as he held the door for her to go through.

'Dancing?' Holly managed on a dry throat, knowing
her face must have been a picture of doom as she walked
past him.

'Something wrong with that?' Ruiz demanded, turning to lock the door.

Where to start? Dancing meant touching each other,
holding each other, moving as closely as two people
could move together, unless they were—

'Those shoes are perfect for dancing. Thank you for
wearing them,' Ruiz said with worrying charm as she
click-clacked across the lobby towards the elevator.

'My pleasure,' Holly said primly, which was the un-
derstatement of the year. Well, she could hardly leave
the shoes alone in a box while she went out, could she?
They might fade, or something.

'Tonight should make very good reading for your column,' Ruiz observed as they stood waiting for the lift to
arrive.

Holly forced a small laugh. Not too good, she hoped.
She'd given up on the thong and was wearing really big
knickers instead.

They crossed the road and walked through the park
with a good three feet of air between them. Where was
Ruiz taking her? Holly wondered as he turned off down
a cobbled side street where the mews houses would go
for millions and any club would be exclusive in the extreme. She was feeling extremely self-conscious by the
time Ruiz stopped outside an iron-studded door where
the faint strains of South American music could be heard

on the street. But the club did look intriguing—all dark and mysterious like the man at her side.

'A Brazilian friend of mine owns the club,' Ruiz explained. 'They have great food and even better dancing. A place like this will be dynamite for your column. Ready, Holly?'

As she would ever be, Holly thought, taking a deep breath.

When would she get another chance like this? Holly asked herself sensibly. The humour in Ruiz's eyes reassured her, though when he rested his arm across her shoulders as they waited for the doorman to examine their faces through the grill, she had to tell herself that Ruiz was just doing his thing and that it was in his nature to make people feel good.

Richly carpeted steps led down to a luxurious, stone-flagged basement, where lead-paned glass glinted in the sultry glow of candles. The heavy polished furniture and rich draperies in ruby reds and regal purples gave the club an established sense of luxury and indulgence. Ruiz was right about it providing food for her column. It was not only packed, she could see now through the archway leading into the main dining room and dance floor, but, judging by the clientele, it was the hottest place in town. Her readers would definitely be interested, Holly thought as Ruiz held her coat. 'Is that a samba they're playing?'

'Very good,' Ruiz remarked as he handed Holly's coat to an attendant. 'I can tell you're eager to dance—'

'Oh, no,' Holly exclaimed as her pulse raced off the scale. 'I'm only here to observe.' But in her head she was already practising the steps. She had taken some classes a while back with a friend, but her heart thundered at the thought that Ruiz might put her to the test. She reassured herself that the samba had been one of the easiest dances to learn: *back, forward, forward*. There were only three steps to remember, for goodness' sake—

'You do dance the samba…?'

Ruiz's eyes were dancing with laughter, Holly noticed. 'And how do you know that?' she challenged him.

'You're mouthing the steps.'

'No, I'm not,' Holly argued, relieved when the maître d' arrived to escort them to their table. He had seated them right at the edge of the dance floor, which was fantastic for watching the dancers, but terrible if, like Holly, you didn't want to be so dangerously close to the action.

'The steps will soon come back to you,' Ruiz assured her with an amused smile.

'I'm sure you're right,' Holly agreed as the maitre d' removed the reserved sign with a flourish.

'And I think you're going to be very good at it,' Ruiz prompted when Holly gave him a look. 'Dancing, I mean.'

As Ruiz lounged back in his comfortably padded chair all Holly could think about was the scary dance teacher, yelling at her to *Bounce, Valiant, bounce! For goodness' sake, lift your feet, girl!* Before she fell over them presumably. Would samba lessons delivered in her local community centre by a moustachioed teacher help her now? Holly wondered as she gazed at the slinky couples moving effortlessly around the floor. Somehow, she doubted it. This samba was faster, cooler, and way sexier than she remembered, especially when she compared it to her shambling attempts. But then she had been dancing with an equally uncoordinated girl. Men had been thin on the ground in the classes, so most of the women ended up dancing together, Holly remembered, glancing at her rugged companion. Dancing with Ruiz Acosta might be somewhat different, she suspected.

He was impatient when people kept on greeting him—especially impatient when he noticed the curious glances they were lavishing on Holly. He should have known better than to bring her here but he had wanted her to have a treat. He had wanted to get her away from the computer and from the shadows of the past for just one evening. He would have liked half an hour with the man who hurt her. She was so inexperienced, so vulnerable. He hated the type of man who took advantage of that. He wondered if Holly had ever known love. Lucia had told him something about her clever friend who had been sent away to school on a scholarship by parents who never visited. No wonder his generous-hearted sister had palled up with sensible Holly Valiant. He could see it all now. Lucia had provided the warmth Holly had so badly needed, while Holly had kept his sister in line—just about.

'What are you smiling at now?' she said.

'Thinking about Lucia…'

'Ah.' She relaxed.

'And I'm enjoying myself,' he confessed, only realising now how true that was. He was completely relaxed—especially now that everyone had taken the hint and seen that he wanted to be alone with his supper companion. Had anyone ever made love to Holly, he wondered, or had they just used her without ever seeing the side of her that Holly kept so close? She was different from anyone he had ever known. He knew most women only wanted him for the material things he could provide—things in which Holly had absolutely no interest.

'Do you mind if I take my shoes off?' she said, distracting him from his thoughts as she pulled a comic face. 'I'll keep my feet under the table so you don't have to look at them—'

He laughed as she kicked the expensive shoes he'd bought her into touch.

She watched Ruiz greet acquaintances with a casual wave. He knew a lot of people in London, or, rather, a lot of people knew Ruiz, Holly amended, and they all seemed inordinately pleased if he noticed them. Perhaps it was she who needed a wake-up call, Holly reflected. Ruiz was an international sportsman and highly respected—

'Are you okay?' Ruiz prompted.

'Of course.'

'I want you to enjoy yourself.'

'I'm sure I shall.' She thought about Ruiz's comment regarding entertaining friends of the family and hoped she wasn't keeping him from his own friends. 'It's very good of you to bring me here,' she said politely.

Ruiz gave her a quizzical look. 'It's very good of you to come with me.'

Was it? Even in jeans and a crisp white shirt Ruiz looked amazing and exuded class, while Holly was increasingly aware of buying something just because it was in the sale that really didn't suit her and that was now clinging unattractively to her bargain-basement body.

'Would you like to dance?' Ruiz suggested.

'With you?'

'Were you thinking of dancing with someone else?' he queried with a sultry growl.

'In front of everyone?'

'That is the usual way.'

'Won't people talk? So many people seem to know who you are.'

'And if they do?'

'I don't want you to be unmasked,' Holly whispered dramatically, thinking she had found the perfect excuse not to dance with the playboy in public.

'Do they give you a byline on the Playboy column these days?' Ruiz asked innocently.

'No, of course they don't put my name on the column. I'm part of a team—'

Stop! Stop Talking NOW, Holly's inner voice advised, before you dig the hole any deeper. Of course no one knew who she was. She was just another of Ruiz's many female friends as far as the people at the club were concerned. 'Shall we chat and eat first?' she suggested, red-faced.

For a moment she thought Ruiz would argue and insist on dancing, but he just said, 'Whatever you like,' and picked up the menu.

And now she was disappointed. A hemp sack and a bowl of lentils was pretty much what she deserved, Holly concluded. Burying her head in the menu, she mentally revisited the conversation where Ruiz had made it clear that this evening was all about entertaining his sister's friend.

'Are you going to relax any time soon, Holly?'

She looked up. 'I'm sorry. I'm just a bit overwhelmed by all this.'

'All this?'

'I feel a bit out of place here, to be honest.' Whereas Ruiz was so confident and so good-looking he was at ease anywhere.

'Out of place? Why should you say that? I can't think of anyone who deserves a night off more than you do, Holly. Since the moment I met you, you've been working all hours.'

'But all these people are so—' She snatched a breath as Ruiz's hand touched her arm.

'Choose something to eat,' he prompted.

Studying the menu, and actually reading it this time, Holly gulped when she saw the prices. When the waiter arrived to take their order she told him that a starter-sized salad would be enough for her. Shaking his head, Ruiz countermanded that idea and ordered for her. 'You don't have to eat what I've ordered for you,' he explained, 'but if you're going to continue working at the pace you do, one lettuce leaf and a spoonful of dressing isn't enough to keep you going.'

Ruiz's amused glance lasted a little longer this time and as she held it something told Holly that if she could relax they might be friends. After all, Ruiz was her best friend's brother, and she loved Lucia…

The meal Ruiz had ordered for Holly was delicious. He had chosen perfectly. The most delicious halibut she had ever tasted came with side orders of buttered spinach, roasted tomatoes, and creamy mashed potatoes. Ruiz devoured an epic steak, and after the meal they drank strong, aromatic coffee as they watched professional dancers giving an eye-popping demonstration of how the samba should be danced. Surely, Ruiz couldn't expect her to do that? Holly thought, imagining how she might interpret the hip grinding and pelvic thrusting, which the professional dancers managed to turn into something so erotic, and yet so stylish. It might look rather different if she took to the floor. And then there were the outfits. The woman's costume was glittery and filmy, barely a whisper of aquamarine chiffon decorated with diamanté, while the man's black trousers might have been sprayed on—

'And now we dance,' Ruiz announced when the applause had died down.

'I don't think so,' Holly protested, sitting deeper in her chair.

Ruiz gave her no option. Making her gasp as he lifted her out of the seat, he lowered her onto a dance floor crowded with couples only too eager to show what they could do. 'You can't force me,' Holly protested, turning to go.

'And you can't resist the music.' He brought her back again.

Short of drawing attention to herself, she had no option but to go through the motions of dancing one samba, Holly concluded. She was just gearing herself up to do this when another man, crowned with the same menacing glamour as Ruiz, strode up to them. Swinging a welcoming arm around Ruiz's shoulders, he exclaimed, 'Hello, my friend. Long time no see.' His gaze remained fixed on Holly's face—assessing and no doubt drawing all the wrong conclusions, she thought. This must be the Brazilian friend Ruiz had told her about, Holly concluded as the two men exchanged a fierce hug.

Ruiz confirmed this when he introduced them. 'Holly, I'd like you to meet an old friend and adversary of mine—'

'Not so much of the old, please,' Gabriel insisted with his gaze still trained on Holly. 'Though I won't argue about our adversarial tendencies.'

'Gabriel,' Holly said politely, hoping she wouldn't get her hand scorched off when she shook his hand. Was there a whole contingent of stunning South Americans living in London? Holly wondered as more, equally striking men joined their group.

'Polo players,' Ruiz explained, slipping out of Portuguese

with Gabriel into Spanish with some of the others. 'My apologies, Holly,' he added politely. 'We will speak only English now,' Ruiz instructed his friends.

Polo players? She would never have guessed, Holly mused wryly, taking in the muscular physiques. All the men looked like athletes and none of them was afraid of staring her straight in the eyes. She wasn't used to such forthright inspection and felt her cheeks fire red. And then Ruiz introduced her by explaining that Holly was an agony aunt, which only brought a fresh blood-rush to her cheeks.

'Holly doesn't look much like your auntie to me,' Gabriel commented dryly.

'If *you* need any help or advice, Holly, don't hesitate to call me,' another man drawled.

'Enough,' Ruiz commanded good-humouredly. To Holly's further amazement, he then placed a protective arm around her shoulders. 'You'll have Holly believing all South Americans are best avoided by respectable women.'

'Respectable women?' Gabriel commented in a low drawl. 'Now there's a rare breed. You must allow me to offer you the hospitality of my club,' Gabriel added, switching his amused, worldly stare from Holly's face to Ruiz. 'At least for the first part of your evening. The rest of the night is up, to you my friends.'

'That's enough, Gabe.' Ruiz cautioned his friend in a low voice in a way that made Holly feel unusually protected.

Not a bad feeling, she concluded, if one she was unused to. Ruiz leaping to her defence was surprise enough, but seeing how quickly the other men backed off when he told them to communicated a lot about Ruiz. 'Thank you,' she said quietly when they were alone again.

'For what?' Ruiz demanded.

'I think you know,' she said.

CHAPTER SIX

*Playing with fire and the consequences thereof.
Someone once told me that dancing is one of the
few things we humans do in perfect rhythm with a
partner, and that the other notable activity, more
often than not, follows afterwards.
Fat chance, is all I can say.
Oh, and I would write at greater length, but tapping away under the table while the playboy briefly
chats with more admirers doesn't give me much
chance to wax lyrical. I can only say that the consequences of the gawkiest redhead in town attending the hottest club in town with the sexiest man in
town, steeling herself to dance the hottest dance on
the planet with a man born to move in rhythm with
a partner, should give you a laugh—*

HER next column would be one heck of a read, Holly
concluded as Ruiz led her onto the dance floor. Seeing
him here outside an environment they shared was interesting. She liked him better if anything. The respect
Ruiz attracted from the other men was a measure of
him, and although she was the clumsiest thing on two
feet she felt confident Ruiz would never laugh at her or
put her down the way her ex had. She only had to see

him with his friends to know Ruiz was all about making people feel good.

'Please excuse my friends,' he said as if he had picked up on her thoughts. 'Waiting for the polo season to get underway frustrates them. I'm afraid they're suffering an overdose of testosterone without the opportunity to work it off.'

'I'm really not that sensitive.'

'In the workplace? I would agree with you,' he said. 'But personally...I'm not so sure.'

'They really didn't upset me,' Holly stressed. 'So *you* can relax.'

'If you ask me to...'

As his lips tugged she shivered with awareness. What was the female equivalent of Ruiz's friends' problem? Pheromone-frenzy? Whatever it might be she had it bad.

'We're all impatient for the polo season to start, Holly,' Ruiz confided, drawing her gaze back to his strong, dark face.

Her name sounded so exotic on Ruiz's lips it must be way past the time to steer her thoughts onto safer ground. 'You must miss polo and Argentina very much.'

'I miss my brothers more than the game. I even miss that wretched sister of mine,' Ruiz admitted wryly. 'I miss the space and the wild free gallops,' he added, drawing her close, fortunately so engaged in his own thoughts Ruiz missed her sharp intake of breath as she collided with his hard body. 'And I miss the warmth of the people.'

There was quite a lot of warmth going on here too, Holly thought as Ruiz pressed against her, but then she noticed he was staring over her head at nothing in particular, as if his thoughts were somewhere else, far away. But when the music started to play and his hand found hers she thrilled at the warmth of his touch. He moved gently at first, easing her into the dance, his confident movements in perfect timing with the beat of the music. He held her so lightly, and yet the music seemed to flow from him to her so that even Holly's awkward body responded perfectly. She was infected by the rhythm, and by Ruiz, Holly concluded, and by the sense that on a cold winter's night there was nowhere else on earth she would rather be than dancing the samba in Ruiz's arms.

Had she gone completely mad?

Probably, Holly thought as Ruiz, having told her to relax, firmed his grip. 'That's better,' he approved as she began to move a little more confidently to the music, but then he added, 'I think you have been less than honest with me, Holly.'

'What do you mean?' Her head shot up.

'You can dance,' Ruiz said, smiling.

She smiled back, feeling good inside. Her hand felt right in his, and with Ruiz's arm around her waist, his fingers lightly holding her, she realised she liked being part of a couple—this couple—however fleeting this chance of being with Ruiz might be. They moved well together, easily, as if they had been dancing this way all their lives. She had never made a show of herself like this before, yet here she was, dancing in public with a man born to use his body expertly, while she was twirling and flirting with her hips and with her eyes—

What was the worst that could happen? She could make a fool of herself? Something told her Ruiz would never allow that to happen.

'You're not even treading on my feet,' he said dryly, dipping his head to direct this observation with a smile into her eyes.

'Nor you on mine,' she agreed.

'Unusual for me,' Ruiz remarked, smiling wickedly again.

She loved it when he teased her. She loved… Unfortunately for her peace of mind, she loved most things about Ruiz.

The samba was fast and flirty. If she had chosen to represent each of them with a dance it would be the passionate tango for Ruiz and an energetic barn dance with more gusto than panache for Holly. But somehow they were meeting in the middle with this highly charged, fast-moving pas de deux that left her little time to wonder if she was doing it right. No time to think, no time to feel self-conscious. Just fun and laughter, flashing eyes, and moving her body to the rhythm of the music in a way she wouldn't have believed possible until tonight.

'Now you're really getting into it,' Ruiz approved as he spun her round.

'You know I'm only doing my best to keep up.'

'No. You have a natural flair,' Ruiz insisted, drawing her close again.

'Not really. There are some great dancers here.' And Ruiz was one of them, as every woman in the club seemed to agree. Thank goodness he couldn't see her face, Holly thought as she relished the unaccustomed sensation of being pressed up close against him. Tough, hard and strong, Ruiz might look like a swarthy bad boy on the rampage, but he moved like a dream.

And this was a man whose reputation made Casanova seem like a choir boy. And what had happened the last time she had allowed herself to be lulled into a trance-like state by a good-looking man? Images of half-empty wine bottles and crisp packets piled up on a carpet of chocolate wrappers crowded into her head. Did she really want to go back there? Not that Ruiz had any need of her money.

'I've lost you,' he chided as the dance floor began to clear. 'Where are you now, Holly? Worrying about the steps for the next dance?' he suggested as the music started up again.

There couldn't be a next dance if she wanted to keep any sense of reality where Ruiz was concerned. Her less than platonic feelings for him could only mean she was setting herself up for a fall. 'Shouldn't we be getting back for Bouncer?'

'The dog?' Ruiz gave her one of his looks. 'Didn't I take him out for the longest walk ever before we came here?'

'He has been on his own for rather a long time.'

'And will be asleep by now, I have no doubt,' Ruiz assured her, his sexy eyes darkening in a smile. And then the infectious beat started up again. The moment his hand found the hollow in the small of her back she was lost. They were good together—frighteningly good.

When the dance ended Ruiz held her at arm's length. 'I don't know when I've enjoyed myself so much, Holly.'

Was he serious? The adrenalin rush that had been brought on by dancing with Ruiz was subsiding, leaving a gap for Holly's self-esteem issues to fill.

'Thank you for tonight,' he said.

'I won't put your toes in danger again, I promise.'

'Where are you going?' Ruiz caught hold of her.

'To get my coat. To call a taxi.' She held up her hand when Ruiz seemed as if he might argue with her. 'You don't have to leave. Thank you for a wonderful evening, Ruiz.'

Dipping his head low, Ruiz stared into her eyes. 'Do

you think I'm going to let you call a cab and leave the club on your own?'

'I'm not a baby, Ruiz. And you don't have to spoil your night just because I'm going home.'

'I brought you here. I'm taking you home. And, anyway, it's too late for you to be out on your own.'

If Ruiz was talking about the dangers of the night he would come top of her list. 'I'll be fine in a cab,' Holly insisted. 'If it makes you feel better, why don't you call a reputable company of your own choosing?'

She was serious, he realised. He had to admire Holly's strength of will. She was an independent woman and he respected that, but all he could think was how she'd felt in his arms when they danced together and how he didn't want the evening to end. Holly was all woman—she just didn't know it yet. Her hair had felt like spun silk beneath his hands and her body was— Now who was writing up a storm? 'I'm taking you home,' he said firmly, flashing a warning glance at his friends who had been viewing their little altercation from the bar.

She slept with Bouncer that night. Much safer. And as far as *sex sells* went, how about a snuffly dog with an ear-splitting snore? How well would that sell? 'Oh, Bouncer,' Holly complained softly as the big dog began to chase rabbits in his sleep. 'I can see I'm not going to get any more rest tonight.'

Retrieving the duvet from the floor where Bouncer had kicked it, Holly glanced at the clock on the wall. Three a.m. Great. There was only one thing for it—she might as well start writing her next column. It wasn't as if she didn't have anything to say. Creeping out of the bedroom, she sat down at her usual place in the living room and began to write, and write. She soon had enough to fill a double-paged spread. Pausing for thought, she started thundering on the keyboard again, hardly realising that she was reasoning out her feelings for Ruiz—

The playboy is the youngest of a notorious band of polo-playing brothers and also the brother of my best friend, so of course we have a bond. He is someone I can be friends with, but nothing more—even if he wanted more, which, obviously, he doesn't...

'Don't stop now—'

Holly swung round in shock to find Ruiz, barefoot in a black tee and boxers, standing behind her, blatantly reading her screen.

'I was just enjoying that,' he protested as she shut the lid on her laptop.

Her cheeks fired with embarrassment. 'Don't you have any manners?'

'In the bedroom? Yes. In the office? No. This is your temporary office, isn't it, Holly?' And then, as if such a wealth of tan and muscle on so broad-shouldered a frame weren't enough to scramble her brains completely, he leaned low to murmur, 'We really have to stop meeting like this...'

'I couldn't agree more,' she said primly, refusing absolutely to acknowledge the way Ruiz was making her feel.

'Can I get you a drink?' he said. 'Hot milk, perhaps? Or cocoa?'

'You can stop teasing me,' she warned. Standing, she drew herself up to her full five feet three, which only succeeded in amusing Ruiz as she had to lean back to look him in the eye. But then she thought about what he'd said. 'Am I really so boring that you think I need hot milk?'

'I wouldn't call you boring.' Ruiz's sexy mouth pressed down in wry conjecture as he pretended to think about it. 'Irritating, maybe—'

'Like an itch you can't reach?' she suggested dryly.

'Oh, I can reach you,' Ruiz assured her softly.

Not quite so sure she wanted to play this game any longer, Holly watched warily as Ruiz walked towards her. She couldn't have been more surprised when he leaned forward to brush a kiss against her lips. Without meaning to, she swayed against him. He moved away.

'See you in the morning, Holly.'

She stared after him, deciding her readers would never know what a close call she'd had.

Tactics that had worked so well for him in the past didn't work with Holly. And he wouldn't want them to, Ruiz concluded as he directed a frustrated punch at his pillow. Was she still working? Was she asleep? Closing his eyes, he tried running the company balance sheets in his head. That had always worked for him in the past, but not tonight, because tonight all he could see was Holly in overlarge pyjamas with her bare feet crossed and tucked neatly beneath the chair while she sat with her head bowed over her laptop, feverishly tapping away.

'Ruiz?'

He shot up.

'I'm sorry to disturb you,' Holly murmured as she opened the door just a crack. 'Bouncer was begging to go out and now he seems to have hurt his paw in the garden.'

'You went outside at night on your own?' He was halfway across the room by this time. 'Don't do that again,' he said, striding past Holly towards the kitchen.

'I didn't have much choice,' Holly insisted, catching up with him. 'I bathed the paw,' she explained as he hunkered down to take a look.

'I can't see anything,' he admitted.

'Neither could I. Maybe he trod on some glass? He was limping when he came back into the kitchen.'

'Did you give him a biscuit when you brought him in?'

'Why, yes, I did,' Holly admitted. 'And once I was sure he was okay I gave him another to reassure him.'

Ruiz grinned as he ruffled the big dog's fur. 'That's one of Bouncer's favourite tricks—limping, and then the hangdog expression. Works every time, doesn't it, boy?'

'He had me,' Holly admitted ruefully, shooting Bouncer a hard stare. 'I'm really sorry for getting you out of bed, Ruiz, especially as it looks like it was for nothing.'

'Better safe than sorry,' he observed, springing up.

He realised then how tiny Holly was in bare feet, and how big and clumsy he was by comparison. More concerning was the fact that he was only wearing boxers and a tee. 'You're not going back to work, are you?' he asked as she turned for the door.

'Maybe—I keep a personal diary too. Remember? I told you. Always have,' she explained.

And wouldn't he love to see that! 'How does anyone find the time?'

'Only child?'

'Ah, yes. Lucia told me. No siblings to distract you.' He realised then that Holly must have had plenty of time to record her thoughts, and that what had been a hobby to begin with had become a habit now. 'So what was it like having my sister as a friend at boarding school?' he asked curiously, not wanting Holly to go just yet.

She laughed. 'Quite a shock to my system. I was an only child used to doing what I was told.'

'And Lucia was a very different animal?' Ruiz's lips tugged. He understood.

How had she become best friends with the most attractive and outgoing girl in the school? Thinking back, Holly remembered Lucia not just being high spirited and up to mischief half of the time, but so incredibly warm, and interested in everyone—not unlike her brother, Ruiz. It was a tribute both to their good nature and to their brother Nacho, who had brought them up.

'Lucia and I made quite a team,' she explained. 'We egged each other on and skated a very thin line between total exclusion from the school and one of our crazy ideas taking off. Lucky for us, one of our ideas worked so well we managed to get a whole pile of money from a government educational grant to develop our ecological project.'

'Was that where the green hair came in?'

'Are you accusing me of deliberately dying my hair green?'

'Should I be?' Ruiz said wryly.

'It may have had something to do with it.'

'So, in summary you were both holy terrors?'

'You don't know the half,' Holly agreed.

'Which is perhaps just as well,' Ruiz commented, his ruggedly handsome face creasing in a rueful grin. 'Well. I suppose I should turn in. Thanks for looking after our mutual friend.'

'Don't you want some ice cream?'

'Ice cream?'

'When it's this late and you don't want to start eating proper food again, ice cream fills a gap, I find.'

'Does it?' Ruiz said in a tone that made her toes curl. She was already rifling through the freezer box by this time, shaking convulsively and not with cold. She had never led a man on before. But this was new Holly, and there was a first time for everything...

Holly licked her lips when she found the carton of ice cream she was looking for. He realised then that had any other woman done that he would have interpreted the request as she would have wanted him to, but with Holly it was different. She was different. Meanwhile, Bouncer might not be the talking dog, but the big mutt had a very eloquent way of expressing himself. Currently stretched out in a contented sprawl snoring softly, Bouncer had clearly forgotten all thoughts of sore paws and looked as if everything in his world was going to plan.

Ruiz took up every available inch in the kitchen. There was no way past his bed-ruffled, barely clad form unless he backed out of her way. Stretching up, she tried reaching for two bowls, then, spotting something else, she changed her mind and grabbed a pack of ice-cream cornets instead. But now her hand was shaking so much she couldn't get the ice-cream scoop to connect with the contents of the tub.

'Here, let me help you with that,' Ruiz offered. 'If we put the scoop in boiling water first—' He stopped. 'Holly? You're really shaking. Are you cold?'

'Yes,' she exclaimed, grabbing the cue Ruiz had given her like a life raft. Could desire do this to you? She had no idea what desire could do, having never felt anything to compare with this before. With her ex she had been so pathetically grateful that he noticed her at all that her own passion had never really come into it. She had been too busy trying to please him, to keep him, to keep his interest—

'Why don't you turn the heating up, while I serve the ice cream?' Ruiz suggested, sounding as normal as ever, as if two people clad in nightclothes—one of them barely clad at all—could have a companionable chat in the middle of the night without feeling as incredibly aware as she did. Could she squeeze past him without touching? She glanced at the climate control on the wall, knowing she wasn't even remotely cold, but it was too late to admit that now.

'Come on,' Ruiz prompted, pressing his muscular form back against the side to let her past.

Was he kidding? This was a really bad idea. She was hardly experienced enough to play flirting games with Ruiz, let alone rub past so much muscle. But she would have to...

Sucking in her stomach, she braced herself. Avoiding contact was impossible. Ruiz tried to help, but she still got stuck. 'This is a tight squeeze,' he observed dryly.

She tried to reach over him to the control, conscious all the time of his hot, hard, naked thigh pressed up against her. 'You're taking up all the space. I can't reach anything. You'll have to move.'

Please, please move—

Ruiz didn't move a muscle. 'I thought you said you needed warming up?' he commented.

'I do—' Her hand flailed about searching for the elusive heat control, while her gaze never left Ruiz's dark, amused stare. He might well look like that when her body had somehow moulded itself around his without any input from her at all.

'Shall we forget about the ice cream?' he asked.

Her breath hitched in her throat as Ruiz dipped his

head towards her, but she had called it wrong. Instead of kissing her, as she had thought he might, he dabbled ice cream on her cheek. Exclaiming with surprise, she pushed him away. 'You—!'

Ruiz seized her wrist and drew her close. 'Don't wipe it off,' he said, frowning. 'What a waste…' She trembled uncontrollably as he moved her hand away and licked the ice cream from her face. She was still reeling from this when he dabbed some more on her neck. 'This is delicious,' he observed as coolly as if they were sharing a meal in a café.

Sweet sensation streamed through her veins, making her more reckless and excited. She reached one hand out, cautiously feeling for the tub, but Ruiz saw what she was doing and dodged out of her way, and the best she could manage was a glancing blow to his cheek. 'How's your temperature?' she demanded, backing away to a safe distance.

'Red hot,' Ruiz assured her.

CHAPTER SEVEN

*Have you ever felt that you were about to do some-
thing you might regret and yet were utterly powerless to stop yourself? Well, that's where I am now. I
could do with a gang of you turning up at the penthouse to drag me back from the lustful brink. But
I should warn you that if you do I might not be all
that pleased to see you.*

*Tomorrow's another day? Yes, and I might need a
hug by then. Maybe I'll know what sex can be like
when you choose the right man, but we all know
that for every good thing that happens there's the
flip side of the coin, so I could be about to make
the biggest mistake of my life.*

*And the playboy? The reason I'm telling you this
is because there's a look in his eyes I haven't seen
before, and after months of telling myself I don't
need men I suddenly thought, Do I want to spend
the rest of my life wondering what I've missed?*

COULD she remember all that? She could hardly race to
the laptop now. 'The writer of this column is otherwise
engaged and seems likely to be so for quite some time'
was one heck of a headline, but was this moment something she wanted to share with the world? 'How is it pos-

sible I'm covered in ice cream while you have a magic ring of protection around you?' Holly demanded excitedly, playing for time. She shrieked as Ruiz prowled closer, while he just grinned and shrugged.

Why was she out of ammunition? Holly's chaotic thoughts refused to assemble into a coherent form as she backed away. It wasn't a fresh tub of ice cream she needed, but a long, cold shower and a few miles' distance between them. What had she been thinking? That she could play games with Ruiz and there would be no consequences? 'Okay. I give up.' She raised her hands in defeat. 'You're better at this than I am—'

'What do you expect with three brothers and a sister? I've been having food fights since I could lift a spoon.'

An only child could only dream of having this much fun, but at least Ruiz had ceased hostilities for now. She breathed a sigh of relief as she tried to retrieve a blob of ice cream that had landed on her chest before it could trickle any lower. But this brief pause in the ice-cream war didn't mean she liked losing. Sneakily reaching for the tub, she launched a counter attack, and, though Ruiz had the reflexes of a fighter pilot, she managed to score a hit on his mouth.

'You'll pay for that,' he warned, wiping his lips with the back of his hand.

Holly sincerely hoped so. The fears that had haunted her for so long had been consumed in the fire burning in Ruiz's eyes. It was enough to make anyone hot and reckless. She held her breath as he prowled closer. Seconds ticked away and then they both launched an attack at the same moment. A fast and furious battle ensued. Ruiz was so much stronger and faster than she was, but she was fast enough, and fiercely competitive. Everything became a blur of limbs and flying ice cream. She managed to put the island counter between them, a barricade that gave her chance to draw breath. Lifting her chin, panting and gloating, she taunted Ruiz across the gleaming stretch of granite.

He vaulted over it. 'Now what are you going to do?' he said, holding her in front of him.

She hummed, glaring at him defiantly. Struggling was pointless. Ruiz's grip was light, yet firm, while she was consumed by excitement and covered in sticky ice cream. This was hardly the moment to assume the moral high ground. Resting back in his arms, she began to laugh.

'What?' he said.

Every part of her was tingling and aware. She was free. 'Nothing you need to know,' she said, straightening up to deliver a challenging stare into Ruiz's eyes.

He had never wanted her more. His virtuous resolutions to steer clear of Lucia's friend were history. He was more interested in licking Holly clean. He kissed her cheek, her neck, tasting her, and then he tasted her some more. 'You're delicious,' he commented as she wriggled in his arms, helpless with laughter.

'And so are you—'

He wasn't prepared for her whipping up his tee, and holding it while she licked the sugared cream from his chest. He sucked in a sharp breath and his surprise didn't lessen with the look she gave him. Her eyes blazed with fire and the sort of confidence he knew was buried deep inside. 'Kiss me,' she demanded fiercely, making it sound like a challenge as she locked her hands behind his head.

A challenge? This was a pleasure. The kiss was long and hot and deep. She tasted warm and sweet, and fiercely female. There was nothing girlie, soft, or vulnerable about Holly now. This was an equal match between a woman intent on claiming her mate, and a man who rejoiced in her strength as he lifted her.

She had never done anything remotely like this before—had never clawed at a man's clothes, hungry to feel his naked body hard against her. There was nothing delicate or tender happening here. She was burning up from the inside out.

Buttons from her pyjama top flew across the kitchen and skittered across the floor as she yanked Ruiz's top over his head. He only paused briefly to protect them both, and then he took over, resting her on the side as he pushed the top from her shoulders and the pyjama pants from her legs. His clothes dropped to the floor. Excited sounds escaped her lips. Ruiz's naked torso was stronger, harder, warmer, more beautiful than even she had imagined. The wide spread of his muscular shoulders was enough to turn her on, but it was the look in his eyes that really did it for her, because that promised more excitement than she had ever known. Holding Ruiz's darkening gaze, she traced the pattern of muscle and sinew from his breastbone to his shoulder, then down over his biceps to his forearms, and on to his hands and the lean, elegant fingers. 'Now,' she whispered urgently.

He brushed his mouth against her lips—a promise that wasn't enough for her now. 'Don't tease me,' she warned him. But he did, brushing his lips and his stubble against her neck and her cheek, and then her lips, promising, always promising, yet pulling away before she could taste him. He repeated this until her body was a furnace and she was wild for him.

As Holly pressed herself against him he tested her and found her ready. He still took his time, teasing her for as long as he had with kisses. She moaned with need when he gave her the tip and then exclaimed with disappointment when he took it away again. She shivered and opened herself more for him, pressing her thighs back as he touched her, crying when he paused. He dipped again, a little deeper this time, and then retreated. She was so moist, so warm, so completely ready for him, but even with the thought of that tight wet grip waiting to claim him banging at his brain he knew it would be better for her if he made her wait.

'I can't stand this,' she raged in a shaking voice.

'You have to,' he whispered. 'It will be all the better for it—'

'Really?' she exclaimed, and, arching forward without warning, she took him. She took him. He gasped and shuddered with surprise, slammed by an overload of sensation. 'Steady,' he cautioned as her fingers bit into his buttocks. 'If you do that,' he warned as she bucked and arced against him, 'it will all be over too soon—'

She ignored him. Screaming out his name, she plunged headlong into the first climax. It was a battle to hold her in place as she thrust her hips frantically to claim each wave of pleasure as it hit her. 'You're so big,' she groaned with satisfaction as the storm subsided.

'I aim to please,' he managed to say wryly, keeping up a steady rhythm until she was ready to start again. 'I trust that wasn't a complaint,' he added in a husky whisper against her mouth, unable to resist the temptation to kiss her again.

'A complaint?' she murmured when he released her. 'I trust that was just a sample?'

He laughed. She was ready for more and this time she didn't want any distractions. Taking him in an even firmer hold, she ground out, 'Don't tease me— Don't wait— Don't stop—'

'You're incredible,' he said. And it was true. He'd met his match.

They feasted on each other, and neither of them tired. He persuaded her to hold her thighs back so he could increase her pleasure. It was then he discovered that she loved to watch. 'You're quite something,' he murmured, accommodating that wish too. Arranging her comfortably with one leg over his shoulder and one tiny foot on the counter, he worked steadily to keep her hovering on the edge, but this was the hottest woman he'd ever known. Could *he* hold on? 'I'll tell you when,' he instructed, staring deep into her eyes.

Her retaliation was swift and fierce, 'Don't make me wait,' she warned him. 'Don't you dare make me wait—'

'Now,' he commanded, taking her with a firm, deep thrust. The sound of her voice—the language she used—all of it increased his pleasure tenfold and this time they rode the storm together, inventing a new erotic dictionary along the way.

They must have been unconscious for a few moments, Holly thought as she slowly came round to find Ruiz resting against her, breathing steadily, still holding her safe in his arms.

'What?' he murmured, raising his head to look at her.

A sudden rush of doubt swept through her at the thought of what they'd done. Without the same hunger driving her she had too much time to think.

'Holly?' Ruiz prompted, sensing the change in her.

'Nothing,' she said. But there was something wrong, and they both knew it. A game that had started out so innocently had turned into something so much more.

'Do you regret it?' Ruiz asked with concern.

'No, of course not.' Reaching up, she closed her eyes and kissed him, but the doubts refused to go away.

'You're not frightened of me, are you?' Ruiz demanded softly when they broke apart.

Nothing could be further from the truth. She wasn't frightened of Ruiz. She was frightened of her feelings for him.

Cupping her chin so she couldn't avoid his gaze, Ruiz demanded, 'Is there someone else?'

That was so ridiculous she laughed. 'There's no one else,' she exclaimed. But Ruiz was partly right, even if he was wholly wrong. She was completely here in the moment with him, but the past couldn't be erased, and she couldn't forget that when her ex had come on the scene she had been so grateful, so thrilled by the attention he lavished on her, she had fallen for it—for him—to the extent that she would have trusted him with her life. Fortunately, she had only trusted him with her bank card, but her small pot of savings had disappeared just the same. No wonder she doubted her own judgment now.

Ruiz eased her carefully down, making sure she was steady on her feet before he let her go. 'Forget him,' he said in a voice she had never heard him use before. 'Whoever he was he can't hurt you now. I won't let anyone hurt you, Holly. You have to learn from the past and move on. Don't you think you can? Why not? When we first met you weren't sure you could make it as a journalist, but look at you now. Where has that woman gone?'

'On permanent vacation?' She smiled wryly to make light of it, but Ruiz wasn't in the mood for a joke and told her so. 'It's time to give yourself a break, Holly.'

'And it's time you stopped being kind to me for your sister's sake,' she fired back, knowing even as she said it that she was allowing the past to spoil things for her.

'You think I'm being kind to you?' Ruiz said.

'What can I think when you've already told me that

being kind to me for Lucia's sake is what you feel obliged to do?'

'You're twisting my words. You should have more confidence in yourself Holly.'

She dragged in a shuddering breath as Ruiz's lips brushed her cheek and then her neck, and finally her mouth. She wanted nothing more than to believe him.

'You're still too serious,' he said, drawing back to look at her, but then his wicked mouth tugged in a smile, 'and here was me thinking I had done everything possible to make you smile.'

She huffed and relaxed a little. Everything they had shared was reflected in Ruiz's eyes. It was both arousing and terrifying.

'More ice cream?' Ruiz suggested, refusing to be drawn into her dark mood.

'You're very bad.' But her voice was trembling as Ruiz's lips brushed her neck.

'It's your turn to lick me clean,' he observed, staring down at her with a mock-stern expression on his face. 'You started this game and now you have to finish it.'

She laughed. Holly touched him in a way no other woman had. He was so acutely tuned in to her he could feel all her hopes and fears, and not for the first time wished he could meet the man who had hurt her so badly. He wanted to keep her safe—

Safe from him?

He brushed that thought aside as she stared at his lips. He had never felt this way before. He had always held his feelings in, knowing Nacho had had enough to contend with bringing up three brothers and a sister. Holly had always kept her feelings in—they both had; that was their bond.

'What are you thinking?' she said quietly.

That Ruiz the fixer had always managed to fix himself, but now there was Holly in the frame. 'Are you refusing to finish this game?' The heat was rising. He could see it in her eyes. He wanted Holly to forget the past with all its false promises and disappointments. 'As it's you I'll permit the use of a clean cloth rather than your tongue,' he teased. 'I realise now that licking is only for the advanced class.'

'Don't you take anything seriously?' she asked, wondering how she was supposed to resist a man whose eyes were always so warm.

Ruiz pretended to think about it. 'The health of my polo ponies? I take that sort of thing very seriously indeed. But ice cream fights?' His lips curved in a wry smile as he shook his head. 'Sorry to disappoint you, Holly.'

'What are you doing?' she said as he drew her close.

'Now I know you're not that naïve.'

'Ruiz—' That was as far as she got.

'I want you,' he said. 'What you see is what you get with me, Holly. There is no hidden agenda. And I think you want me too. Am I wrong?'

How could she deny it? Confronted by this much strength of will she might have expected to feel weak or vulnerable, but she felt neither of those things. She felt strong. The strongest man she had ever known had made her feel confident in her own right.

'Are we going to stand here all day?' he demanded, brushing his lips against her cheek and then her neck. 'Or am I going to take you to bed?'

She was on fire for him, and as Ruiz's hold softened into a caress she linked her hands behind his neck and let him lift her.

Ruiz carried her into the bedroom and laid her down

carefully on the bed. Every instant apart from him seemed like a minute, every minute an hour. She reached for him hungrily, wanting him so strongly nothing could stop this. Ruiz's kiss was like the first time all over again, and so gentle her eyes stung to think he could be so tender. She hadn't expected such reverence. She was a plain, down-to-earth woman and expected to be treated as such, but Ruiz was kissing her as if she were made of the finest glass and might shatter in his arms if he held her too tightly. 'You're beautiful,' he murmured.

'No, I'm not.'

'If I say you're beautiful you should believe me.'

'I'm far too big,' she interrupted, trying to cross her arms over her breasts.

'How can you be too big when the top of your head barely reaches my chest? And your breasts are beautiful.'

She didn't argue when Ruiz lay beside her. Or when she shivered with pleasure as he dipped his head to lave first one nipple and then the other with his tongue so skilfully she writhed urgently on the bed, instantly hungry for him. When one powerful thigh pressed against her legs she welcomed him with a sharp cry of need, responding greedily by arching against the brutal thrust of his erection, demanding release.

She might have known he'd make her wait, and now she was all the more excited, knowing what lay in store for her. He protected them both again. Protection was for the woman to think about, she remembered her ex telling her—

She must have been mad. And desperate, Holly thought as Ruiz took her in his arms. 'No more shadows,' he whispered as if he knew where her thoughts had been straying. 'You're beautiful, and I want you, Holly. It's that simple.'

Stroking the hair back from her face, he kissed her repeatedly, and when she felt the tip of his erection brush against her she almost lost control. 'Greedy,' he murmured, soothing her when she groaned with complaint. Moving on top of her, he warmed her with kisses, cupping her buttocks as he positioned her for pleasure. This was more leisurely, allowing them to relish each sensation to the full. She pressed her hands against his chest, staring up into his eyes.

'Good?' he murmured.

'So good…' Holding his gaze, she was able to share the moment when the smooth warm tip of Ruiz's erection probed delicately before withdrawing again. It was an incredible sensation, and sucked every last shuddering breath of air out of her. He repeated the action so it was like the first time every time. He was giving her a master class in foreplay with such a concentration of sensation it wasn't long before she had to thrust towards him and take him deep—and she was still astonished by the size of him.

'How about we take it more slowly?' Ruiz suggested with amusement.

'You dare,' she warned him, wondering if it was really possible to be stretched like this and survive the pleasure. 'I'll take it anyway you like,' she managed shakily.

Ruiz soothed her with one hand while he increased her pleasure with the other. 'Don't be scared, I've got you,' he said, reading her.

'But it's too much,' she exclaimed frantically. 'Too big…'

'I decide when,' Ruiz told her, perfectly in control.

She trusted him and stared deep into his eyes as he

held her firmly in position to take her on an effortless slide into a world of sensation. 'I can't hold on,' she cried at last.

'You're not supposed to,' Ruiz assured her with amusement. Taking her deep with several firm, sure strokes, he thrust her over the edge where she had no option but to fall, clutching at him wildly as a starburst of sensation exploded in her head.

He held her in his arms as she slowly subsided. Holly was like an open book, pure and true, but was he ready for this wealth of feeling? He had often joked with his brothers about finding a woman who meant more to him than any other. They had tossed the idea around and concluded that as the youngest, it definitely wouldn't be Ruiz first. Probably wouldn't be him ever. Where would he find someone to put up with him? And if he did it would be years from now. He was too wild, too selfish, too unworthy of the sort of commitment and responsibility that came with devoting himself to one person, because that was what love meant to him—

Love?

He actually laughed out loud, and then felt guilty when Holly lifted her sated face to search his eyes. Smoothing the hair from her damp brow, he reassured her with murmured words and kisses. But she wasn't entirely convinced. 'What was that about?' she murmured groggily.

'You,' he said. 'You're lovely—I can't believe you're here with me.'

'Didn't you get that the wrong way round?' she queried sleepily.

'I got it exactly right,' he said. And she didn't deserve to be hurt.

'Lovely?' she said, wrinkling her nose. 'You really think I'm lovely?'

'Lovely and funny, and…you make me laugh,' he finished, not used to such feelings bombarding him. 'You're a lovely person, Holly.'

'Ah,' she breathed, turning her face into his chest.

Reading her insecurities, he could have kicked himself. 'Don't you dare,' he warned. Holding Holly in his arms, he realised the past haunted them both. He had worried his little sister could hear their parents fighting. And like the rest of the Acosta boys, he had struggled to understand his father's infidelities. He'd seen the hurt in his mother's eyes. He'd seen the so-called perfect family torn apart, until all that was left was a band of brothers with a sister to protect. He would never go down that road. The thought of turning out like his father was his worst nightmare. He had no intention of settling down with a woman until all the fire had left his veins and the only thing that mattered to him was holding someone's hand…

'Where are you now?' Holly murmured. 'And where are you going?' she said as he grabbed a towel from the bed and made for the door. 'I'm going to take a shower,' he said, securing the towel around his waist. His heart filled and when she smiled back at him his mind was made up.

She could use a break, Holly concluded wryly, stretching her glowing limbs contentedly. She was still in a wonderfully dreamy recovery state, and had been worrying that she might not be able to gather herself fast enough to satisfy a man like Ruiz. Keeping up with a man like that would require regular training sessions, she reflected happily. She looked up with surprise when he came back into the room, but it was only to drop a kiss on her swollen mouth. 'Where are you going now?' she demanded softly, reaching up to him.

'Goodnight, Holly…'

Smiling drowsily, she stared into the impossibly beautiful eyes, wondering if now was the moment to admit that Ruiz had exhausted her, but with a little sleep she'd be—

'Try not to oversleep,' he was telling her. 'I know you've got work tomorrow and I don't want you to be late because I kept you up half the night. Would you like me to set your alarm for you?'

She started to frown, realising that all the heat had gone from his eyes.

'I'd never forgive myself if I were the cause of putting a curb on your career,' he murmured, caressing her face.

He was talking about work now? Ice filled her veins. This wasn't good. 'There are plenty of things to worry about apart from work,' she said. 'Wasn't that what you told me?'

'So I did,' Ruiz agreed. 'And there's something else. The repairs on my town house are nearly complete so I'll be getting out of your hair soon.'

And that was good? Ruiz seemed to think so. Maybe her brain had been blown to mush by so much amazing sex, but that did not sound good to Holly.

Lifting the duvet, Ruiz pulled it up to her chin—an action that smacked more of consideration for a maiden aunt with an attack of the vapours than a crazy-for-you, I-want-to-keep-you-warm-for-the-very-few-minutes-I'm-away-from-your-side action. 'I don't want to get too comfortable,' she complained, throwing it off again. 'I might go to sleep if I do—'

'You should sleep well now, Holly.'

'Only for a few seconds.' She laughed, but something warned her to stop talking—that this was a train wreck and she was in the middle of it. Reaching up she put her hands flat against Ruiz's chest. They'd been as intimate as two people could be, but instead of feeling any response from him all she could feel was the play of muscle beneath her hands. 'Polo must be some game,' she said lamely.

'It is.'

And Ruiz had already left her, she registered.

What had she done? What had she done wrong?

She had allowed herself to want more than Ruiz was prepared to give her, Holly reasoned as he walked across the room. She wanted all of him, not just the sex. She wanted his warmth and his humour, his intelligence and perception, and the friendship that brought them close, making them, she had believed, trusting and trusted. She did not want this cold little voice inside her saying this same thing had happened to her before.

Not quite the same—

Not the same at all, Holly reassured herself. Not so many kisses and caresses, and no genuine affection of any kind. No affection at all, in fact. Her ex had been nothing like Ruiz.

'Sleep now,' Ruiz whispered from the door.

Burying her face in the pillow, she went tense all over as if that could shut out what was happening, but she only knew one way to give and that was wholeheartedly. She couldn't divide parts of herself off and hold them back. Perhaps men could do that.

Okay, she could deal with this, Holly told herself fiercely, swinging off the bed as the door closed. Chasing after Ruiz wasn't the answer. She had no one to blame but herself. Good-looking man notices plain, uncertain Holly, and bam! She's grateful. Worse. She's hungry for affection and blind to common sense—

But Ruiz had made her feel beautiful...

No. She had allowed Ruiz to make her feel beautiful and desired, because that was what *she* had wanted. She had bought into the fantasy while telling her readers so earnestly that casual encounters weren't cool, they were dangerous—especially for anyone with an iota of feeling inside them. Regrets? She only had to think about the letters pouring into the agony-aunt office to know that the majority of people writing those letters lived with regret. And now she was one of them. How badly had she let her readers down?

She took a shower, thinking that would help, but she was left with exactly the same absurd impression that Ruiz was special and mustn't be allowed to slip through her fingers. That he was one of a kind—one of *her* kind; the only man she would ever want and would measure every other man against—

Oh, to hell with that! Holly thought impatiently, tugging on fresh nightclothes. This wasn't love, it was lust. Those sexy eyes, that incredible body and the humorous curve of Ruiz's lips would be any woman's downfall.

No. Dropping onto the bed to stare blindly at the ceiling, she was finally prepared to admit that Holly Valiant's downfall was all her own doing and that Ruiz had merely been a willing accomplice.

And love?

Love didn't come into it, Holly told her inner voice coldly. Ruiz had been caught up in the moment and she had too. At least he hadn't presented her with a bill, which was pretty much what her ex had done. Shaking her head, Holly remembered that classic excuse when she had challenged her ex about emptying her bank account. 'Consider it payment for services rendered,' he'd said. 'You don't think I'd do it for free with you, do you?'

With that ringing in her ears it was no wonder she had a few issues where men were concerned—

But Ruiz wasn't that man. And she was a survivor who could put experiences like that behind her. Hadn't she already shown she could do that? Wasn't that why she was here now? She just had to get a handle on how she felt about Ruiz and remember that thunderbolts struck other people—in novels, mostly. They certainly didn't strike Holly Valiant. Tonight she had lapsed from the path she wanted to take, but she would be firmly back in control by tomorrow.

She lay in bed listening to the wind in the trees, and remained in the same lifeless position until everything in the apartment went quiet. It occurred to her that Ruiz wouldn't be lying in bed staring at the ceiling as he raked over the events of the night. This was, after all, just one day in the life of a playboy. Turning her face into the pillow, she wished briefly with amusement that she had her own agony aunt to write to and ask for advice, but then accepted she'd got it right from the start with rule number one: rely on no one but yourself.

Holly was a fixture in Ruiz's head the next morning as he pounded down the staircase to the street rather than taking the lift in the penthouse. He couldn't stop beating himself up about what had happened. She was new to London—and vulnerable. And his sister's friend. And he didn't need reminding about the world of inexperience on Holly's side and the equal amount of should-know-better on his. Exiting the building he saw his breath turn to frost. It made him long for the warmth of Argentina. Seeing Holly in Argentina away from her computer and the fantasy life she was weaving, Holly relaxed and happy, living in the real world for once… But he had meant it when he'd told Holly he would never stand in the way of her career. She had come so far since moving to London and had never made any secret of the fact that her career meant everything to her. He should be exhilarated at the thought of returning to Argentina, just as he should be happy for Holly. She was a proper city girl now—a survivor, successful and driven—

But he had hoped for more.

Ruiz frowned as he gunned the engine and pulled out onto an almost empty London street. Thank goodness today was all about business and he'd have no chance to think about Holly at all. It had to be early, he reflected wryly, for the streets of London to be this deserted. He'd lain awake after he'd left her, thinking, trying not to feel... In the end, he just left her a note warning her how cold it was and advising her to wrap up—

Holly...

He wasn't doing all that well at shutting his mind to her, Ruiz reflected. But he must. He would. He had to fly to Argentina for the match and would stay on for a while. Resting his chin on his arm as he waited for the lights to change, he remembered how Holly had felt in his arms, and her fresh, clean smell with the hint of vanilla—

Put Holly out of his mind? He might as well try to stop the breath in his chest. Nothing could steal away that look in her eyes when she gazed into his. Holly, dazzling and tender, quirky and funny, had a permanent place in his head. Holly wry, Holly angry, Holly spirited, taking him on. Holly hot as hell and sexy as sin—

Holly innocent and vulnerable.

Regrets?

She had them. And now he did too.

CHAPTER EIGHT

I have allowed myself to believe the playboy and I have something going on. How? Last night we got close—closer than I'm comfortable sharing in a public forum such as this.

Then he said his place was fixed and he'd be out of my hair shortly. Please don't pity me! I can do that for myself. And he wasn't proposing to turn the penthouse into a gilded cage where I can recline and paint my toenails until he finds time to visit, because as far as the playboy is concerned I am yesterday's news. Better to have lusted and lost than never to have lusted at all? Maybe we've all thought that at one time or another. Maybe we've all been wrong.

And the playboy? He's just the same—i.e. confident and busy, leaving me to get on with my life while he gets on with his. Which is ideal—or it should be, but I want someone to share things with, without getting laughed at or dismissed and he would never do that. I'd like to be part of his life—the private part that doesn't get written about—little things like sharing glances and second-guessing each other that's nothing and everything in the end. Maybe I deserve your pity after all...

SHE had got exactly what she deserved for allowing reality and fantasy to collide, Holly concluded, impatiently dashing away tears as she walked back to the penthouse after taking Bouncer for his early morning walk. She and Ruiz might have clung to each other and gazed into each other's eyes, and in the throes of passion she might have believed anything was possible, but he was still going back to Argentina.

Leaving her to get on with her career. Wasn't that exactly what she wanted? What she should want? What it was safest to want? So, why did she feel as if the bottom had just dropped out of her world?

This was all grist to the publishing mill, Holly concluded as she opened the door on an empty apartment. She should make use of the angst and write something to entertain. No one read the 'Living with a Playboy' feature to hear her moaning. She'd make something funny out of it—

Really?

So the idea just hadn't come to her yet, Holly reasoned, gazing out of the window at the frigid London street with its powdering of frost. But it would, she determined, stripping off her coat. Flinging her beanie and scarf onto a chair, she tossed out her hair. Ruiz was right about it being freezing outside. But why should he care if she was well wrapped up or not? Perhaps he didn't like the idea of his dog-walker-in-chief getting sick—

Enough Ruiz.

Enough! Enough! Out of my head now!

There was something she wanted to do before she left for work, and it did run contrary to rule number one: rely on no one but yourself. But desperate times called for desperate measures. Most of the mail for the agony-aunt column came in anonymously—and who needed help more than she did? She hurried to her laptop and quickly created an e-mail address for this one, very special purpose, and then, typing in the message, she pressed Send before she had the chance to change her mind.

So this is what it feels like to be a dedicated career woman, Holly reflected, ready for work, having applied more make-up than usual. Were her lips supposed to feel as if they were superglued together? Grimacing as she peeled them apart, she removed the overdose of gloss with a tissue, then reclaimed her nightclothes from the floor where Ruiz had flung them the night before. Resolutely shutting her mind to thoughts of how they had come to be on the floor, she tossed them into the washing basket, but then she couldn't resist plucking out the top again on the pretext of checking if it had more than one button missing. She held it briefly to her face and inhaled, as if Ruiz's spicy scent might still linger in the brushed cotton folds.

What was she doing? She wanted no reminders of last night. Dropping the top into the basket, she picked up the cryptic note Ruiz had left her about the cold weather and aimed it at the bin. She was ready for anything now—and positively buzzing with ideas for the column. Last night was another learning experience in her new London life, and this morning was a reflection of the woman she had become, i.e. tough Holly—tougher, anyway. Holly who could handle anything, Holly who had grown up overnight and who no one would ever accuse of being naïve again.

She carried that thought to the office, where she was relieved to be rushed off her feet. It gave her no time to think—except about Ruiz, who coloured all her thoughts. They were so busy on the agony-aunt column it looked as if they might have to recruit more people to handle the level of traffic the web site was attracting, not to mention the circulation boost the magazine had received.

All thanks to your column, Holly was told to her embarrassment. 'We're a team,' she insisted as everyone from the neighbouring offices gathered round her.

'And the team loves reading about your disastrous love life,' someone commented, which made everyone else laugh.

'Who doesn't love to sit knitting at the foot of the guillotine?' another colleague added with brutal honesty and an ironic laugh.

But it was just that bad, Holly thought, wishing she could write her own happy ending. Then one of the men from marketing distracted her by brandishing a copy of the magazine. 'Your private life's not your own any more, Holly. It belongs to all of us now.'

'Great.' She forced a laugh.

'Listen up, everyone,' one of the girls announced, reading from the monitor. 'You won't believe what some idiot has written.'

Holly knew. She knew immediately and only wished she could disappear in a puff of smoke, but it was too late as her colleagues had already rounded her up and were shepherding her towards the screen.

The girl started reading Holly's message: '"I've just met a really hot guy, which is great. What's not so great is that I slept with him on practically the first night when I know the relationship isn't going anywhere. It certainly can't now as he just told me he's moving on. I know you'll say I should forget him and move on myself. And I would. I really would, but I think I've fallen for him…"' Can you believe anyone would be that stupid?' the girl demanded, directing the question at Holly.

'Don't be harsh,' Holly blurted, blushing furiously.

'No, you're right,' the girl agreed when everyone had finally calmed down and stopped laughing. 'That was bitchy of me. And we've all been there, haven't we?'

When Holly's colleagues finally calmed down and agreed with this, their team leader, who was in the best of moods for once, called for silence. 'I've got some really good news for all of us. Since the playboy told our beloved redhead Holly that they were splitting, hits to the web site are threatening to crash the system.'

'Hasn't the "Living with a Playboy" feature almost run its course?' Holly suggested desperately, not wanting to go any deeper into this. 'Should we be thinking of going out on a high? Maybe trying to come up with a new idea for a fresh column?' She was clutching at straws, Holly realised when she saw the disapproval on her team leader's face.

'Are you mad?' he demanded. 'Don't even think about finishing it. Most of the hits are on your page. Your love life is such a mess everyone feels confident writing to you.'

'Oh, good. My life is a disaster, so everyone's happy—'

'Don't be so naïve, Holly. This is fiction. Keep up the misery,' the team leader advised. 'It sells almost as well as sex.'

Everyone laughed except Holly, who had closed her mind to the problems of real life and was already constructing her next headline: *Fall in love with his dog by all means, but don't fall in love with him—especially if you expect the same level of loyalty and affection you get from his furry friend.*

When she got back to the penthouse Holly's heart almost stopped when she found Ruiz already back from work.

He was lounging on the sofa in the living room with one jean-clad leg crossed nonchalantly over the other, the sleeves rolled back on his checked shirt—

Forearms bared meant action, Holly thought, feeling a jolt as her sixth sense kicked in. Ruiz had made no secret of the fact that he would be leaving soon for the polo match in Argentina. How soon? Very soon? She could sense change in the air. And then she saw what he was looking at. 'What's this?' he demanded, swinging his laptop round so she could see the screen.

'Fiction,' she said flatly. He'd read her latest article, which was less than complimentary about him and even less kind to her. It was the type of relationship screw-up the team leader had asked for, and, because she was still stinging from Ruiz's cold dismissal and the thought of him leaving for Argentina, for once she'd given her team leader what he'd asked for—no holds barred. 'Don't you like it?' she asked Ruiz, aching inside.

'It doesn't matter what I think,' he said, closing the lid. 'It's up to your readers, though you make your feelings clear enough.'

Wait until he read tomorrow's column, Holly thought, wondering briefly if she should tone it down, and then deciding not. 'I'm a journalist, Ruiz.'

'You mean you make things up,' he said, his eyes dark and watchful.

'You know I do. I've never made any secret of the fact that the "Living with a Playboy" feature is a fiction—a piece of light entertainment to increase reader interest in the agony-aunt column.'

'A feature for which I am the inspiration.'

'I have never made a secret of that either.'

Ruiz wouldn't look at her. But he had always known what she was doing. She must appear as nonchalant as he did. The sex had been spectacular between them last night, but acting cool the morning after was the only thing she could do to protect herself. So what would she tell her readers? She would heap on the misery as she'd been asked to, Holly concluded. 'What's wrong, Ruiz?'

'You say this is fiction?' He glanced at the laptop. 'But I think this must reflect your true feelings, at least a little.' And as such it hurt like hell, Ruiz concluded angrily. On the back of it he'd made a lot of changes—like hiring a housekeeper to take care of Bouncer while he was gone. 'I think you've started believing your own fiction, Holly.'

'What?' She laughed incredulously. 'It's just work. That's what I do.'

'Then I don't like what you do.'

The room hung in frigid silence. Holly felt as if the sword of Damocles were hanging by a thread above her head. She knew the sword had to fall, it was just a question of when and how fast.

So get out of its way—

'I'll go and put these things away, if you don't mind?' she said, glancing at the shopping bags of food she had brought in.

'When you've done that, come back. We need to talk.'

She felt dead inside. There was nothing in Ruiz's voice to suggest that last night had meant anything to him. Just as she had suspected, he had already moved on.

She went into the kitchen, where Bouncer came snuffling up to her, his big brown eyes soulful as if the dog sensed her tension and wanted to defuse it. 'I won't leave you,' Holly vowed fiercely. 'I'll find somewhere to live where you can come with me.' She glanced at the door behind which the man she had been so confident she could turn into a fiction, and who had somehow become so much more than that, was waiting for her.

She'd miss him when he left.

Squeezing back tears, she made do with hugging Ruiz's dog. 'I love you, Bouncer,' she said passionately, releasing some of the tension. It wasn't right to feel like this about a man. No excuses. She'd known all along how dangerous it was to risk her heart.

'I thought you were going to put that shopping away and then come back and talk?'

Collecting herself quickly, Holly looked up to find Ruiz lounging in the doorway. His arms were folded across his formidable chest, and his voice, his body, his eyes especially—eyes she had stared into with love, and into which she had placed her trust—everything drew her to him. She couldn't change her feelings where Ruiz was concerned just because it was safer to do so or because she willed it. She could write whatever she liked in the column, but reality refused to be manipulated. 'I'm just sorting stuff out,' she managed casually.

'Well, don't take all evening.'

The playboy might be a fictional figure, but Ruiz was all too real. And so were her feelings for him. Finding the doggy treats she'd bought at the supermarket, she tried telling herself it wasn't all bad as Bouncer's tail thanked her profusely. At least she'd made one good friend in London. But there was really only one friend and lover she could ever want, and he plainly wasn't interested.

She took her time, had a shower and changed into jeans before returning to the living room where Ruiz was working on his laptop. 'You're leaving soon, aren't you?' She had to challenge him before he could make the announcement. Ruiz's answer was to indicate the space next to him on the sofa. She sat as far away from him as she could, determined not to let him see how she felt about his silence. She wondered then if Ruiz had any lingering memories of her touch, or her kisses, as she had of his. Did men even bank physical memories like a woman, to pull out and review later?

She had to stop thinking like that, or she'd break down. She should have had a good howl in the shower to get this out of her system. The way Ruiz was acting, so casual and normal as if this was just another day, she couldn't bear it. The greatest intimacy of all seemed to have pushed them apart, and she of all people should have known the risks: *don't tie me down, don't ask me to commit.* It was, after all, a favourite topic in the column. Friends were bound by loving ties even if they didn't see each other for years, but sleep with a friend and that changed everything, because you ran the risk of becoming a nuisance, a potential curb on your friend's freedom.

'Are you okay?' Ruiz glanced at her with concern as she sucked in a couple of steadying breaths.

'I'm fine, thank you. So when are you going?'

'Soon. Very soon. But that's not what I want to talk to you about.' He picked up a set of keys. Was Ruiz offering Holly the keys to his house? Why? 'Do you want me to keep an eye on the place while you're away?' She was happy to do so.

'No, that's okay—but thanks for the offer. I have employed a live-in housekeeper who will have her own apartment on site.' He ruffled Bouncer's ears. Having padded into the room in search of company, the big dog had settled down between them. 'The town house is a much better option than here,' Ruiz went on. 'There's a proper garden, plus a large communal garden that leads on to the park.'

'That's great.' She kept it light. 'But I'm not sure I can afford the rent…'

'That's very funny,' Ruiz said, shaking his head, but his eyes were cold as he stared at her. 'I'm talking about Bouncer moving back there. You'll stay here, won't you, Holly? At least until you find somewhere else to live. No hurry,' he stressed.

'Of course.' She laughed. She smiled. She died a little more inside. She should have known Ruiz's forward planning was all about his dog. 'Don't worry, I won't be here long. I've found several flats to look at in the next couple of days—'

'Well, that's great,' Ruiz agreed. 'But you know you can stay on here as long as you want.'

'I'd rather not.'

'Okay.' He shrugged. 'Whatever you want, Holly…'

'I thought I'd move closer to the office.'

Ruiz made no comment and it was a relief to get up and turn away. New Holly didn't long for things she couldn't have. She didn't risk her heart or her bank account. And she certainly didn't risk her career, Holly told herself fiercely, fighting back tears.

CHAPTER NINE

Concerned you might be left on the shelf? Don't be. Just think—no shirts to iron, no meals to cook, and you can eat chocolate éclairs for supper every night of your life.

Light-bulb moment, why? Because wallowing in misery isn't for me, the new me. Friend to lover and back to friends again. I'm told this shift of position is possible if handled correctly. And because I love this man's sister as if she were my own and I don't want to hurt her, I'm determined to make it back to friends with him.

And the playboy? Who knows what he thinks? He's off to Argentina and a life of which I will never be a part. I have to say he seems preoccupied. Perhaps he's concerned he's been out of the game too long and might not come up to scratch when he returns to play top class polo. Whatever his problem, one thing I'm sure about—it has nothing to do with me.

HOLLY kept her head down next day at the office. Work was the only thing that numbed the pain of thinking about Ruiz resuming the life of a playboy in the next couple of days, surrounded by sloe-eyed *señoritas* in

Argentina. Work, as well as time-tabling visits to likely
rental properties throughout the capital...

'You haven't forgotten it's the Christmas party tonight, have you?' Freya reminded Holly later that same
afternoon.

'Hmm?' Holly barely looked up as she hammered
away on her keyboard.

'Didn't you hear me?' Freya pressed.

'I heard you, but I have to work.'

'For goodness' sake, Holly. You haven't even stopped
for lunch,' Freya protested.

'We're not letting you get out of it,' several more girls
chorused as they gathered round Holly's desk.

'You haven't forgotten the Christmas party is at the
samba club, have you?' Freya prompted, exchanging
glances with her friends.

How could she forget? Another good reason for not
going to the party, Holly reasoned, thinking of Ruiz and
keeping her head down when the girls shrieked *'Ole!'*
while putting in a bit of skirt-twirling and pouting practice.

'Hot men, fast music, free drinks. How can you pass
that up?' Freya demanded.

'Easily,' Holly murmured, keeping her attention fixed
on the screen.

'Well, we're not going without you,' Freya said flatly.

'Then none of us will go,' Holly flashed, immediately
regretting her outburst when she saw the hurt and surprise on Freya's face. But how could she go to the samba
club with all that it meant to her? It had been such a special night with Ruiz—a night she would never be able
to recreate or forget, and she didn't want to try. 'Please,
Freya. I've still got so much to do,' she pleaded, offering

her last piece of chocolate, which Freya refused. 'Some other night, perhaps.'

'Holly, this is the Christmas party,' Freya pointed out. 'It won't come around again until next year. You never stop working. You're in serious danger of—'

'Don't say becoming boring. Please don't say that,' Holly cut in.

'I was about to say, you're in danger of burning out,' Freya told her with concern.

'I'm sorry,' Holly admitted. 'Truly, I am.' And when Freya smiled encouragement, she added in a very different voice, 'Okay, so whose bright idea was it to hold the Christmas party at the samba club?'

Freya's face brightened immediately. 'The guys in marketing. Does that mean you're coming?'

'If you'll have me,' Holly said wryly.

Freya's answer was to switch off her screen. 'Go and get ready,' she insisted. 'We'll wait for you.'

She had made some good friends in London, Holly reflected as the girls bustled her out of the office. She should make more time for them, but somehow there didn't seem to be time for anything these days.

Having tested every part of his body at the gym and found it all in good working order, Ruiz took a long, cold shower and tucked a towel around his waist. He was just opening his locker when the call came through on his phone. 'Gabe? To what do I owe this honour?'

'That pretty little thing you brought to the club that time?'

'Do you mean Holly?' Ruiz was instantly alert, all thoughts of cutting Holly out of his life forgotten.

'ROCK!' is having its Christmas party at the club and the guys are well into the party spirit. I'm not sure your

friend is too happy about them trying to get her to dance. Would you like me to intervene?'

A muscle in Ruiz's jaw flexed. 'I'm only across the road at the gym. Can you keep an eye on things until I get there?'

'Count on it.'

He didn't pause to dry his hair. Throwing on the same running clothes he had arrived in, he collected Bouncer from the girls on Reception and headed off.

How was she going to do this nicely without causing offence to people she had to work with? How was she going to get out of dancing with men who'd had too much to drink, and who should have learned by now that no meant no? She couldn't help but remember Ruiz, and how safe she'd felt with him.

'Ow! You're hurting me,' Holly protested, freeing her arm from one man's grasp. 'Please don't touch me,' she exclaimed, whirling round to try and catch another culprit. But the more Holly resisted, the more the men seemed to think it was a game. Where was Freya? Where were all the other girls she worked with? Holly frantically scanned the dance floor, but it was so packed she couldn't see anyone she knew.

And then her heart rolled over. 'Ruiz?'

Dressed in running shoes and gym clothes, his hair still damp from the shower, Ruiz was framed in the entrance to the club with Bouncer sitting patiently at his feet. With his dark eyes narrowed Ruiz was also searching the dance floor, every fibre of his pumped and muscular body poised for action. The moment he caught sight of her he strode purposefully forward. A path cleared in front of him. No wonder, Holly thought. The expression in Ruiz's eyes was murderous. With their reflexes dulled by drink, the men around her took a little longer to realise what was happening, but thankfully some primal warning mechanism must have kicked in and they peeled away just in time.

'Are you all right?' Ruiz demanded tersely.

She was now, Holly realised, feeling massive relief.

'I heard you were having trouble.' Before she could question this, Ruiz added, 'Let's get your coat.' And putting a protective arm around her shoulders, he led her towards the reception area.

'You've come straight from the gym,' she said as they collected Bouncer.

'No, I always dress like this for a night out.'

'Ruiz, I—'

'Don't say it.'

'I will say it. I always seem to be such a bother. So, thank you.'

Ruiz grunted and held the door for her.

They walked home at a brisk pace through the park, icy air billowing in silent clouds from their mouths. They both had plenty to think about, but neither of them voiced those thoughts, and Holly could feel Ruiz's tension. Only Bouncer seemed perfectly at ease as he trotted along between them. She was grateful to the big dog's softening influence on a situation that showed no sign of easing any time soon. Ruiz didn't speak until they reached the penthouse and then he turned at the door of the elevator. 'What will you do when I'm not here, Holly?'

'Work,' she said as the doors slid open and they stepped inside.

Ruiz firmed his jaw, staring straight ahead as they waited for the elevator to reach the penthouse floor. While she knew she had done nothing wrong Holly felt as if something light and good had died inside her and she didn't know how to get it back. 'I suppose you can forgive the people at the Christmas party. Thank goodness it only comes round once a year.'

Ruiz remained resolutely unimpressed by her attempt to make light of something that could so easily have turned nasty without his intervention. When the lift doors opened he stood aside to let her pass. She wasn't even sure he was going to get out with her. 'Thank you for coming to the club. I don't know what I'd have done if you hadn't been there.'

He indicated that she should move and he would follow. 'If you will excuse me, Holly,' Ruiz said, holding the door for her, 'I'm going back home to bed.'

'You're taking Bouncer? Of course you are,' she said quickly, remembering Bouncer was living at the town house now. 'I'm really sorry to have put you to all this trouble, Ruiz. The silly thing is I didn't even want to go out. I'm so bogged down with work I can't spare the time.' She stopped when she saw his expression.

'I think you have some decisions to make about how you live your life, Holly. Success is great, but—'

Ruiz's shrug said it all.

'I need to get some sleep,' he said, turning. Before he made the long journey back to Argentina, Holly guessed, as the man she loved and his dog left her life without a backward glance.

He didn't sleep. Luckily for him he'd packed for the trip ahead of time. He tossed and turned, thinking about life and what he wanted out of it, and he came up with the same answer every time: Holly. She was all he wanted. He couldn't make sense of his longing for her, or come up with anything more concrete than the fact that his life was empty without her. He wanted her, not just for a fling, but for longer—for ever, maybe. He'd started to get to know her and he wanted to know more. A lot more. He wanted to give them a chance. He wanted to run with the crazy redhead and see where it led. Almost certainly nowhere, Ruiz concluded, since Holly seemed completely wrapped up in her career. But was that because she really didn't care about anything apart from her job. Or did Holly's lack of confidence in her personal life mean she only felt safe when living vicariously through her column? There was only one way to find out.

If the team leader wanted misery he could have it, Holly reflected the next morning as she hung up her coat at the office. The only consolation was that she wasn't alone with her hangdog expression. Everyone was a little under par after the party, moving in slow-mo and speaking in mumbles, and then only when necessary. But all that changed when she reached her desk. 'What?' she said, looking at the mob surrounding it. 'What's happened?'

As her colleagues peeled away from Holly's work station Holly saw the envelope propped against the monitor. She knew immediately who it was from. Thousands of letters arrived each week addressed to The Redhead, but this was addressed in bold, black script, To Holly.

'Well? Open it,' Freya insisted.

Picking it up, Holly held the envelope to her chest almost as if she hoped that would make it invisible. 'This is private,' she said, hoping everyone would go away.

'Open it here,' Holly's team leader insisted with his usual insensitivity. 'Then if it's anything to upset you, one of us can take over your work so at least something will get done today.'

'He's all heart,' one of the girls murmured discreetly, adding, 'We're all on your side, Holly. And judging by the size of that envelope there could be something more inside it than just a private note.'

And why should she care if it was from Ruiz? Holly reasoned. He'd made it clear enough last night that what he wanted was a clean break. Perhaps she'd left something behind in the club and he was returning it, though she couldn't remembering doing so—

'It's a folder from an airline,' Freya informed her colleagues as Holly peered inside the envelope. 'And there's something else,' she exclaimed, poring over Holly's shoulder.

'Do you mind?' Holly said shakily. Walking over to the window, she turned her back on everyone. She read the handwritten note first. It was another of Ruiz's succinct wake-up-calls: 'Have you thought about your life yet, Holly? About who you really want to be? Maybe the enclosed will help. Ruiz.'

'Are you okay, Holly?' Freya demanded when she remained rooted to the spot. 'Have you checked the airline tickets yet?'

Airline tickets, Holly thought numbly, turning her attention to the rest of the envelope's contents. 'Oh, my God! This is ridiculous—'

'What is?' Holly's team leader demanded.

'First-class return tickets to Buenos Aires, leaving tonight. And a VIP pass to a polo match.' Holly held them up as if she needed everyone else to confirm that they were real. When the shrieks of excitement died down, she shook her head. 'What a waste.'

'A waste?' her team leader queried sharply.

'Well, I won't be using them.' Going back to her desk, Holly sank weakly into her chair. 'How can I, when I've got so much work on here?'

'Have laptop, will travel,' the team leader argued

briskly, swinging his chair round. 'You can send copy from anywhere in the world with Internet access, Holly. And if you don't take up that offer, you can consider yourself fired.'

'Fired?' Holly exclaimed, springing up.

'Wasn't it you who told me that the "Living with a Playboy" feature had almost run its course?' her boss reminded her. 'Don't you think this trip to Argentina is the key to reviving it?'

And put her life through the wringer again? Did she want that? Wouldn't it be so much easier to make it all up in the column as she went along and walk away from this? 'I can't afford to take time off,' she said flatly.

'We'll cover your expenses and pay your wages while you're away, as long as you keep submitting the column,' the team leader said, growing in enthusiasm as he thought through his idea. 'You've just been appointed *ROCK!*'s foreign correspondent. Just think what that will do for reader figures,' he added, rubbing his hands with glee.

Reader figures. Great. But she felt empty inside. What was wrong with her? She finally had the career she'd always wanted.

And what a hollow victory that had turned out to be. What about the guy? What about Ruiz?

The thought of seeing Ruiz again was a terrifying and uncertain prospect. She didn't know what to expect. Could she do it? Could she be with Ruiz again, write about him, and remain aloof? 'What about me?' she blurted as desperation took over.

'What about you?' the team leader demanded. 'You're part of a team, Holly. The clue's in the word.'

He was right, Holly realised. She couldn't let the team down—all of their jobs were on the line, not just hers.

And nothing was ever achieved by hiding away. She had to get out there and confront life—and Ruiz—head-on.

'I don't know what you're standing there for,' he added impatiently. 'Shouldn't you be going back home to pack? According to this ticket you've got four hours to catch your flight!'

CHAPTER TEN

Hope I can read my writing later with all the turbulence—this must be the messiest diary entry I've made in a while.

Did I have any option but to accept Ruiz's invitation? Having already messed up my non-existent love life, can I afford to risk my job as well? And then I have to ask myself this: If I can't trust myself to take a professional approach and write an article about the playboy without wailing, what kind of journalist am I going to make?

So here I am after a thirteen hour flight, taxiing towards the stand at Aeropuerto Ministro Pistarini airport, more commonly known as Ezeiza after the city close to Buenos Aires in which the airport is situated. Did you hear that? Buenos Aires! Where the weather, according to our hip young captain, is a bikini-basting twenty-eight degrees. Before you get excited, he wasn't directing that comment at me. With my red hair and freckles I don't feel a bit out of place amongst all the sultry whip-thin señoritas seated here with me in First Class. As if! I feel more like a suet dumpling than ever—a fact no doubt observed by said captain when he took the precaution of performing a talent-trawl in the

*First Class cabin before lowering his landing gear.
But I will be spending Christmas with the playboy
at his family's fabulous country-sized estancia and
no one else can say that. I think you'll agree this
takes 'Living with a Playboy' to a whole new level.
Buckle your seat belts, my friends; something tells
me we're in for a bumpy ride.*

THE first thing Holly saw in the terminal building was
a huge poster advertising the polo match featuring the
Band of Brothers. Ruiz Acosta, ten times life size and
easily the best looking of four astonishingly handsome
brothers, staring down at her. She swallowed deeply.
Everywhere she looked there seemed to be another
poster—another heart-stopping reminder of the darkly
glittering glamour that had so easily attracted her. Even
the limousine Ruiz had sent to collect her had a Band of
Brothers sticker on the back window. A crowd had gathered round to stare and comment and swoon, and by the
time she had collapsed onto the back seat her heart was
thundering like a pack of wild mustangs.

Surely, this had to be a dream…

But it wasn't a dream, and as the luxury vehicle ate
up the dusty miles between the airport and the Acosta
family's *estancia* Holly felt her throat grow increasingly
tight. Her anxiety wasn't eased by the sight of numerous
billboards advertising the match. Ruiz was a national
hero it seemed. But how could this swarthy, dangerous-
looking man with his burning stare, earring and tattoos
be the same man who had held her in his arms and made
love to her—

Forget that. Forget him. You're here to do your job,
that's it.

She couldn't think of anything but Ruiz. Even this

harsh land was right for him. London, with all its neatly packaged districts, felt a lifetime away as the driver took her deeper into the interior. She had been commissioned to write an article and nothing more, Holly reasoned, trying to calm down: 'Christmas with the Playboy'. She would also have the chance to watch Ruiz play polo, to see this rugged man with his thighs wrapped around the flanks of some prime horseflesh.

'The game will have started by the time we arrive,' the driver informed her. 'But you'll see plenty of it,' he assured her in heavily accented English. 'That's if there's anyone left alive on the field for you to watch by the time we get there.'

He laughed. She didn't laugh.

Another colossal billboard loomed in front of them like a vivid punctuation mark amidst miles of arid scrubland that seemed to mock her with just how far she was from civilisation and any form of escape. She stared blindly out of the window. What was she doing here? Why had she come? She could have refused.

She should have refused.

And lost her job?

A road that had been deserted for hours was suddenly clogged with vehicles all travelling in the same direction. Hundreds more were already parked up on the roadside and in lines across the fields. Holly gasped with alarm when her driver, using the simple avoidance tactic of pulling onto the wrong side of the road, overtook everything at speed. With a final thump on his horn to warn the other vehicles, he swung the wheel and steered the limousine beneath an impressive archway that led to an immaculately groomed drive lined with trees. 'Welcome to Estancia Acosta, Señorita Valiant,' he said, continuing to drive at a speed that had the crowds spraying to either side on the road ahead of them. 'I'm going to take you straight round to the pony lines where you will find Ruiz, if he isn't on the polo field.'

'I'll be fine here. You can drop me anywhere.' But preferably not beneath this billboard, Holly thought anxiously as they drove through what looked more like a very busy small town than a family ranch.

'You might get lost if I leave you here,' the driver insisted. 'And then I'd be in trouble.'

With whom? she wondered. With Ruiz?

'My orders are quite specific,' the driver went on. 'This is the most popular event of the year.'

It looked like it, and she was thrilled to see real gauchos, the Argentine equivalent of a cowboy, for the first time. Leather chaps to protect their breeches were held up by coin-decorated belts, while their hats were festooned with bands and laces. There were socialites too—the girls as immaculately groomed as the flashy polo ponies they had come to see. While I am more your sturdy hunter, Holly thought wryly. But then she was hunting for a story, not a husband.

But that didn't stop her finger-combing her hair as the driver started to slow the car. They were approaching the pony lines now. Mashing her lips together, she decided against lipstick because her hands were shaking too much to put it on. She couldn't see the polo field as it was hidden by the towering stands, but polo players were stalking about like muscular gods of the game. They wore white, jean-style breeches and either black shirts with a skull and cross-bones embroidered on the pocket, or 'Acosta' emblazoned in white in capital letters on the back of red shirts. Some of the players were already mounted with their faceguards down, their dark eyes shielded behind stylish eye-protectors, but so far there was no sign of Ruiz.

'He must be playing,' the driver said as a cheer went up somewhere out of sight. 'These men are the reserves—warming up and standing ready in case of injury.'

Holly's stomach lurched at the thought of Ruiz being injured.

'Shall I take you to see him play?'

'Would you?' she said gratefully, though the thought terrified her at the same time.

The stands were vast and impressive and ran the length of the field, which was about six times the size of a football pitch and packed to the rafters with noisy supporters. Seats had been reserved for them on the front row and as she sat down Holly's gaze instantly locked onto Ruiz. She'd have known that muscular body anywhere, though she had never seen it at full stretch like this. As he thundered past the stand in a blur of red top, and white mud-streaked breeches, she felt a reckless punch of full-blown lust. Ruiz's face guard was down, but she didn't need to see his eyes to know that he was on a mission and everyone had better keep out of his way. The romantic idea of polo was one thing, but seeing Ruiz's superb horsemanship firsthand, along with his tactical expertise and sheer physical courage, made it impossible to keep her thoughts confined to business. She was ashamed to admit, even to herself, how much she wanted him.

No, she didn't, Holly told herself firmly, turning like the rest of the crowd to watch Ruiz. She wasn't going there. She was a professional journalist with a job to do. Ruiz had stopped abruptly at one end of the field. Turning his horse, he charged the pack at a gallop, mallet raised. Leaning at such an acute angle, he seemed to defy gravity as he deftly hooked the ball and smacked it down the field. The crowd went wild as the band of brothers closed ranks behind him. Everyone sprang to their feet, screaming encouragement as Ruiz swung his mallet a second time and scored a goal. Forgetting herself, Holly screamed hysterically with the rest.

'What a man,' the woman next to her exclaimed, fanning herself with her hand. 'What wouldn't I give to spend the night with him?'

So that was why she had come to Argentina, Holly thought wryly.

No, it wasn't!

'Ruiz stole that ball from the great Nero Caracas,' the driver on her other side was explaining to her excitedly. 'Ruiz's brother Nacho Acosta and Nero Caracas are considered to be the top players in the world.'

'And yet Ruiz got the better of him,' Holly agreed with pride. Oh, yes, he did.

She watched Ruiz settle back into the saddle and take easy control of his horse as the two teams cantered down the field to change ends after his goal. He was so relaxed, so sexy. The excitement of the match had made her forget how nervous she had been at the prospect of seeing him again, but now the butterflies were back. What would a man like that think of a distinctly unglamorous, plane-rumpled Holly Valiant? Would he sigh heavily, and wonder why on earth she had agreed to come to Argentina? Ruiz must know why she had accepted. The public reason was that she had no option if she didn't want to lose her job. The private reason was hers alone.

She sat tensely as the match started up again. The camaraderie between Ruiz and his infamous brothers was obvious, as was the strong bond between them. The way he praised his horse touched her, just as the quiet confidence on his ruthless face made Ruiz even more attractive. She envied him for belonging so strongly to something and somewhere, and having the family bond she had always hankered after. How wonderful for Lucia to have grown up under the protection of brothers like that, she thought briefly, but then she added wryly, how terrible. With four warriors watching over her it was no wonder Lucia Acosta had felt the need to break away. The Acosta brothers were such a formidable force it would be easy to be eclipsed by them.

When the match had been declared a draw and the players awarded their medals, they cantered off the field. Holly felt weak with longing, and tense with anticipation at the thought of this first meeting. She left her seat to go and find Ruiz. The teams were coming into the yard by the time she arrived, steel horseshoes clattering across the cobbles. The men made quite a sight—all of them muscular and rugged, with shoulders wide enough to carry an ox. She stood beneath the shade of some trees, watching discreetly as the men chatted to each other as if they hadn't been mortal enemies only minutes before. Ruiz had his mallet resting on his massive shoulders, and was holding the reins casually in one hand. He was so achingly familiar, and yet a stranger in so many ways. Thinking herself hidden in the shadows she exclaimed out loud when he looked straight at her and came cantering over.

'Welcome to Argentina, Holly Valiant,' he said.

She gasped with surprise when he dipped out of the saddle to kiss her cheek. 'I'm glad you decided to accept my invitation,' he said, staring down at her with all the knowledge and humour in his eyes she remembered.

She hoped she mumbled something vaguely polite in return as Ruiz sprang down from the saddle. Handing over his sweating pony and mallet to a waiting groom, he turned to face her. 'Did you enjoy the match?' Her heart thundered in response as Ruiz removed his helmet and ran one hand through his wild black hair.

'It was fantastic. You were fantastic…' Her voice tailed away. She felt incredibly self-conscious all of a sudden, and realised that Ruiz must receive such unsophisticated compliments all the time.

'I'm glad you enjoyed it,' he said, a sincere smile planting an attractive crease in his cheek. 'Did you see my goal?'

'Yes, I saw it,' she confirmed, realising that even national heroes needed reassurance from time to time. 'It was brilliant.' And now she was smiling. How could she not smile when Ruiz was around? She had lost the art of playing it cool where Ruiz Acosta was concerned—if she had ever had it in the first place.

Ruiz's massive shoulders eased in a self-deprecating shrug as he glanced after his horse. 'I owe it all to my pony. I saved my best horse until the last chukka.'

'I think it might have something to do with your skill too,' she suggested dryly, growing in confidence because Ruiz was so relaxed.

Her heart bounced as he stared intently at her. 'Are you attempting to flatter me, Señorita Valiant?'

'Maybe, Señor Acosta,' she agreed. To have Ruiz teasing her again in that warm, husky voice was alarming and yet strangely reassuring too. It was as though nothing had changed between them, as though they were still close, and had always been close, and only she had imagined the yawning gulf growing between them.

'Come on,' he said, taking hold of her arm.

'Where are you taking me?'

'Does it matter?'

Ruiz's gaze was dark and disturbing, and she had to

remind herself that this was a research trip. 'Not one bit,' she said. 'Your driver told me you and your brothers own some of the top ponies in the world…' Not the best conversational opening gambit she had ever come up with, but she had to try something to distract her wandering and highly erotic thoughts.

'Have you ever wondered why there isn't a polo world series?' Ruiz demanded, staring down at her.

She looked into the dark, compelling gaze. 'I'm sure you're going to tell me.'

'Argentina would clean up every time. We have the best ponies in the world. And the best players.'

'The most modest too,' Holly observed dryly.

'You're right,' Ruiz agreed, his eyes dancing with shared laughter. 'We're just about perfect.'

She hadn't imagined it would be so easy to relax with him. But she mustn't read too much into it, Holly warned herself. Tensions had never existed between them for long and she was Ruiz's guest in Argentina.

'I notice you're not taking notes?' Ruiz observed, adopting an expression that made her smile even more.

'What notes?' she said, frowning. And then she laughed again, knowing her reputation for work.

'I was led to understand that the only reason you agreed to accept my invitation to come to Argentina was because your boss at *ROCK!* told you it would be a good idea to write a polo feature for the magazine.'

'Correct,' she said. That was the only reason.

'And there was no other reason?' Ruiz probed in his deep, husky voice.

'Should there be?' If she couldn't fool herself, what hope was there of fooling Ruiz?

'You tell me,' he said.

* * *

'This is my family home,' Ruiz told her as they approached a grand old house.

The building had an air of permanence and was much loved, Holly decided, noticing it was immaculately maintained. When they went through the impressive entrance she found herself in a large hall crammed with people. 'Too many people for proper introductions,' Ruiz determined, leading her towards an impressive sweeping staircase. 'You should have some privacy now so you can rest up and take a bath before you meet everyone. You might even like a sleep to recover from the journey?'

'I'll be fine. I'm far too excited,' Holly admitted, which drew a sharp glance from Ruiz. 'If you can just give me half an hour or so to take a shower and change my clothes…?'

'But no face masks,' he said dryly.

'Promise,' she said, trying hard to curb a smile.

'I need to freshen up too,' Ruiz pointed out, breaking what had turned into a long moment of mutual inspection and assessment. 'Then I'm going to take a tour of the stables to check on the ponies.'

'Can I come with you?'

'If you promise not to bring your phone or your notepad.'

'I haven't even switched it on yet.' And only now remembered her oversight.

'Then do so,' Ruiz prompted. 'You should let people know you're safe. Though your working hours at the *estancia* will be between one and four in the afternoon while I'm taking a siesta.'

She laughed. 'So I work while you rest?'

'Sounds good to me,' Ruiz observed with another heart-stopping flash of humour.

'And what am I supposed to do for the rest of the time?'

'Live a little?' Ruiz suggested.

I will, she thought as he turned to go.

She had so much research material already and she'd only been here five minutes, Holly reflected as she leaned back against the heavy wooden door in her bedroom. Decorated in shades of palest coral and cream the room Ruiz had chosen for her was light and sunny, and beautifully feminine in a way Holly had never had the luxury of enjoying before. There was lace on the bed and silver on the dressing table, with a clutch of satin cushions on the elegant chaise longue positioned to take in the view over the ponies in the paddocks beyond the formal gardens.

The scent of beeswax tickled her senses as she waited for the data to upload on her phone. It was then that she noticed the family photographs arranged on the antique chest of drawers. There was a shot of the brothers as teenagers with their much younger sister, all of them smiling and instantly recognisable—dangerously handsome even then. She might only have been here five minutes, Holly reflected as her heartbeat increased, but it was long enough to know she would write about sexy polo players in general, because some things were better kept private. She couldn't bear the thought of everyone laughing at her if she admitted how hopelessly in love she was with one polo player in particular.

Having made the necessary calls, she took a shower in the old fashioned, but immaculate and beautifully maintained bathroom, before sorting out her clothes on top of the high, intricately carved four-poster bed with its dressing of crisp white linen and lace. When she was ready she went to find Ruiz and her heart juddered when she bumped into him on the landing. Like her, he was just going downstairs. 'Do you have everything you need?' he asked.

She looked at him and thought not. 'My room is lovely. Thank you.' And then the question uppermost in her mind had to be asked. 'Why did you invite me here, Ruiz?' It was impossible to tell what he was thinking.

The dark eyes gave nothing away. 'Your editor's pleased you're here, isn't he?'

'Yes, of course he is.' But that didn't answer her question and Holly's shoulders slumped as she watched Ruiz walk ahead of her down the stairs. Her heart yearned for him, but her head said, Don't set yourself up for another disaster.

CHAPTER ELEVEN

Another column I only hope makes more sense to you, the reader, than it does to me right now. My head is full of one man: the playboy. He's so hot and sexy with a torso that would eclipse the centre-fold on any magazine you care to mention. To see him control a horse, effortlessly and completely, is the biggest turn-on of all. The polo match was spectacular. He was spectacular—

Am I getting a little selfish here? If I am, this is for you: the quotient of thighs like smooth, muscular tree trunks, and forearms like hairy steel bars was totally off the scale—

But the playboy is the only man I'm interested in. To seem him in full battle mode cracking the ball down the field at a gallop was so thrilling I would have fallen in love with him on the spot if I weren't in love with him already.

Yes. You can safely say I am a lost cause. I don't seem to have any sense of reality when it comes to men. I can't find a safe man with carpet slippers and a newspaper. I can't even find a slightly risky man with a set of golf clubs and a year's subscription to the local squash club. All I can find is a Playboy with a capital P and a stonking great mallet.

Ruiz was in the kitchen drinking coffee, with a house-keeper bustling at the stove. He put his cup down when Holly came into the room and got up immediately. 'I want you to see something,' he said, leading her back towards the door she had just entered.

His touch on her arm was so familiar...so achingly familiar. She liked it. A great deal too much.

Ruiz took her across the baronial hall with its burnished wooded floor and muted, jewel-coloured hangings to another passageway leading off the grand entrance hall. Opening the door onto a room with a very different personality, he followed her in. Leaning back against the door, he said, 'Well? What do you think?'

She was finding it hard to concentrate right now.

'Take a look around,' he said. 'I think you'll find everything you need here...'

It was an office, she realised. Ruiz had brought her into a very modern office. All teak and cream furnishings, and sunlight slid through crisp white blinds to create the perfect working environment.

'I thought you would appreciate having a room of your own to work in quietly,' he said. 'Somewhere away from the rest of the house and the hubbub of polo and family life. This is where I come when I want to get away, and where I do some of my best thinking. Let's hope the same vibes work for you. Consider this your room for the duration of your stay, Holly. No one will disturb you here.'

It was a beautiful room. So why did she feel so flat? Maybe because Ruiz wasn't part of the package? 'Thank you.' No one had ever been so thoughtful before. Her family home had been small and cramped with parents at war, so the local library or the coffee shop down the road had been her office. A room of her own, even for her brief stay here, was luxury indeed. There was only one thing missing, Holly realised as Ruiz turned to go.

'Don't spend all your time in here,' was his parting shot.

'I won't.' She was determined to keep it light. 'I won't have anything to write about if I do!'

But he'd already gone. The door had shut behind Ruiz, leaving Holly to her own devices in his fabulous office. Great. She was here to work, so this was brilliant.

Well, get on with it, then…

Nothing. Her mind was empty. There wasn't a single idea in her head. There was just a keyboard, a blank screen, and the sound of confident footsteps walking away.

There were times when you had to cast your net into the water rather than wait on the bank doing nothing, Holly reflected when the longest ten minutes of her life had passed. There was everything here in this office, except for the one thing she needed. Picking up the internal phone, she dialled the kitchen. Ruiz picked up immediately. 'Problem?' he demanded.

'I need something to write about.'

'I'll be right up.'

There was nothing in his tone to suggest that this was going to be anything more than a courtesy call, but Holly's heart turned over at the sound of a knock on the door. 'Well?' Ruiz demanded, walking in.

Her brain seized up. Right now she just wanted to look at him. There'd been a Ruiz-drought in her life and now she just wanted to drink him in. Big, refreshing gulps! Propping one lean thigh against the desk, he stared down at her, frowning. 'I hope you haven't brought me up here for nothing?'

'No…' Her senses were full of him. She loved it when he glowered, and Ruiz was close enough for her to feel the warmth of his body and smell the soap he'd used in the shower.

'Why aren't you working?' he asked, straightening up.

'I am,' she protested.

'Well, work faster,' Ruiz prompted, 'and remember that when you leave this room your work stays here. Agreed?'

She loved it when his lips firmed. 'Agreed,' she said faintly.

'Louder, Holly.'

'Agreed.'

'That's better,' Ruiz murmured. 'Now come here. We haven't said hello to each other properly yet.'

She stood. Taking a couple of small, prudent paces forward, she stretched out her hand to shake his.

Ruiz took hold of her and dragged her close. 'Hello, Holly,' he murmured, laughing down into her eyes.

She stared into the dark, amused eyes, and then at the firm, sexy mouth only a whisper from hers. 'I thought you said this room was to work in,' she protested without much force.

'It is,' Ruiz agreed. 'Here's your next headline.'

His kiss took her breath away. It was both fierce and tender. Two dams had burst at once, she thought as Ruiz swung her into his arms. 'You can't do this in the office.'

Shh you crazy woman, and savour the moment!

'I can do anything I want, anywhere I want,' Ruiz assured her. 'Just so long as you want it too…'

'All I want is you,' she said softly, opening her heart when caution couldn't save it.

'If you're sure?' He held her above the sofa. 'I can always leave you here to work.'

'You dare,' she said, feeling excitement spring inside her. 'And you know what they say about too much work.'

'I know what I say,' Ruiz commented under his breath.

'Where are we going?' she said as he carried her towards the door.

'To bed,' Ruiz said bluntly. 'This might take some time and I'm not confident the sofa springs will hold up.'

She could hardly breathe for anticipation as he strode down the landing with her in his arms. Opening a door at the end, he walked into a spacious room and kicked the door shut behind them. He carried her straight over to the bed and she barely had time to register that this was a very different room again: elegantly furnished in the Italian style rather than in the heavy traditional manner of the rest of the house. 'I like a man who knows what he wants.'

'And a woman who knows how to give it to him.'

She wouldn't argue with that, Holly thought as her breathing quickened. Ruiz's bed was big and firm, and had been recently dressed in crisp white linen. She was sure she could smell sunshine coming off the sheets. Lowering her onto the bed, he joined her and then, cupping her face, he kissed her. 'You're in a rush,' she said, fighting to catch her breath when he released her.

'Would you have me any other way?'

'Absolutely not,' she admitted. And then, because she was a glutton for punishment, she added, 'How about me?'

'Stop hiding behind the column,' Ruiz said frankly.

'And live a little?' Holly suggested.

'No.' He paused. 'Live a lot.'

Her body responded urgently as Ruiz kissed her again.

She loved the feel of his arms around her and the touch of him beneath her hands. She loved the taste of him and the smell of him, warm, clean and musky with rampant maleness. 'I'm so glad you invited me.'

'Don't play prim with me.' His lips tugged in a grin. 'I know what you want.'

'Seriously, Ruiz.'

'Seriously?' he queried, stopping her with a kiss. 'I know what you want. And you should know by now that I'll call you any way I have to, as loudly as I have to, from as far away as I must.'

She wasn't used to this feeling, this safe, sure, happy feeling. Maybe Ruiz was right and this was living. It was certainly risking everything for one man. And it was better this way. She stared into the dark amused eyes and knew then that for her this was the only way.

'Now stop trying to kid yourself and me,' Ruiz told her in a husky voice. 'We both know you're a very bad girl. So, what's holding you back, Holly?'

'Nothing,' she said, moving down the bed.

She took her time tracing the lines of Ruiz's muscular thighs. Then, pulling up his top, she traced the band of muscles across his belly. As her fingers trailed lower she had the satisfaction of hearing him suck in a fast breath. 'Was the belt really necessary,' she murmured. Cupping the arrogant swell of Ruiz's erection over the fabric of his jeans, she directed a teasing stare into his face. 'Is all this for me? You shouldn't have.'

Holly gasped out as Ruiz swung her underneath him. 'But I have and I will,' he promised as he began unbuttoning her shirt. 'And if you can't give me a very good reason for keeping me waiting for this, I shall just have to pleasure it out of you.'

'Oh, no. Please don't do that,' she murmured, watching

as Ruiz reached back to tug his top over his head. Tracing the formidable muscles on his chest, she turned her attention to his jeans. 'You are massively overdressed,' she complained, wrestling them off him. And massively erect, she discovered with excitement.

'And you are as forward as I remember.' Ruiz paid her back by whipping her top off and tossing it away.

'Lie on that bed, *Señor*,' she warned, stripping down to bra and pants. 'There is some unfinished business requiring my immediate attention, and it cannot wait.'

'Go easy, *señorita*,' Ruiz growled. 'I've been waiting a long time for this.'

'Are you saying the renowned playboy has lost his self-control?' she taunted, kneeling over him.

'I'm saying that with you it might be impossible to hold on.'

'Don't touch,' she warned when Ruiz reached for her breasts. Currently threatening to spill over her bra, her nipples were deep rose pink and erect.

'Do your worst,' Ruiz encouraged in a husky Latin whisper.

'Don't worry, I will,' she promised, slipping her fingertips beneath the waistband of his boxers. It was Holly's turn to suck in a fast, excited breath when she had removed them. Ruiz was magnificent in every department and most especially in this. She dipped her head to take him in her mouth, relishing his smoothness and the sheer size of him as she traced the veined surface with her tongue. She tasted and suckled gently, before licking him while cupping him with her hands. She wanted to hold him now, to feel the promise of pleasure beneath her hands. She needed both her hands.

'That's enough,' he exclaimed suddenly, swinging her beneath him.

'Can't you hold on?' she challenged him.

Ruiz's eyes were equally wicked. 'Let's find out, shall we?' he teased.

'Oh, yes. Let's,' she agreed with enthusiasm as Ruiz lost no time removing her remaining clothes. Nudging her legs apart with one powerful thigh, he tested and positioned her, using a pillow to raise her hips to an even more receptive level. After protecting them, he eased inside her with infinite care.

'That feels so good.' She breathed out a shuddering sigh as Ruiz lifted her.

'And now you can see,' he said.

She hummed, pretending that didn't matter to her. But it did. And now Ruiz had started to move his hips from side to side, so skilfully massaging he stole the breath from her lungs. Would it ever be possible to breathe normally again, she wondered, while Ruiz was inside her and stretching her so incredibly?

'This feels so good…' he said as he continued to roll his hips.

The pleasure was incredible and she gasped when he combined the massage he was giving her at the end of each stroke with a deep and steady movement back and forth. What made it even better was the way he withdrew completely each time, only to repeat the action again and again, until who would lose control first was no longer in doubt. 'Keep your legs wide,' he said, helping her to do so by placing the palms of his hands flat against the inside of her thighs and pressing them apart. 'I want you to do nothing, think nothing. All you have to do is feel, Holly, feel me…'

All she had to do was accept this steady pulse of pleasure growing inside her, while Ruiz worked to a dependable rhythm. A soft wail escaped her throat as the tension began to build to an unsustainable level. She tried to lie still as Ruiz had told her, but she couldn't blank her mind to what he was doing to her and knew it couldn't be long now... Perhaps one stroke, perhaps two—

He was ready for her, and when the strength of her climax threw Holly into his arms, he held her firmly as she bucked against him lost in pleasure. This felt so right. She felt perfect. Cradling her in his arms, he stared deep into her eyes to watch the fire rage and subside again into a series of pleasurable waves, each of which brought a groan of contentment from her lips. 'I think you liked that,' he murmured. His mouth tugged in a grin as he dropped a kiss on her parted lips. 'I think you liked that a lot...'

'I did,' she confirmed groggily. 'But now you have to keep that standard up.'

'You know I have very high standards.'

'And there's only one way to maintain them,' she murmured.

When he queried this with a raised brow, she murmured again, 'Regular practice.'

'Then I can only be grateful I rescued you from the samba club when I did.'

'You never told me how you knew.'

'Gabe called me at the gym,' he confided in a whisper against her mouth. He was already hungry for her again.

'Of course,' she whispered. 'So, what did he say, exactly?'

'He said that the pretty little thing he'd seen me with at the club was having trouble with some men.'

'Pretty little thing?' Holly queried, pulling back her head to stare at him. 'Are you sure he was talking about me?'

'Size is a matter of scale, isn't it?' he said, smiling

against her mouth. 'Or in your case, Holly, it's all in your mind.' He lavished an appreciative look down the length of her naked body.

She stretched extravagantly, no longer self-conscious or inhibited. 'You are rather large,' she said. 'I might hang onto you to keep me looking small.'

He laughed. 'You do that. Now, have I answered all your questions? Or would you like to talk some more?'

'Talk? No. Talking can wait,' she said, reaching for him. 'Don't be selfish,' she complained when he teased her by pulling away. 'You can't show off goods like that and then deny me the pleasure of them.'

'Again?' he said. 'So soon? Are you sure?'

'It's been at least thirty seconds,' she observed impatiently.

'Well, if I must,' he agreed, moving over her.

Ruiz was incredible. Big and hard and muscular didn't begin to describe him. Dangerously dark, with a wicked sense of humour, but even that didn't begin to scratch the surface of a man who meant so much to her. She was head over heels in love with him—in over her head—and it felt so good. There could be no half measures with a man like Ruiz, Holly reasoned gratefully as he probed and stretched and stretched her some more. 'I'm glad you came to my rescue at the club,' she managed to gasp before he took her mind off conversation. 'And now you can come to my rescue again.' Arching against him, she seized him with her muscles.

'Whoah, tiger,' Ruiz husked, responding just as she had planned. 'That's very forward of you.'

'Don't pretend you don't like it,' she said grasping him again. 'I know you better than that.'

He brushed her swollen lips with his, and then dipped his head to suckle her nipples as he thrust firmly into her. She sucked in a noisy breath. Nothing could have prepared her for this level of sensation. 'Brute,' she complained, balling her fists against his chest when he proceeded to ride her with the same easy control he used on his polo ponies.

'You love it,' he said confidently, maintaining the rhythm she adored. Cupping her face in his hands, he kissed her as he made love to her, and when he pulled away she thought that seeing her responses mirrored in Ruiz's eyes was the most erotic experience she had ever had. And now his kisses had grown deep and tender. 'I want you,' he murmured.

'I want you too.' He had no idea how much.

Burying his face in her breasts, Ruiz drew on her scent as she eased back her legs to give him greater access. Pressing her knees back, he brought her to the edge again. 'Now?' he teased her.

'Please,' she begged him, and only moments later she was bucking out of control with only Ruiz's firm hands to guide her and keep her safe.

'That was so, so good,' she murmured a long time later.

Kissing the soft swell of her belly, he moved on to Holly's heavy breasts to show them the appreciation they deserved. From there he kissed his way down the silky length of her body until he could bear no more, and, turning her on top of him, suggested she ride him.

'I'm not sure I've got your excellent technique,' she said.

She looked sultry and hot in the mellow light of early evening. Her red gold hair, burnished in the last rays of the sun, tumbled in glorious disarray over her breasts. 'Enough with the excuses,' he murmured, starting to guide her hips with his hands. 'Remember, practice makes perfect. This is almost as easy as the samba. That had three steps. This has two, forward and back…

'Who knew you'd be such an able pupil?' Ruiz commented with appreciation after a few minutes of this.

'At a guess?' she said. 'You.'

He groaned with contentment as she picked up the rhythm. It wasn't as if she hadn't made love with this man before, but being in control like this, directing his pleasure, took her feelings to a new level. She loved being in control. She loved teasing him by making him wait. She loved to see the tension growing in him as she brought him to the brink, though she couldn't keep him hovering there as he had kept her hovering, because she wanted to fall so badly too—

They fell together in a bucking, thrusting tangle of limbs as the pleasure waves hit them. She knew nothing more after that for a long while, and, as a slave to sensation, she was glad to be lost. When she woke she was still safely wrapped in Ruiz's arms. Their legs were tangled around each other and his sensuous face was relaxed. Thinking he must be asleep, she took hold of his hand to kiss each sensitive fingertip in turn.

'I trust you're satisfied,' he murmured.

'For now,' she agreed sleepily, turning her face towards him on the pillow.

'You'll exhaust me,' Ruiz complained, but his lips were already tugging in a wicked smile.

'I'm going to do my best to,' Holly agreed, 'though I think I still have some way to go,' she observed, registering the pressure of Ruiz's erection against her belly growing more insistent by the second.

Lifting himself up on one elbow, Ruiz smiled against her mouth. 'More?' he murmured, teasing her.

'Much, much more,' she agreed.

But first he caressed her with all the care and tenderness she had always dreamed of. Emotion wedded to strong sexual attraction was a wonderful thing, Holly had discovered, and Ruiz's stamina had never been in doubt. She exclaimed with the anticipation of pleasure as he turned her, touched her and entered her. She was on her side with her back to him, her legs drawn up in what was at once the most comfortable, as well as the most receptive position. She arched her back, offering herself for pleasure, while Ruiz held her and rocked her until the excitement became too much for her to bear.

Would he ever get enough of Holly? It seemed not, and it was torture holding back. She had no idea how much he wanted her or how deeply he had come to care for her. He hadn't realised that himself until he'd seen her here in Argentina. He had hoped she would accept his invitation, but he'd played it cool, played it down, because he had wanted this to be Holly's decision. He'd left airline tickets—a long shot based on nothing more than his belief that Holly had the same gut feeling he did that there was more ahead of them. The proof that he had been right to bring her to Argentina had blazed from her eyes the moment he'd seen her after the polo match.

Something vital had changed between them, Holly thought as Ruiz caressed her face. She hadn't been imagining things before; they were bound on more than a purely physical level. Breath shivered out of her in a soft moan as he cupped her buttocks in his warm, strong hands. 'You can't help yourself, can you?' she murmured, gratefully positioning herself.

'Maybe not, but I can help you.'

She drew back her knees to encourage him as he eased inside her. 'You're always so gentle with me,' she said.

'Until you tell me otherwise,' Ruiz agreed, 'and even then I'll be gentle with you.'

'Not even a little bit rough?' she said, provoking him as she wrapped her legs tightly around his waist.

'Fast and deep and hard is as rough as I'm prepared to get with you—'

'Get rough, then,' she said, smiling wickedly as she egged him on.

They made love for hours. Whenever Holly was briefly sated Ruiz coaxed her back into a state of arousal until she clung to him, rocked with him, moaning rhythmically as he coaxed her on to yet another welcome release. Not that she needed much coaxing. And when at last she did fall asleep for any length of time he kissed her and lay watching over her, knowing that he had never felt like this before. His feelings for her beat against his brain. They had never been in doubt, but what exercised his mind was how to make it possible for them to be together. Because they were going to be together. He was going to make it happen.

Rolling onto his back, he stared at the ceiling to think about his dual life in Argentina and London. And then there was his loyalty to the Band of Brothers. The London house he so badly wanted to make into a family home, the family *estancia* and the pampas he loved. And that was before he even got started on his horses and the polo—his whole crazy life. How could he ask Holly to share that when she was so gifted and career-oriented? He couldn't expect her to trot along meekly at his heels.

Like Bouncer?

He couldn't even be in the right place at the right time for the dog, let alone Holly. Come and live with me and fit in? Was that what he was saying? Try to shoehorn your life into mine—or into whatever small space I can spare for you? He had nothing to offer Holly. Throwing himself back on the pillows, he knew he would never ask so much of someone he loved. So what then? How could he keep her? And he must. They belonged together.

By giving her all the freedom she could want. By letting her go. By allowing Holly to make her own decisions.

Dios! That wasn't satisfactory. He was accustomed to being in control.

He was accustomed to being alone. Did he want her or not?

He had to wake her.

'What?' she murmured groggily as he kissed her awake. Reaching for him she was trusting like a child. She touched him tenderly, her fingers trailing down his arm, her eyes seeking reassurance in his. He wanted this. He wanted it for ever and not just for now. He wanted this closeness, this tenderness, this caring for each other, for ever and for always.

She smiled slowly. 'So you're still here,' she said.

'Of course I'm still here,' he confirmed, frowning as if anything else were inconceivable to him. And it was. It already was. It was unthinkable that he should be anywhere other than with Holly. The French called it a *coup de foudre*—a thunderbolt to the heart. He just knew it as love.

Ruiz introduced her to his brothers. They were dangerously good fun and ridiculously good-looking. Only Nacho remained a little reserved, but Holly felt his approval. 'You're good for my brother,' Nacho told her after supper that evening. 'I've never seen him so relaxed.'

Holly glanced at Ruiz, exchanging a look with him

that told her how pleased he was she fitted in and liked his family.

Fitted in for now, Holly mused the next morning after another spectacular night of love-making with Ruiz. Soon she would have to go back to London and return to work. Before then she had an article to write, but, though she sat and stared at the screen in the room Ruiz had set aside for her, the page remained resolutely blank. She turned with surprise when Ruiz walked in, managing to look sexier than ever in his knee-length riding boots, form-hugging breeches and tight-fitting top. 'Aren't you supposed to be training?' she queried.

'I changed my mind,' he said. 'It's no fun on my own.' Walking up to the computer, he typed in: FUN. 'That's what you need more of, Holly.'

'Didn't I have enough fun last night?' She rested her chin on her hand to stare up at him.

'That was then and this is now,' Ruiz argued. 'When I first met you Holly Valiant, you embraced fun. You couldn't get enough of it.' Putting his arm around her shoulders, Ruiz emphasised this comment with a kiss that made it hard to remember work. Holly stared down at the powerful forearm currently resting against her chest, all deliciously nut brown and muscular, and shaded with just the right amount of dark hair...

'Holly,' Ruiz warned softly, swinging her chair round so she had to look at him. 'You have to stop doubting me.'

'How do you always know what I'm thinking?'

'I just know you,' he said.

'So, why *are* you with me, Ruiz?' She searched his eyes.

'Let me think,' Ruiz murmured dryly. 'Could it be because I love you? Have you thought of that? Or are you just too frightened to put love in the frame in case you get hurt again?'

'Frightened? No.' She certainly wasn't frightened of Ruiz. She trusted him. 'You love me?' she said as if her brain had only just computed it.

'I love you, Holly Valiant,' Ruiz said, staring into her eyes.

'You can't say that just because we had good sex.'

'Surely you mean amazing sex?'

'Naturally, that's what I meant to say,' Holly agreed, adopting the same teasing tone. 'But that doesn't mean you love me,' she said, turning serious again. 'How can you be so sure of your feelings?'

'We've got plenty of time on our hands if you want me to prove it to you now.'

'Ruiz, please be serious—'

'I have never been more serious in my life,' he said, losing the smile. Taking both her hands in his, he stared into her eyes and then he kissed each of her hands in turn. 'I know you've been hurt in the past, but I will never hurt you, Holly. I want to be with you and to care for you always. If you'll have me…?'

For that split second she thought Ruiz looked as vulnerable as she felt. 'Who wouldn't want you?' she said. 'Not that I'm giving you licence to find out.'

'The only licence I want is one with both our names on it,' Ruiz assured her.

'Cheesy, but it might just work,' Holly said, starting to smile. This was happening. This was really happening. Holly Valiant had a boyfriend. And he loved her.

'It will work,' Ruiz said with confidence. Drawing her into his arms, he stroked Holly's hair back from her face. 'When will you go public with this?'

'In the column?' She gave him a cheeky look. 'You'll just have to wait and see—'

'This isn't for the column,' Ruiz said, turning suddenly serious. 'I'm asking you to marry me, Holly.' As he waited for her to say something he felt as if he were balanced on the tip of a mountain peak on one foot. 'I want to be with you, and I don't want anyone else,' he said. 'I want to share everything I have and everything I am with you, and I don't want to waste another second of our lives debating this. I want our future to begin now—here—right this minute,' he declared fiercely. 'I'm asking you to be my wife, but to be your own person too.' He stopped, knowing Holly's answer would be final, and that nothing in his life had meant this much to him before.

'Your life is so wildly different from mine,' she said, managing to smile and frown all at the same time.

'Wild is about right,' he agreed. 'But isn't taking chances what life is all about? There never will come a point where things are easy and straightforward, but if we can work through the challenges together we can make this work. And hopefully, there are some problems you wouldn't want to be without.'

'Like you?' she suggested.

'I'd rather think of myself as a challenge,' he teased her.

'I agree. Life would be boring without challenges, but endless problems are depressing.'

'Then let's not make a problem out of this. Do you accept my challenge?'

'I do,' she said.

'I love you, Holly Valiant.' He folded her in his arms.

'You love me?'

'I love you.'

'You love me,' Holly repeated, as if testing the words and finding them, not only plausible, but gradually, slowly, oh, so slowly, believable. 'You love me.' This time she smiled as she looked at him.

'Yes, I do,' he confirmed. '*Dios* send an angel to help me convince you,' he muttered beneath his passionate Latin breath. 'And if it takes a lifetime to prove it to you, then that is what I will do, Holly Valiant. So,' he said, 'having got the main challenge out in the open and sorted out, have you worked out yet what the missing link is where your writing is concerned?'

'I only wish I could,' Holly admitted worriedly, raking her hair with frustration. Her mind was so scattered, she could hardly concentrate. He loved her?

Focus, Valiant, focus!

'Let's take a shower.'

'Together?' she said, frowning.

'Is there any other way?'

'Your writing will be fine now,' he said later when they were both standing in front of the silent computer. 'Before, you had just shut your mind to anything that frightened you, stifling original thought.'

'And I suppose you've just done me a favour in the bedroom by opening it up again?'

'It certainly helped,' he said. 'I think I can give you some further help if you need it,' he added, glancing at the sofa.

'Don't you think of anything else?'

'With you around?' His lips pressed down. 'Rarely.' Grabbing her hand, he pulled her across the room. 'I bet I can give that imagination of yours a real kick-start.'

'I'll try anything once,' Holly said, gamely.

'Excellent. First play and then work—'

'If you think that's the solution,' she said, 'We'd better get to it.'

'I couldn't have put it better myself. I think you're going to write the best article of your life after this, Holly Valiant, and then I'm going to teach you to ride.'

She laughed. 'And after that?' she queried.

'After that we're going to show everyone how to dance the samba—'

'You're completely mad,' she exclaimed as he lowered her down onto the cushions.

'Mad for you,' Ruiz agreed, unfastening his belt.

CHAPTER TWELVE

When Holly was lying quiet and contented in Ruiz's arms, she asked him, 'Did you mean it?'

'Did I mean what?' he said, opening one wicked eye.

'You know,' she prompted.

'Say it, Holly.' Ruiz raised a brow as he waited.

'When you said…you love me.'

'Of course I did—I do.'

With a hum she settled back in his arms again. 'I'm glad you didn't go riding right away.'

'Oh, so am I,' Ruiz agreed in a mocking tone and with a smile Holly didn't see. 'But I am going to try out a new horse in a while, so you'll have plenty of chance to write your article.'

'Slave driver.'

'Don't tell me I haven't filled you with enough inspiration yet?' Dipping his head, Ruiz stared with laughing eyes into Holly's sated gaze. He knew this was the only way they could both be happy—if he let her be free to explore her talent and her career.

'You've certainly given me enough to go on for now,' she said, reluctantly staggering a little as she got to her feet and walked to the desk.

'Just call me back if you need any more help,' he said, springing up and adjusting his clothing.

'Don't worry, I will,' she said, already logging on.

Being singled out by Holly meant more to him than she could ever know. He was so used to being one of the Band of Brothers: Ruiz, the youngest, the fixer, the travelling glue pot for the family. The man who made things right again. He was so busy sorting things out he had never stayed anywhere long enough to form a lasting attachment, let alone with someone as precious to him as Holly. And now he wanted to do something special for her. She had to know how much he cared about her, how much he loved her. It was almost Christmas, and Christmas Day was also her birthday. Gifts for his brothers were easy—anything for their horses. Lucia was almost as easy. He could take his sister on a virtual shopping trip and let her choose anything she liked, but he didn't want to do that with Holly. He wanted to choose something that had meaning for her. He wanted to spoil her because she had never been spoiled, and surprise her because he loved to see her laugh.

She had bought Christmas presents for the Acosta family, knowing she would be staying over the holidays with them, but she couldn't find the perfect gift for Ruiz, the man who had everything—or who could buy it in the unlikely event he found a gap.

She had an idea. She'd have to work on it, and she'd have to work fast, Holly concluded, pressing Send on her latest 'Living with a Playboy' feature, along with a second message marked 'URGENT'. The main article for *ROCK!* was still work in progress, and something told her that unless she wrote a couple of alternative endings she would have to wait until after Christmas to complete the final draft of that.

'Are you ready for your riding lesson?'

She turned as Ruiz entered the room. 'As I'll ever be!'

'Not chickening out, I hope?' he said, smacking a whip against the side of his sexy, calf-moulding riding boots.

'You wish,' she said.

'No, I'll leave that to the pony,' Ruiz said, laughing. 'Come on.' Throwing an arm around her shoulders, he led her out of the room.

Ruiz put her up on a young, dark bay gelding called Dulce. 'Can I have hand rails?' Holly asked nervously, feeling she should have a safety harness at the very least.

'Hang onto me,' Ruiz suggested, springing onto the back of a waiting stallion. 'Dulce is very light on the mouth, but he'll be kind to you. Squeeze your knees together and he'll go forward.'

'Not sure I can squeeze my knees together...'

Ruiz laughed. 'Then do the best you can.'

'Well, I blame you if I can't get them to move together.' But, experimenting, she discovered her knees still worked. She found the small horse remarkably biddable too, and with Ruiz at her side, patiently advising her, she also discovered confidence flooding in. 'I like it,' she exclaimed with surprise, urging the kind pony to pick up his stride.

'Do you like him?' Ruiz asked when she had successfully completed a couple of circuits of the ring.

'I love him,' Holly admitted, stroking the pricked, velvety ears as she rested her cheek against Dulce's firm, warm neck.

'He's yours.'

'What?' She sat up. 'You can't do that.'

'Who said I can't? Happy Christmas, Holly.'

'But when will I be able to ride him?'

'Whenever you come to Argentina with me.'

'Are you serious? Who will ride him in the meantime?'

'The grooms will ride him. What will it take to convince you?' Ruiz demanded, riding alongside. 'Shall I call my brothers over and ask them to convince you that I never joke where horses are concerned?'

'Don't do that,' she said, flashing a glance at the posse of impossibly tough-looking bad boys busy training fresh young ponies in the next paddock. 'I've got more than enough trouble on my hands as it is. So,' she said, narrowing her eyes as she stared at Ruiz. 'If you never joke about horses, how about women?'

'There are no women.' Ruiz gave her a long, intense stare. 'There's only you.'

'Good, because I tweeted our news resulting in a mega uplift in hits to the site.'

'Oh, I'm delighted,' Ruiz said dryly.

'A love story contained in one hundred and forty characters isn't bad editing.'

'Not bad at all,' Ruiz agreed. 'You should think about taking up writing as a career...' He dodged out of the way as she aimed a swipe at him.

'So if we're going to be together do you think I should kill the column?' she said.

'Of course not,' Ruiz argued.

'You don't think the readers will grow bored now they know the outcome?' Holly said, frowning.

'I'm disappointed in you, Holly. What has happened to that imagination of yours? There should be at least three spin-offs from this piece of news.'

Would that be the engagement, the wedding, followed swiftly by the first baby? Holly wondered.

Ruiz swiftly disillusioned her. 'Cleaning his tack, ironing his shirts, and cooking the playboy's meals should do it.'

'You mentioned dancing?' she said as he helped her to dismount.

'Yes. We're having a party at the *estancia* this evening.'

Holly hummed. 'I'd watch your toes if I were you.'

The Christmas Eve celebration was being held in the main courtyard and, dressed in jeans with her hair piled up high, Holly had pitched in with the staff to help them dress the walls and balustrades with garlands of flowers to augment the colourful blossom in the garden. The cobbled area was lit by candlelight and torches held in high brackets on the walls, and there was a full moon that cast a spotlight on the glittering fountains. The band was already playing sexy South American music and there were professional dancers on hand to demonstrate the various styles of dance to the guests, as well as enough food and wine to feed an army. The banquet had been set out on trestle tables dressed with crisp white linen, boasting silver cutlery and twinkling crystal. Holly was just about to go and get changed when the biggest surprise of the night waylaid her. Lucia had arrived under cover of darkness to surprise her brothers. The two girls had been in touch by e-mail in order to spring a few more surprises before the night was out.

'It's just like the old days at school,' Lucia commented, handing over Holly's Christmas present. 'All this subterfuge, with the added amazingness of you and my brother falling in love—' Lucia broke off to give Holly the biggest hug ever. 'Come on, sister-to-be, let's go and get changed. You can hardly arrive at the party wearing jeans.'

The outfit Lucia had chosen for Holly was spectacular. The slinky dress in vivid red had a low vee neck and the highest of high hemlines. Lucia had also chosen a pair of silver sandals with stratospheric heels to wear with it.

'You look fabulous,' Lucia exclaimed when they had sneaked into Holly's bedroom and locked the door securely behind them. 'Now get those sandals on,' she prompted. 'If Ruiz loved you before, his tongue will be sweeping the floor when he sees you wearing this…'

'I'd rather Ruiz kept his tongue in his mouth,' Holly remarked dryly, turning her head to examine her back view in the full-length mirror.

'The answer is no,' Lucia assured her. 'It doesn't look big. It looks perfect. You look perfect.'

'And you shouldn't be spending so much money on me.'

'And you weren't supposed to pay me any rent,' Lucia countered. 'I couldn't believe it when I saw the amount you put into my bank account.'

'The column is going well.'

'That doesn't matter. Whoever gave you my bank details is so dead!'

'Take the money. I can afford to pay you the going rate,' Holly reminded her best friend. And didn't that feel good. 'You look pretty fabulous for a change,' she added wryly, staring with renewed interest at her beautiful friend. 'What's the special occasion, Lucia?'

'Only pretty fabulous?' Lucia said worriedly, examining her back view in the same mirror.

'You know you look as gorgeous as you always do,' Holly volunteered. 'But you still haven't told me what the special occasion is…'

'Why does it have to be special? It's just a family party.'

'And you are making a very special effort,' Holly noted as Lucia checked her make-up in the mirror.

'Okay, so I hear Nero Caracas is bringing his polo team as well as his new wife and baby tonight,' Lucia explained off-handedly. 'Which means Luke Forster, that American polo player, will be at the party. Don't look like that, Holly. Luke's far too stern and serious for me. And he's about ten feet tall.'

'Poor man,' Holly murmured, remembering she had seen the good-looking American commanding the field of play quite a few times during the game.

'But I might enjoy teasing him,' Lucia added thoughtfully as she arranged her ample breasts in the low-cut dress.

'Excellent news for Luke,' Holly agreed tongue in cheek. 'So are you ready to spring our surprise?'

Ruiz, meanwhile, was pacing up and down his bedroom with the phone gripped so tightly in his hand it was threatening to break apart. 'What do you mean you couldn't arrange it? I told you well in advance what I wanted. Plus there's an agreement between our two countries so there shouldn't have been a problem. What has happened to the vet? How can he have left on another flight when I booked him? I booked the jet, damn it!' Ruiz thundered. 'Who the hell countermanded my order?' Ruiz whirled around as one of his brothers poked his head round the door. He waved him away. Business was all-important, and when it was business concerning Holly nothing came before that.

'Are you coming to the party, Ruiz?' his brother Diego asked him, refusing to be so easily dismissed.

'When I'm ready,' he snapped.

'Would you like me to look after Holly for you?'

His answer to that was to lob a polo ball at the door, which his brother dodged. 'Only asking,' Diego murmured, closing the door.

So his surprise for Holly was ruined, Ruiz raged inwardly. Lucky for him the jeweller in Buenos Aires hadn't let him down. Checking the breast pocket of his jacket, he decided he'd better go down to the party, but he was nowhere near ready to give up on his other surprise for her yet.

Holly and Lucia had barely walked into the party when three of the Acosta brothers spotted their sister and came straight over. Their reunion was touching and Holly envied their closeness. This wasn't the constant squabbling and petty jealousies Lucia had described at school. It was the deep and abiding affection of people who knew everything there was to know about each other, and made Holly long for her own family.

With all the constant squabbling and petty jealousies that might involve, she thought with amusement as Lucia batted the most formidable of her brothers, Nacho, on the head with her frivolous party purse. 'How dare you summon me back like an employee, you great oaf? And what have you done with Ruiz?' Lucia demanded, swinging round. 'Holly has a special surprise for him and he's not even here. Don't tell me you've sent him back to London to work?'

Nacho huffed dismissively. 'I can't tell your brother Ruiz what to do.'

'Quite right,' Lucia agreed dryly. 'Ruiz is too busy telling me what to do.'

As Lucia kissed each of her brothers in turn Holly

grew increasingly anxious. Was her surprise for Ruiz going to fall flat?

'Last time I saw Ruiz he was pacing his bedroom like a bear with a sore head,' Ruiz's brother Diego murmured discreetly in her ear. 'I'd give him a few minutes.'

'Thank you.' Holly smiled her thanks.

As the darkly glamorous men peeled away to welcome their guests other men were drawn like moths to the two girls standing on the edge of the dance floor. Holly was quite relieved to see the driver who had brought her from the airport amongst them. He bowed so politely over her hand she was only too delighted to accept. He was fun, she remembered, as her portly partner chuffed his moustache before leading her onto the dance floor. The dress Lucia had given her was really working its magic, Holly thought as she started dancing. She had never worn such a beautiful party dress before. She glanced grate-fully at Lucia, noticing with amusement that Lucia had just walked straight up to the attractive American polo player, Luke Forster, only to veer away at the very last moment on the pretext of tugging one of her brothers onto the dance floor. It was also interesting to see Luke Forster's brooding amber gaze following Lucia as she sashayed off.

Holly had only been dancing with the driver for a few minutes when another man tapped the driver's shoulder and cut in. This man spoke no English, but he danced well and held Holly at arm's length so their bodies al-ways had air between them. She was really enjoying herself, though still worrying about Ruiz and wonder-ing where he could be. And then a younger man, who had clearly had too much to drink, decided it was his turn to take Holly on a drunken lurch around the floor. Unfortunately his grip was so secure she couldn't break free, and now Lucia was making frantic signals from the edge of the dance floor. Like a drama slowly unfolding that no one could stop, Holly saw Ruiz emerge from the house and stand at the top of the steps to scan the dance floor. The young man who had Holly in his grip decided that this was the perfect moment to launch his assault. Wet lips pursed, he darted his head forward, and as she whipped her head away to avoid him a big black shape launched itself on Holly and her partner, barking wildly as it knocked them to the floor.

'Bouncer?' Holly exclaimed, wiping muddy paw marks from her arm. She looked up to find Ruiz dressed in full evening rig standing over her. He looked more magnificent and formidable than she'd ever seen.

'No harm done,' Ruiz said in a tone Holly had never heard him use before as he brushed the man's suit down and called for one of the gauchos to escort him away. 'How the hell did Bouncer get here?' he demanded with frustration.

'Please don't be angry with Holly,' Lucia begged him, hanging onto her brother's arm.

Easing himself free, Ruiz took hold of Holly. 'Well?' he murmured.

Their faces were very close. Ruiz's mouth was almost touching hers. Everyone at the party was frozen to the spot, sensing drama. There was no music, no chatter, not a sound to be heard—until Bouncer whimpered and both Holly and Ruiz knelt simultaneously on the ground to make a fuss of him. As if this were the signal everyone had been waiting for the music started up again and the dance floor came back to life.

'Happy Christmas, Ruiz,' Holly murmured, staring across Bouncer's head into Ruiz's eyes. 'I think Bouncer had this planned from the first moment we met, though

Lucia brought him over in the private jet with the vet,' she explained, 'and as Bouncer has had all his shots and has a pet passport and Argentina has the same arrangement for allowing pets to travel as the EU…'

'This I know,' Ruiz assured Holly, softly holding her within an inch of his mouth as he lifted her to her feet. 'I do deal quite a lot with the authorities in both countries, you know? Shipping ponies?' Ruiz's lips tugged in his trademark smile. 'I tried to bring Bouncer over to surprise you for Christmas too, but it appears you beat me to it.'

His brothers, hearing this, congratulated Holly.

'Nice to know someone can get the better of you, Ruiz,' the great Nacho Acosta commented dryly before moving away to ensure the party didn't flag.

'I thought it would be better for Bouncer to live here on the pampas than in London,' Holly admitted. 'Your brothers agreed. But then I hesitated until Nacho said you had mentioned the same thing to him.'

'Nacho agreed to Bouncer coming to live here?" Ruiz demanded with surprise.

'He did more than that. Nacho arranged the jet,' Holly explained. 'He said it was a long journey for a rescue dog to take unaccompanied, but with Lucia and a vet on hand he thought it might be possible.'

Dios! Ruiz glanced at his brother who raised a glass.

'Are you pleased with your surprise?' Holly asked anxiously.

'I couldn't be more pleased,' Ruiz said, holding Holly a little closer as the dance floor filled up. 'But you've left me without the possibility of giving you a surprise.'

'Oh, I don't know,' she said. 'I can't believe we've exhausted your repertoire yet…'

Ruiz's wicked mouth tugged in a grin. 'So you don't need a surprise right here, right now?'

'In front of all these people? Absolutely not,' Holly murmured.

'What am I going to do with this, then?'

She stared at the small jewel box. 'What is it?'

'The next headline for your column,' Ruiz said dryly.

'If that's what I think it is.'

'It is,' Ruiz murmured, 'but I think you'd better get out of that dress first.'

Holly sucked in a breath, remembering only now that her dress was ruined and covered in mud.

'We have very good dry cleaners in Argentina,' Ruiz reassured her, slipping the jewel case back into his pocket.

'But I couldn't possibly let you pay the bill...'

Their faces were very close as both of them relived a day in London that seemed such a long time ago now.

'Shower?' Ruiz murmured with a very particular look in his eyes.

'As soon as possible,' Holly agreed.

'Ruiz and Holly. I like the sound of that,' Ruiz commented as they strolled back to the house together arm in arm.

'Holly and Ruiz,' Holly corrected him.

'I'll go for that,' Ruiz conceded. It was an easy victory for Holly. He was just quietly celebrating that the world and everything in it was his now, while Bouncer, who was safely back in Lucia's keeping, barked his satisfaction at a job well done.

'So what do you think, Holly?' Ruiz demanded as Holly stared in thrilled delight at the huge ruby on her wedding finger.

'I think you're a very dangerous man,' she said as Ruiz moved behind her.

'Have you only just noticed that?' Ruiz murmured against her neck.

As she turned in his arms Ruiz's gaze slipped to her lips. 'Stop it,' she warned him softly as he whispered a world of wickedness in her ear.

'No one will notice if we don't return to the party right away…'

Ruiz had a point. He also had a formidable erection. And as they were both standing naked beneath the shower she thought it rude not to seize the moment.

It's big and red and fits me perfectly. Rubies are the perfect choice for a fiery redhead, Ruiz told me. You can know his name now, seeing as the playboy and the redhead are going to be headline news in the next issue of this magazine—front cover too. And the column?

This column will continue, for, as my polo-playing bad boy points out, I can send copy to ROCK! from anywhere in the world, and there should be plenty more headlines to come—especially as Ruiz has three gorgeous brothers and a baby sister, my best friend, Lucia. You can read all about them here— The Good, The Bad, and The—

Well, not ugly, since all of them are stunningly glamorous, lead the most riotous lives, and are the best fun to be around. You'll have to stay tuned to find out.

Hasta la vista! Here's to the next time we meet.

* * * * *

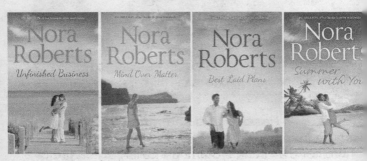

5_ST_12

MILLS & BOON®

The Thirty List

*cover in development

At thirty, Rachel has slid down every ladder she has ever climbed. Jobless, broke and ditched by her husband, she has to move in with grumpy Patrick and his four-year-old son.

Patrick is also getting divorced, so to cheer themselves up the two decide to draw up bucket lists. Soon they are learning to tango, abseiling, trying stand-up comedy and more. But, as she gets closer to Patrick, Rachel wonders if their relationship is too good to be true…

Order yours today at
www.millsandboon.co.uk/Thethirtylist

MILLS & BOON®
By Request

RELIVE THE ROMANCE WITH THE BEST OF THE BEST

A sneak peek at next month's titles...

In stores from 15th May 2015:

- **Unbuttoned by the Boss** – Natalie Anderson, Robyn Donald & Kira Sinclair

- **The Ryders: Jared, Royce and Stephanie** – Barbara Dunlop

In stores from 5th June 2015:

- **Baby for the Tycoon** – Emily McKay, Karen Rose Smith & Emily Forbes

- **His Summer Bride** – Joanna Neil, Abigail Gordon & Leah Martyn

---

Available at WHSmith, Tesco, Asda, Eason, Amazon and Apple

Just can't wait?
Buy our books online a month before they hit the shops!
visit www.millsandboon.co.uk

These books are also available in eBook format!